A QUESTION OF LOVE

Isabel Wolff was born in Warwickshire and read English at Cambridge. Her first novel, *The Trials of Tiffany Trott*, was an international bestseller and was followed by *The Making of Minty Malone*, *Out of the Blue*, *Rescuing Rose*, and *Behaving Badly*, all of which have been published worldwide. She lives in London with her family. For further information, visit www.IsabelWolff.com

To receive regular updates on Isabel Wolff, visit www.harpercollins.co.uk and register for AuthorTracker.

PRAISE FOR ISABEL WOLFF:

'Too clever for chick-lit.'   *Time Out*

'A generally superior confection . . . Wolff's writing quirks are charming.'   *Independent on Sunday*

'Compulsive.'   *She*

'A warm, witty romantic comedy. Perfect! Isabel's work has a lot of substance as well as fun.'   Helen Lederer, *Express*

'Wolff has a light touch and a slick prose style that makes this story flow effortlessly.'   *Marie Claire*

'A brilliant look at love and life.'   *You*

ISABEL WOLFF

A Question of Love

HarperCollins*Publishers*

HarperCollins*Publishers*
77–85 Fulham Palace Road,
Hammersmith, London W6 8JB

www.harpercollins.co.uk

Published by HarperCollins*Publishers* 2005
1 3 5 7 9 8 6 4 2

A catalogue record for this book
is available from the British Library

ISBN 0 00 717828 X

Set in Sabon by
Palimpsest Book Production Limited,
Polmont, Stirlingshire

Printed and bound in Great Britain by
Clays Ltd, St Ives plc

Acknowledgements

I am indebted to a number of people who kindly helped me in the planning and research for this book. For the background to the world of TV quiz shows I am grateful to the *Fifteen to One* team who were very generous with their time – William G. Stewart, Janet Mullins, Chris Shoebridge, Angus McDonald, Elizabeth Salmon, Tim Eaton, Sian Roberts and Brenda Haugh. The Quizzing.co.uk website was also a very helpful resource. For information about independent television companies, I would like to thank Richard Bradley of Lion TV. I am also very grateful to Angus Broadbent of the Broadbent gallery, to Zsuzsanna Szekeres for enlightening me about all things Hungarian, to Glenn Livingston from 'Pygmy Goat Secrets' and to Jane Kerr of the *Daily Mirror*. I owe a debt of gratitude to Jim Parton of Families Need Fathers, and the three women at the SecondWives.Com website who shared their stories with me, but prefer to remain anonymous. I would also like to thank Tom Maxey of Groom Bros., Spalding for information about floriculture, and Suzanne Noot of St. Thomas' Hospital. Tim Bamford of Withers kindly gave me copyright advice, Jackie Freeman of W. W. Thompson advised me about patent applications, and Sarah Anticoni of Charles Russell provided me with information about various aspects of divorce. I am also indebted to Kate Williams, Roz Hanna, Eliana Haworth, Louise Clairmonte and Caroline Heroux who all gave me helpful contacts and raised my morale along the way.

As ever I would like to thank my agents, Clare Conville, Sam North and everyone at Conville and Walsh. I have very much appreciated the wonderful editorial guidance I have had from Maxine Hitchcock at HarperCollins and from Rachel Hore and Jennifer Parr. I am extremely grateful, as ever, to everyone at HarperCollins – especially Lynne Drew, Amanda Ridout, Fiona McIntosh, Steve Newall, Jane Harris and David Swarbrick. I would especially like to thank Greg for his love and encouragement throughout the writing of this book and for being so tolerant of the long hours required. Finally, I am lucky enough to live in a very happy 'blended' family of my own, and it is to the three children, who make it so worthwhile, and such fun, that I dedicate this book, with much love.

For Alice,
Freddie and George

'A pound of knowledge
is worth an ounce of love.'
John Wesley

ONE

'A very good morning to you,' said Terry Wogan, his voice as smooth as Guinness. 'It's ten to eight, and, if you've just tuned in, then a warm welcome to the show.'

'Thanks,' I murmured as I opened Nick's small mahogany wardrobe and surveyed his clothes with a sinking heart. To the left were his suits – two woollen ones, three linen, and some casual trousers. To the right were ten or twelve shirts. I ran my hands over them, masochistically imagining, for a moment, Nick's chest filling them, then I stopped at the dark blue silk one with the short sleeves. Patterned with tropical fish, and now faded, it had been his favourite. He'd worn it on our last holiday, four years ago.

'Now,' Wogan went on in that cheery way of his. 'Here's a song I've always been fond of . . .' I heard the opening bars, and flinched. '. . . "Just When I Needed You Most".'

I pulled out Nick's shirt, then pressed it to my face. As I inhaled the masculine aroma mixed with the faint scent of the sea, I remembered him wearing it in Crete. He was standing on our hotel balcony, his face alight with laughter, his glass of retsina uplifted as though he hadn't a care.

I miss you more than I missed you before . . .

Breathing slowly to steady my nerves, I set to work.

1

Now where I'll find comfort, God knows . . .

I removed the shirts, put them over my arm, then carried them down to the spare room. *Because yo-oo-ou . . . left me, just when I needed you most.*

'Yes, Nick,' I breathed. 'You did.' As I opened his father's old wooden trunk and placed them inside I wondered what other women in my position might have done. Many would have taken their husband's clothes to Oxfam long ago – but I couldn't. Somehow it just didn't seem right.

'Now . . .' I heard Wogan say as I went back into the bedroom and unhooked Nick's suits from the rail. 'Here's a question. A bit of a trick question, really. Do you know what day it is?'

'Wednesday,' I replied, as I laid the suits on the bed. 'The ninth of February.' My hands shook slightly as I buttoned up the jackets.

'It's the first day of Lent.'

'So it is.'

'A day, traditionally, for a little sober reflection, and of course a day for giving things up. So what are you all giving up for Lent then, hmm . . . ?'

I carried Nick's suits into the spare room and put them in the trunk, carefully folded between sheets of newspaper.

'Chocolate?' I heard Wogan ask as I stood up, back aching slightly. I glanced into the garden. A light snow was falling. 'That would be a tough one now, wouldn't it? Or maybe booze?' I returned to the bedroom, lifted Nick's jumpers out of the chest of drawers, then put those in the trunk as well. 'Fast food, maybe? Or sweets . . . ?'

Now I took out his shoes, then carefully unthreaded his ties from the rack. I fingered the blue and gold cashmere one he'd worn for our wedding and was nearly felled by a wave of grief.

'Swearing?' Wogan persisted. 'Smoking? Reading *OK!* and *Hello!*? Come on now everyone – let's give it some serious thought, shall we? What are we all giving up for Lent?'

I looked at our wedding photo over the bed, then reached up and took it down. 'What am I giving up? That's easy. My past.'

You have to try and get over things don't you? You have to move on, or, rather, 'let go' as they say in the popular jargon. And so, at long last, I am. I've finally put Nick's things away because I no longer want to live with a ghost. But, although I know it's something I have to do, at the same time it still feels wrong. As though I'm somehow denying that Nick ever existed or, that for six years, we had a shared life.

The hardest thing of all has been the answerphone. In three years I've never changed the message – I couldn't bring myself to – but now, at long last, I have. So, as from this morning, callers will no longer hear Nick politely saying, *Hello, we're sorry we're not here* . . . – that used to freak people out. Now they'll just hear me, on my own. *Hi – you've reached Laura* . . . I say with casual cheerfulness, as though I'm publicly acknowledging that he's gone.

This is something my sisters have been urging me to do for ages. 'It's *unbearable*!' my elder one, Felicity, would exclaim every time she came round. 'You can't carry *on* like this, Laura! The flat's a mausoleum! You've got to accept what happened and move *forward*!' My younger sister, Hope, who's more restrained, would just say, 'If you're still not ready to change things, then . . . *don't*.' But in January I finally decided that I was. My New Year resolution was to redecorate the flat – that's made a big difference to the feel of the place – and to put away all of Nick's stuff. I haven't disposed of his things – that seemed callous – I've simply hidden them, so that the outward evidence of his life here has gone. His computer, his books, his pictures and now his clothes, are all packed away in the spare room, out of sight. In one way it feels like a liberation, in another, like a betrayal. But, rationally, I know that it's not.

I miss Nick. And I still feel angry with him. They say that's a common reaction – especially if you're young. Of course it's got easier, over time. I've got used to it – I've had to – but even now, I can still be tripped up. Whenever a letter arrives for him from someone who still doesn't know, for example, and I have to write back and explain. And the way my neighbours sometimes react can upset me. This morning, for instance.

I was coming out of the flat at about nine thirty, on my way to work. For the first time in ages I was feeling energized and optimistic, ready to move forward. And I'd just locked the front door when I saw Mrs French from over the road leaving her house with her shopping trolley, on her way to Portobello. So I smiled at her, and she smiled back, but, as usual, her smile was tinged with sympathy and I almost heard her compassionate 'tut-tut'. And I realized that being, as I still am round here, an object of pity and curiosity, is going to make moving forward quite hard. Take Mrs Singh, next door. She's the same. Whenever she sees me she comes up to me and lays her hand on my arm, and asks me, very sweetly, if I'm 'all right'. And I always reply, as non-defensively as I can, 'Yes, thanks. Of course. How are you?' I don't like it, but I can't blame them because they remember Nick, and this is a gossipy little street, so I've become 'that poor girl at number eight'.

Dunchurch Road is at the far – unfashionable – end of Portobello just off Ladbroke Grove. Many of my neighbours have lived here for years, and not all of them are as charitable as Mrs French and Mrs Singh. Twice now in our tiny local supermarket I've overheard that hatchet-faced woman from number twelve telling the manager in a loud, authoritative whisper, that I must have 'driven him to it, poor man'. But then, when it happened, I know that there were a number of unpleasant theories doing the rounds. Some people blamed me – I don't know why as Nick and I were very happy, thank you. Others thought he must have lost it with the emotional stress of his work. The most generous view of it was that Nick must have got himself in such a terrible mess that he just couldn't make sense of his life. What that mess might have been, in the absence of any firm evidence (and, believe me, I looked), was open to conjecture of the most lurid kind. But I suppose it was inevitable that there'd be rumours, not least because it got in the papers because of Nick's job. So, one way or another, I've had a lot to cope with; but now, as I say, I'm determined to move on, and to leave this sad phase of my life behind.

So, disconcerted by my encounter with Mrs French, I did some positive thinking to lift my mood. As I walked up Portobello – the sleety snowflakes whirling and eddying against my face – I reflected that work-wise at least, things have improved. As I passed the tattoo parlours and the halal butchers I reminded myself of how hard my financial position had been. There's no insurance payout in cases like mine, and Nick had left his affairs in a mess. On my TV researcher's salary I'd struggled to pay the mortgage alone, and, in my situation, I wasn't able to move. The Halifax gave me three months' grace, my family helped, and my boss, Tom, kindly gave me a rise. Now, as I passed the stalls selling cheap pashminas and tie-dye shirts, I remembered how, even so, I'd accumulated huge debts – but how I'd then found a good way to make ends meet.

Last March I saw an article in *The Times* about a company called InQuizitive which compiles quizzes for pubs. It mentioned that they were looking for freelance question-setters so, being a general knowledge junkie, I got in touch. I knew it was something I could easily do and, apart from the cash – £2.50 per question – it distracted me from my distress. Every evening after work I'd sit there with my reference books, totally absorbed, making up questions. 'Who designed the first petrol-driven car?' (Karl Benz). 'What is stored in a mattamore?' (Grain). 'How many squares are there on a Scrabble board?' (225). 'What is the capital of Ukraine?' (Kiev). I enjoyed it. It was relaxing, and yet at the same time it gave me a buzz. And now, as I turned left down Westbourne Park Road, I thought, as I often do, about how that one newspaper article had changed my life . . .

One Friday afternoon last June I'd been in Trident TV's tiny 'boardroom' with Tom, who owns the company, and Sara the other full-time researcher – we're a very small company – and we were bouncing around ideas for new programmes to pitch at the broadcasters.

'Things are very tight, money-wise,' Tom had begun, as he twanged a rubber band between thumb and forefinger in the slightly distracted way that he does. He narrowed his blue eyes, as though drawing on one of his occasional cigarettes. 'So I think we may have to do something a little bit more . . . commercial,' he continued with slight disdain. I'd been with Trident for five years then – right from the start, when it was just Tom and me – and we'd done some quite heavyweight stuff: two series about the first world war for the History Channel, for example; a drama-documentary about Helen of Troy for BBC Two, a four part series on the ethics of bio-technology, and a half-hour programme about the Turin Shroud. We'd also done a few corporate videos, to pay the bills, but we'd become well known for our factual work.

'It's very nice being nominated for the Baftas and all that,' Tom went on. He leaned back and clasped his hands behind his head. 'But what we *really* need now, is a money-spinner.' My heart sank. I liked the kind of serious-minded programmes we did. I've never wanted to do cookery programmes, or silly lifestyle shows or pander to lowest common denominator taste. Tom slowly swivelled his chair from side to side. 'So . . . ?'

'A money-spinner?' I repeated.

He winced. 'Yes – not least so that we can have a bit of a refurb round here –' he glanced at the floor – 'this carpet must be due for its bus pass. So . . . any ideas for something a bit more . . . popular?' He looked at me.

'Well . . . how about . . . "Celebrity Wifestyles"?' I suggested. 'Or "Maisonette Makeovers"? Or "Bungled Bungalows" or, erm . . . "I'm a Nonentity, Get Me Into Here"?'

Tom fired the rubber band at me. 'There's no need to be facetious, Laura. I'm not suggesting that we start making *crap*.'

'Sorry, Tom. I'm just a bit tired.'

'Been partying?'

'Hardly. Burning the midnight oil.'

'Doing what? If you don't mind my asking,' he'd added politely.

I shrugged. 'I don't mind at all. Compiling pub quiz questions.'

'Really? Why?'

'Firstly, because I need the money and, secondly because I enjoy it – it's interesting.'

He leaned forward. 'And how does it work?'

'Well, usually the company I do it for asks for a batch of questions on different subjects. Last night was a bit heavy because –' I stifled a yawn – 'they needed twenty on the history of Russia, and another twenty on Scottish Premier League football clubs. I ended up dreaming that Catherine the Great played for Queen's Park Rangers.'

'Hmm.' Tom had steepled his fingers and was gently bouncing them against his lips.

'I make up the questions,' I went on, 'they have them verified, then they put the quizzes together and sell them to the pubs. Tonight I've got to prepare fifteen on the plays of Ibsen, then tomorrow I'm going to do fifteen on the Roman Catholic Church. In a good month I can make an extra five hundred pounds, which God knows, I can do with.'

'Quiz questions . . .' Tom repeated. He was just staring at me, saying nothing. Usually I feel comfortable with Tom

7

– we have a great working relationship – but I found this unnerving.

'Anyway, can we get on with the meeting?' I said after a moment. 'I wouldn't mind going home a bit early tonight, as I say I'm a bit tired and . . .'

'*We* should do a quiz,' Tom said suddenly.

'Yes,' said Sara, her face lighting up. 'That's just what *I* was thinking. That's a *great* idea.'

'A quiz,' Tom repeated. 'A really *good* one. I don't know why I've never thought of it before.'

'Probably because there are any number of good quizzes out there already,' I suggested drily.

Tom pinged another rubber band out of the open window. 'That doesn't mean we can't do one as well.'

'It'd have to be different,' said Sara. She took off her little black specs and began cleaning them on the hem of her skirt, which is what she does when she's fired up about something. 'It would have to be unlike anything that already exists.'

'In short it would have to be original,' said Tom. 'But the question – irony intended – is how?'

So for the next hour or so we'd talked about the different quiz shows and tried to analyse why it is that they work. With *Who Wants to be a Millionaire?* we decided that it was the Greed Factor combined with the brilliant tension that Chris Tarrant creates. With *Mastermind* it was the sinister atmosphere – the menacing music, the Black Chair in the harsh spotlight – inspired, according to Tom, by its creator's experience of interrogation as a prisoner of war. The appeal of *University Challenge* was seeing young people answer such difficult questions, and the attraction of *The Weakest Link* seemed to be the mesmerising spectacle of the contestants' meek submission to Anne Robinson's bile. But underpinning the ever-growing success of the genre was, we agreed, the simple fact that we all like to show off what we know.

Watching a quiz makes us revert to our eight-year-old selves, shooting up our hands in class, bursting to answer.

'Yes,' mused Tom. 'A quiz . . . what do you think, Laura?'

I shrugged. I like television quizzes as much as the next person but I'd never for a moment thought that we might do one.

'Well . . . I think it'd be fine. In fact, I like the idea – as long as it's a proper general knowledge quiz,' I added quickly. 'Real information – not trivia. I couldn't stand having to compile questions about soap opera plots or . . . I don't know . . . how many A-levels Prince William got.'

'Quite,' said Tom nodding; then he looked at me. 'How many A-levels *did* Prince William get?'

'Three. Geography, Art History and Biology. He got an A, a B and a C.'

'But what could be the format for our quiz?' Tom swivelled from side to side in his chair again, his hands clasped behind his head. 'How could ours be different?'

When we came in on the Monday, we knew. Over the weekend Tom had thought up an idea for one which was original – if not actually quite radical. He said it had just come to him, in the bath. He swore us all to secrecy, we planned a pilot, and for the next month we worked like dogs. Tom produced, I compiled the questions, Sara, our P.A. Gill, and our incredibly annoying receptionist, Nerys, stood in as contestants and, to save money, I fronted it. Within a week of being pitched, *Whadda Ya Know?!!* had sold to the new cable channel, Challenge. They bought it, however, with one quite unexpected proviso – that I should present it myself.

Now, as I turned left into Tavistock Road, I remembered how Tom had been as amazed at this as I was. I'd had zero experience in front of the camera and we'd assumed that Challenge would want to bring in a star. But Adrian, the Commissioning Editor, said he wanted me to present it

9

because I was female – there are few women quizmasters – and, more importantly, young.

'Most quiz show hosts are middle-aged,' he'd said as Tom and I sat in his leather-scented office, the ink on our signatures still wet on the contracts in front of us. 'It would be a refreshing change to have a quality quiz presented by a thirty-something rather than a fifty-something. I also like the fact that you're –' and here he'd hesitated – 'interesting looking.' I winced. 'Now, don't get me wrong, Laura,' he added, much too quickly. 'But you're, well, rather . . . unusual. What some people might call *"une jolie laide".*'

'That means "jolly ugly" doesn't it?' I quipped, to cover my annoyance.

'Oh, no, no – it doesn't mean that at all. You're an attractive woman,' he added, again too quickly I thought.

'She is,' said Tom. 'Laura's lovely.'

'Of course she is,' Adrian went on. 'You're very . . . attractive, Laura . . . erm . . .'

'In a way?' I said pleasantly.

'Well, it's just that your looks are –' he squinted at me, cocking his head to one side – 'unconventional.' By now I felt like the Elephant Man. 'You're a bit like Andie McDowell . . .'

'Gone wrong?' I suggested.

'Well – ye-es. You *could* say that. I hope I didn't hurt your feelings,' he blundered on.

'You didn't,' I said politely. 'Really.' In any case I'm used to it. My sisters may be pretty but I'm what you'd politely call 'characterful': I've got Dad's angular jaw line, and his over-long nose. The galling thing is that I was a lovely baby – I was the pretty cygnet who became a duck.

'But the thing I really like about you,' Adrian went on, 'is the fact that you have authority.'

'Do I?' I said wonderingly. This had never occurred to me, though I liked the idea. Perhaps I should have been a policewoman – or a dominatrix.

10

'You have natural authority – which is the quality that quiz show presenters most need. They can get it in various ways,' he continued. 'On *The Weakest Link*, Anne Robinson exudes a kind of authority by being vile; Jeremy Paxman has authority on *University Challenge* because he's a serious journalist, ditto John Humphreys on *Mastermind*. But you have authority too, Laura. I think the viewers would feel that they're in safe hands with you and that you could probably answer many of the questions yourself.'

'She could,' Tom interjected. 'She's incredibly well-informed.'

'Misspent youth,' I explained. 'Too many books.'

'Plus you've got a fantastic memory,' Tom added warmly. I shrugged. But, to be honest, it's true. Facts and figures – however useless – stick to my mind like chewing gum sticks to the pavement. I only have to read something once for it to sink in. I've always regarded this as an oddity – a bit like having perfect pitch, or a sixth toe – but it can come in handy sometimes. No need for shopping lists, for example. Excellent recall of names and dates. No problem remembering what had rolled by on the *Generation Game* conveyor belt – *Cuddly toy-Teasmaid-Toaster-Carmen Rollers* – and, when I was nine, I won a family trip to Paris by being able to recite all fifty states of the Union in reverse alphabetical order.

'Yes, well,' Adrian went on, 'I think the viewers would feel that you're not just reading the questions out; and with this format – particularly with its highly unusual unique selling point – that's what the show really needs.'

Tom was delighted that I was to present the show. As I say, we have a good rapport – though it's strictly professional, mind you. I like Tom; he's clever and laid-back and very kind and yes, if I stop to think about it, he's definitely good-looking, and he's got this attractive, north American voice. But I could never see him as anything more than a colleague because a) he's my boss and it could be awkward and b) I know he once did something that just wasn't . . . great.

But, to go back to the quiz, Tom had been worried that no established 'star' would want to present it. But then there were serious risks. It could have been utterly humiliating for them if they were no good – they could have got a really bad press. But the thing that makes *Whadda Ya Know?!!* so dangerous for the presenter is precisely what makes it riveting to watch. And so, last September it went to air. Being on cable, it didn't have a huge audience to start with – just two hundred thousand, but we were hoping to build. Then a tiny piece appeared in *Time Out* describing it as 'hip' and 'subversive'. Before we knew it, Channel Four had poached it, outbidding Challenge for the second series by £30,000 per show.

So tonight is a very big night because *Whadda Ya Know?!!*'s going to be aired nationwide for the very first time. And you might think that presenting a prime-time TV show would make me happy, and of course in one way, it does – but, in another way, it fills me with dread . . .

There are drawbacks you see. Huge drawbacks, I reflected nervously as I turned right into All Saints Road. In one way I'm hoping that the show *won't* be a success, because, if it is, then what happened to Nick might be raked up.

I stopped at the newsagents and bought the *Independent*. I felt a surge of adrenaline as I turned to the TV listings. There it was, in the 8pm slot, and next to it, it said *See Choice*. My eyes scanned to the top of the page. *Hey – Whadda Ya Know?!! Another new quiz show! But, whadda ya know, this really is one with a difference. Newcomer Laura Quick (right) looks brainy – and she'll need to be. Riveting.*

My stomach was churning, but as I crossed the road into All Saints Mews I felt my tension recede. To me it's the prettiest street in London; even on a cold, sleety day like today. It's wide for a mews, and the houses are painted in seaside tones of pink and lemon and blue. Well-behaved climbers trail neatly up their exteriors twining through elegant balconies of wrought iron. I caught the scent of the white *Clematis Armandii* as I passed number twelve, and admired the pots of freckled mauve hellebores.

Trident TV is half way down on the left, and occupies two white, shuttered houses that were knocked together in the seventies to make the only office premises in the Mews. Without being obviously commercial looking, the building has a pleasantly businesslike air. I shook my umbrella, then pushed on the door. There was Nerys, sitting behind the desk of our tiny reception area.

'So then *I* said to her . . .' I heard her say in a loud whisper as I folded my umbrella, 'and then *she* turned round to me and said . . . . well, *no* . . . that's *right*. She *has* got a nerve, and so I thought, well, I'm *not* standing for this, so *I* turned round to her and said – oh just a minute Shirl . . .'

'Good morning,' I said pleasantly. I may not like Nerys much, but I am always polite to her.

'G'morning Laura. I'll ring you later, Shirl.' She replaced the receiver. 'These are for you . . .' she nodded conspiratorially at a bouquet of yellow tulips, white roses and golden mimosa. She patted her hair, which was the colour of marmalade and lacquered to the texture of candyfloss. 'They were delivered about an hour ago.'

'How *nice*,' I said wonderingly, my irritation with Nerys vanishing. The vanilla-y scent of the mimosa was delicious. I unpinned the card. 'I wonder who they're from?'

'They're from your sister, Hope, and her husband.'

I felt a stab of annoyance. 'How do you know?'

'Because she phoned up to check they'd arrived.'

'I see. Never mind,' I added briskly. 'I've always thought lovely surprises *quite* over-rated.'

She examined her nails. 'Well, I'm sorry, Laura, but you *did* ask.'

'It was a rhetorical question,' I explained sweetly as I took off my coat.

Immune to the rebuke – she has a pachydermatous hide – Nerys was now staring at my top half. 'You're not going to wear that jacket on set are you?'

'Yes.' I looked at her. 'Why?'

She cocked her head to one side. 'Well, if you ask *me*, I don't think that colour really suits you.'

'I didn't ask you, Nerys.'

'Take it from me, that lime green –' she sucked the air through her teeth 'Ooh, no – it's *all* wrong. You should wear pink,' she added as the phone trilled out. 'Or peach. In fact, you know what you *should* do – you should get your colours done. You look like a Summer to me. Go-od *morn*-ing – Trident Tee-*veee* . . .'

When I say I don't like Nerys much, what I really mean is that I actively *dis*like her. So much so that I sometimes entertain fantasies about chopping her into human nuggets and feeding her to next door's cat. I have often wondered why she has this effect on me. Is it because of the amount of time she spends making personal phone calls? That's not my business – Trident belongs to Tom. Is it because she's deliberately unpleasant? She may be jaw-droppingly tactless, but she's not. Is it the way she keeps saying, 'You'd never think I was fifty-three, would you?' Why shouldn't she delude herself? No, the reason why Nerys drives me to near insanity is because she's one of these annoying people who always know *best*. Whatever the subject, Nerys has the answer. 'Take it from me,' she likes to say, or 'If you want my advice . . .' or 'I'll tell you what *I* think . . .' And because this is quite a small, open-plan building it's all too easy for her to do just that.

We'll be discussing something to do with the show, and we'll suddenly hear her pipe up from the front desk with her opinion on the matter, her conviction matched only by her ignorance. The other day, for example, I was talking to Dylan,

14

who's our new script editor – he's a bit of a boffin really, perfect for the quiz. We were discussing Wallis Simpson for one of the questions; we compile them ourselves – Dylan does the science, geography and sport ones, while I do politics, history and the arts – and we were talking about the Duke of Windsor's stint as Governor of the Bahamas.

'It was Bermuda, wasn't it?' we suddenly heard from reception. 'The Duke of Windsor was Governor of Bermuda wasn't he?'

'No, Nerys,' Dylan shouted back politely. 'It was the Bahamas.'

'Really?' There was a moment's stupefied – and, frankly, impertinent – silence and then we heard, 'Are you sure?'

'Yes, Nerys. We're quite sure,' Dylan replied with saintly patience.

'Because *I* thought it was Bermuda.'

'Honestly, Nerys,' I said. 'It really *was* the Bahamas because a) it just *was* and b) Dylan and I have checked it in two reference books and on the net to make one hundred and ten per cent certain. Because that's what we always do.'

'I see,' she replied, before adding, as if making a gracious concession, 'Oh well then – if you're sure.'

In many ways it's unreasonable of me to dislike Nerys as much as I do because the fact is I know she means well. That's the worst thing about it – she's genuinely trying to *help*. There's nothing in the world she likes more. I've seen her practically mug tourists in order to give them directions to Portobello, and several times I've heard her give unsolicited advice to strangers in shops. *You don't want to pay fifteen pounds for that ... they've got them for a tenner in Woolworths ... yes, that's right – a tenner ... it's not far ... second left, third right, straight on for 800 yards, first right, fourth left, past Buybest, opposite the ABC Pharmacy ... that's okay, it's a pleasure – no really ... it was no trouble – honestly, please DON'T mention it.*

And that's the other thing. Nerys thinks that everyone's indebted to her, and basks in their imagined gratitude. She deflects our exasperated put-downs like a Sherman tank deflecting ping-pong balls; they bounce off her completely unfelt. And though she drives us all mad, Tom keeps her on for the very good reason that a) having a receptionist gives out the impression that we're a bigger, better company than we actually are and b) she adores working for him. In the two years she's been here she's always turned up on time, never taken a day off and, in her own way, she does the job well. She opens up the office in the mornings. If the photocopier breaks down, she gets it repaired. She does all the clerical work and arranges our transport to and from the studio. She changes the light bulbs, and waters the plants. Tom appreciates her loyalty; he also feels responsible for her as he says she's so annoying she'd never get a job anywhere else. Needless to say, Nerys fancies herself as a bit of a quiz buff and is thrilled about *Whadda Ya Know?!!* 'It's a pity I can't go on it myself,' she often says. 'I think I'd do *rather* well.'

I went through to the office, which increasingly resembles a small library – every inch of wall space taken up with the huge number of reference books we need to compile the quiz. The dilapidated shelves groan with *Halliwell's Film and Video Guide*, the *Penguin Dictionary of Art*; all twenty-nine volumes of the *Encyclopaedia Britannica* and the *Complete Book of the British Charts*. We have the *Oxford Dictionary of Quotations*, the *Guinness Book of Records*, the *Science Desk Reference* and *Debrett's*. Plus the *Concise Dictionary of National Biography*, the *Encyclopaedia of Battles*, the *Compendium of British Wild Flowers* and *Who's Who*.

Dylan was at his desk, on the phone, absently winding his bootlace tie around his index finger, while Tom hovered over the central printer, which was spewing out reams of script.

'Hi,' I said to Tom above the clattering of the laser jet.

Normally Tom wears jeans, but today being a studio day – we record six weeks ahead – he was wearing his one suit – a Prince of Wales check.

He looked up. 'Hi, Laura.' His blue eyes creased into a smile, the fine lines spoking out from the corners. 'Now. I need to ask you a *very* serious question.'

'Go on then.'

'Who sent you the flowers?'

I smiled. 'My sister Hope and her husband – to wish me luck. Why?'

'I thought they must be from an admirer, that's all.'

'Nope.' I went to my desk. 'I don't have any.'

'Sure you do.'

'I don't, I tell you. I haven't been on a date for *so* long.'

'Then it's high time you did. You're young, Laura.'

'*Ish.*'

'You're beautiful.'

'Hardly, but thanks.'

'So you've got to get out there and . . . seize the day.'

'Yes,' I said. 'Maybe you're right.' A new relationship – however scary the idea – would help me move forward, and, without wishing to sound heartless here, it's hardly as though Nick's in any position to object.

'Anyway, today's a big day for you.'

My stomach turned over. 'It is a big day – dead right.' Today, I thought, my life could change forever.

Tom pulled out the last sheets of script and began shuffling them into order. 'So are you feeling okay?'

I shook my head. 'I'm feeling horribly nervous to tell you the truth.'

'The critics will love you, Laura. Have confidence.' He picked up a red stapler and began clipping the pages together.

'That's not what I mean.'

The stapler stopped in mid air. 'Oh.' His voice had dropped. 'Because of . . . Nick.'

I nodded. Tom knows what happened. Everyone here does – but then it was too big to hide.

'I feel like I'm a target, Tom, waiting to be shot at.'

Tom looked at me, then carried on stapling. 'Well, that's the risk you took. We talked about it when you agreed to front the show, remember?'

'Yes,' I murmured. 'I do. But at that time it was only going to go out on cable – we had no idea it would ever hit the network, let alone at peak time.'

'I hope you don't regret it.'

'No,' I sighed. 'Of course not – I was thrilled – I still am. But now that I'm laying myself open to media scrutiny, I can't help feeling . . . *terrified*, actually.'

'Well, don't be.' He straightened up. 'In any case, Laura, what happened to Nick wasn't your fault. Was it?'

I stared at him. *Your fault* . . .'No. No, it wasn't my fault.'

'If the show's a success,' he went on, 'then yes, the story might get picked up. So make sure your nearest and dearest are primed to keep schtum.' I made a mental note to remind my sisters to stay quiet. 'But in any case, you've done nothing *wrong*. You've got nothing to be ashamed of, Laura, have you?'

To be ashamed of . . .'No. No, I haven't. That's right.'

'Anyway, there's a friendly little piece in *The Times* today,' he said. 'Here . . .' He handed it to me. It was very complimentary about the show's 'unique format' – with its 'unexpected twist' – and about my presenting skills. I showed him the one in the *Independent*.

' "Riveting . . ." ' Tom read. 'Good.' He nodded. 'Well, I think it *is* riveting – if I'm allowed to say that about my own baby.' I looked at him. 'Anyway, I'd better get over to the studio.' He reached for his coat. 'Ner-ys,' he yelled, 'Is my car there yet?'

I saw her peering through the slats in the blinds. 'He's just pulling up.'

'I'll see you there in about an hour, okay, Laura?' Tom said. I nodded. 'Don't be late.'

'I won't. I'll just get Dylan to run through the script.'

I put the flowers in water, then sent Hope a virtual thank you card, and by the time I'd pressed 'Send' Dylan was winding up his phone call, and waving at me. He used to be a question setter on *Mastermind,* and is now script editor on *Whadda Ya Know?!!* He decides which questions should go in each show, and in what order, then he goes through them with me before we record.

'Right then, Laura.' He picked up his clipboard. 'Your starter for ten. What is the name for an alloy of copper and tin?'

'Brass!' we heard Nerys shout from the front desk.

'Bronze,' I replied.

'Correct. What is the Roman numeral for a thousand?'

'C!' she yelled.

'It's M.'

'What is the capital of Armenia?'

'Ulan Bator!'

'Yerevan.'

'It's Yerevan,' said Dylan, rolling his eyes. I sat down at my desk.

'What is a hoggerel?' I heard him say as I fiddled with a large paperclip.

I looked up at him. 'A what?'

'A hoggerel.'

'Pass!' Nerys called out. 'Anyway, that's much too difficult if you want my opinion. Good *morn*-ing, Trident Tee-*veee* . . . ?'

'A hoggerel?' I repeated. 'No idea.'

'It's a yearling sheep – you can accept "young" sheep. Who discovered the source of the Nile?'

'Livingstone,' I replied absently. 'No, not Livingstone – erm . . . I mean – *Speke.'*

'In which Scottish mountain group is Aviemore?'

'The Cairngorms.'

'What's the traditional Muslim colour for mourning?'

'White.'

'In human biology what term describes the hollow ball of cells that is an early stage in the development of the embryo?' I felt my insides shift.

'I'll have to hurry you . . .' I heard Dylan say. 'Don't you know it? Sure you do – a well-informed woman like you.'

'Yes. I do. It's a blastocyst.'

'Correct.' I visualised a tiny blob, smaller than a full stop, but already heaving with life, burrowing into the dark softness of the uterine wall.

'Are you okay Laura?'

'What? Yes . . . of course. Carry on.'

He flipped over the page. 'What is the Hindi name for India?'

Sindh, I wondered? No, that's a province . . . The Hindi name for . . . begins with a 'b' surely . . . a 'b' . . . a 'b' . . . a 'b' . . . 'Bharat, isn't it?'

'Correct.'

'So have we covered all areas?' I asked after we'd been through all sixty questions.

Dylan nodded. 'The whole shebang.' He took a deep breath. 'History, Politics, Science, Literature, Religion, Philosophy, Geography, the Monarchy, Classical music, Pop music, Entertainment, Architecture, Ballet, the Arts and Sport.'

'Comprehensive then.'

'And are you happy with the script?'

I quickly scanned it. 'It looks fine.'

'Your car's here, Laura!' I heard Nerys shout. I picked up my bag.

'Are you coming with me, Dylan?' He grabbed his leather jacket and helmet.

'No – I'll see you there; I'm on my bike.'

'You be careful on that motorbike now!' I heard Nerys call out as he left the building. 'You want to be careful!'

'Yes Nerys. I always am.'

As I passed her desk Nerys handed me a large envelope. 'It's the list of contestants. Sara asked me to give it to you before she went to the studio this morning.'

'Thanks. I'll look at it on the way.'

'Good luck then, Laura.' She looked at me appraisingly. 'Yes – you're a Summer. I can tell from your skin tone. Good *morn*-ing, Trident Tee-*veee* . . .'

The studio we use is in Acton, so from Notting Hill it doesn't take long. But today the traffic was slow because of the weather – the snow had turned to driving rain. Then we were held up for ten minutes at White City because someone had broken down, and then we hit roadworks, and the driver was ranting about Ken Livingstone, and what he'd like to do to him, and it was only then that I remembered the list. I don't meet the contestants beforehand – Sara auditions them – but on the day I'm given a brief biography of each one. And I was just about to open the envelope and read the four names and the brief descriptions of who they were, what they did, and what their hobbies were etcetera, etcetera, when my mobile rang. I rummaged in my bag.

'Laura!' It was my elder sister, Felicity. She loves to chat – unfortunately about only one thing. I braced myself. '*Guess* what Olivia discovered this morning?' she began breathlessly.

'Let me see,' I replied, as I glanced out of the window. 'A cure for cancer? Life on Mars? The square root of the hypotenuse?'

There was a snort of derisive, but delighted, laughter. 'Don't be *silly* Laura. Not yet.'

'What has she discovered, then? Tell me.'

'Oh it's so adorable – her *feet*!'

'Really?' I said as we pulled up at a zebra crossing. 'Where were they?'

'On the end of her legs of course!'

'Isn't that where they're usually located?'

'Yes, but babies don't *know* that, do they? They suddenly discover it when they're about six months and they're *fascinated*. I just wanted to share it with you.' I suppressed a yawn. 'You see this morning, there she was, lying on the changing station gurgling and smiling up at me in that adorable way of hers – just looking at me and smiling – weren'tyoumylovelylicklesweetiedarling?' she added in a helium squeak. 'Then, she suddenly looked at her feet in this really quite profound way, Laura, and then she grabbed them and started *playing* with them. It was quite amazing actually . . . just playing with her toes and . . . are you still there, Laura?'

'Yes . . . yes, I am.'

'Don't you think that's *incredible*?' I thought of the microscopic blob, its cells dividing, and doubling.

'It's a miracle.' I glanced out of the window.

'Well, I wouldn't go *quite* that far. But it is an important little milestone,' I heard Felicity add proudly. 'And what's so fantastic about it is that Olivia's only five months and three days – so she did it a month *early*. Your niece is very advanced – aren'tyoumylovelylicklebabychops?' Her voice had suddenly risen two octaves again. 'You'revewyVEWYadvanced!'

'So the breastfeeding's obviously paying off then,' I said with as much enthusiasm as I could muster.

'Oh, absolutely. It definitely makes them brighter.'

'I'm not sure, Fliss. Mum only breastfed us for two weeks and –'

'I *know*,' she said in a scandalized voice. 'Just think how intelligent we *would* have been! Oh God, she's just puked *all* over me . . . hang on – it'sokaymylicklesweetiedarlingit-doesn'tmatter – where's that muslin? I can *never* find one when I need one . . . damn, damn, damn – oh, here it is . . . Laura? Laura – are you still there?'

'Yes, but I'm just on my way to the studio right now and –'

'Did I tell you I'm just starting her on solids?' she interrupted again.

'*Yes*, Fliss. I believe you did.'

Felicity, being the world's biggest Baby Bore, tells me everything about Olivia – her development, her mental alertness, her weight gain, her hair growth, her superior prettiness compared to other babies of her acquaintance – and about the general joys of being a mum. She doesn't do this to be smug – she's a nice, warm-hearted person – but because she can't help it because she's so over the moon. And as the three of us are close, and as Hope and I don't have kids – she's never wanted them – Fliss likes to share it all with us both. She sees it as a gift to her childless sisters, to include us in every single detail of Olivia's life. And although she means well, it does annoy me sometimes. Yes, to be honest, it can . . . get to me. But whenever it does, I just remind myself of what she went through to have a baby. 'I'd walk over broken glass,' she once said to me, in tears. 'I'd walk over broken glass if that's what it took.' And in a way, that's what she did, because having Olivia took her ten years and six failed cycles of fertility treatment. The fact that she was a Montessori teacher had only made her frustration worse.

She tried everything to boost her chances – yoga, reflexology, acupuncture and hypnosis; she completely overhauled her diet. She had the house feng shuied – as though shifting the furniture around could possibly have helped! She gave up alcohol, coffee and tea. She even had her amalgam fillings replaced with composite ones. She went on a pilgrimage to Lourdes. Then, at thirty-eight, out of the blue, she conceived. Now, having finally managed motherhood, Felicity worships, fanatically, at the shrine of Babydom – she adores every burp, gurgle and squeal.

'So how's it going with the sweet potato?' I enquired politely.

'Oh it took a couple of goes – you should have *seen* her

screw up her little face the first time – but she loves it now, don'tyoumygorgeouslittlepoppetypops?' she added. 'I mix it with a bit of courgette.'

There then followed an exposition about the dangers of giving babies too much carrot because they can't digest vitamin A and turn bright orange, followed by yet another lecture about the environmental horrors of disposable nappies – a subject with which Felicity's obsessed.

'They're filling up our landfill sites,' she said vehemently. 'It's *so* disgusting – eight million of them a day – and they *never* biodegrade, because of the gel. Just imagine, Laura, in 500 years' time Olivia's descendants will *still* be trying to deal with her Pampers! Isn't that a dreadful thought?'

'It is rather. So you're using the cloth ones then are you?'

'God you must be joking – too much hassle, not to mention the pong. No, I've started using these Eco-Bots gel-free disposables – I get them from Fresh and Wild. They're *very* environmentally friendly if a teensy bit expensive.'

'How much?'

'Forty-five pence each.'

'Forty-five pence? Blimey.' I did a quick mental calculation. Babies need six changes a day on average don't they, which is £2.70, multiplied by seven equals £18.90 a week, times fifty-two weeks equals . . . £980 give or take, multiplied by two and a half years' average time in nappies equals almost £2,500. 'Poor Hugh,' I said.

'Well, he didn't *have* to give up his job, did he?' she countered crossly.

'Mm, I suppose that's true.'

I like Hugh – Felicity's husband. He's a nice, rather attractive, easy-going man – but I feel a bit sorry for him. He used to work, very successfully, for Orange, which enabled them to buy their house in Moorhouse Road. But on the day Felicity ecstatically showed him the second blue line on her pregnancy test, he announced that he'd just resigned. For years he'd wanted to pursue an entirely different career. So far his pipe dream is not going well.

'How *is* the father of invention?' I asked as the car turned in at the gates of the studio car park. 'Anything patentable on the horizon?'

There was an exasperated sigh. 'Of *course* not – what do you think? Why he can't just get himself a proper job again I don't know, or at least invent something *useful*, like the wheel!'

'Anyway, I must go Fliss, I've just arrived – we're recording today.'

'Well, best of luck. And I'll be watching tonight – as long as Olivia's gone to sleep, that is.' And then she started telling me about how she's trying sleep training on Olivia to stop her waking at 4am and what she has to do to get her to drop off again and I was thinking, Why don't you just shut up? Why don't you just shut *up* about the baby? Yes, she's a *very* sweet baby and I love her *very* much, but I don't actually want to know *any* more about her today *thank* you, Fliss, because let's face it, she's *your* baby isn't she, she's *your* baby she's not *my* baby – when Felicity suddenly said, in that impulsive way of hers that never fails to catch my heart, 'You know, Laura, I'm so proud of you.'

'What?'

My frustration melted like the dew and I felt tears prick the backs of my eyes.

'Well, I just think you've been so wonderful. I mean, here I am going on about Olivia, boring you to bits most probably . . .'

'Oh . . . no,' I said weakly. 'Really . . . I –'

'But just look at what *you've* achieved! The way you've coped with everything – the sheer bloody awfulness of it all and of what *he* did. The not-so-dearly departed,' she added sardonically, because that's how she always refers, rather blackly, to Nick. 'But you've pulled yourself up again in the face of all the hideous difficulties he left behind, and – my God – look at you now! Your life's going to be *fabulous* and *brilliant* and, from today, you're going to be a famous television presenter.' At that, I felt my heart sink. '*And,*' she added with an air of triumphant finality, 'you're going to meet someone *else*!'

'And live happily ever after,' I murmured cynically as I opened the car door. 'In a whitewashed cottage with pink roses round the door and a Cath Kidston apron and two . . . *Labradors,* no doubt.'

'Well, actually, I'm quite sure you are. If you'd only *let* yourself,' Felicity added with her usual benign vehemence. 'Anyway, drop by after work tomorrow and we can chat – I haven't seen you for ages – and you can have a cuddle with Olivia. She'd love that – wouldn'toomylittledarling?' she added in a soprano ripple. 'Oo'dlovetohaveanicecuddle-withyourAuntieLauramylittlebabykins?' I could hear Olivia yodelling in the background. It tore at my heart.

'Okay then. I will.'

I took a couple of deep breaths to compose myself then looked at my watch. It was twenty-five past one and the studio session started at two. I ran inside, got the lift to the fifth floor and went straight into the small make-up room. Marian, the make-up artist, looked at me appraisingly.

'Nice jacket,' she said. 'Great cut.' Ya boo sucks, Nerys, I thought. 'But I'm not too sure about that green.' Oh. 'It's a bit acidic for your skin tone. Here . . .' she grabbed an oyster-pink one from the wardrobe rail. 'I think this might look better.' To my surprise, it did. Oh well, Nerys is clearly right about some things, I decided generously as I buttoned it. Small things at least. Now, as Marian put up my hair, and sponged foundation on to my cheeks, adrenaline began to burn through my veins. Over the tannoy I could hear the murmurs and giggles of the studio audience as they were ushered into their seats. Then I heard Tom welcoming them to the programme and explaining that, although we record as live, there would be a few retakes to do at the end. Then he asked them not to raise their hands, or fidget or cough, although it's not really possible to cheat on this show.

'And please *don't* shout out the answers!' I heard him say. There were titters. 'You may laugh, but it has been known.'

Then Ray, our sound technician – popped in. 'You've got three minutes, Laura.' He clipped the tiny microphone on to my lapel, then tucked the talkback pack into the back of my jacket and handed me the earpiece. 'Give me some level would you?'

'Hello, one, two, three . . . I had toast for breakfast . . . and I was late getting to the studio . . . and I *still* haven't looked at the list of contestants.' I rummaged in my bag for it again, while he repositioned the mike. 'Where the hell *is* it?'

'Thanks Laura, you're sounding fine.'

'And would you now please give a warm welcome to our four contestants!' I heard Tom say over the loudspeaker. The audience applauded enthusiastically as the four players went up. I heard their footsteps tap across the wooden stage.

'What are they like?' I asked Marian as I stared at my reflection. She had done their make-up before she did mine. 'Will you tell me about them as I can't find my list?'

'Well there are two nerdy ones,' she replied as she dabbed concealer under my eyes. 'Complete train-spotters. Plug ugly.'

'Par for the course.'

'Then there's quite a pretty girl in her mid-twenties, and, I must say, one absolutely *gorgeous* man. I was quite taken with him actually,' she added with a giggle. 'He made me come over all funny. Wonderful eyes,' she confided as she pulled mascara through my lashes. 'And it was obvious that he was rather excited about meeting *you*.'

I looked up at her. 'Was he?'

She tucked a hank of ash-blonde hair behind one ear. 'Oh yes.'

'Why?'

'I really don't know.' She selected a lipstick from the ten or so standing on the counter in their metal cases, like bullets. 'He told me how much he was looking forward to it – so I just assumed he was already a fan.'

As Marian blended two lipsticks together on the back of her hand, I carried on rummaging in my bag for the list of contestants, but still couldn't find it. *Damn*.

'Look up please, Laura,' Marian said.

As she applied the lipstick with a small brush, then dabbed on some gloss, I heard Tom giving the contestants his usual advice.

'Make sure you listen to each question properly,' he said. 'And don't just blurt out the first thing which pops into your head because, on this show, if you get it wrong, you *lose* points so it's important to *think* before you speak.' Then, as Marian swiftly stroked on some blusher, then brushed powder on to my brow, I heard Tom say, 'Well, I think we're ready to start.'

'Are you finished in make-up, Laura?' I heard Sara say into my earpiece.

'Yes,' I replied as Marian sprayed my hair.

'Okay, Tom, she's on her way,' I heard Sara add. 'Cue intro.'

'So, here to quiz you today is *Whadda Ya Know?!!*'s presenter – Lau-ra *Quick*!' Marian whipped off the black gown then I half walked, half ran the few yards down the corridor into the studio and stepped up on to the stage. As I did so I was momentarily blinded by the lights hanging from the rigging. I was aware of their heat, and of the oily smell, and of Tom extending his right arm to me by way of welcome; then he turned to the audience and raised both hands above his head to prompt applause, so I looked at them and smiled. As he walked off stage, I glanced up into the gallery at the back of the auditorium. There, behind the glass, was Sara, who produces the show, and the production assistant, Gill. Next to Gill I could see Dylan with his headphones on, then the vision mixers and technical team. As the clapping began to fade, I surveyed the set – four tall, illuminated blue columns of varying heights on either side; the massive pink question mark in the middle of the floor; at the back, the show's title in huge, loopy green letters; the enormous yellow clock. The whole thing was deliberately kitsch. And standing before me, behind their electronic lecterns, were the four contestants. Without taking in their faces, I smiled.

'Welcome to today's recording,' I began, squinting slightly into the spotlights. I lifted my hand to my eyes. 'I'd like to wish you all good luck, and I look forward to chatting to you afterwards but, in the meantime, as Tom says, just relax and, above all, please try and enjoy yourselves!' As I glanced at the names on their lecterns I became aware that while three of them were looking apprehensive, one of them was quietly smiling; then I saw that he was smiling at me. Now, as the spotlights were adjusted, I could see him properly. I felt as though I'd been plunged into a frozen lake.

'Right, ready to start then, Laura?' I heard Sara whisper as I tried to cover my involuntary gasp with a throat-clearing cough – for a moment I'd thought I might faint. And it was on the tip of my tongue to say, 'Well you can't start yet, actually, Sara, because I'm struggling with the fact that my first serious boyfriend – who I haven't seen for twelve years and who broke my heart and who, if I'm being honest with myself, I never *really* got over – is standing just ten feet away.'

'Counting down now, Laura,' I heard her say. 'So it's in five . . . four . . . three . . . two . . . one and . . . go music!' I heard the jaunty theme tune strike up, then the audience burst into applause.

Aware of a pounding in my chest, I turned to the camera. 'Welcome to *Whadda Ya Know?!!*,' I began with as much confidence as I could muster. Now, as the autocue scrolled

29

down, I felt not so much cold as red hot. 'I'm Laura Quick and I'll be asking the questions tonight, but first, let me explain how the show works. In my hand, here, are the questions.' I held up the cards. 'All of them are open to any of the contestants to answer – it's a case of whoever gets to the buzzer first. But once the players have buzzed they *must* answer – but they have no more than five seconds in which to do so. Now, if you look at the screens on the front of their lecterns, you'll see that they each start with one pound. This will double with every correct answer they give, when we'll hear *this* . . .' There was a loud *Ker-ching!* like the pinging of a colossal cash register. 'If, however, they give a wrong answer, or fail to answer in the five seconds, then their money will be halved, and we'll hear *this* . . .' There was a downward glissandoing *Whooooop!* 'The winner will be the player who's accumulated the most money. He or she will then get the chance to double it, if they decide to Turn the Tables – and ask *me* a question. But this carries a risk. If I get it wrong, their total money is doubled.' *Ker-ching!* 'But if I answer it correctly then it will be halved.' *Whooooop!* 'So, without further ado, let's meet today's four contestants!'

I turned back to the players as, *University Challenge*-style, they introduced themselves. I glanced at Luke, mentally kicking myself again for having lost the list – at least I'd have had less of a shock.

'*Relax* Laura,' I heard Sara whisper into my earpiece. 'You look very tense.' I softened my monkey grimace into a professional smile. 'That's better. And don't go too fast.'

'I'm Christine Schofield,' I heard number one say. She was, as Marian had described her, blonde and attractive. 'I'm from York and I'm a teacher.'

'I'm Doug Dale,' said the next. He was one of the trainspotters – late forties, bearded, bald and monkish, with large square glasses. 'I'm from Islington and I write business reports.' Standing next to Doug made Luke look even more attractive, with his fine cheekbones, and dark wavy hair, curling over his collar. All that suggested the passage of time was a nest of fine lines beneath his eyes. 'I'm Luke North,' he said, with a self-conscious smile. 'I'm an art dealer and I live in West London.'

'Hi, I'm Jim Friend,' said the next contestant, a tall, scraggy-looking man in his mid-fifties. 'I'm a mature student, studying psychology, and I live in Bedford.' There was another, polite round of applause. I held up the cards. A hush descended.

'Right. Here we go. First question. What was the Roman name for the city of Bath?'

Doug Dale's lectern flashed gold as he pressed the buzzer first. 'Sulis.'

'Technically, Aquae Sulis – but I'll allow it.' *Kerching!* 'Which berries are used to flavour gin? Christine.'

'It's juniper.'

'That's correct.' *Ker-ching!* 'What is the capital of Liberia? Luke?'

'It's Monrovia.'

'That's right.' *Ker-ching!* How bizarre, I thought, that the first words Luke should have said to me in twelve years were not 'Hello, Laura,' or 'How lovely to see you again,' or even, 'I'm sorry I hurt you so badly,' but 'It's Monrovia.'

'Which Bronze age civilization was based on the island of Crete?'

'The Minoans,' said Jim correctly. *Kerching!* Now they all had two pounds.

I looked at the next question card. 'Which canal, spelled backwards, is the name of a Greek god?' Luke buzzed first.

'Suez.'

'Correct.' *Kerching!* 'Making Zeus, of course. Who, in 1700, wrote *The Way of the World*?'

Doug Dale buzzed first. 'Congreve.'

'Yes. William Congreve.' *Kerching!* 'Which French royal house gave its name to a biscuit? Christine?'

31

'Nice,' she said confidently. *Whoooooop!*

'No – it's Bourbon.' Her two pounds went back down to one. 'Edgehill was the opening battle in which war? Luke?'

'The Civil War.'

'More detail please.'

He looked momentarily nonplussed and I was aware of the second hand moving noisily forward on the clock.

'Oh. The *English* Civil War.'

'Yes.' *Kerching!* 'Who was the Roman god of fire? Doug?'

'Prometheus?'

'No.' *Whoooooop!* 'He *stole* it from the gods – it was Vulcan. What is the common name for a solution of sodium chloride in water? Christine?'

'It's brine.'

'That's correct.' *Kerching!* 'Which South American country was named after an Italian city? Doug?'

'Argentina.' *Whooooop!*

'No – it was Venezuela, which was named after Venice. What is the meaning of "Caprine"? Luke?' He was laughing for some reason.

'Goat-like,' he said firmly.

'That's the correct answer.' *Kerching!* 'As in capricious,' I added. 'From the Latin, "caper".'

And so it went on. 'Who was the first woman to fly across the Atlantic? . . . No, not Amy Johnson.' *Whooop!* 'It was Amelia Earhart . . . What is a duiker? That's correct, Jim – a small antelope.' *Kerching!* 'What do the five Olympic rings represent . . . ? No takers for this one? The world's continents. Who discovered the source of the Nile? No – not Livingstone.' *Whooooop!* 'It was Speke. What is the Roman numeral for a thousand? M is correct, Doug.' *Kerching!* 'What is a hoggerel? No.' *Whooop!* 'It's a yearling sheep. What is the world's best-selling book? Luke? That's right. The Bible.' *Kerching!* 'Which planet has a pink sky? Mars is correct, Jim.' *Kerching!* 'Of what colour is "Leukophobia" a fear?

Doug? No.' *Whooooop!* 'Not yellow – it's white . . .' And all the time I was asking the questions, aware of the scores doubling and halving, the players' fortunes yo-yoing up and down, into my mind would flash images of Luke and me lying on the college lawn beneath the huge copper beech; cycling over Clare Bridge; sitting at the same table in the library, feet gently touching; entwined, like rope, on Luke's narrow bed.

'Five minutes left,' I heard Sara whisper in my ear. 'It's going great.' As I turned over the next card, I quickly glanced at the scores again. Doug Dale was leading with £4096, which meant he'd got twelve questions right, while Luke was one question behind with £2048 and Christine and Jim were trailing in the low hundreds as they'd answered recklessly. Behind me I was aware of the audience, silent and focused.

'Which animal features on the State flag of California?'

There was a second's silence, then Doug buzzed. 'The eagle?' *Whooooop!* He winced with frustration.

'No, I'm sorry – it's the bear.' Now he and Luke were level-pegging.

'Three minutes to go,' I heard Sara say. I looked at the next question.

'How many cards are there in a deck of Tarot cards?'

'Seventy-eight,' said Luke.

'Correct!' *Kerching!* His score doubled to £4096.

'Two minutes, Laura,' I heard Sara say.

I looked at the next card. 'Which artist designed the uniform of the Pope's bodyguards, the Swiss Guard?' Luke buzzed again, but then the answer seemed to elude him. He closed his eyes for a moment as he struggled to remember, and I was aware of the second hand, clunking forward. He only had three seconds left . . . Two seconds . . . One . . . He was about to lose four thousand pounds.

'Michaelangelo,' he blurted out. 'It was Michaelangelo.'

'Correct.'

KERASHHHHH!!! The huge gong which signalled the end of the round had sounded. Luke was ahead by one point. He'd answered thirteen questions correctly, which meant that he was on £8192.

I turned to Camera One. 'Let's take a look at the scores. In fourth place is Jim with £512, in third place is Christine with £1024. Doug is in second place with £2048. But this week's clear winner – with £8192 – is Luke North!' The audience applauded loudly and he smiled. 'But it's not over yet,' I added, 'because it's now time to Turn the Tables. The question is, Luke . . . Do you *want* to?' I turned to the audience. 'How many of you think that Luke *should* Turn the Tables? If he does, he risks losing £4,000. On the other hand, he could win another £8,000. So would you all please now cast your votes? They pressed the voting panels attached to the back of each seat, and the result was flashed up on a big plasma screen.

'Sixty-eight of you think he should,' I said, 'with a hundred and ten believing that he should hang on to what he's got.' I turned to Luke. 'The audience clearly think that you should quit now, Luke, but what do you want to do?'

'I want to Turn the Tables.'

'Are you sure?'

'Yes,' he said with a smile. 'I'm quite sure.'

'Okay then.' I turned to the camera. 'If I can't answer Luke's question – in the usual five seconds – then his prize money will double. If I can, then it will be halved. But I can assure you all at home, and here in the studio, that I have absolutely *no* way of knowing what he's going to ask me beforehand. Right then, Luke. Go ahead.'

He pulled a piece of paper out of his pocket. I prayed he hadn't come up with some question about pop music – not my best area – or football. I braced myself.

'Right . . .' he began. There was a drum roll. 'What I'd like to ask you *is* . . .' He paused, then cleared his throat. 'Erm . . .' He ran a nervous finger under his collar. 'Okay . . . Here goes.

My question . . .' he looked at me. 'My question . . . *is* . . . erm . . .' What was his *problem*? 'Would you have dinner with me sometime?'

There was a stunned silence from the audience, then nervous giggling.

'What the *hell's* he *playing* at?' I heard Sara exclaim.

By now most of the audience were laughing, and so was Luke.

'Will you have dinner with me Laura?' he repeated. 'That's my question.' But I didn't get the chance to answer it, because at that moment Tom shouted 'Cut!'

TWO

'*Now* we know why he was so interested in meeting you again,' said Marian as she removed my make-up. I looked at her reflection as she wiped off the foundation in long, firm strokes. 'It must have been a bit of a shock.'

'You can say that again.' I looked at my hands. They were still trembling. 'It was bad enough just seeing him again, without . . . that.'

'So he was a bit of a live wire then, was he, when you knew him before?'

'Yes. Yes, he was. He was . . . fun.'

'And gorgeous,' she repeated as she tore off another wad of cotton wool. I breathed in slowly through my nose to calm myself.

'Yes.' And clever, and charismatic and entertaining and slightly eccentric, and rather flirtatious and utterly . . . *maddening*.

'Has he changed much?' Evidently not. 'I mean, to look at?' she added.

'No. He's more attractive, if anything.'

'But how weird seeing him again – and like that!' And now, at last, I looked at the list of contestants, which I'd finally located in my coat pocket. I rapidly scanned the piece

36

about Luke. *Luke North, 36, read Art History at Cambridge, then worked at Christie's for a number of years. For the past three years he has been running the Due North Contemporary Art gallery in Bayswater. He lives in Notting Hill.* I read it again. Then again. Then again. Then once more.

'Was it serious?' I heard Marian ask.

'What?'

'Was your relationship with him serious? It's okay,' she went on with a smile. 'You don't have to tell me. But I can't help wondering, after what he's just done.'

'I don't mind at all,' I replied. In any case I felt so churned up that I wanted to talk about it, and I find Marian sympathetic. 'It was serious,' I explained. 'I was reading Classics, he was doing Art History. We argued a lot – but that was part of the fun. It was one of those volatile, passionate relationships – it was exciting . . . it was . . . intense . . . it was . . .' A bitter sigh escaped me. 'The happiest time of my life.'

'So what went wrong?' she asked gently. 'Did you decide you were too young to settle down?'

'No. No, it wasn't that. We were going to get a flat together in London after we'd graduated – we'd even found one to move into but then –' I was too embarrassed to tell Marian the humiliating truth – 'it all just went horribly . . . wrong.' A silence descended, then Marian put her hand on my shoulder. 'Anyway,' I looked in the mirror at my thirty-four year old face with its incipient lines. 'It was a very long time ago.' I stood up, then pulled off the gown. 'I suppose I'd better get up to the post-show party.'

'Well, good luck. I assume he'll be there.'

I got the lift to the top floor, my pulse racing, my mind wrestling with conflicting feelings. I felt dismayed that Luke had gate-crashed my life again, flirting with me – upsetting me – but, at the same time, I also felt . . . *glad.* Now, as I walked down the corridor, I could hear the hubbub emanating from the hospitality suite. I paused for a moment at the doorway, then ventured in. The air reeked of sandwiches, coffee and cheap white wine – the usual, rather dreary post-show fare. Most of the crew were up there already, chatting to the contestants, and, as they spotted me, one or two of them smirked. As I made my way inside I heard Dylan explaining to Christine that the show would go out at the end of March, while, to my right, Jim and Doug seemed to be having some sort of quiz-nerd discussion.

'It's not a "herd" of rhinoceri,' I heard Jim say. 'It's a "crash".'

'Are you sure?' said Doug.

'Absolutely – I know my collective nouns. It's used for hippo as well.'

'*I* thought it was a "bloat" of hippopotami.'

'You *can* use "bloat", but "crash" is more usual.'

'What about giraffes then?'

'That's easy – a "tower".'

And there, in the corner, by the window, talking to Sara – a sight which, even then, twelve years on, made me feel wildly, and quite unreasonably, jealous – was Luke. He suddenly saw me and waved. Then, with characteristic effrontery, he beckoned me over. Had Sara not been standing there, I would have ignored him. I was determined to be cool and aloof.

'Hi Laura.' He smiled. As Marian had said – wonderful eyes. Fringed by thick, dark lashes, they were a rich, warm brown, like the brown of tobacco, with radiating fibrils of topaz and gold. I never believed that I'd see him again, let alone that I'd be standing this close. I'd sometimes spotted men who'd looked a bit like him, and had found myself staring, overwhelmed by regret.

'Hello Luke,' I replied.

'I'm sorry about that. Did I embarrass you?'

'Yes,' I replied. 'You did. But then you probably meant to.'

'I didn't, actually.' He nodded towards Tom. 'Your director seemed a bit cross.'

'I think he thought you were trying to ruin the recording.'

'Not at all. It was just –' he shrugged – '*fun*.'

'Anyway, the retake worked out fine,' said Sara, diplomatically. 'So let's not worry about it.' We had re-done the end so that Luke decided not to Turn the Tables.

He lifted a sausage roll off a passing tray. 'But they did say that I could ask you any question.'

'Any general knowledge question,' I corrected him.

'Still, it was a very good, fast-paced show,' Sara interrupted. 'You were a great contestant, Luke, and there was no harm done. Anyway, I'll . . . leave you two to it,' she added tactfully. 'You've obviously got some catching up to do.'

As Sara retreated, Luke smiled at me again, quizzically, as if slightly bewildered by my frosty demeanour, but what did he expect? Why should I be warm and effusive when he'd embarrassed me like that, not to mention what had happened between us twelve years before?

'Can I ask you something?' I said.

'Of course.' He grabbed another sausage roll. 'That's your job now, isn't it – asking people things. Gosh I'm hungry – I didn't have lunch.'

'Did you plan to do that?'

'No. I was going to ask you something perfectly sensible –' he wiped the crumbs off his lips – 'but then I suddenly felt this overwhelming compulsion to ask you out to dinner instead.'

'I see,' I said. 'So it was a "caprice" then was it – an "impulsive change of mind"?'

He smiled. 'I suppose it was.'

'And why did you laugh when I asked you what "caprine" meant?'

He rolled his eyes. 'It would take *too* long to explain – I'll tell you over dinner. You will come, I hope. It's been such a long time.' He smiled again, and as he did so, I was suddenly acutely aware, despite my turmoil, of the familiar longing that I had once had for him resurfacing. I wanted him to wrap his arms around me, like he used to. 'Will you?' I wanted to bury my face in his neck. I wanted to trace the lovely curve of his lips with my fingertips. 'Will you?' he repeated.

'I really don't . . . know.'

'Playing hard to get, Laura?'

'No, but . . .' I suddenly surfaced from my reverie. 'Look, Luke – you've got a *nerve*. You waltz back into my life in this . . . *bizarre* way, and now you're just assuming I'll have dinner with you, when we haven't actually *spoken* since 1993, have we?'

'No. But that's not my fault.'

'It *is*!' I lowered my voice, aware of eyeballs swivelling discreetly in our direction. 'It *is* your fault.'

'That's not true. You wouldn't answer my letters or calls. You airbrushed me out of your life as though I'd never existed.'

'Who could *blame* me?' I enquired. 'In the *circumstances*?' A silence descended.

'This is just like old times,' he said happily. I realized, with a jolt, that he was right. Two minutes in each other's company and we'd already stripped down to our emotional underpants.

I tried to wrest the conversation back to neutral ground. 'So what was the sensible question you were going to ask me then?'

'Ah – well, I gave that very careful thought. I didn't want to ask you anything that you might not know, because of course the last thing I wanted was for you to be humiliated in front of the watching millions.'

'How considerate.'

'So I decided I'd ask you a question that you'd be able to work out.'

'Namely?'

'How many times a day does the human heart beat?'

I looked at him blankly. 'That sounds like one of your classic snippets of Useless Information.'

40

'It is. But your mental arithmetic was pretty hot, I remember, so I knew you'd get it.'

'But it would almost certainly have taken me longer than five seconds, so you could have doubled your money there, Luke. Your little joke was rather expensive, wasn't it?'

'Oh well.' He shrugged. 'Eight grand's enough.'

'For what – if you don't mind my asking? I mean, why on earth did you want to take part?'

'Do you really want to know?'

'I *do*. I was surprised to see you, to put it mildly.'

'Okay. I was put up to it by a couple of friends. I was complaining to them that I needed a few grand because I'd like to go to art school – I've always wanted to go. Don't you remember that?'

'Yes, I do. Of course.'

'And I've got a place at the Slade to do a part-time diploma. But I'm very short of cash at the moment for various reasons which I won't bore you with, so they suggested that I try and get on *Whadda Ya Know?!!* When I discovered that you were the presenter it was a bit of a shock, to put it mildly, and I decided against it. But the more I thought about it, the more I realized how much I'd like to see you again – especially when I found out that your office isn't far from where I live.'

'Then why didn't you just write to me there?'

'Because I didn't think you'd reply. You probably wouldn't have done, would you?'

'I don't . . . know. I . . . probably . . . *not*.'

'Exactly. So I decided that I'd just get myself on the show. To be honest, I thought you'd know beforehand.'

'I should have done, but I hadn't read the list of contestants.

He glanced at his watch. 'Crikey – I must get going – I've got to pick up Jessica.' Jessica? 'She's my girl,' he explained proudly. I felt a sudden sagging, as though all my buoyancy had gone. 'She's the love of my life.'

'I see.

'She's really gorgeous. She's got big blue eyes . . .'

'How nice . . . I really *must* talk to the other contestants.'

'And this *fantastic* smile.'

'That's great.' I held out my hand. 'It was nice seeing you again, Luke.' I gave him a brittle smile, then turned away.

'Do you want to see a photo of her?'

'Sorry? No – not particularly, since you ask.'

'Hang on . . . here you go . . .' He'd removed a small folding leather frame from his pocket and now handed it to me. Staring out at me was an angelic little girl, smiling gappily.

'She's your daughter?' He nodded enthusiastically. A wave of relief flooded over me, in a way that took me aback. 'I didn't know you'd had a baby.'

'Didn't you?'

I shrugged. 'I didn't have a clue *what* had happened to you.' I didn't add that I'd avoided finding out. I'd dropped all our friends because I couldn't bear the association. I looked at the photo again. 'She *is* gorgeous. She's really beautiful.'

'Well, I think so obviously, but thanks.'

'She's, what, five?'

'Just turned six.'

'So you – got married and all that, did you?'

'I did.'

'Uh huh.' So that was that then.

'Anyway . . .' He fished his car keys out of his pocket and jingled them. 'I'd better be off – it's my turn to collect her from school. So . . . I guess you don't want to have dinner with me.' He shrugged. 'Oh well . . .'

'I didn't actually *say* that, Luke.'

'Well you didn't say that you *did*.' He picked up his scarf. 'So you've changed your mind have you?'

'How could I have changed it when I hadn't made it *up*? You're being so . . . bloody . . . *manipulative*.'

He smiled. 'I'm not actually – I'm being direct. I'm asking

you if you'll have dinner with me – how about Friday? Now, I'm in a hurry so, if you don't reply, I'll take your silence as assent. I'll pick you up at eight shall I?'

'But . . .'

'But what?' He looked at me then slapped his brow. 'Of course . . . but I don't know your *address*. Silly me. Give it to me now then will you?'

'No Luke – that wasn't what I meant. I meant – what about your *wife*?' My heart was beating so loudly I thought he'd hear it. 'You said you were married – won't your *wife* mind? I rather imagine she will.'

He shook his head. 'I'm not going to tell her.'

'Oh. Well, I don't think that's on.'

He rolled his eyes. 'Get off your high horse will you Laura. I'm not going to tell her – for the simple reason that I don't have to. We're separated.'

'Oh dear,' I said. My heart sang. In fact it wasn't just singing – it was jigging and pirouetting and twirling and hopping. 'I *am* sorry to hear that. Since when?'

'Last May . . . Anyway, Laura, I've got to leave right now. So what's the answer then?' He picked up his coat.

'Well –' and now, for the first time, I allowed myself to smile – 'the answer *is* . . . a hundred thousand. The human heart beats a hundred thousand times a day doesn't it?'

'That's right.' He kissed me on the cheek. 'Sometimes more.'

They say the first cut's the deepest – and it's true. Seeing Luke again seemed to have cast the whole world in an entirely new light. All that was familiar looked oddly unfamiliar – as though the prism through which I'd viewed everything had changed. As I opened my front door that evening, it was as though the past had risen up to overwhelm the present and I was seeing the flat for the very first time. I went straight to my desk and took out a carved wooden box in which I'd kept things too personal for public display. There was a black and white photo of my parents, kissing; there was a be-ribboned lock of my grandmother's hair, there were my engage-ment and wedding rings in their velvet boxes and, at the bottom, one of Luke's drawings of me. I'd burnt all the others – he'd done dozens – but, for some reason, I'd kept just this one. He'd sketched me while I slept one Sunday morning at the end of our first month together when everything had been heightened – intense. Now, as I looked at my younger self, my naked form caught in dark blue pastel lines and smudged shadows, I thought of how different my life might have been.

I poured a glass of wine, had a couple of large, steadying sips, then lay on the sofa, eyes closed, thinking about Luke, allowing all the memories that I had pushed away for so long to wash back on a nostalgic tide . . .

Thump! Thump! I opened my eyes. 'Oh God.' *Thump! Thump!* I looked at the ceiling. 'Not again.' My new upstairs neighbour is a medium and her séances can get a bit noisy. *Thump! THUMP! THUMP!!* I rolled my eyes, imagining the curtains swishing, light bulbs popping and furniture flying round the room. I haven't met her yet, though I caught a glimpse of her when she moved in – she's one of these glam-orous brunettes *d'un certain age*. But I know what she does, because for the past month people have been buzzing my intercom, and asking me if I'm 'Psychic Cynth?' *Thump! Thump!!* According to the letters she gets, her real name is Cynthia del Mar. *THUMP! THUMP!!!* I see her cat sitting on the fire escape sometimes.

THUMP!! THUMP!!! 'EEEEEEHH!!!' This really was a bit much. Why couldn't she show a little consideration, or at least clock off at a reasonable time? I glanced at my watch. It was a minute to eight – time to turn on the TV; with luck it would drown out her noise.

'Fingers on the buzzers now everyone,' said the continuity announcer cheerily. 'Because it's time for Channel Four's brand new quiz show – *Whadda Ya Know?!!*' The opening

credits rolled. And there I was, asking the four contestants –
two men and two women – to introduce themselves. We'd
recorded this edition in early January.

'My name's Peter Watts and I'm a civil servant.'

'I'm Sue Jones and I work in I.T.'

'I'm Geoff Cornish and I'm a poultry wholesaler.'

'My name's Kate Carr and I'm a librarian.'

'Here we go. First Question . . .'

I felt disconsolate, watching it alone, but there wasn't
anyone to watch it with. My parents live in Yorkshire, Hope
and Mike were out, and I hadn't wanted to go round to
Felicity's because I was seeing her the following night. It would
have been nice to have watched it with Tom, but he was obviously busy. I think he might be seeing someone – I've got
that feeling. Now, as we got to the third or fourth question
I heard, from above, 'Oh! – oh! – OOOOOH!!' *THUMP!!*
THUMP!!!

Living below a spiritualist might bother some people, but
it doesn't bother me because I don't believe in the paranor-
mal – I'm a rationalist, so I only believe in facts. But although
it doesn't spook me, I do object to the noise. And Geoff the
poultry wholesaler had just got the question about Noël
Coward completely wrong (the answer was *Blithe Spirit*, not
Hay Fever), when there was the sound of rapidly descending
footsteps, then urgent knocking.

'Hell-oooo!!!' I heard, in a pleasantly husky, but oddly
over-elocuted voice. 'Is there anybody there? Is there anybody
th-e-r-e?' I wearily got to my feet.

'You're a medium,' I muttered. 'So you should know.' I
opened the door. There was Cynthia, looking desperate.

'I'm *awfully* sorry,' she breathed, clasping the architrave
with both hands. 'But I've got a problem.'

'Yes?' I said wonderingly, inhaling the overpowering aroma
of her *Knowing*. I've a good memory for scents as well as
facts.

'I'm Cynthia.' She offered me a bejewelled and beautifully manicured hand. 'I know we haven't met properly, but I wonder if you could help me.'

'Sure. If I can do. How?'

'My blasted television's broken down again. It usually responds to manual violence, but not today for some reason.' Ah. That explained the noise. But what did she think *I* could do? Thump it myself? Call Radio Rentals? 'And there's this new quiz show I'm *dying* to watch.'

'I see.'

'It looks like a real goodie actually.'

'Hmm.'

'So I wondered if you'd mind if I watched it down here.' Oh.

'Well . . .'

'I'm *so* sorry,' she breathed. 'I know it's an *awful* imposition.' Why not, I thought? In any case my encounter with Luke had made me feel expansive and generous.

'It's . . . okay. I really don't mind. I'm just watching it myself actually.'

She clapped her hand to her chest, rattling her string of large pearls. 'Oh that *is* kind of you! You see I *adore* quizzes,' she explained, as she barged past me and installed herself on the sofa. 'I watch them all. I'm rather *good* at them if I say so myself. Ooh, is that an open bottle? I'd *love* a glass.'

I wouldn't have minded Cynthia's presence – or the speed with which she consumed most of my Merlot – were it not for her non-stop commentary on the show. She sat right forward on the sofa, staring at the screen intently. If she'd had a tub of popcorn she would have been rattling it.

'What an awful shirt that man's wearing . . . And she *really* should get her teeth fixed . . . It's the Ngorongoro crater you *moron*! Ngorongoro! . . . The presenter's a bit weird-looking, don't you think . . . ? No, no, it's *not* a monkey house, you steaming great ignoramus – it's a place where *bees* are kept!'

At times her exasperation with the contestants would almost lift her on to her feet. At other times she would shoot me a complicit smirk before returning her gaze to the screen. 'No, not the *Titanic*, you *idiot* – it was the *Lusitania*! How many properties are there on the Monopoly board? Forty! Oh. Twenty-two is it? Hmmm . . .' Sometimes she'd try and hurry the contestants, as though she was the compere. 'Come on, now . . . Come *on* . . .' Then it came to Turn the Tables time. 'My God,' Cynthia gasped. 'He's going to ask *her* a question. *That's* novel! I bet Anne Robinson wouldn't like that!' We watched as the leading contestant, Geoff, the poultry wholesaler, asked me, with a smug little smile, as though he was convinced I couldn't possibly know the answer, 'What is a quadrimum?'

'A quadrimum?' Cynthia repeated with an appalled expression. 'I haven't the *faintest* idea. Poor girl, she'll *never* get that – how humiliating. I can't bear to watch.' She covered her face with her hands. We could hear the stage clock ticking as the five-second countdown began. 'Quadrimum?' Cynthia repeated quietly from behind oblonged fingers. 'Fiendish. Absolutely *fiendish* . . .'

'It's the best or oldest wine,' Cynthia and I heard me say. 'It has to be at least four years old.'

'That's . . . correct,' said Geoff with an expression that combined horror, surprise and naked disappointment – after all, he'd just lost two grand.

'*That* was good,' Cynthia said. She looked at me, her eyes like satellite dishes. 'I was *amazed* she knew it.'

'It's not that hard. It's in any dictionary of difficult words – I used to make myself learn five new ones every day – and of course studying Classics helped. That word features in a beautiful poem by Horace.' I made a mental note to re-read it. I glanced at the shelves – I knew I'd got it somewhere.

'Even so, it's impressive, I mean . . .' She was looking at me again, and now her expression had changed. 'I mean . . .' She stared at me openly then turned her head back to the screen. By now the penny was rolling around in the gutter, tinkling loudly. 'It's *you* . . .' she breathed. 'I didn't . . . notice . . . I didn't . . . realize . . .' She'd clapped her hand to her mouth. 'But it *is* you, isn't it?' I nodded. 'Of *course* – you're called Laura.' She looked at the TV. 'And so is *she*.'

'That's . . . right.'

Having looked mortified, Cynthia suddenly brightened, as if seeming to glimpse the possibilities of the situation. 'Well . . . that's *rather* good. I've got a celebrity neighbour. A real live television presenter!' she concluded happily. 'Now, tell me – *how* did that come about?' As the closing credits on the show scrolled up the screen, I quickly explained how I'd got the job.

'So you've had fame thrust upon you, then.'

'Well I certainly didn't go looking for it.' I thought, sinkingly, of Nick. 'Fame's the *last* thing I want. And you?' I went on. 'You're a . . . medium aren't you?' I poured her another glass of wine. 'A spiritualist?'

'Oh *no*.' She looked appalled. 'I wouldn't be seen dead at a séance, and I do *not* communicate with the deceased. Too creepy,' she added with a shudder. 'I did do a course in mediumship skills some time ago but I had a rather unpleasant experience with some ectoplasm.'

'So what *do* you do then?' I asked as I topped up my own glass.

'I'm a psychic. I have the gift of clairvoyance and I use it to give people advice, or to help them achieve their goals. I can help with all sorts of matters – matrimonial crises, professional problems, family difficulties – I even help to find missing pets. Some people think of me as their spiritual guide, or even angel.'

'Well – ' I regard it as complete baloney but tried to think of something nice to say. 'That sounds fascinating.'

'It is, although, *confidentially* . . .' her brow had pleated with anxiety, 'I could do with a few more clients. In fact it's a bit of a worry. It's *hard,* isn't it – having to make one's living,' she added distractedly.

'Well,' I shrugged. 'I'm . . . used to it.'

'So if you know anyone who's in need of a little clairvoyance . . .'

'Oh. Yes. Of course. Have you put an ad in the local paper?'

'I have – and I've got a website – but the problem is that there are so *many* psychics in London. The market's saturated – oh *hello* Hans!' Her cat had just wandered in through the open door and was now winding itself in and out of her ankles, purring like a tiny Ferrari. 'You don't mind cats do you?' she asked as it sprang on to her lap.

'No. I like them.'

'And she's very sweet.'

'She is. Erm . . . why do you call her Hans, if she's female?'

'Because I found her outside my old flat in Hans Place.'

'Hans Place in Knightsbridge?' She nodded. 'That's a nice address.'

'Oh it was,' she said regretfully. 'It was *heaven.*'

'So what brings you here?' I asked. 'Ladbroke Grove's a bit . . . different.'

'I know. But, well . . .' she sighed. 'My circumstances changed. You see, my last flat didn't belong to me. *Unfortunately.*' She snapped a breadstick in half. 'So, when that . . . arrangement . . . came to an end I decided I really *must* buy my own place. This was all I could afford, but it's a nice flat.'

'But how did you get into the psychic . . . business?'

'Well, that's quite a story actually . . . Do you want to hear?' I didn't – but I nodded politely. She sat back, and cradled her wine, gazing into the middle distance as she began her trip down Memory Lane. 'It was all because of a seagull,' she began. 'A psychic seagull, to be precise.' I looked at her. 'It saved my life.'

'Really?'

'Without a doubt. You see, this time last year I was feeling very, very low – I'd reached . . . a major turning point in my life. So I went to stay with my sister in Dorset and one afternoon I went for a walk on the cliffs. And I must have been too near the edge, because I slipped and fell about twenty-five feet. And I was lying there, on the beach, trapped between two boulders, in great pain with a broken leg, quite unable to move – like *this*.' She'd clapped her arms stiffly to her sides to help me visualise her predicament.

'How awful.'

'It was *terrifying* – not least because I knew the tide was coming in. I kept calling out, but the beach was deserted; and as I lay there, sincerely believing that I was going to *die,* a seagull came and hovered overhead. And it wouldn't go away. So, in desperation, I shouted at it. I yelled, "For God's sake, go and get *help*!" To my *very* great surprise, it flew off.' She leaned forward, her large grey eyes widening. 'But *this* is the incredible part. I learned afterwards that it had flown to my sister's cottage, where it tapped on the kitchen window with its beak, and flapped its wings and made a *huge* noise. My sister tried to shoo it away, but it persisted, so she decided that it must be trying to tell her something. So she followed it outside, and on it flew; but it kept stopping and looking back at her to make sure that she was still following, then on it would fly again. When it alighted at the cliff edge, it looked over, and my sister looked over too and saw me lying there, and called the fire brigade.' Cynthia sat back again, shaking her head in bewilderment. 'Don't you think that's an incredible story?'

'I . . . do.'

'But it's quite true. Here . . .' She pushed the cat off her lap, then lifted up the hem of her rather smart silk dress. Through her stocking I saw a large scar above her left knee, the indented stitch marks like teeth on a zip. 'And I kept thinking afterwards, *how* did that wild bird know that I was in distress? And how did it know the means to summon *help*? I decided that there could be only *one* explanation . . .'

'Which was?'

'That I had somehow been able to communicate with it psychically, which had enabled it to save my life. This made me realize that I had the precious gift of clairvoyance – a gift I mustn't waste. So *that* is how I became a psychic,' she concluded. 'If you like, I'll give you a reading by way of saying thank you for being so neighbourly.' She put her hand on my left wrist. 'I can do one based on the electrical vibrations your watch emits.'

'Thanks.' I withdrew my hand. 'But I don't believe in that sort of thing.'

'You don't?' She seemed flabbergasted.

'No.' Her surprise annoyed me. 'And I don't believe in Father Christmas either, or the tooth fairy, or elves, or ghosts or little green men or the Loch Ness Monster, and I must say I have my doubts about *God*. I'm afraid I believe only in what can be proved. It's facts that ignite me, not fantasy.'

Cynthia was shaking her head. '"But there are more things in Heaven and Earth, Horatio", etcetera etcetera . . .'

'That may be true. But I tend to the belief that phenomena have natural, rather than miraculous, causes.'

She looked disappointed. 'Well, that's up to you. But are you *sure* you don't want a reading?'

'Quite sure. Anyway,' I went on, determined to change the subject, 'what did you do before you became a psychic?'

'I used to be an . . . actress.'

'Really? What were you in?'

'Oh, a number of films.'

'Anything I might have seen?'

'Well, this was a long time ago – in the late fifties, but I was very young, just out of school.' From this I figured that she must be in her early sixties – at least ten years older than she looked. 'I was a Rank Charm School starlet.' Ah. That explained the Fenella Fielding-like voice. 'They were only B movies but it was *thrilling*. I was shipwrecked five times, kidnapped twice, abducted by aliens four times and eaten alive by giant killer ants.' She smiled wistfully. 'It was a *marvellous* life.'

'And what were you in after that?'

'Oh, well, once I got to my late thirties my career seemed to . . . well . . . you know how it is with acting . . .' She seemed reluctant to elaborate and I didn't want to seem inquisitive. 'Look, are you sure you don't want me to give you a reading?' she persisted. 'I'd really *like* to because I find your aura rather fascinating. I can *see* it you know. Quite clearly.' She sat back and looked at me appraisingly. 'It's green and yellow with a hint of lilac. *Do* let me.'

'No. Thanks all the same. To be perfectly honest, Cynthia, I think all that stuff's a load of bunkum.'

'In which case there's *no* problem,' she declared triumphantly. 'Because, if it *is* a "load of bunkum" then what harm could it *possibly* do you to have a reading, hmm?'

Defeated by her logic, I agreed.

She clasped my left wrist with her right hand and closed her eyes. Then she suddenly opened them again, and stared into the middle distance, her large, grey eyes narrowing as if she was trying to focus on something that kept bobbing below the horizon.

'You're going in a new direction,' she announced. That's *very* insightful, I thought cynically. 'You've been unhappy.' Yeah. Who hasn't? 'But your mood is lifting.' Stunning percipience, I said to myself. 'Romance is in the air.' Her guesses were getting warmer. I thought happily of Luke. She closed her eyes, inhaled noisily – the end of her nose twitching like some woodland mammal – then she opened them again. 'You're taking control of your life,' she declared. Like most professional women of my age. This really was tosh. I'd humoured her long enough. But now Cynthia closed her eyes again, as though she'd fallen into a deep, deep sleep. In the ensuing silence I found myself gazing at her eyelids, which were crepey with age, and frosted with silver eye shadow. I was aware of the tick of my carriage clock – a wedding present from my parents – on the mantelpiece. And I was just wondering how long Cynthia was going to stay like that and at what point it would be polite to wake her, when she suddenly re-opened her eyes, wide, and stared at me with an intensity which startled me.

'You're missing someone,' she said in a voice that was no longer husky and theatrical, but clear and penetrating. 'Aren't you? Someone's missing from your life. Someone who was very important to you. But there was a . . . *tragedy*, and now he's gone.' I was aware of a strange, warm feeling, from my toes to my sternum, as though I'd been dipped in hot wax. 'You've been bereft, Laura.' She closed her eyes again, inhaling deeply. 'Bereaved.' Another silence descended which seemed to hum and throb. Then she opened her eyes. 'Isn't that right, Laura?' I stared at her. *'Isn't* it?' I could hear myself breathe.

'Yes. It is.' I heard myself say.

'I *knew* it!' she exclaimed happily, evincing more delight at the apparent accuracy of her analysis than any concern for me. 'I sensed it the *second* I laid eyes on you. I could *feel* it –' she looked around the room, then shivered slightly – 'there's a very high vibratory level in here. Anyway,' she added. 'Let's carry on.'

'I'd rather not,' I protested. But still she kept hold of my hand. 'Really, Cynthia.' I tried to withdraw it. 'I think we've done *enough*.' She looked into the distance again, this time blinking rapidly. Then she clapped her left hand to her chest.

'I can see him.'

'You what?'

'I can *see* him. Quite clearly.' Now I felt not so much warm, as chilled. 'He's standing in a field . . . a field full of . . .' she drew in her breath, her eyes widening in wonderment, '. . . *flowers*. Beautiful flowers. He's *surrounded* by them. It's a *marvellous* sight. But even though he has all these exquisite flowers around him, he's looking mournful and sad.'

'I'd like to *stop* now.' I reclaimed my hand with a sharp tug. I could still feel the pressure of her fingers on my wrist. 'He *isn't* in a field of flowers. That's absurd.'

'No. It's *not*. It's quite *true*. But that's not all. There's someone else.' I felt sick. 'Isn't there?' I stared at her.

'What do you mean?'

'I mean that there isn't just *one* person missing from your life – there are two.' I felt the hairs on my neck rise up. She closed her eyes for a moment, then opened them again. 'I can't see the second person, but I can *feel* their . . . presence. I can *feel* it.' I got to my feet. 'You didn't know them for long . . . but you loved them. You didn't want it to end . . . Now,' she said benignly, 'does that mean anything to you?' I stared at her, aware that goose bumps had stippled my arms. 'Does it?'

'No,' I said. 'Not a thing. No.'

'It gave me the creeps,' I told Felicity the following evening. I was sitting at her kitchen table in Moorhouse Road with Olivia gurgling on my lap, while Fliss washed the salad at the butler sink. 'She said that she could see Nick standing in a field of flowers. What do you think?' Felicity stared out into their small walled garden where dusk had just descended.

'It sounds much too good for him. Positively Paradisal.' She tucked a hank of tangled blonde hair behind one ear. 'He didn't deserve such a pleasant fate.'

'Oh come on, Fliss. Don't be too hard.' Via the baby monitor, we could hear Hugh, moving about upstairs in the bedroom. Every time he shifted, it caused the arc of lights on the display to flicker and ripple.

'No, Laura,' Felicity went on. 'I'm not afraid to say it. Nick was a shit to do what he did – and with no warning! I know some people might take a more compassionate view but he caused you too much pain for me to forgive him.'

'It isn't for you to forgive him, Fliss,' I said quietly. 'It's for *me*. In any case the idea of either of us forgiving him is somewhat academic in the circumstances.'

'I guess it is – as he's on eternity leave.' She laughed darkly.

'That's horrible, Fliss.'

'Sorry.' She smiled guiltily. 'But did this Madame Arcati character say anything else?' I thought of what Cynthia had said right at the end, but I didn't tell Felicity. Although she's always been so open with me about *her* life there are some things she's never known about mine. 'Couldn't she communicate with Nick?' she went on. 'Ask him why he did it, maybe? Put us all out of our misery?'

I shifted in my seat. 'She's not a medium, and I wouldn't want her to try. As for why he did it . . . the fact is we'll probably never know. But please, don't mention what happened to him to *anyone*, Fliss. It's *very* important because I *don't* want it getting in the press.'

She tipped the salad into a bowl. 'O . . . kay.'

'Afaclathaollaollagazzzagoyagoyagoya,' said Olivia.

Felicity turned round and beamed at her with a smile so wide I thought her face would split open. 'Is *that* what you think my darling? I love the way she talks,' she added with a giggle. 'She sounds like a little alien with her strange, unworldly utterances.'

'Thekzellagoyaobbadobbagertertergoya.'

'Is that what they speak on the planet where you come from my little babychops?'

As I held Olivia's plump little person on my lap, her fair, downy hair brushed my chin. I stroked her soft arms with their little pillows of fat, and dimpled elbows. I squeezed her podgy knees. I love Olivia, but it's a bittersweet kind of love.

'You're so . . . adorable, Olivia,' I said longingly. 'You really are.' I kissed the top of her head.

She twisted round to look up at me, her big blue eyes gazing unflinchingly into mine, with benign interest. Then she raised her right hand, with its stubby little fingers, like a starfish, and touched my cheek. 'Thizclalefafffooohethana-gagoygoyagoyagoya.'

'Goyagoyagoya to you,' said Fliss, coming over and plant-ing a kiss on her cheek with a noisy smack. Olivia giggled, so she did it again, then went back to the sink. 'I stand over her cot,' she confided quietly. 'At night. When she's asleep. I lean right over her cot, and feel her lovely breath on my cheek, like a tiny zephyr, and I still can't believe that she's mine. I love her so much,' she said as she began to slice a tomato. 'I could spend all my time just gazing at her; kiss-ing her little face, I love her more and more each day, I –' I heard her voice catch – 'I never knew that one could feel such love.'

'I know,' I murmured. Felicity's knife stopped for a moment. 'I mean, I can . . . imagine.'

'And it's a completely different kind of love from anything one's ever felt for a *man*. To be perfectly truthful, Laura, I find the relationship I have with Olivia totally fulfilling. I almost envy single mothers,' she confided, guiltily. 'It must be rather cosy if it's just you and the baby, with no-one else to consider.' As she said this, we heard Hugh sniffing and coughing slightly as he walked about, opening drawers and cupboards. 'He'll be down in a minute for supper.' She took the top off a baby bottle and handed it to me. 'Would you give Olivia her milk? She gets formula in the evenings because by then my boobs are all in.'

While I settled Olivia in the crook of my arm, Fliss opened the fridge and took out some steak, a pot of cream, and a tub of butter.

'Are you on the Atkins diet, Fliss?' She certainly needed to be. The average weight gain in pregnancy is twenty-eight pounds, but Felicity, voluptuous to start with, had managed to put on four and a half stone.

'Atkins? You must be joking.' She opened the freezer and grabbed a bag of chips. 'I love my carbs too much. Anyway, I'm still breastfeeding so I shouldn't be dieting at all. That's my excuse.'

'But the milk's drawn directly from the mother's fat reserves, so if you did lose a few pounds, you'd still be fine, Fliss.' *For weeks*!

'I know I should.' She pinged the elastic waistband of her old maternity trousers. 'I'm still two stone over.' *And the rest*! 'But *I* thought –' she frowned – 'that if you carried on breast-feeding the weight just fell off.'

'That's a bit of a myth. You do lose weight when you first breastfeed, apparently, but then it often plateaus and remains . . . stuck.'

Felicity gave me an odd look. 'How do you know?'

I stared at her. 'I read it somewhere.'

'Anyway,' Felicity went on. 'I'm too happy to care how fat I am, and Hugh's too busy with his silly inventions to notice. On the rare occasions that I need to look smart I wear my atomic knickers to flatten the lard.'

'Don't neglect yourself, Fliss. That's what the books all say.'

'Oh it'll come off in the end,' she said airily. 'And Hugh isn't shallow.' I didn't think he was either, but hoped she was right. 'Anyway, don't give me a tough time about it – okay? It's hard enough for me as it is, having two slim sisters.'

Noticing an expensive looking little bag on the high chair, I changed the subject. 'What have you been buying?'

She reached for a towel and dried her hands. 'Something scrumptious.' She opened the bag, and pulled out a sheath of pale yellow tissue in which lay a miniature pink cardigan of exquisite softness. 'Isn't it *gorgeous*?'

I felt my throat constrict. 'It is.' Olivia grabbed at it, trying to stuff one sleeve in her mouth. 'It's cashmere,' I added as I stroked it.

Felicity grimaced. 'I know. It cost eighty quid and she'll only wear it for three months, but it was *so* delicious I couldn't resist. In any case, why shouldn't my little girl have the best of everything?'

Olivia has that all right. She is dressed in beautiful baby clothes from Oilily, BabyDior and Petit Bateau. She sleeps on linen sheets. She is transported in her Bugaboo Frog pram, which cost £500, and her sheepskin-lined Bill Amberg sling. Her beaming face adorns a personalized tote bag from Anya Hindmarch, and her newborn feet were cast in solid bronze. The silk christening gown Felicity has had made for her baptism this Sunday is costing £220.

'Can you afford it?' I asked as Olivia sucked contentedly on the bottle.

'Of course not,' she replied. 'But I don't care because I'm on my babymoon, Laura, so I'm not going to stint, because I will never have this time again.' This is a frequent theme of Felicity's. That she will never get back this special time of her life, so it must be perfect in every way. Then she began talking about the christening and about how much she likes the vicar, and how it's a nicely high church, not a 'ghastly happy-clappy one', and about all the lovely music there's going to be, and the top-notch caterers she's booked, and all the people she's invited, and the new suit she's going to wear.

'And when are you going back to work?' I asked her as I tilted the bottle up for Olivia. 'Your maternity leave must be up soon.'

Felicity drew in her breath. 'I'm not.'

'What?'

'I've decided, Laura.' She opened the fridge. 'I'm not going back. At least, not for three years,' she corrected herself as she rummaged around. 'But *don't* mention it in front of Hugh.

I only told him this morning, and he's not taking it very well.'

'I'm not surprised.' I knew they had a huge mortgage, not least because of all the fertility treatment. 'It'll be hard for him, Fliss.'

She shrugged. 'That's his own look out – he had a good job. I know you'll think me hard-hearted,' she went on as she took out a bottle of French dressing. 'But for seventeen years, I've looked after other people's little darlings, and now I want to devote myself to my *own*. I expect Hugh to support me for a while and that's all there is to it. If my decision forces him to go back to work again, then so much the better, because this bloody inventing lark's not going to work out.'

'I don't know – he might come up with something, really, you know . . . handy.'

'They haven't exactly been brilliant inventions so far, have they? That thing that looks like a Pritt Stick, but is filled with butter instead of glue, "to save washing up"; those two tiny umbrellas you clip to the front of your shoes . . .'

'Oh yes. To protect them in the rain.'

She rolled her eyes. 'That's right. The umbrella with a skylight so you can check if it's stopped raining without getting yourself wet . . .'

'Mmm – and those edible picnic knives and forks.'

'I know. *Useless*,' said Felicity with a bitter laugh. 'Whatever next? An inflatable dartboard?' I heard a creak on the stairs. Then Olivia sucked the last of the milk with a contented sigh.

'She's finished it, Fliss.' I dabbed the corner of her mouth.

'That was quick. Here, darling . . .' she took Olivia, lifted her aloft, kissed her twice, then put her on her left shoulder. 'I mean, I can think of some useful things Hugh could invent.'

'Like what?' said Hugh, slightly stiffly, as he came in. He's very tall – six foot three – and slightly shambling-looking in his old corduroys and his Guernsey jumper, but he's very handsome, in a boyish sort of way. 'Hi Laura.' He beamed at me, then gave me a fraternal kiss. 'What useful things would you want me to invent, Fliss?'

'Well, things we really *need*,' she replied. 'Like nail varnish which dries in one second for instance, or tights that never run, or a microwave with a "Reverse" button for those times when I overcook things, or a voicemail system which lets you go back in and delete the stupid, incoherent message you just left someone, or, let's see – oh God she's puked!' A tiny white lagoon had formed on Felicity's shoulder and was now oozing down her back. 'Where's the muslin?' She cast her eyes about. 'I never, *ever* have a muslin when I need one.'

'Which explains why you look like a walking Jackson Pollock,' said Hugh.

'Could you grab me some kitchen roll?' He tore some off and wiped her baggy black t-shirt. 'Blast – I'll have to wash it again. Oh well,' she sighed. 'Spit happens, and at least she's kept most of it down.' By now Olivia's blonde head was sinking on to Felicity's chest. 'She's *so* tired, the little darling. Could you put her in her cot, Hugh, while I carry on with supper?'

'I was about to pour myself a drink. I've had a long day.'

'You can have a drink *afterwards*,' she said as she handed him the baby, 'but I want her in bed *right* now.' Hugh took Olivia, then gave Fliss a mock salute.

'Rog-er. Nighty-night Auntie Laura,' he squeaked, offering me the baby to kiss. 'Your quiz was fantastic by the way.'

'Thanks.'

'Everyone we know watched it so I guess you got a good audience.'

'We did. The overnight viewing figures were amazing for a first outing – almost three million. We "won the slot" as they say in the trade.'

'And did you see that little piece in the *Standard*?'

'Yes. They seemed to like it.'

'They loved it,' said Fliss. 'And so did we.'

'Quadrimum,' Hugh muttered. 'I like that. Anyway, come on Mrs Baby – up we go.'

'I'm really trying to crack the sleeping problem,' said Felicity as I got the knives and forks out of the drawer. 'She wakes at least twice. It's exhausting.'

'Doesn't it bother Hugh?'

'No – he's still in the spare room.'

'Really?' I picked up a tiny white sock embroidered with a garland of pink roses. 'Doesn't he mind?'

'I don't think so. He doesn't complain. Which is quite something considering that we haven't –' she lowered her voice – '*you* know, for ages.'

'Really?' I said politely. As I say, Fliss likes to share everything with me. I've always found it touching, even if I've never been the same with her – but Fliss has this need to tell. Confidences gush out of her like oil from a tanker. She's the opposite of Hope, who's controlled and contained.

'*No* nookie,' she explained. 'Not since before the baby was born.' She reached up and got down three plates. 'I haven't felt like it.'

'Well, that sounds a bit . . . risky, Fliss. I wouldn't neglect him . . .'

'*Baby love, my baby love . . .*'

Over the monitor we could hear Hugh crooning to Olivia as he changed her nappy.

'*I need you, oh how I need you . . .*' We could hear her giggle and gurgle.

'I mean, he's a good-looking man, Fliss.'

'*But all you do is treat me bad . . .*'

She laughed. 'Oh Hugh's *far* too straight-laced to stray.'

'*Break my heart and leave me sad . . .*'

'Anyway, who'd *want* him?' she added as she lit the hob. 'He's not even *earning*. He just sits in the shed all day.'

'*Do be doo, be do be doo, 'cause baby love, my baby love . . .*'

'Well, the baby books all say that you should make a fuss of your husband.'

'*Been missing ya, miss kissing ya . . .*'

Felicity gave me an odd little look. 'How do you know *what* the baby books say?'

'Well . . . I . . .' I nodded towards the bookshelf. 'I've looked at that *Baby Whisperer* book of yours – I love reference books – and it advises new mums not to ignore . . . *that* side of life.'

'*Do be do be do do be do be do do da da do be do do be do be do . . .*'

'I don't know Laura,' she sighed. 'I find sex perfectly easy to live without – I don't miss it at all.'

'*I* do,' I said dismally as I laid the table. 'I haven't had so much as a cuddle in three years.'

Felicity got down three glasses. 'Well that's just plain *crazy*! I've always said you should have looked for someone else.'

'How could I? I was too depressed, plus I had zero self-confidence – and who'd have *wanted* me? With *my* baggage?' I concluded bleakly.

'Well, yes, I admit that your situation hasn't been . . . great. But, look, what about your boss?' she asked as she poured the dressing into the bowl. 'Every time he picks up the phone when I ring you at work, I can't help thinking how nice he sounds – or maybe I'm just mesmerized by his gorgeous voice.'

'No, Tom is nice. And he does have a lovely voice, that's true. I'm so used to hearing it, I don't often think about it.'

'Where does he come from?'

'Montreal. The English-speaking part, though he's lived here for ten years now.'

'What about him then?' I shook my head. 'Don't you like him?'

'Not in that way.'

She began to toss the salad. 'You mean you don't find him attractive?'

'No. It's not that, because he *is* attractive. Very attractive actually.'

She dribbled in some more dressing. 'What does he look like?'

'Well . . . he has a boy-next-door kind of charm. Brown hair, receding slightly; large blue eyes, medium height, medium build. He's a bit like Tobey McGuire.'

'And do you think he likes you?'

'God, I don't . . . know. I don't suppose he's ever *thought* of me in that way. He's . . . fond of me I guess, but that's all.'

'He was good about Nick, wasn't he?' She put the top back on the French dressing.

'Yes, he was. He was a real . . . rock. And we've worked together for six years now – right from the start – when it was just him and me, so we've a very good professional rapport.'

'Then why not make it a personal one too?'

'Well, because a) he's my boss, so it could be extremely awkward and b) – and you are *not* to repeat this – '

'I promise,' she said seriously.

'– he did something pretty awful, a few years ago. I've never told you before, out of loyalty to him – but the fact is that although he *is* wonderful in many ways I find it . . . off-putting.'

Felicity's eyes were like saucers. '*What* did he do?'

'He left his wife –'

'Oh,' she began to toss the salad again. 'So *what*? That happens all the time. You can't hold *that* against him, Laura. You *do* tend to be judgemental, you know.'

'– a month after their baby was born.' The salad servers stopped in mid air.

'Oh. I see. That *is* awful.' She pulled a face. 'The poor woman.'

'Quite.'

'Did he have some sort of crisis about becoming a dad?'

63

'No. He just left her for someone else.'

'God . . .'

'It was in the gossip columns.'

'Really? Why?'

'Because the woman he went off with was Tara McLeod.'

'The actress?'

'Yes. She'd had the main part in that drama-documentary we made about Helen of Troy – that's how they met. The affair didn't last long, but it was curtains for his marriage. But because Tara was up and coming then, there was a bit of press interest, and one or two of the pieces mentioned how devastated Tom's wife, Amy, was.'

'But the papers print all sorts of rubbish, so how do you know it was true?'

'Because a) I saw him and Tara together a number of times, and b) his own sister told me. She was in London not long after that – she's a non-executive director of the company – and we had lunch together, the three of us; and while Tom was away from the table she just started talking about it, as though she wanted to explain.'

'She was probably a bit embarrassed.'

'I think she was. She said she assumed I knew about him leaving Amy, so I said I did, and then she just shrugged, and said that it had been a "coup de foudre". So I guess he must have developed some sort of fatal attraction which skewed his judgement.'

Felicity got out a bottle of wine. 'Leaving your wife for another woman when she's just had your child is just about as skewed as it gets.' I thought, as I often have done, of how incongruous it seemed that someone as decent as Tom could have behaved so badly. But then – as I know only too well, because of Nick – the 'nicest' people can surprise you in the most terrible ways. 'And does he have any contact with his child?' Felicity continued.

'I don't think so. His wife divorced him then went back

to Canada, so whether he ever sees his child on trips home I don't know. He never mentions him, and he doesn't have a photo of him in his office, so I suspect the answer is no. But . . . it's affected how I view him – on a personal level at least.'

'Well, I don't blame you for not getting too close. Just keep it as it is, warm, but strictly business-like.'

'That is what I do. In any case I find it hard to think of Tom – or anyone at work – in anything other than a professional way.'

Now, as Felicity rummaged in the drawer for a corkscrew, I thought how odd it is that I should spend so much of my waking time with my colleagues, yet know so little about how they live. I know that Dylan has a girlfriend who's a producer on *Richard and Judy*; I know that our production assistant, Gill, is engaged. I know that Sara's boyfriend's a teacher, and that Nerys lives alone in Paddington, with a couple of budgies. And I know that Tom left his wife a month after the birth of their child.

'Is there anyone else you might be interested in?' I heard Fliss say. She handed me the bottle and I started to peel off the thick metal foil. 'I'm inviting a very eligible man to the christening by the way.'

I looked at her, appalled. 'Please Fliss, *don't*.'

'I taught his daughter some years ago.'

'I don't *want* you to.'

'I bumped into him again recently in Portobello and he told me he'd got divorced.'

'Especially not at a family occasion.'

'He's called Norman, and he's a stockbroker.'

'It's not *appropriate*. Oh this damn foil won't come off.'

'Sorry, but I've already invited him.'

'Why?'

'Firstly, because I've invited loads of people, so it won't matter if he's there too and secondly – and this is the main reason – because I want you to *meet* someone.' She looked at me. 'Laura, in June you'll be thirty-five. I want *you* to have the chance of a family. I want *you* to know the bliss of being pregnant.' I shifted on my chair. 'I want *you* to experience the joy of knowing that a baby is growing inside you – *your* baby,' she added with evangelical fervour as I struggled with the metal foil. 'I want *you* to know the indescribable happiness of holding your baby for the first time . . .'

'Shut *up*, will you Fliss! Oh shit!' Blood was suddenly seeping from my index finger. 'Now I've *cut* myself!' I wailed. 'Just stop lecturing me will you and get me a *plaster.*' I wiped away an angry tear.

'I'm sorry to be so forthright, Laura,' said Felicity quietly. 'But I can see I've touched a nerve.'

'No you *haven't*. It's just the shock. I *hate* the sight of blood!'

She wrapped a wet tissue around my index finger and it instantly became tinged with crimson. I felt sick.

'I'm sorry I upset you, Laura.' Felicity put her arm round me, and I felt my anger subside. 'But I just want you to be happy,' she said softly. 'Look how hard it was for me to get pregnant – who's to say it wouldn't be hard for you too?' My stomach lurched with dismay. 'I don't want you to miss out on this wonderful area of life – and that means you've got to meet someone *soon*. Haven't you?' she insisted. 'I'm only trying to help you.'

I looked at her. 'Well . . . maybe I don't *need* your help.' I peeped at the cut. It had almost stopped bleeding.

'Why not?' Felicity tore open a Band Aid. 'What do you mean?'

'Maybe I already *have* met someone. You see, something extraordinary happened yesterday . . .' And now, as Felicity applied the plaster to my finger, I told her about my encounter with Luke.

'*Luke?*' she exclaimed with a smile. 'Oh I *liked* him – well,

66

we *all* did, didn't we? I mean, he was such *fun*.' She pulled the cork out of the wine bottle and poured two large glasses. 'He always had some snippet of useless information or other up his sleeve – I can still remember some of them – what was it? – oh yes, that a hippo's breast milk is pink – I've never forgotten it – and that Virginia Woolf wrote all her books standing up. Yes . . .' she nodded delightedly. 'Luke was great. I'm *thrilled* you've bumped into him again. What happened before was . . . a pity.'

'You're right. Finding him in bed – or rather bath – with someone else *was* a pity.'

'That's true – but then, come on, Laura, he *was* very young. You both were.' She sipped her wine. 'And it was only a one-night stand wasn't it?'

'That's what he claimed. But I felt as though I'd stepped on a landmine – everything seemed ruined – I couldn't deal with it.'

'You might have been able to now. Our perspective changes as we get older.'

'I suppose you're right. And after what Nick did, there's not much I couldn't cope with. But that wasn't now – it was then.'

'And this is *now* . . .' She gave me a meaningful look. 'This is a second chance, Laura. A *second chance*, to ignite an old flame – so you must absolutely grab it with both hands. You've waited long enough. Emotionally, you've been . . . frozen, but now you must get out there, and . . . seize the day!' Funny. That's just what Tom had said. '*Carpe diem!*' Fliss added gaily. 'So, tell me – were there any sparks?'

'Well, yes. I'd often wondered what would happen if Luke and I ever met again – and now I know. The chemistry was *just* the same. Except that he's now a separated man with a six-year-old daughter and I'm a . . .' I swallowed. I always find it hard to say.

'And you *are* going to see him again, aren't you?' said Fliss.

There was a pause. '*Please* tell me you are, Laura. *Don't* be tricky. I *know* you.'

My heart looped the loop.

'I'm having dinner with him tomorrow night.'

THREE

On some TV quiz shows there's a degree of preparation in the way the questions are asked. On *Mastermind*, for example, John Humphreys will say; 'In classical music, what does the term "Legato" mean?' rather than, simply, 'What does "Legato" mean?' Or he'll say, 'History; and when was the Diet of Worms?' rather than, just, 'When was the Diet of Worms?' This gives the contestants a split second in which to tune into the next subject and prepare. But on *Whadda Ya Know?!!* they don't have that luxury – they just get the questions – boom, boom, boom. 'Of what was Hecate a Greek goddess?' (The Underworld); 'What is the alternative name for a wildebeest? (A gnu); 'Which line of latitude provides the border between North and South Korea?' (The 38th Parallel); 'Which river runs through the Peak District?' (the Dove). We do it that way because it's harder, and because it adds to the tension and pace. As I walked up Ladbroke Grove to meet Luke on Friday night a similarly rapid inquisition formed in my mind. 'Did you cheat on me more than once during our two years together? How many girlfriends did you have after that? Is your wife pretty? Is she clever? Is she successful? Why did you break up?'

'Don't look so serious, Laura!' There he was, standing on

the corner of Kensington Park Road, outside E & O. He kissed me on the cheek, then held his face for a moment against mine, and, again, I felt the old familiar longing for him stirring. I had once loved him so much. As we walked into the restaurant I felt the light pressure of his hand on my back. It made me feel elated.

'At first I misheard you,' I said, as we were shown to a quiet table in the corner. 'I thought I was being invited to the ENO for a bit of opera.'

'We'll do that next time.' I felt my face heat up with pleasure at the notion of a next time. 'Okay?'

I suppressed a smile. 'Maybe.' I glanced around the monochrome interior, with its blond floor and dark lacquered wooden screening. 'This is cool.'

'Didn't you ever come here with your husband?' He had used the quiet, respectful voice that people use when they mention Nick.

'No. We didn't eat out much. Money was tight.'

'He worked for a charity didn't he?'

'He was the director of SudanEase – a small development agency.'

'That's a tough call. He must have been a good person.'

'He was.' I always hate talking about Nick in the past tense; it upsets me. 'He was a very good person in many ways.'

'I meant to write to you,' Luke said as he unfolded his napkin. 'I even started a letter – but it was . . . awkward. I just didn't know what to say.'

'Don't worry,' I said with a brittle smile. 'Lots of people had the same problem.'

Luke's expression suggested that although he was curious about Nick, he felt he might be intruding – so he enquired about my family instead. As we sipped our champagne I told him about my parents retiring to the Pennines to run a B & B and about Hope's success in the City, and about how she doesn't want to have kids, but is happy with that, as is her husband, Mike. Then I told him about Fliss.

'I saw her,' he said. 'Pushing a pram along Westbourne Grove.'

'They live round there.'

'So do I – in Lonsdale Road. It's such a goldfish bowl I'm surprised I hadn't seen her before. I wanted to speak to her – I was dying to ask her about you actually.'

'Why didn't you then?'

He shrugged. 'I felt . . . awkward. I assumed I'd be *persona non grata* with members of your family.'

'But it was such a long time ago.'

'I know – but, even so, they must have disapproved of me.'

'Oh, no . . .' I lied.

'Really?'

'Well, okay . . . Yes. They did. But mainly because I had to be Felicity's bridesmaid the week after . . .'

'I remember.'

'And I was in a total state.'

'Oh dear.'

'I wept all the way through the service.' I paused while the waiter put our dim sum on the table. 'My mother had to tell everyone that it was the emotion of the occasion.'

'I see.'

'And when Fliss chucked the bouquet at me I threw it back.'

'Crikey.'

'I was in a bad way.'

'So it seems. Look –' he parted his jacket. 'See this?' He fingered his shirt. 'Pure horsehair.'

I rolled my eyes, then smiled. 'Pure horse*shit*, don't you mean!'

'And I've brought a small whip with me for the purposes of self-flagellation – or you can do the honours if you like. But seriously, Laura . . .' he lowered his voice '. . . can we

71

get this all out of the way right now – so that we can have a nice evening? Can I just say I'm really sorry I did what I did? I know it was a *long* time ago, and I was a very young, silly man; but just in case you still bear me any vestige of a grudge – which I see you do – I'd like to apologize from the bottom of my heart. I was a bastard to you in June 1993. You didn't deserve it. I'm *sorry*. Now – will that do?' Any lingering frigidity I'd felt evaporated in a puff of steam, as though I'd just been pan-seared.

I smiled. 'Yes. Thanks. That'll do. Nicely.' I snapped open my chopsticks.

'Mind you, I paid a very high price. You just packed your things and left. You ignored my calls. You returned all my letters. Your determination to cut me out of your life was . . . impressive.'

'I couldn't cope. Seeing you – with her. Like that.' Into my mind flashed the unpalatable image of Luke, lying in the bath of the house we shared, up to his chest in bubbles, with Jennifer Clarke standing, naked, at the sink. I will never forget the frozen horror on Jennifer's face as she looked into the mirror and saw me . . .

I'd gone home the previous day for a final dress fitting for the wedding. I hadn't been due back until the late afternoon. But I'd returned early because Luke and I had rowed before I left and I'd wanted to make up with him again, and surprise him. But the person who was most surprised was *me*. Jennifer, who, to be fair to her, was good looking – with a sheet of long, smooth hair of the kind I've always coveted – had been a fellow team-mate in the *Universally Challenged* inter-college pub quiz competition we'd narrowly won the week before.

'I'm really sorry,' Luke repeated. 'It's actually the one and only time I've ever done that. It was an awful mistake – I just wish I hadn't made it with you.'

'And why did you, do you think? Now that we're on the subject.'

He narrowed his eyes as he considered the question.

'It was because I was young I suppose, and very immature, and because we'd just taken finals and it was a release – and because I was in a panic about graduating and having to find my way in the big wide world. And we'd been arguing a lot, if you remember, and then you were *away* and Jennifer was . . . keen. Plus I'd been faithful to you for two years and maybe I wanted to be let off the leash. But it didn't mean I didn't love you – I *did*.'

'It's okay, Luke.' I'd learned all too well since then that the people who love us, can still hurt us. 'But I didn't think Jennifer Clarke was a great choice.'

Luke grimaced. 'You're right. She wasn't much cop. I don't like to be in*delicate* –' he leaned forward as he prepared to be indiscreet – 'but she didn't even know that the capital of Cuba is Havana.'

'Or that *La Dolce Vita* was directed by Fellini. Remember that?'

'Or that the Hermitage is in St Petersburg. She thought it was in *Paris*!'

'Pathetic. I don't know how she got on the team. It must have been because you fancied her.'

He chewed his lower lip. 'Maybe – her general knowledge was crap. Thanks to her we almost lost. Do you remember how close it was?'

'I do. I mean, she didn't even know that the largest organ in the body is the liver.'

'Or that the best selling novel of all time is *The Valley of the Dolls*.'

'Is it? More than *The Da Vinci Code*?'

'Yes, it's sold thirty million copies.'

'Really? Thanks – we'll use that on *Whadda Ya Know?!!*'

He reached for my hand. 'Do you forgive me, Laura?'

'Yes.' I smiled. 'Of course I forgive you – now – but I couldn't have forgiven you then. You'd hurt me too much,

Luke – it was like a physical pain. Here – right *here* –' I tapped my sternum – 'as though someone had taken a bite out of my heart. I was *happy* with you, Luke. Happier than I've ever been. Maybe I'll never see you again, so I don't mind you knowing that.' I felt a pang of guilt about Nick, but dismissed it. What he had done to me was far worse.

'We *were* happy,' said Luke. 'We were very young, but it *meant* something.'

'It did.' I remembered how alive Luke had made me feel. His exuberance and vitality had ignited me, when I'd been so quiet and bookish before. He'd made me confident, where I'd been introverted. He'd made me feel beautiful, when I'd thought myself plain. I'd had a passion for him that I'd felt for no other man. He'd been . . . yes . . . the love of my life. If I'd known that then I might have forgiven him, as he'd begged me to. Instead, I'd left him, without a word or a glance and had gone down a different path.

By now the air between us was so clear it was positively Alpine.

'So,' I said. 'What happened to you after that? You got into Christies, then?'

'I did. I was there for eight years. I started as a porter, and ended up as director of the Modern British department. On the personal front I had one or two unsatisfactory flings. Then, in the summer of '96 I met Magda.'

'Was it love at first sight?'

He considered the question. 'No. But I was very . . . attracted to her.' I felt a stab of jealousy. 'I found her fascinating, and slightly intense. She's Hungarian – although she'd lived here for twelve years by then – and she had this captivating, arty sort of air. She wore vintage clothes and she had these big blue eyes, and this long blonde hair that she'd pile on top of her head.'

'How did you meet?'

'At . . . life drawing classes.'

'So she's artistic too.'

He sipped his wine. 'We saw each other for a few months and I'd started to feel under pressure because she was five years older and was keen to settle down; but I'd begun to think it wasn't right.'

'Why?'

'Well, although she could be delightful, she had these . . . dark moods. So I was just steeling myself to break it off when she told me she was pregnant.' He shrugged. 'I was worried because we'd only been together four months and hadn't discussed living together, let alone having kids. But I was also excited at the idea of being a father – so I felt I should do the right thing.'

'And tell me about Jessica.'

He smiled, then shook his head, as if in wonderment. 'Jessica? What can I say? I just . . . adore her. She's the reason I put on my clothes in the morning. She's the reason I go to work. She's the most cherished thing in my life – she means *everything* to me, Laura, she really does – she's the *best* thing, she really is . . . she's just . . . the best, *best* thing . . .' I was shocked to see his mouth quiver; his eyes were shimmering with sudden tears.

'Luke,' I whispered. I put my hand on his. He looked away, ashamed, then lowered his head.

'Sorry,' he croaked. 'I get upset because Jess doesn't live with me any more and I *miss* her. I miss her lovely little presence. I miss hearing her talk and sing, and play. I can't bear seeing her empty room. Sometimes I just sit on her bed and cry.'

'But you see her?'

He nodded. 'Every Saturday. And I often collect her from school.'

'So it's not too bad then.'

He shrugged. 'It could be worse – but I wanted to *live* with my child. Magda and I weren't happy, but I would never have left her, because of Jessica.'

75

'So why *did* you split up?'

He heaved a weary sigh. 'Because having been charmingly eccentric to begin with she began behaving in a seriously bizarre way . . .'

'Doing what?'

'Picking fights the whole time. Hiding my things, or even destroying them. I once took the car when she wanted it, and I'd just started the engine, when she threw a pair of crystal decanters that had belonged to my grandmother out of the window.' He shuddered. 'I can still remember the sound as they hit the path. She flushed her engagement ring down the loo. She was outrageously rude to my friends.' He winced. 'She'd walk out of dinner parties mid-course if someone said something she didn't like.'

'How embarrassing.'

'It was. She even did it when we were at my boss's house once – I was worried it could affect my career. She'd make these . . . *awful* scenes. I took her to the Connaught for her birthday and she asked me to order for her while she went to the loo. So I ordered salmon, which I knew she liked, but when she saw it she started crying, really loudly – everyone was staring. So I whispered, "What's the *matter*, Magda?" and she shouted, "But I wanted *trout*!!!"'

'Wow. Erm . . . why do you think she did things like that?'

'She loved the drama – and the attention, of course. And she seemed to find normal married life boring, so she'd engineer these break-ups so that we could have wonderful make-ups. But I just found it wearing.'

'And didn't you want more children?'

'I did; she didn't – perhaps because she's an only child herself – but in any case by then it wasn't looking good. I felt that she was trying to provoke a separation, which I didn't want, because of Jess, so I did my best to keep calm. But then – and this is what really drove us apart – she began keeping goats.'

'*Goats?*' He nodded. *Ah.*

'Pygmy goats. Her grandmother had kept them, apparently, in the Carpathians and they brought back happy memories. Anyway, I came home one day, and there was this tiny goat in the garden happily chomping on my dahlias. "Meet Heidi," Magda said, with an air of triumph. So I thought to myself, fine, I can cope with a miniature goat – and I thought it might have a calming influence on Magda. But then, without telling me, she had Heidi mated, and she had twins – Sweetie and Ophelia. Then, a few months later, Heidi had two more – Phoebe and Yogi. And when I said I found it unreasonable to have so many, she laughed and said I'd wanted more kids, and now I'd got them. So there we were in fashionable Notting Hill with livestock in the back garden. Everyone was sniggering.'

'So that's why you laughed when I asked what "caprine" meant.'

He nodded. 'There's not much I don't know about them. They were sweet actually. I was rather fond of them.'

'Don't they smell?'

'Not the females and the castrated males. But of course they'd get out, and I'd have to go and look for them, or they'd wander into the house and I'd find them on top of the wardrobe; and they have to have this special alfalfa hay and these mineral salts which it was now *my* job, apparently, to procure. Anyway, at weekends Magda would take off to these agricultural shows with them – she'd got this little trailer. And I'd find a note on the kitchen table saying that she'd be away *all* weekend at some county jamboree or other and could I look after Jess. We had flaming rows about it. The next thing I knew she was packing her bags.

'I tried to stop her, because of Jess – I was distraught. I wondered about applying for a residence order, given Magda's eccentric behaviour, but a legal fight would have been too destructive – not to say expensive – plus I was worried that it would upset Jess.'

'So have you started proceedings?'

'Not yet – there's been no particular reason to – and it would distress Jessica. The terrible thing is that she thinks it's *her* fault. She's got this idea that if she'd been "better", then her mum and I would never have split up.'

'Poor little thing.'

'I know. I keep telling her it's not true – that she's a *good* little girl, and that these things just happen.' He shook his head. 'But she can't work it out. Sometimes, when she's with me, and it's her bedtime, she says her prayers. And she always ends by praying that her mum and dad will live together again.' He looked away. 'It breaks my heart.'

'So . . . where do she and your ex live now?'

'In Chiswick, in the house Magda owned before she met me – it had been let. The garden's bigger than mine so the goats are happy, and it's not too far away. I pay the mortgage on it and all the bills, and Jessica's school fees . . .'

'Doesn't Magda work?'

'No. She used to be an interpreter – she was well-paid – but she won't do it any more.'

'That's tough for you.'

'I know. Luckily the gallery's been doing okay. I *just* managed to hang on to Lonsdale Road with extra borrowing but money's been tight. I've really had to duck and dive.'

I dipped a prawn dumpling into the soy sauce. 'Which is why you wanted to get on the quiz?'

'Partly – because, as I told you, I've got this place at the Slade. But I also did it because . . . well, I wanted to *see* you, Laura. I'd never ever forgotten you.' He stroked the back of my hand. 'I thought of you so often – particularly since hearing what had happened – and I'd like to believe that you thought of me too.'

'I didn't let myself,' I said quietly. 'I'd push you away. But you'd come back to me in my dreams.'

He smiled. 'I knew you'd have dinner with me.'

78

'Really? How could you be so sure?'

He nodded at my hands, clasped under my chin. 'Because I saw that you were wearing my watch.'

I glanced at my left wrist. On it was the slim gold watch Luke had given me for my 21st. It had cost him the whole of that term's grant.

'Well,' I shrugged. 'I . . . like it . . . and . . . it would be silly to . . . waste it, wouldn't it?'

Suddenly his mobile phone rang. He glanced at the screen, then winced. 'Sorry, Laura. I'll be right back.' He went outside and, through the large plate glass window, I saw him standing on the damp pavement, beneath the street lamp, then slowly pacing back and forth. Once or twice he ran his left hand through his hair in an intense, frustrated way. Then I saw him snap shut his phone.

'Childcare arrangements,' he said, as he came back to the table, purse-lipped. 'Magda was trying to suggest that her bloody boyfriend drop Jessica off tomorrow morning. She was only saying that to hurt me – silly cow. I told her I'd collect *my* daughter *my*self!'

'And what's the boyfriend like?'

'He's called Steve – he's mid forties, an accountant – divorced with three teenagers. How he feels about goats I have no idea, but Magda misses no opportunity to tell me what a paragon he is, how successful, how nice – and what a "marvellous stepfather," he'd make,' he added bitterly.

'And have *you* been out with anyone else?'

'No. I've been too upset – I've lived like a monk; plus I'd been through enough pain with her and I didn't want to risk any more with someone new.' He stared at me. 'But what about *your* life, Laura? *Your* marriage?'

My heart sank. I hate talking about Nick, but I wanted Luke to know exactly what had happened.

'How did you meet?' he asked.

'At Radio 4.' I had a large sip of water. 'I'd set up an

interview with him about the Sudan, and I politely chatted to him while he was waiting to go on air, and afterwards, to my surprise, he asked me out.'

'When was this?'

'Eleven years ago now. In the spring of '94.'

'Not that long after we split up then.'

I pushed a piece of tempura round my plate. 'That's right.'

'And were you in love with him?'

'That's a very direct question.'

'I'm sorry. But I want to know. Were you?'

'I think so. I mean – yes. Of course I was.' I stared at the flickering tea-light in its glass holder.

'You sound like Prince Charles with Diana.'

'Look Luke, Nick was honourable and kind, and he was doing something worthwhile. Plus he was very keen on me, so, yes, I guess that . . . helped. Okay, he wasn't exciting, like you were. But he was very interesting, and he was a *good* person. And I didn't think that he'd hurt me.' I gave him a bleak smile. 'That seems rather ironic now.'

'And didn't you want kids?' I shifted on my chair. 'I know that's a very direct question too – but I feel no barriers with you, Laura, just talking to you like this again.' He gently took my left hand in both his and stroked the tips of my fingers. It made me feel almost faint with desire. 'So . . . ?' He looked at me expectantly. 'Didn't you want a family? I've always imagined you with children.'

'We never . . . got round to it.' I withdrew my hand, then fiddled with my napkin. 'We were both forging our careers. And then, well . . . you heard what happened. So that was that,' I added bitterly.

'I'm sorry,' he said again. 'When exactly was it?'

'On the first of January, 2002.'

'So he did it on New Year's Day? Just to add to your grief, I suppose.'

'It was wonderful timing – you're right. And of course it's

ruined every New Year's Day since. A permanent reminder.'

'I suppose what he did –' he lowered his chopsticks – 'is just about the worst thing anyone *can* do to their partner.' I nodded. 'The pain that it leaves behind. And the *questions* I suppose. The unanswered questions . . .'

'Oh yes,' I said bitterly.

'But you're getting over it now?'

I thought of Nick's stuff, buried in boxes.

'I have laid his memory to rest.'

A silence descended. I glanced out of the window. People were scurrying by with umbrellas. Collars were upturned. I could hear the swish of wet tyres on the road.

'And do you think there's any chance he might ever . . . come back?'

I inhaled slowly. 'That's . . . highly unlikely.'

'But it does happen sometimes.' I looked at him. 'I'm sure I read that somewhere.'

I shook my head. 'It's almost unknown. Especially after so long. If Nick *was* going to come back then he'd have done it a long time ago – probably within the first three months. That's what the experts all say. They say that the longer a missing person has been away then the harder it is for them to return. I suppose they're afraid they'll be in serious trouble, because they know they've caused so much misery and stress.'

'So he just . . . disappeared? Out of the blue?'

'Into the blue, I often think. His car was found by the coast.'

'And how did it happen? If you don't mind talking about it?'

'No. In fact I'd like to tell you.' I had another sip of water. 'We'd been on the London Eye. I thought it would be a nice thing to do on New Year's morning. We'd had a few . . . difficulties . . . and I said that it would give us a positive perspective on everything. And I did remember, afterwards, that when I'd said that, he'd smiled this strange, rather sad little smile.'

'And he disappeared later that day?'

I nodded. 'It was around six o'clock – I know that because I was listening to the news on the radio as I did something in the kitchen, and I heard him call out that he was just going to get a pint of milk. So I said fine, but half an hour later he hadn't returned. And after an hour had passed he still wasn't back, and by then I had a very bad feeling, and I opened the fridge and saw that we already had a full bottle of milk. So I ran to the little local supermarket and asked the woman at the check-out if she'd seen him, and she said she hadn't. Then I looked for the car, and it was gone. So I called his office in case he'd gone there, but there was no reply – and he wasn't answering his mobile phone. I waited another two hours, and by now I was in a real state. By the time it got to ten I was frantic. So now I rang my parents, and they told me to call the police. But the police said that I couldn't report him missing until he'd been gone for twenty-four hours. You can imagine what those next twenty hours were like.'

'Agony.'

I nodded. 'Fliss came round and spent the night. Every time the phone went it was like an electric shock; I felt as though my nerve endings were attached to twitching wires. But I clung to the belief that there must be some perfectly rational explanation and that I'd suddenly hear his key in the door. But I didn't hear it. Not that night, or the next day – or ever again.'

Luke shook his head. 'Did he take anything with him?'

'Just the car. Three days after he'd gone they found it abandoned on the Norfolk coast, just outside Blakeney, where he used to go on family holidays as a boy. In it were his phone, his house keys, and his wallet – the credit cards untouched. Then, the next morning, they found his scarf. It had been

82

washed up on the beach.' I shuddered at the memory. 'So then a massive sea search was launched, with helicopters and divers, but they failed to locate a body. But they said that if he *had* committed suicide – which I refused to believe because I knew him well enough to know he'd never do that – then he'd be washed up further down the coast, probably within three weeks. But a month went by and nothing was found.'

'The waiting must have been terrible,' Luke said. My stomach lifted up and down just thinking about it. 'For his family too.'

'He didn't have siblings, and both his parents had died. His mother years ago, when he was a student, and his father three months before Nick disappeared. The National Missing Persons' Helpline were very supportive. They put up posters in Norfolk and London. They also advised me to talk to homeless people down on the Embankment, just in case Nick was living rough. So I spent a month trudging around, going into pubs and cafes, showing people his photo, asking if they'd seen him. I had to bear in mind how, if he was living rough, his appearance might have changed. He'd be unshaven, maybe bearded. He'd be thinner than he was – he was a big, well-built man. He might be walking in a different, less confident way. And I went to Leicester Square every day for those four weeks, just sitting there on a bench all afternoon, watching the people go by, thinking that I might suddenly spot him. And I remember, once, running after a man who I was convinced *was* Nick – I even called out his name, but he didn't hear, so I grabbed his arm from behind. And he turned, and he looked *so* shocked . . . He clearly thought I was mad.' I clutched my napkin. 'I think I *did* go mad for a while.'

'And what about your work?'

'I had to go back. It was hard, but I needed the money – and the distraction. But I wanted to stay in the flat in case Nick phoned, or even turned up. I had this fear that if he came back and I wasn't there, then he'd just take off again.

So my boss, Tom, let me work from home. He was wonderful actually.' I remembered again how supportive Tom had been, despite the fact that he was having his own marital crisis. He'd drop off the books I needed. He'd bring me funny videos, to cheer me up – I remember he gave me a boxed set of Ealing comedies and five series of *Frasier*. He'd make sure I had enough in the fridge.

'So you never went out?

I shook my head. 'Hardly ever, and then not very far. I had a new phone line put in, so that our main one was always clear in case Nick called. When I did have to leave the flat, which was rare, I'd leave a note for Nick on the door. I left all his things completely untouched. Our marital home was like the *Marie Celeste*.'

'And how long did this go on for?'

'Two months. By then, of course, I was a wreck. Day in, day out, I lived in this . . . *void*. I was in such a state that I could hardly eat. It was as much as I could do to wash. But then in early March I got these two silent phone calls – one in the afternoon and one the following morning. I could hear faint breathing at the other end, and I just knew it was him, so I said "Nick, please don't hang up. Please, *please* just talk to me." Both times I heard a sigh, or he might have been trying to whisper my name. But then the line went dead – and that was all the contact I had. Until . . .' I paused while the waiter took away our plates.

'Until . . . ?'

'The middle of April. *The World Tonight* did a feature about missing persons, and they interviewed me.'

'I heard it. That's how I knew.'

'And the following morning, my case manager at the Missing Persons' Helpline phoned me to say there was *fantastic* news – Nick had just made contact. I was so *happy* . . .' I heard my voice catch. 'I was . . . *elated*. I just kept saying how wonderful it was, and I kept thanking them for their help, over and over . . .' My throat was aching with a suppressed sob. 'Then I asked them when I could see him, but they didn't answer. So I asked them again. I said, "When can I see him? I want to see him." And there was this odd little silence. And they told me that he'd phoned their 24-hour "Message Home" line and had said he was safe and well –' my eyes were brimming, the tears tickling my lower lashes – 'but that he wanted no further contact.'

'No further contact?'

I covered my face with my hand. 'The *relief* . . . The *relief* of knowing that he was all right – but at the same time the knowledge that he didn't want to *see* me. The *cruelty* of it – after all I'd been through.' I felt a hot tear slide down my cheek. 'Sorry,' I murmured, 'but I can never talk about it without crying.'

'Who could blame you?' Luke murmured. He discreetly passed me his handkerchief. 'But at least he wasn't dead, thank God.'

I swallowed. 'Yes. That's what I told myself. "At least he's not dead." Although, in one way, he *was*. And that's what it's been like ever since. I've been in this awful limbo in which I feel like a widow – I even got letters of *sympathy* – and yet my husband's alive. And it was impossible to start again with anyone else, because, technically, my marriage wasn't over – although, of course, it was. Even if he did come back, which he's not going to after so long, we could never go back to being a "normal" couple. Can you imagine my resentment? Plus I'd never trust him not to do it again.' I thought again how ironic it was that Nick, who had seemed so 'safe' after my heartache with Luke, should have done something so terrible.

'Why can't you just get divorced?'

'Because you can only divorce without consent after five years. And I couldn't face the idea of going on dates, and having to explain that I was still married, but that my husband was a missing person – that he was out there, somewhere, but I didn't know where, because he didn't *want* me to know. I felt stigmatized by what Nick had done – as though I was such an awful person he couldn't bear to see me, or even talk to me, or separate from me honestly and openly. It totally destroyed my morale.'

Luke reached for my hand again, but this time I didn't withdraw it.

'You're lovely, Laura. It's about him. He'd obviously got terrible emotional and mental problems which had nothing to do with you.'

I could feel my face tingling at the light pressure of Luke's fingers on my skin. 'Maybe . . . Yes . . . I guess. I don't . . . know.'

'So doesn't he ever make contact?'

'Not with me. Every few months he sends the Missing Persons' Helpline an e-mail, saying only that he's okay but not where he is. The last one came just before Christmas.'

'And can't they be traced?'

I shook my head. 'He uses a different e-mail account each time so it's impossible. He's just "disappeared" himself – but the awful thing is, that's his right. It's not a crime for a man to go missing, and that's what thousands of men do every year. They just walk out of their lives, and there's nothing their families can do except wait, and wonder, and hope. I can't *make* Nick come back, even if I knew where to find him. I just want this chapter of my life to end.'

'And he wasn't mentally ill?'

I shook my head. 'And there were no irregularities at his work. There was speculation that he might have done something dishonest, but the charity's trustees said that the accounts were all fine. I know some people believed Nick had a mistress somewhere, or even another wife; but I found nothing in his e-mails or diary or on his mobile to suggest any kind of double life. Some people thought *I'd* had an affair

86

and that it had sent him over the edge, or that he was gay, and couldn't cope; or that he wanted to have a sex change, or had joined a cult, or had found out that he was terminally ill – or was living on the moon with Elvis for all we knew . . .'

'I suppose people tend to think there must be a reason for it,' Luke said.

I shifted on my chair. 'Yes, that *is* what they think.'

'They can't believe that these things just . . . *happen*.'

'That's . . . right. But being at the centre of so much gossip was vile. And I couldn't hide it because there were a few small pieces in the press – "Charity Director Disappears", that kind of thing – so everyone got to know.'

'What about your friends? Were they supportive?'

'Only at the beginning – which is probably why I became even closer to Felicity and Hope. They might drive me mad in their different ways, but at least I could *rely* on them. I did have one close girlfriend, but she moved to the States with her husband not long afterwards. All my other friends were ones Nick and I'd had jointly. And they were kind at first of course, but as time went by they started avoiding me – but then what *do* you say? At least in widowhood there's dignity, but with this there's only pity, and curiosity . . . and talk. And now I'm on national TV I'm terrified that one of the tabloids will pick it all up – so you must never *ever* mention it to anyone. Do you promise me?'

'I do. I solemnly swear. But do you have any idea why he might have done it?'

I fiddled with the stem of my wine glass. 'No . . . No, I don't, I . . . don't . . . know. He'd recently been to the Sudan again, and had come back depressed. He was also badly affected by his father's death. He'd worked for the UN and Nick had idolized him; he'd died of a heart attack six weeks before – he was only sixty-three – and after that Nick became rather withdrawn. And then, well, there was *one* thing . . .'

I sighed. 'We'd had a car crash. Two weeks before Christmas we'd spun off the road on our way back from a party in Sussex.'

'Were you okay?'

I paused, remembering again the strobing blue lights of the police cars, and the whoop and wail of the ambulance. The kindness of the nurses. *Don't worry,* they'd said to me. *It'll be fine.* But it wasn't.

'Nick took a bad knock to the head. He had concussion, and after that he didn't seem quite . . . himself.'

'Is that what you meant when you said you'd had difficulties?'

'Ye-es. And I thought, maybe . . . he'd suffered slight neurological damage, or had some kind of amnesia . . .' My voice trailed away.

'And how do you feel about him now?'

I heaved a profound sigh. It seemed to come up from the very depths.

'I just feel . . . so . . . incredibly . . . *angry.* Because *he* knows where he is – and *I* don't. It's like this mortal game of hide and seek. And there are many, many times when I *hate* him for putting me through such hell.'

'But he must have been in turmoil, poor guy.'

'Yes,' I sighed. 'Of course. And on one level I feel sorry for him – but the point is he left turmoil *behind.* Quite apart from the stress of it, I suddenly had to pay the mortgage on my own – £900 a month – when I wasn't earning a huge amount. There are no insurance payouts if your husband disappears. You're left completely high and dry. I found part-time work, compiling quiz questions, and my parents and Hope lent me some cash.' I remembered again how kind Tom had been. He'd given me a 'bonus' of £2000, despite the fact that he was in the middle of an expensive divorce.

'Why didn't you just sell the flat?' I heard Luke ask. 'Move somewhere smaller?'

'Because if the property's in joint names, you can't.'

'And does he ever take money out of his bank account?'

'No. But we discovered afterwards that he'd drawn £5,000 out of his own savings, ten days before, so he'd clearly been poised for flight. He *knew* he was going. That makes it even worse. Anyway,' I sighed. 'Now you know.'

'But you're getting on with your life.'

'I am. I've waited three years and I'm not going to wait any more. Nick's made it clear that he doesn't want to see me again.'

Luke put out his hand. 'But I *do*.' I looked at him. 'I *do* want to see you again, Laura. So . . . can I?' he asked gently. He glanced at his watch. 'You've got five seconds to answer by the way.' I looked into his eyes. 'The clock's ticking . . .' His pupils were so black, I could see myself in them. *Drriinggg!* 'Time's up! And the answer *is* . . . ?'

'Well . . .'

'I'm sorry, I'll have to hurry you.'

I half-smiled then I said, 'Yes.'

'*Really?*' I nodded. He lifted his hand to his chest with relief. 'Well, that's . . . great. So . . . what day? Let's see . . . I'm busy tomorrow as that's my day with Jessica, but how about Sunday afternoon? That would be lovely for me – I find Sundays very difficult as Jessica goes back to her mum. We could have a nice lunch somewhere. Would you like that?'

'I'm afraid I can't this Sunday. I've got Olivia's christening.'

'Okay then – Monday. In fact Monday would be perfect.'

'And why's that?'

'It's Valentine's Day.'

FOUR

On Saturday morning I stayed in bed late, wallowing in the delicious aftermath of my date with Luke. I felt a new contentment – a real sense that my life, which for so long had been crawling along on all fours, was now speeding forward again on all fronts. At nine thirty the phone rang. Maybe it was Luke, phoning to wish me a good morning. I let it ring four times then reached out my hand.

'Laura?'

'*Tom*! Hi there!'

'Hi. You sound cheerful.'

'Hmm,' I said. 'I *feel* cheerful. And how are you doing?'

'I'm fine – and I'm sorry to ring you on a Saturday –'

'You can ring me any time, Tom, you know that.'

'I do. But I just wanted to ask you a *very* serious question . . .'

'Yes . . .' I said, smiling. 'And what might that be?'

'Have you seen today's *Daily Post*?'

'*No.*' I pushed myself up. 'Why?'

'There's a fabulous review of the show. Nerys phoned me and I ran out to get it. We've had some good write-ups, but they've all been small. This one's *big* – and it's *great*.'

I clutched the duvet to my naked shoulders. 'What does it say?'

'It's by Mark McVeigh . . . that critic who's always – what is it?' I could hear the rustle of the newspaper – '"Witty and Waspish."'

'Pithy and poisonous more like – he's commonly known as Mark McVile.'

'Well he's been nothing but Mark McLovely about you. His review's headed "Quick-Witted".'

'Good God!'

'He likes the show's fast pace,' Tom read. 'He also likes, "the combination of the low-brow set with the high-brow questions", and, above all, he likes your "assured and authoritative" presenting style . . . Here we are. "The fact that Ms Quick shows neither Robinsonian astonishment when the contestants answer correctly, nor Paxmanesque derision when they get it wrong, makes this clever young woman a refreshing change. She is the natural heir to British TV's greatest quizmeister – Bamber Gascoigne. As with him, you feel in very safe hands. And, as with him, you suspect Ms Quick could answer most of the questions herself – *without* needing to phone a friend."' I felt giddy with delight.

'I told you that the critics would love you,' Tom went on. Suddenly I heard his mobile trill out. 'Oh, hang on a moment, Laura . . . Hello?' I heard him say. 'Oh *hi*! . . .' I wondered who he was speaking to. 'I'm just on the other line . . . Yes, I'd *love* to . . . okay then . . . I could come over to you . . .' It's funny – we know each other well, yet we never discuss our private lives. 'Why don't we meet in Ravenscourt Park? Ten thirty? By the playground? *Great.*' I found myself wondering who it was. 'Sorry, Laura. What was I saying? Oh, I know – I just wanted to warn you that a bit of media interest in you is starting.'

I felt my insides coil. 'Already?'

'It's because the viewing figures were so good – plus there's a real buzz about the show. The market research said the viewers like seeing the presenter put on the spot.'

'Well, that's our USP. But I *won't* do newspaper interviews because I know they'll ask me about Nick and I don't want to talk about it.'

'That's fine. But the Channel Four press office do want you to do *some* publicity.'

'Fair enough – it's just a question of what.'

'The *Daily Mail* and the *Sunday Post* have both asked you to contribute short pieces to their lifestyle pages – Nerys has e-mailed you the details. Have a great weekend.'

I padded over to the computer, clicked on my inbox and read the two requests. They were both for those celebrity filler columns you see dotted all over the press. Usually I find these pieces either fatuous – *My Cottage, My Second Bedroom* – or horribly confessional: *My Biggest Mistake, My Prolapse, The Worst Day of My Life*. The one from the *Sunday Post* was called *My Pet Hates*, and I had to list three. 1) Nerys, I thought meanly, 2) my nosy neighbours, and 3) the way Felicity bores on about the baby. I could hardly use those, so as I showered and dressed I gave it some *serious* thought. My three pet hates . . . People who queue-barge; the dark – I really hate the dark – and – oh *yes* – those prisoners on probation who sell dusters and dishcloths door to door. I can't stand them, not because I'm unsympathetic, but because they always turn up *at night*. As a woman living alone I find it alarming to encounter a strange man on my doorstep after dark, saying he's on day-release from Wormwood Scrubs and would I be interested in some rubber gloves? They seem to work this area a lot, as a result of which I have two hundred tea towels and thirty tubs of *Astonish*.

The request from the *Daily Mail* was to do *The Last Five Things On My Credit Card* – innocuous enough – and, as it happened, there were things I needed to buy. I hadn't got Olivia's christening present, and I wanted something special to wear – Felicity had issued the family with strict instructions that the dress code for us was 'smart'.

So half an hour later I made my way slowly up Portobello, through the throng of Italian and Japanese tourists, then browsed in the antique shops. I bought Olivia a Victorian silver jewellery box lined with midnight blue velvet, then turned down Westbourne Grove. Five years ago this area was full of antique shops but now the area's become like a mini King's Road. Put it this way, it's got the only Oxfam shop I've ever come across which has regular 'Prada Promotions'.

I bought a copy of the *Post* then sat at a table outside Café 202, sipping a latte in the spring sunshine while I happily read Mark McVeigh's TV review. Then I crossed the road to Agnès B. As I wandered around I luxuriated not in the clothes themselves, but in the delicious knowledge that lack of money was no longer the gut-churning problem it had been for so long. For the best part of three years I'd bought nothing that wasn't essential, but now, with a presenting fee for each show on top of my normal pay, I could afford to indulge myself. So I went into Dinny Hall and spent £200 on a pair of gold and pearl earrings, for the simple reason that I *could*. The novelty of such extravagance was delicious. Except that it didn't feel like extravagance at all. It felt like a reward to myself for having survived such a tough time. Then I looked for something to wear.

I tried on tie-wrap dresses in Diane von Furstenberg, and floaty chiffon skirts in Joseph and Whistles, and cashmere cardigans in Brora, before going into L K Bennett and opting for a dark pink, fitted wool crepe suit which I knew would also look good on the show. I didn't much like their shoes, so I crossed over the road to Emma Hope, and was just waiting for the assistant to get me a pair of crimson slingbacks in my size when I glanced out of the window. My heart stopped. There was *Luke*. He was walking past on the other side of the road, hand in hand with Jessica, his face alight with love and pride.

My first instinct was to run out of the shop waving and yelling – but he looked so happy, I felt I shouldn't intrude. Jessica was half-walking, half-skipping, in her blue anorak and her polka-dot wellies, her white-blonde pigtails swinging behind her. Then she must have said something funny because he threw back his head and laughed, then hugged her to him. I felt my heart expand. As I watched them walk over the zebra crossing, past the church and down the road, until they were almost out of sight, I allowed myself to entertain a little fantasy in which Luke and I were living together – with Jessica, Magda having agreed to give Luke custody so that she could spend more time with the goats. And the three of us had such a nice life . . .

We went to Holland Park every Saturday and played in the adventure playground there, and as Luke and I pushed Jessica on the swings, she'd be shrieking with laughter, head thrown back, hair flying; then we'd all go home and have tea. And I'd have made her a chocolate cake, with loads of icing, and she'd get it on her face, so I'd wipe her mouth and hands. Then I'd help her with her piano practice, or her reading, or teach her to knit, or help her sort out her dressing-up box. And I'd tell her about the tickets I'd got for us to see *Swan Lake* at Covent Garden the following week, and about how first we'd go shopping together to get her something special to wear. And her face would be radiant with amazed delight.

And in the evening the three of us would watch a video together, something really fun and wholesome like, I don't know, *Shrek*, or *The Princess Diaries* – and Jessica would snuggle into Luke on the sofa while I sat a tactful distance away. And, as the credits rolled, she'd yawn like a little cat, and Luke would say, 'Okay, time for bed my little girlie – say nighty-night to Laura.' And Jessica would come and give me a hug and I'd feel her soft little face against mine, and I'd remind her that I was taking her for a riding lesson in Hyde Park the next day because she's mad about ponies, and she'd sigh with happiness and then, to my joy, I'd hear her whisper, 'Oh, I'm so lucky to have *you* as my stepmum, Laura . . .'

'Blah blah blah blah blah . . .'

And I'd reply, 'Oh no, Jess – I'm so lucky to have *you*. I love little girls, I just *love* them, and you're the *sweetest* little girl there's ever been . . .'

'Blah blah blah blah shoes, madam?'

'Hm?'

The assistant swam into focus. She was holding up the slingbacks. 'Your shoes. Size 41.' I stared at them. 'Are you all right madam?'

'What?'

'Are you all right? Would you like a glass of water?'

'Oh. No . . .' I thought of Monday, and of my date with Luke. I smiled. 'It's all right, thank you. I'm *fine*.'

'Don't *you* look fine and dandy,' said Mum as I met her and Dad outside St Mark's church at half past two the next day.

'So do you,' I said, as I kissed her – or tried to; our hats collided. 'Though I feel a bit overdressed to tell you the truth.'

'Me too,' Mum confided. 'But then it isn't every day your first grandchild gets christened, and our Fliss did say she wanted us to scrub up.'

We were so worried about being late that we'd arrived a good twenty minutes early; so we went in and sat in the third pew on the right hand side. Swords of spring sunlight sliced through the stained glass, scattering splinters of colour like the fragments of a broken rainbow. We inhaled the sweet aroma of beeswax and dust. As the organ began to play, I perused the elegant Order of Service that Felicity had had specially printed. I read the dedication – a fragment of a poem by Emily Dickinson.

As if the sea should part
And show a further Sea –
And that – a further . . .

That must be how parenthood makes you feel.

'Look at all these lovely readings and hymns,' I heard Mum whisper next to me. 'It's a bit posh, isn't it?' she added with a giggle.

'It certainly is.'

But that had been obvious when the invitations arrived. The card was so stiff it was practically self-standing; the embossing on the flowing black italics so pronounced you could have read it with your fingertips, like Braille. Despite their stricken finances, Felicity had eschewed the idea of a simple family christening for something much more lavish. Behind us, in the organ loft, the large choir was assembling. In front of us a string quartet was discreetly tuning up. On either side of the altar were two white floral arrangements the size of obelisks. A large posy of white and pink anemones hung from every pew.

'It's more like a wedding really,' said Mum, as Hope and Mike arrived and squeezed past us.

'A Royal one,' Hope added with a smile. 'She's got an official photographer outside, and there's someone videoing the whole thing.'

'Totally over the top,' Mike breathed. I glanced at him. He's normally good-natured, but I thought that was sharp.

'Well, why shouldn't she go to town?' said Hope fairly. She opened her Hermès Birkin bag and removed an elegant compact. 'This is her special day after all.'

I remembered Felicity's last 'special day', twelve years before, and how miserable I'd been, and by delicious, but unexpected contrast, how elated I felt today.

'You look smashing, Hope,' said Mum proudly. It was true.

Hope is always immaculately turned out in her expensive, perfectly accessorised little suits, with her neatly shod feet, and her glossy tights, and understated make-up and her perfect, face-framing bob, as smooth and shiny as a helmet. She's dark and petite – the physical opposite of Fliss, who is voluptuous and milk-maidy blonde. I resemble neither of my sisters – gangly, frizzy, and with strong, slightly angular features. Luke used to say that if I was a painting I'd have been a Modigliani. Felicity, being fair and fleshy is pure Rubens while Hope . . .

What was *she,* I wondered as I stole a glance at her profile. A Dora Carrington, maybe? Small and sharp. Inscrutable. Efficient-looking. She tends to radiate a slightly chilly competence. She was flicking through the hymnal, marking the relevant pages with tiny Post-It notes.

I always find it amazing that the same ingredients could have produced both my sisters. Where Fliss is untidy, expansive and spontaneous, Hope is highly organized, reserved and self-controlled. It's almost as though she's the responsible eldest, and Fliss the indulged baby. I've always been the pivot between the two. When we were in our teens we discovered that Mum had had another pregnancy between Fliss and me but that it hadn't worked out. I think about that lost baby sometimes . . .

From behind us now we could hear muted conversations. The pews were beginning to fill.

'How many people has Felicity invited then?' Dad asked as he had a swift look behind us.

'A hundred and fifty,' said Hope, as she brushed an imaginary speck off her cuff. 'I imagine that as it's a Sunday she'll have a pretty good take-up – probably seventy per cent – so there should be at least a hundred of us.'

'Ridiculous,' Mike muttered, folding his arms. If I hadn't liked him I would have felt angry at this second swipe, but I decided that his ill-temper was due to stress. He and Hope both work in the City – she as head of PR for the metal exchange, he as Vice-President of an investment bank – and I knew he'd been working all hours on some massive deal. But, although he looked exhausted – and I noticed that his close-cropped dark hair was greyer than before – I felt his intolerance was due to more than fatigue. He had a tetchiness about him as though he really didn't want to be here. But then christenings probably bore him to bits.

Mike and Hope don't have children – by mutual agreement. Mike's never shown the slightest interest and Hope has always joked that she's 'anti-natal'. And it's *not* a front to protect herself against possible disappointment – it's a sincere and deliberate choice. 'I have *no* maternal feelings,' she says happily if the subject ever comes up. 'Absolutely *none* – *not* interested.' She was always like that. When she was ten, for example, my parents offered her a rabbit, but she refused. So they offered her a gerbil, and she politely declined that as well. She explained that she didn't want to look after a rabbit or a gerbil or a mouse or, in fact, anything, thank you – and that resistance extended, in adulthood, to kids. She told me a long time ago that she didn't want the responsibility of children, or the 'chaos' and 'mess'.

She's nice with other peoples' babies mind you. She'll jiggle them and play 'peek-a-boo' with them and do 'round and round the garden' – but then she's genuinely happy to hand them back. She and Mike have been married for six years, and on their first date she told him that she didn't want kids and that she would never change her mind, so it was essential that he knew that right from the start. Because he was so besotted, he accepted it. Felicity once asked him whether he didn't ever mind. He just shrugged and said it was 'a question of love'.

But he and Hope have a fabulous life. They have a large house in Holland Park – creamily luxurious, fitted with every mod con, including an oven which cost them six *grand*, but which they hardly use, because they eat out all the time. They go on amazing holidays – you should have heard them whining about Concorde being taken out of service! They have weekends in Paris and Prague. Hope has got just the life she always wanted. I don't think she'd ever *allow* anything to go wrong.

I glanced at the back of the church. Fliss and Hugh still hadn't arrived. I didn't mind. It was nice just sitting next to my parents, quietly chatting. They can't come to London much because of their bed and breakfast – a large farmhouse – plus they live a long way north. We grew up in Ealing, but five years ago they retired to Nether Poppleton, the beautiful Yorkshire village where Mum grew up.

'Now, our Laura,' she said to me, as the organ began to play a Pachabel toccata. 'I don't see as much of you as I'd like, so tell me –' I braced myself – 'how's your *personal* life? Have you made any new *friends*?' she enquired meaningfully. 'I understand Fliss has invited one or two single lads for you today.' My heart sank. I'd completely forgotten.

'She doesn't need them,' said Hope, as she flicked dust off her Gucci pumps with a silk hanky. 'She's seeing Luke again.'

'I hadn't told you that yet,' I protested.

'Felicity told me. You know how she blabs. She phoned me up specially, she was so thrilled about it.' I rolled my eyes.

'Luke?' Mum repeated wonderingly. 'Luke from *university*?' I felt blood suffuse my face. 'You're seeing *Luke* again?'

'Well . . .' I didn't want to overstate the case. 'I've just met him again, that's all.' I told her about his surprise appearance on the quiz.

'Oh I *liked* Luke!' she exclaimed. This is what she had kept saying after we broke up, I now remembered. 'I *liked* Luke,' she'd say regretfully, about ninety times a day. 'Oh, I *did* like him.' It had driven me mad. 'Derek –' Mum was nudging Dad in the ribs now. 'She's seeing Luke again.'

'Who?'

99

'Luke. Our Laura's seeing *Luke* again. *You* remember Luke? The one she knew at Cambridge. You know. The one who *broke her heart.*'

'Mum!'

'Sorry, love, but your father's hearing's not what it was. But I *liked* Luke,' she said again. 'Now *he* was a laugh.' This, I knew, was a dig at Nick, who they'd always found too serious – which is probably why I'd gone for him in the first place. Felicity, in particular, had never warmed to him.

'Too bloody worthy,' I'd overheard her telling my parents a week before our wedding. 'I know he's a good egg and all that, but he's not much *fun*, is he?' This had stung me. Because I knew she was right. Nick *wasn't* exactly the life and soul of the party. But he was interesting and affectionate, reliable and good; and he was 'safe'. Or so I thought.

'I remember Luke always had some snippet of trivia up his sleeve', Mum added appreciatively. 'Some of the things he used to come out with like – what was it? – oh, that's right, that a mosquito has forty-six teeth. Can you imagine? Forty-six teeth! A mosquito! I've never forgotten it. I mean, that's more than we've got isn't it?'

'Not if you count our milk teeth,' said Dad. 'That would give us fifty-two.'

'It isn't forty-six,' I said. 'It's forty-seven. And in any case that isn't Trivia, Mum.'

'Isn't it?'

'No. It's Useless Information.'

'Same thing.'

'No it's not the same thing – it's very important to distinguish between the two. Trivia is stuff about popular culture – who's doing what to whom in soap operas, or how much footballers get paid, or who paints Victoria Beckham's toenails. Useless Information is quite different – it's the study of fascinating, but entirely irrelevant facts like, for example, the fact that Anne Boleyn had three breasts.'

100

'*Did* she?' they all said.

'Yes – and six fingers on her left hand. Or the fact that babies don't have kneecaps.'

'*Don't* they?'

'No – they don't develop them until they're two. Or the fact that an octopus has three hearts.'

'Really?'

'*That* is Useless Information,' I explained. 'Luke has always excelled at it,' I added proudly. Which is how, I now remembered, we first met.

I'd noticed him of course – around college – but I'd deliberately ignored him because I found him so attractive, but knew that he was out of my league. But then, one evening, he'd sidled up to me at a party, where I was leaning against a wall, watching the dancing, and he'd just stood there, saying nothing, swigging his bottle of designer beer. Then, without any introduction, and without actually *looking* at me, he'd said, '*Did* you know that the fingerprints of koala bears are indistinguishable from human ones?'

'Really?' I'd returned, indolently, despite the fact that my heart was racing.

'It can lead to confusion, apparently, at the scene of a crime.' He had another sip of beer. 'Miscarriages of justice, even.'

'How terrible.'

He'd nodded regretfully. 'It is. And did you also know . . . that a snail mates only once in its entire life.'

I glanced at his profile, and felt my legs turn to rubber. 'I can't say I did know that, no.'

'And did you *also* know –' and now he'd looked at me – 'that both Adolf Hitler and Napoleon had only one testicle?'

'What? Between them?'

He sipped his beer again, then shook his head. 'Each.'

'That *is* fascinating,' I'd said.

And then some girl had come up to him and dragged him

on to the dance floor and I didn't get to speak to him again. But every time we met after that, usually in the library, he'd sidle up to me and say, very quietly, '*Did* you know . . . ?' followed by some intriguing, but one hundred per cent useless, fact. Until the day when he came up to me and said, '*Did* you know . . .'

'Yes?' I'd replied politely.

'That I've fallen in love with you?'

'So what's happened to Luke then?' Dad enquired now.

'Separated. One little girl. Has an art gallery. Where's Fliss?' I glanced to the back of the church. As I did so, a bald, bespectacled fifty-something man sitting about five rows behind, gave me a little wave. As I hadn't the faintest idea who he was, I pretended I hadn't noticed: in any case, Felicity had just arrived. I half expected to hear 'The Arrival of the Queen of Sheba' as she progressed in stately fashion up the aisle. Felicity loves being the centre of attention. She should have been the TV presenter, not me.

Hugh was holding Olivia, who did look angelic in her hand-embroidered, antique lace-trimmed silk christening gown complete with detachable frilly bib in case she puked. Felicity also looked surprisingly good in her new suit, and she was definitely wearing her nuclear pants as she didn't actually look too vast. But beneath her huge hat, her fixed smile and her professionally-applied make-up, I could see that she was furious.

'Everything under control?' Dad whispered as she sat down in front of us.

'No!' she snapped, still smiling like a ventriloquist's dummy. 'The bloody vicar's cancelled – he's got 'flu. So they've dug up some piss-poor locum – the man's a complete idiot.' Suddenly said vicar appeared. He looked about twelve – but was probably thirty. He was very long-sighted, his eyes swimming behind thick, old-fashioned magnifying lenses like fish in a bowl.

'Welcome to St Mark's,' he said benignly. He held out his hands. 'Welcome to you *all*. And what a *remarkable* turnout!' he added as his eyes focused and he took in the unusual size of the congregation – there were well over a hundred of us. 'We are here to celebrate the Holy baptism of this lovely child – Olivia Clementina Sybilla Alexandra Margarita . . .'

'Piña Colada,' I heard Mike mutter sardonically. Hope jabbed him in the ribs.

'. . . Florence Mabel Carter,' the vicar concluded unctuously, 'and to welcome her into God's house. So let us now joyfully sing our *first* hymn, "All Things Bright and Beautiful".'

So far so good. In fact he conducted the service well, though he seemed taken aback by the number of godparents. There were five godmothers – including, at Felicity's insistence, Hope and me, even though she knows I'm not a believer – and five godfathers. Frankly, I thought this was ludicrous – we'd only ever had one of each.

'Do you reject Satan?' the vicar asked us as we stood by the font. I always find that bit thrillingly primitive.

'We do,' we answered seriously.

'And all his works?'

'We do.'

'And all his empty promises?'

Most of them, I thought. But then – and here I understood Felicity's reservations – the vicar gave this toe-curling sermon, all about what baptism means. It took the form of an idiot-level Q and A session – as though we were in Sunday School.

'Now . . . Jesus was the son *of* . . . ?' He looked at us expectantly, then cupped his hand behind his right ear. 'Come on – can anyone tell me? Who was Jesus's Dad then?' There followed a silence so excruciating we could hear each other swallow. 'C'mon now – I know *you* all know, but I just want you to tell me. So. Let's all *shout* it out, shall we? Jesus was the Son *of* . . . ?'

'God?' Dad piped up, sportingly.

'Yes! *Well* done! Absolutely right! And who is the Holy *S* . . . who helps God, particularly in the sacrament of baptism? The Holy *S* . . . anyone?' We were too catatonic with embarrassment to reply. 'Holy *Spppppp* . . .' he went on, helpfully.

'Spaceman.' I heard Mike mutter.

'No – *not* the Holy Spaceman,' the vicar said indulgently, shaking his head.

'Spirit!' said Hope loudly to cover her shame at Mike's rudeness.

The vicar beamed at her. 'Yes! That's *right*! It *was* the Holy Spirit.' From in front I heard Felicity's tortured sigh.

'And who can tell me the name of the John who Jesus baptized in the River Jordan?' he enquired benignly. 'Here's a clue – it *wasn't* John Lennon, though some people might say that it was. It was actually John the . . . ?' He'd cupped his hand behind his ear again. 'C'mon folks. Begins with a B . . . ? Buh . . . Baa . . . . *Baaaa* . . . ?' By now you could have used our toes to take corks out of chardonnay. Indeed the embarrassment was so palpable it had even got to Olivia as, for the first time, she started to cry. My theory is that Felicity had pinched her – if so, it did the trick. She started wailing like an ambulance, the dreadful sermon came to an abrupt end, and there was a collective sigh of relief. Then there were two more readings, another hymn, the choir's a cappella rendition of a Micronesian lullaby, a final blessing, and that was that.

'Thank *God*,' Felicity muttered, still smiling like a contestant in a game show. 'And to think I gave the church a donation of two hundred pounds! If I'd known we were getting this pantomime artist, I'd have made it fifty. Anyway,' she handed Olivia to Hugh, 'at least I won't have to bother again until she gets confirmed. Right – let's head home for the champers and cake.'

It was obvious to anyone who'd never been there before

which was the right house. Pink and white helium balloons inscribed with Olivia's name flew gaily from the gate and there was a large posy of white flowers on the door. We all poured inside and, with the aid of a small pink and white striped marquee, somehow we all squeezed in. And I was just making my way over to a second cousin of ours who I hadn't seen for years, when the man who'd waved at me in the church came up to me, a look of eager anticipation on his face.

'Laura?' he said. He was blocking my way, which I found rather rude.

'Yes?' I replied, looking at him blankly. 'I don't think we've . . .'

He thrust a bony hand at me. 'Norman Scrivens.' Good God . . . I was astounded – for this, I now saw, was my 'date'! 'Felicity told me to look out for you,' he explained happily.

'Really?' I said weakly. I felt his eyes flicker over me, appraising me. His scrutiny made me feel sick.

'So here I am then!' he said with jokey desperation. 'Very nice to meet you.' His hand felt dry, like snakeskin. 'I met Felicity through the school.'

'Really?'

'She taught my daughter a few years ago.'

'I see.'

'Very nice christening service,' he observed. 'If a tad grand,' he added gratuitously; then he rolled his eyes – bloody cheek! Did he really think that slagging off my sister would endear him to me?

'I thought it was beautifully done actually,' I said coldly. 'Felicity went to a great deal of trouble.'

'Oh yes, yes of course, but that vicar was an unprepossessing fellow wasn't he?' he smirked. Not half as unprepossessing as you, I wanted to say. He was as bald as a tortoise and, on closer inspection, looked nearer sixty. He had a thin, hard face, with beady blue eyes behind a pair of steel rimmed glasses and when he smiled – which he was now doing, idiotically – his neck pleated into a stack of creases and folds.

'Felicity told me all about you,' he observed. He was practically smacking his lips.

'Did she?' The thought filled me with utter dismay.

'And of course I recognized you from the TV,' he added enthusiastically. So he'd done his homework. 'I must say you *are* a clever girl aren't you?' I felt my jaw go slack. 'The things you know.' I anaesthetised myself against the horror with another large swig of champagne. 'Quadrimum . . .' he chuckled. 'Mind you, I seem to remember that word featuring in some Latin ode or other at school. Thoroughly boring,' he added.

'Not at all. It's by Horace and it's a hymn to the pleasures of life and youth. Horace coined the phrase, "*carpe diem*". His poems are lovely. They make you rethink your life.'

'*Carpe diem*, eh? Anyway, I happen to know quite a bit about wine myself,' he went on. Then he launched into this brain-numbingly dull monologue about his 'large cellar' in his 'house' – 'in Chelsea,' he slipped in casually, as though I could care! – and how he liked 'driving holidays in France' but also greatly enjoyed 'hill walking' and 'collecting antiques'. After ten minutes of this I was wondering why he hadn't just stuck a Personal Ad to his forehead and saved himself the trouble.

'Well it was great meeting you,' I said, as politely as I could. 'But I must circulate.'

'Of course – we'll catch up later.'

I didn't reply.

I went through to the marquee and chatted to my aunt and uncle, but within a couple of minutes I was aware of Scrivens, on the periphery of my vision. Why couldn't he take the hint? Then I went into the dining room and chatted to people there and, within two or three minutes, there *he* was

106

too. In order to discourage him, I entered into an in-depth conversation with a former colleague of Hugh's, who was grilling me about quizzes.

'Are there things you can do to improve your chances?' he asked.

I told him that there are – that you can learn the elements in the periodic table, for example, or the world's capital cities, or the roll call of American presidents, or England's kings and queens, or the key works of famous composers, or famous historical dates, or the planets in the solar system, or a comprehensive selection of collective nouns – my all time favourite of which has to be a 'smack' of jellyfish, closely followed by a 'murder' of crows.

'And of course you should read the papers, and listen to the radio and watch TV and generally be very aware. But the main thing you need to be good at quizzes is a grasshopper mind. My short attention span has got me a long way,' I joked tipsily. 'Being good at quizzes is not really about intelligence, so much as memory and retrieval, which means you can't spend too long on any one thing. Anything more than three seconds and you might be so deeply ensconced in the sexual peccadilloes of Henry VIII or whatever it is that hours will have passed, wasting the opportunity to learn hundreds more superficial, but interesting, facts.' I had another large swig of champagne. 'Who cares about psychological motivation or insight in the field of general knowledge?' I concluded jokily.

Meanwhile Hugh was chatting animatedly to a university friend of Felicity's – a solicitor called Chantal Vane. Fliss seems to adore her, but I've never warmed to her – she's a cold fish.

'More champagne, madam?'

To my surprise, my glass was empty again. 'Why not?' By now I knew, for a fact, that I was pissed. My happiness had made me drink far more than normal. I was with my family: I felt secure; my confidence was high. I'd had a long period of anxiety and misery, but now things were looking good. But still I felt Scrivens's eyes boring into me, trying to make contact. And – oh no – I could feel him coming towards me again. Why didn't the man read my body language? I might as well have been standing there, shouting 'Fuck *Off*!' So I shot upstairs to the sitting room where by now the party was beginning to thin out. I had a brief chat with the next-door neighbours, who I'd met before, and I had another glass of champagne, then suddenly there Scrivens was again.

'Laura – here,' he handed me his card. 'We must have lunch sometime. Do you have a card – or shall I ring you at work?'

I tried to think of a way of extricating myself without giving offence. 'Well . . .' I could say I needed the bathroom, but that would seem crass . . .

'I know a super place in St James. So do you have a card?' he repeated.

Or I could pretend I'd just spotted someone I hadn't seen for twenty years, but the room was emptying now. 'I'm afraid I don't have any on me, no.'

'Any particular day good for you?' he persisted.

Or I could just faint . . . 'Friday's usually good . . .' he continued. But then – yuck – he might try to revive me. 'Or, of course, if it's difficult to take a lunch break from your quizzing, we could have dinner – in fact, yes, dinner would be better for me.'

I could just throw up. I felt in danger of doing so right now as I suddenly realized how much I'd drunk, plus his stale breath was making me ill.

'Erm . . .' I stuttered, swaying slightly. Or I could just say, 'I'm sorry, but I have to go now. Goodbye.'

'Right . . .' he said, getting out his diary. 'Let's fix it up *right* now. As you say, "*carpe diem*" and all that. So . . . when's it going to be?'

'Never,' I wanted to say. 'It's going to be never.' And I was just praying for someone to come and rescue me from his persistent and unwelcome attentions, when – Hallelujah! – my mobile phone rang.

'Oh, I'm *so* sorry,' I said, as I rummaged in my bag. I looked at the number. It was Luke. '*Hi*!' I said, with deliberate delight. 'How *lovely* to hear from you. *Sorry*!' I mouthed happily at Norman. He looked crestfallen, and then irritated when he saw that I was taking the call. He hovered for a moment, then turned on his heel and headed downstairs. I ran upstairs into Felicity's bedroom, shut the door, then flopped backwards on to the bed.

'How *are* you?' I heard Luke ask as I stared at the ceiling.

I closed my eyes, and the room began to spin. 'A bit pissed – but otherwise fine.'

'I hope you don't mind my calling you at the christening.'

I gazed at the cornice. Its egg and dart detail was blurring. 'Far from it – I was delighted, to tell you the truth.'

'Why?'

'Because I was just being chatted up by this *dreadful* man.'

'Really? Who was that then?'

'Oh this stockbroker, Norman Scrivens. Felicity was trying to set me up with him.'

'*Was* she now?'

'Yes. But that was before she knew I'd seen you. Even so, I don't know what she was thinking of! He's at least fifteen years too old and totally unappealing. He's thin and bald with glasses – and *tedious*. Felicity says he's desperate to meet someone because his wife left him – I'm not surprised she did.'

'Don't be too hard, Laura. You can't blame the poor guy for trying.'

'I guess I *am* being a bit mean. But it's because I've had *far* too much champagne . . .' I closed my eyes again. 'And because he's been pestering me *all* afternoon and because he has *no* appreciation of Horace's ninth ode which is one of the most beautiful poems I've ever read – I used to recite it to you, if you remember? – and oooh . . . I've got the whirlies – hang on! *Hic!* – oh blast. Now I've got the hiccups too. But he really was – *hic!* – *so* pushy, Luke – trying to make me agree to a date. He even – *hic!* – got his diary out! But then – *hic!* – thank God, *you* phoned; but anyway why the – *hic!* – hell would he assume I'd be remotely interested. He was much too old, and, frankly, pretty hideous – plus he had bad breath!'

'Oh dear.'

'Exactly. Oh dear. Oh God – *hic!* – I've had *far* too much fizz. Think I'm gonna be sick. Wonder if Fliss's got any water up here.' Now I pushed myself up with one hand, and stared at her bedside table where, amongst the face-creams and books and baby wipes a tiny red light was steadily shining. 'Whass tha?' I muttered. I leaned forward, peering at its white casing. And then I realized what it was.

'Oh. *Shit.*'

FIVE

'It was *so* embarrassing!' Felicity hissed twenty minutes later. The party was over, and I was slumped over the kitchen table, sipping my fifth pint of water. 'Absolutely *everyone* heard.'

'How many?' I asked.

'At least thirty. And it was *quite* clear, from your eloquent description, who you were talking about. They were *riveted*. I turned it off the second I realized, but by then it was too late. He was standing *right* by the monitor – which was on full volume – and he was *incredibly* offended. The look on his face as he left!'

'Well I'm *sorry*, Fliss.' I heaved an inebriated sigh. 'I'd drunk *far* too much – largely because he'd been pestering me – and I had *no* idea the monitor was on. Why *was* it on anyway? It didn't *need* to be did it – so actually this is all *your* fault.'

'We always have it on,' she explained crossly. 'Plus it was hidden behind this christening card, otherwise I'd have noticed and turned it off.'

'I'm sorry,' I sighed again. 'He'd been bugging me all afternoon and I was just letting off steam. I had no *idea* anyone was listening.'

'It was *so* embarrassing,' Felicity repeated, her nostrils

flaring. I half-expected to see smoke shooting out of them.

'Well, *I* thought it was rather funny,' said Hugh, who'd also had a bit too much to drink. 'More christening cake anyone? The icing's lovely.' For someone on the verge of bankruptcy he seemed very cheerful.

'Hugh – it's *not* funny to offend our guests!'

'Oh come on, Fliss. We hardly knew the guy and you only invited him along to meet Laura – and frankly, I think Laura's right. He *was* far too old for her – and yes, too unattractive. I don't know what you were thinking of.'

'Thanks for your support Hugh,' she snapped, as I beamed at him.

'You haven't got it.'

'It was just a bit unfortunate,' said Dad.

'And no real harm done,' Hugh shrugged. 'Scrivens works in the City so he's not going to know anyone who knows Laura, even if he did want to talk about it, which *I* certainly wouldn't do if I'd been in his shoes.'

'Who are you talking about?' said Hope. She had nipped out to the car to get Olivia's present and had missed the conversation.

Fliss explained. 'His name's Norman Scrivens. I taught his daughter a few years ago. He's a stockbroker.'

'Norman Scrivens?' Hope repeated. 'Was *he* here? He isn't a stockbroker.'

'Isn't he?' said Fliss.

'He used to be, but he was made redundant from Cazenove's so he became a financial journalist. He's now City Editor of the *Daily Post*.'

'Is he?' Fliss said. 'Oh . . .'

I had a vague sense of unease.

'He's very close to the editor, Richard Sole – commonly known as R. Sole – king of the tabloids, and animal nut. Apparently Scrivens looks after his portfolio. I've never met him,' Hope went on, 'but he's an utter toe rag.'

112

'How do you know?' said Hugh. 'He seemed affable enough.'

'Because last year he interviewed Carol Stokes, the most successful woman dealer on the Metal Exchange. She's single and very attractive, but she wasn't receptive to him, so he was vile about her in the piece. I'm not sorry that Laura offended him.'

'Anyway, he can hardly write about *me*,' I said. 'I'm of zero interest to his readers.'

'That's true,' Hope conceded.

'And I'm sure he'll just want to forget the whole thing – which is what I intend to do.' A silence descended. 'Good. So that's that then. Incident closed. Any further comments on the subject from anyone?' They all shrugged.

'Aladadazagoyagoya,' Olivia said.

The following morning I woke with a raging thirst, a blinding headache, and a vague sense of unease.

'Ooh, I *do* hope I didn't say anything silly and *embarrass* myself,' I croaked as I staggered into the bathroom. 'Oh well,' I muttered as I ran my bath. 'Too late to regret it – *forget* it.' I looked in the mirror. My eyes felt like peanuts and were about the same size. I had three espressos on my way to work.

'So *she* turned round to me . . .' I heard as I pushed on the door. 'And so *I* turned round to her and said . . . no, that's *right*, Maureen, she did – she turned *right* round to me and *she* said . . .'

That's another thing that drives me mad about Nerys. The fact that no one she knows ever just 'says' something. They have to 'turn round' first, for some strange reason, and then say it. All that twirling and spinning must be exhausting. Just hearing about it made me feel giddy, adding to my postalcoholic distress.

'You look peaky,' Nerys said as she put down the phone.

113

Her hair was the colour of ketchup. She dyes it a different shade of red every week.

'I feel peaky,' I replied. 'Alcohol poisoning.'

'You know what you need, don't you?'

'A blood transfusion, probably.'

'No. Some sodium of bi-carb – *here* . . .' She scrabbled in her drawer and plonked down her emergency tub. 'Simple, but reliable,' she added, tapping the top with a sharp, claret-coloured fingernail. 'Take my advice – there's no better cure.'

'It's okay, thanks. I'll get Tom to trepan me – I'm sure there's a tin-opener in the kitchen.'

'Anyway, you've got some very nice mail today Laura,' she added. 'That'll perk you up.' She nodded conspiratorially at my pigeon-hole. 'You've got *five* Valentine's cards.'

'Really? That makes up for having had none for the last three years.'

'Tom's got one too,' Nerys added casually.

'Has he?' I remembered the conversation I'd overheard him having on Saturday. I peeped at the large, red envelope in his pigeonhole. The address was typed so there was no telltale handwriting, and the post-mark was smudged with rain.

'I wonder who *that's* from then,' I said, hoping that Nerys would be unable to resist enlightening me, if she knew, which she probably did, because she would have spoken to his new woman on the phone – whoever she was.

'Well Tom's *very* popular,' she teased. 'But then he's an attractive man. Clever with it. *Oh* yes – *very* clever, is Tom.' You'd think he was her own son the way she boasts about him. 'Don't you think so Laura?'

'Oh, well, yes. I do.' My happiness at having five Valentines made me feel expansive. 'Of course I do. Tom's *very* attractive, *extremely* clever, and a *great* boss.'

'A wonderful boss,' she concurred happily. 'He's a marvellous man.'

'He is.'

'Plus he's so reliable.'

'Mm. That's right.' I thought of his poor wife and baby.

'He's a catch,' Nerys added. 'An absolute *catch*.'

'He . . . is. And I'm sure whoever reels him in will be a very lucky woman, Nerys. Whoever she is.'

'*Well* . . .' she began. She was fiddling with the gold locket she often wears. I've sometimes wondered who she keeps in it.

'Shall I tell you what *I* think?'

'Yes, Nerys.' There was a silence.

She gave me a sly sort of look, as though she had a particularly delicious piece of gossip. 'Well, what *I* think –' Suddenly the phone trilled out and she adjusted her headset. 'Good *morn*-ing, Trident Tee-*veeee*.' Oh well, I thought. 'Oh *hello*, Joan . . .' I'd get it out of her another time. 'No, it's okay. Yes. *Ye-es*. I *do* know her . . . *Really* . . . ?'

The first of my Valentines was from an anonymous viewer with a number of suggested questions for the show – all of them concerning the dimensions of a particular part of his anatomy. I put it straight in the bin. The second and third were from two guys who were desperate to get on the quiz and thought I might be impressed by their egghead credentials. *I was Radio Wales's Pub Quiz runner-up,* said the first. *I was 'Britain's Brainiest Estate Agent'*! declared the second. The fourth card was from the Merseyside Quiz League. *There aren't 22 properties on the Monopoly board,* they'd written. *There are actually 28 if you include the four stations and the two utilities. But there are 22 property* squares. *But, apart from that glaring, and frankly surprising error, we love the show. Yours in quizzing, MQL.* The fifth card was from Luke. I opened it last because I recognized his hand-writing. It was a sketch of me, in red chalk, on brown paper, in the shape of a heart. *I'll pick you up at seven thirty,* he'd written. *We're going on a mystery date . . .*

At six thirty I was at home trying to tame my hair with

industrial quantities of de-frizzing mousse and my hair-straightening iron when I heard the buzz of the entryphone. I opened the door. A young, fit-looking man was standing there, with a large holdall.

'Please Miss,' he began, holding up a photocard, 'I'm a prisoner on day-release from Wandsworth . . .' My heart sank. 'But *don't* shut the door in my face; *don't* send me away on a cold night without buying *something* from me, just a dish-cloth, or a duster . . .'

And that's another thing I don't like – the lachrymose sales pitch these guys always give you. I ended up adding another tub of *Astonish* to my vast collection, then carried on trying to smooth my hair. At ten past seven, as I was putting on my mascara, I heard the entryphone buzz again. I heard Cynthia's door open, then her descending footfall.

'Ooh, *so* sorry,' I heard her simper. 'I thought you were my seven o'clock. *Laura*!' I could hear her strings of pearls clicking against each other. I opened the door. 'You've got a gentleman caller,' she smirked. Luke was standing on the threshold, clutching a huge bunch of flowers.

'Thanks, Cynthia,' I said. I'd been avoiding her since last week so I decided to be friendly – not least because I was happy. As I ushered Luke inside, I noticed her scent – *Intuition* – and her sand-coloured cashmere cardigan; as usual, she was expensively dressed.

'Sorry,' he said, 'I'm a bit early.' Suddenly his mobile phone rang and he winced as he looked at the screen.

'You did say romance was in the air,' I reminded Cynthia pleasantly as he stepped outside again.

'Yes,' she said, slightly smugly. 'I *did*.' I smiled at her. She was okay really. Just a bit odd. She nodded at Luke. 'But not with him.'

'I'm sorry?'

'Not with *him*,' Cynthia repeated patiently, as Luke walked wearily down the steps. I stared at her. Bloody cheek!

116

'Yes, Magda', we heard him say. 'Well, no, it's *not* a good moment actually. Okay – o-*kay* . . .' He turned and rolled his eyes at me. 'No Magda, you've got that *all* wrong . . .'

'Thank you Cynthia,' I said, 'but I don't need any more of your predictions. To be honest, I don't find them very accurate.' She was driving me mad. Okay, she'd identified that Nick was missing, but she could easily have got that from one of my neighbours. Knowing them, she probably did. Plus the stuff about the flowers was quite obviously crap.

'Would you like me to video *University Challenge* for you?' she enquired pleasantly, ignoring the slight.

'No,' I said, rather sharply. 'No thanks.'

'It's the first semi-final – should be very exciting – Loughborough v. Leicester.'

'It's okay. I really don't mind.'

'I'm sorry about that,' said Luke as he came in again. 'It was my nightly ear-bashing.'

'About what?'

'Oh everything,' he replied. 'Just . . . everything. Anyway – this is where you live.' He'd walked me home on Friday, but hadn't come in, so I gave him the guided tour. 'All your Classics books,' he said as he looked at the shelves. He ran his finger along the spines. 'I remember them,' he sighed. I wondered where Horace was, I hadn't been able to find him.

'The flat's a good size,' he added as we went down the stairs. I unwrapped the flowers – candy-striped tulips with exuberantly frilled petals. 'I know red roses are traditional,' he said. 'But I remembered how much you liked tulips.'

'I do. I love them – there are so many gorgeous ones, and these are wonderful. They're called "Burgundy Lace".' They were so frilly they looked as though they were doing the can-can.

'Your neighbour seems friendly,' he observed. 'She thought I was her seven o'clock *what*, though? It sounded rather dubious.'

117

I handed him one of the flyers she leaves in little piles in the hall.

'"Let Psychic Cynthia solve all your problems,"' he read. '"This gifted lady will tell you your past, present and future."' He smiled. 'What a laugh.'

As I arranged the flowers in two vases I thought again of what she'd said about Nick. 'It is – it's utter bunkum. There – how gorgeous. Now . . . drink?'

'No thanks – we should be on our way.'

I picked up my bag. 'So where are we going?

'To the flicks.'

'To see . . . ?'

'Well, do you remember that Valentine's Day when we saw *Casablanca* at the Arts Cinema?'

'Yes,' I said wistfully. 'We sat through it twice.'

'Well . . .' he said, smiling at me in a way that made my knees turn to jelly.

'Is that what we're going to see? *Casablanca*? I'd love that.'

'Nope. We're going to see *The Satanic Rites of Dracula*. They've got a Hammer Horror season at the Electric.'

'How . . . lovely.' I put on my coat. 'You always did like scary films. You were a connoisseur of horror.'

'That's right. I'm a regular shockaholic,' he quipped.

As we walked up Portobello, Luke gave me an exposition on the unique blend of blood and eroticism that had made Hammer films so successful.

'They veered towards self-parody in the end,' he said, 'but these early ones are wonderful. They're camp, and over-the-top gruesome in the manner of *Grand Guignol*, of course . . .'

'Of course,' I said happily as we went in.

'Plus they're really *rather* sexy,' he explained as we had a snack at the bar and a glass of champagne.

It was a clever choice of date. The warm, velvety darkness of the cinema – together with the scariness of the film – invited physical touch. As we sank into the leather armchairs

118

Luke helped me out of my coat, and as his arm went round my shoulder, I felt the hairs on my neck rise up. As the film got underway our forearms brushed against each other, tentatively at first, then more boldly. As Christopher Lee sank his fangs into Joanna Lumley's neck, Luke placed his hand over mine, interlocking our fingers. I was aware of his smell – a familiar blend of lime and vetiver. I could feel the rise and fall of his chest.

'That was terrific,' he said, as the lights went up. 'I love a good scare. It's so . . . *refreshing*. Now . . .' he looked at his watch. 'It's five past eleven. How about some more champagne and some Belgian double chocolate ice cream?'

'Where? It's rather late.'

'Thirty-eight Lonsdale Road.' My heart did a swallow dive. 'Is that okay, Laura?' he said softly now. He leaned towards me and held his mouth to my ear. 'Would you like to come home with me?' I didn't reply. 'I've got a new toothbrush you can have. It's hard,' he murmured. My face was aflame. 'You always liked a hard bristle didn't you?' he whispered, with fake innocence. 'And you never wore pyjamas so that shouldn't be a problem?' I shook my head. 'So is that okay then?' I nodded again, the erotic charge between us so intense now as to have bereft me of speech.

'If we'd only just met, I suppose we'd have to be more . . . proper,' he said quietly as we left the cinema. 'We'd have to go on at least – what? – four chaste dates before we . . . you know . . .' he lifted an eyebrow and I felt my skin tingle. 'But because we already *know* each other we can fast forward right through all that . . . bashful restraint can't we?'

'Hmm,' I concurred dreamily as he took my hand in his.

'In *our* situation, two dates is perfectly acceptable – don't you think?'

'Perfectly,' I agreed. My body was humming with anticipation.

We walked in silence through Westbourne Grove. Luke's house was at the scruffier end of Lonsdale Road, close to the Colville Estate. He unlocked the front door and turned off the alarm. The answerphone on the hall table was flashing angrily, but he ignored it. He put on the light. Every inch of wall space was filled with abstract art.

'Most of them are my clients' paintings,' he explained as he took my jacket. 'I'd rather have them on the walls here than locked away in my stock room.' I looked at a large, swirly oil over the fireplace.

'That's a Craig Davie. We're doing a major retrospective on him at the end of March. I love his work.'

'And I love this one,' I said. 'It's a Luke North.'

It was an ink and wash portrait of Jessica – strong and unsentimental; and even though she was so young, and so innocent, it imbued her with charisma, and *power*. Her presence was evident throughout the house. In her tiny pink trainers by the door, and her blue coat on the rack; in her books and her Barbie dolls in the sitting room, and in the glitter pictures that festooned the walls. There were also dozens of photos of her in large clip frames. As Luke opened the champagne I looked at the ones in the kitchen. There she was, aged eighteen months or so, beaming happily into the camera; as a newborn, cradled in Luke's arms; in her paddling pool with just a sun-hat on; riding her little pink bike. There were a couple of her feeding the goats, and one of her at Disneyland, standing between her parents. As I looked at this one, I felt myself tense . . .

There was Magda. She was exactly as Luke had described her. Petite, and very pretty. I felt a dart of jealousy. She had a skein of long, enviably smooth blonde hair piled into a topknot, a style which, with her floral vintage frock, gave her a curiously old-fashioned air. There was an oddly defiant glint in her large blue eyes, as though she was spoiling for a fight.

120

'Do you really want some ice-cream?' I heard Luke ask.

I turned away from the photo, and felt my face suffuse with warmth.

'No,' I whispered. 'I don't.' Desire had robbed me of my appetite. I felt a physical longing for Luke that made my bones ache. He took my hand, and led me upstairs. At the top of the first flight, I paused. For there, on a small mahogany table, was a large silver frame containing a black and white portrait of Luke, Jessica and Magda. Seeing further evidence of their family life made me feel uneasy, as though I were intruding, so I reminded myself – as I would often come to do – that Magda had left Luke and lived elsewhere.

'Do you mind?' he asked quietly.

'No,' I lied. I noticed, again, the same pugilistic gleam in Magda's big blue eyes.

'I keep it there for Jess,' he explained as we went into the master bedroom. 'As I say, the separation's been hard for her, so I tend to downplay it.'

'I understand.'

He shut the door behind us, and held my gaze for a moment. Then he stepped forward and kissed me, then unbuttoned my shirt and pushed it off my shoulders; then he gently pulled down the zip on my skirt. If he was someone new, I would have been scared of exposing my flaws – my *self* – for the first time; but Luke knew me, and I knew him.

'Laura,' he breathed. His mouth was on my ear. 'My lovely Laura . . . I can't believe you're *here*.' There was no shyness. The twelve years fell away as naturally and easily as our clothes slipped to the floor. Our bodies remembered each other as we moved together in the darkness, then lay, limbs entangled, and slept.

I woke at six, with Luke's arm around my waist, pulling me close, his hands cupping my breasts, his legs warm against my own.

'It's so lovely to hold you again,' he sighed, as he ran his

121

hand over my hip. 'I never, ever forgot you, Laura.' I turned towards him and buried my face in his neck, speechless with contentment. I felt reconnected not just to Luke, but to a time of my life when everything looked positive, and full of promise, and good.

Luke stroked my hair, tucking it behind my ears, then held my face in his hands, caressing my cheekbones with his thumbs.

'I'll never let you go again,' he murmured. He kissed me again.

'No,' I whispered, as I closed my eyes. 'Don't . . .' Luke had drawn me back to him, ineluctably. He was my magnetic North . . .

From outside now came the gentle whine of a milk float, then birdsong. A triangle of opalescence was visible through the curtains. We lay there as the room filled with a gauzy light.

'I guess we'd better get up,' he said dreamily. 'What time do you have to be at work?'

'Not till ten.'

'Let's have a shower together then.'

'Hmm.'

'Like we used to, remember?'

'I do.'

'Then we'll have breakfast in bed – I'll go and get some Florentines.'

'My absolute favourites.'

'I remember that too. I remember so many things about you,' he murmured.

'Like what?'

'I remember that your grandmother was French, and that you had a hamster called Percy . . . I remember that you locked yourself in a loo on Euston station when you were seven and the fire brigade had to be called out.' I smiled.

'I remember you were afraid of the dark . . .'

'I still am.'

'. . . and that Felicity accidentally broke your nose showing you how to play hockey when you were nine, hence its slightly odd, but fetching shape.' He kissed me. 'How am I doing? Am I through to the next round?'

'You are. Plus you've picked up some bonus points.'

'And are there any other contestants?'

'No. They've been eliminated.'

I went into the *en suite* bathroom and turned on the shower. As I did so I thought of how with Luke I could have the best of both worlds – the delicious tension of a new relationship, with the comforting familiarity of an old one. I could have novelty and history, new experiences and shared memories. With him I could have Now – and Then. As I tested the warmth of the water, I suddenly heard the phone, sharp and insistent, drilling into our mellow mood, like a Black and Decker.

'Yes . . .' I heard Luke say, his voice cracking with fatigue. 'What? No I *haven't* listened to your messages – I came back late. No. I was at the cinema. With a friend, if you *must* know, now what *is* it Magda – it's very early . . . Are you sure it's a crisis? . . . I'm *not* being callous – it just doesn't sound that serious . . . Have you given her Calpol? . . . No – I *don't* want her missing school unless it's absolutely *necessary* . . .'

As Luke spoke to Magda, his voice rising with frustration and stress, I opened the medicine cabinet to see if I could find the promised toothbrush. There were Luke's shaving things and his bottle of Penhaligon's Vetiver. There was a tube of Colgate and some floss, and some Calpol and a tiny pink hairband and a box of *Little Mermaid* sticking plasters. And, on the shelf below, I now saw, there was a bottle of Lancôme foundation, an atomiser of Guerlain, two lipsticks and a wand of mascara, a bottle of Decleor moisturiser, some No. 7 cleansing lotion and an open packet of Tampax. I felt as though my veins had been flooded with fire.

'All right, Magda, all right. Driving over to Chiswick in the rush hour is *not* ideal, and I don't think it *is* an emergency, and I've got a very busy morning at the gallery, but if you can't cope . . .'

She'd left him ten months ago. Why were her things still here? I was so tense I could hear myself breathe.

'No, no – of *course* I'm not saying that you're an incompetent mother . . . far *from* it, Magda . . .' Realizing that this conversation was not going to be brief, I turned off the shower. The sudden silence seemed to resonate, as though I'd just banged a large gong.

'What?' I heard Luke say. 'No-one. No. I'm on my own. That's because I was about to have a shower but now I've turned it off – okay, *okay*, you win; I'll come over *straight* away and I won't shower first. Satisfied? Good. Now will you let me get off the phone?' He sighed as he replaced the handset. 'Sorry about that,' he said as he came into the bathroom and ran the cold tap. 'She constantly stresses me out, as you must have noticed.'

'Why did you say you were alone?'

He splashed water on his face then grabbed a towel. 'Because I don't want to razz her up. If she thought I'd had a woman here she'd have gone *crazy*.'

I flinched, as though I'd been slapped. 'Even though *she* left *you*?'

'Yes.'

'And even though she's got a boyfriend?'

'Yes.' He began to pull on his clothes.

'Don't you think that's rather *unfair*?'

'Yes. But Magda *isn't* fair – plus she's very erratic, if not slightly insane.' He stepped into his boxer shorts, then pulled on his jeans. 'If I annoy her she'll reduce my time with Jessica – that's what she constantly threatens me with.' He pulled on last night's shirt. 'Or she'll try and turn Jess against me . . .'

'Would she be that low?'

'If she was angry enough with me, yes. She's *very* volatile, so I do whatever I can to keep her sweet.'

'Her things are still in the bathroom cabinet,' I said quietly, my heart still pounding from the shock of seeing them there.

'Are they?' He finger-combed his hair. 'I can truthfully say that I hadn't even noticed – I've got so many other things on my mind.' He slipped on his shoes. 'She either forgot them, or couldn't be bothered to take them all when she left. Anyway, I've got to go *right* now.' He kissed me, then wrapped his arms round me for a moment. 'I'm sorry about breakfast.' I felt a pang of disappointment – eating Florentines in bed with Luke would have been heaven. 'Help yourself to anything in the kitchen and just lock the front door with this spare key, then post it back. We'll speak later.' He kissed me again, then left.

It was strange being left alone in Luke's house. As I picked up my discarded shirt, I noticed a photo of his parents looking much the same as I remembered them, and of his sister, Kim, who'd gone to live in Australia, and one of Rocky, his old dog. The wardrobe door was hanging open so I went to close it and, as I did so, I peeped inside. There were Luke's jackets – mostly casual, but three smart ones, presumably from his Christie's days. Next to them were his shirts, subtly striped and finely checked, and one Liberty print one. They've recently become fashionable with men. I could imagine Luke looking good in it. It was that classic art nouveau pattern in turquoise and red. I pulled it out but, as I did so, I saw that it wasn't a man's shirt at all. It was a woman's. I felt as though acid had been spilt on my chest.

Next to it, I now saw, was a black, heavy satin vintage cocktail dress, and hanging alongside that was a velvet jacket – size eight – and, next to that, a pale green silk dress, forties-style, with a lily-of-the-valley print. Then I looked on the wardrobe floor. There were three pairs of high-heeled shoes. She had very small feet. I found myself resenting her as much for this as for the fact that, almost a year after she'd left him, Magda's things still hung alongside Luke's. I suppressed the urge to rip them off their hangers and stuff them into bin liners. But I couldn't resist the masochistic temptation to look for further evidence of her. It was all too easy to find.

On the mantelpiece, in the china bowl in which he kept his cufflinks were two pairs of crystal earrings, a big diamante brooch, some sparkly hair clips and a string of pearls. On the shelf beside the bed was *Bridget Jones's Diary*; a Hungarian-English dictionary, and *The Handbook of Goat Care and Health*. In the bottom of the chest of drawers I found two silk nighties, a hydra of tights and, to my dismay, several pairs of lacy black knickers. In the bedside table on what must have been 'her' side, were a rosary, a hairbrush, a bottle of crimson nail polish and a small leather purse. Everywhere I looked I saw this residue of Magda – a glistening snail-trail of her personal effects.

I sank on to the bed, heart pounding, nausea rising in my throat. Why were so many of her things still here – let alone such intimate ones? Were she and Luke *still* . . . ? I breathed deeply, forcing myself to think rationally. Then I drew back the curtains. By now the sky was a flawless blue. The answer had to be no. Because if they *were*, that would mean their relationship was fine, in which case they'd still be living together, which is what Luke had wanted, because of Jess – in which case he would *not* be pursuing me.

'She *left* him, she lives *elsewhere*, she's with someone *else*,' I said firmly. Even so, I felt confused and distressed. But then, as I stepped into my skirt, I saw something that surprised and consoled me. Sitting on a chair by the window was Wilkie, my old bear. I picked him up and held him, inhaling his musty aroma. His suede-covered paws were shiny with wear, and the green jumper my mother had knitted for him when I was five was badly frayed, but he was otherwise in fairly good shape. I'd given him to Luke when he was recovering from appendicitis because I'd wanted him to have something of mine that I'd loved. He'd kept him all these years, and he'd clearly cherished him. Calmer now, I let myself out.

My equanimity was to be short-lived.

'Hi Tom,' I said when I got in to work a couple of hours later. He was engrossed in the newspaper. 'Morning Tom,' I tried again. He seemed unable to hear me. 'Can you hear me, Major Tom?'

'Oh. Laura . . . er . . . sorry.' He looked uncomfortable. 'Sorry.'

'Anything up?'

'Well . . .' He looked *very* uncomfortable, I now realized. So, it seemed to me, did Dylan and Sara, who seemed to be slinking away. And Nerys had given me a peculiar look when I arrived, but I wondered whether that might have been because, being a shrewd old bird, she'd detected my post-coital glow.

Tom put the paper down, then ran his left hand through his hair. 'I'm afraid there's something in here you're not going to like.' He handed me the paper. The *Incognito* gossip column was dominated by a large photo of me – taken yesterday I realized – walking up Portobello, looking distracted.

QUICK TEMPER it was captioned.

'Wh-at?'

Laura Quick, the host of Channel 4's quirky new quiz, Whadda Ya Know?!!, may have cut the mustard when she made her TV debut last week, but at a party in Notting Hill over the weekend fellow guests were said to be 'appalled' by the Clever Clogs' not so brilliant behaviour. She was 'drunk and obnoxious' said one party-goer. Quick allegedly has personal problems – her husband, charity supremo, Nick

127

Little, went out to buy a pint of milk three years ago, and decided not to come back. Is it any surprise, Incognito can't help wondering . . .

I felt as though I'd fallen down a mineshaft.

'This is terrible,' I croaked. I closed my eyes, breathed in, then looked imploringly at Tom. 'It's just . . . terrible – and they've completely twisted it.'

'I thought they must have done – but what actually happened?' I told him. 'So this Scroggins is obviously both the source and the unnamed "party-goer".'

'Yes – it's Scrivens all right – but it's *trash*.' I snapped through to the City pages: there he was – complete with hideous photo-byline. 'He probably wrote it himself.' Now I thought, with horror, of all the people I knew who might read it. 'I want you to sue the *Post*, Tom,' I said impotently.

'Well, it wouldn't be Trident who sued them, Laura, it would have to be you. And it would be hard to prove defamation given that, by your own admission, you did have too much to drink, didn't you?'

'I was just merry – it was a family christening – and of course my behaviour wasn't "obnoxious". It was just unfortunate that my admittedly unflattering remarks about Scrivens were overheard on the bloody baby monitor. I unwittingly insulted him and here's his revenge.' Tears sprang to my eyes. 'Hope *said* he was a shit and she was *right*! But a million people will read this, Tom. And some of them will believe it.'

'If it makes you happy I'll ring the Channel Four lawyers,' he replied quietly. 'But I know what they'll say. It's tough, Laura, but you'll just have to take it on the chin. You'll also have to be more careful because the show's sparked a *lot* of interest – so what you do or say could get in the press. And you won't have much redress, because the papers will be able to claim that you're a public figure now.'

I laid my head on the desk. My morning had started blissfully but, from the moment Magda had rung, it had gone crashing downhill – as though her phone call had cursed my day.

'This is a disaster,' I moaned. 'Everyone I know will have seen it. I'm just . . . *cringing.*'

'People will forget,' Tom said soothingly. 'I know, because, well, I've been there myself.'

'Oh yes,' I said vaguely, though I didn't feel I should say any more.

'And let's face it,' he went on, "TV presenter drinks too much at party" is hardly an interesting story, is it?'

I pushed myself up. 'No. But the fact that said TV presenter's husband has been missing for three years ago *is* an interesting one.'

'Well . . . yes,' said Tom regretfully. 'I'm afraid *that* is.'

'How *could* you?' I said to Felicity five minutes later. I'd gone up to the boardroom to berate her in private. 'It was bad enough that you invited that creep to the christening, but why the hell did you have to tell him about *Nick*?'

'I'm sorry,' she whined. 'I had no *idea* he worked for a newspaper.'

'Even if he didn't, you had no right to discuss my private affairs with him – or with anyone. I *told* you it was essential to be discreet, but you blabbed. You even told him that Nick had gone out to buy a pint of milk – what a delicious little detail! I was hoping it wasn't all going to be dragged up – or at least not for ages, until I could perhaps cope with it. But now, thanks to my own *sister,* it's right *out* there, on Day *One,* in black and white!'

'I'm *sorry,*' she wailed. 'I was trying to make him feel sympathetic towards you.' I rolled my eyes. I could just imagine Felicity laying it on about how I'd been 'cruelly abandoned' by my 'cowardly husband' who'd just 'run off'. She'd never pulled her punches about Nick, and after he'd 'gone walkabout' as Mum tactfully puts it, she'd really had it in

129

for him. 'I'm *sorry*,' she repeated. 'I was only trying to help.'

'You've done the opposite.'

I put the phone down feeling slightly better for having at least vented my indignation. As I passed Tom's office I noticed that his casement window was wide open and that the breeze was lifting his papers off the windowsill, sending them flying. I went in and closed it, then picked up the bits of script and correspondence that lay scattered about the threadbare carpet. Beneath a letter from the bank was Tom's Valentine card. It was a cute, rather than a romantic, one, depicting a large teddy bear clutching a red satin heart. With a guilty pang I looked inside, unable to resist a quick peek.

To Tom with lots of love from . . . The writing was deliberately childish – and there was a string of hugs and kisses after the signature which was, teasingly, just legible – *S* . . . *a* . . . *m.* So he was seeing someone called Sam . . . Samantha. I left the card there as I didn't want Tom to think I'd been snooping.

As I went downstairs I found myself wondering who Samantha was, and what she looked like, and what she did, and if she was like Samantha in *Sex and the City* and whether he made a habit of asking *her* 'very serious' questions; I also wondered how he'd met her, and how long they'd been together, and what they had in common, and then I realized, with relief, that this train of thought had distracted me from the horror of the *Incognito* piece. In any case I knew I'd have to put it from my mind because today was a recording day. But when I got to the studio I saw that one member of the audience was holding a copy of the *Post*. Just seeing it made me feel sick. I was convinced that he'd read the offending article out loud to everyone and that they'd all been sniggering about it.

'They were giving me funny looks,' I confided to Marian as she did my make-up. 'A few of them were waiting in reception when I arrived, and they were all looking at me in this shifty way.'

130

'They were only doing that because you're the presenter and they were curious,' she said firmly. 'There's no need to be paranoid because of one silly little piece in a cheap newspaper. Just forget it, and put on a good show.'

Somehow, I managed to do so, although my concentration was shot to pieces. I felt hot with indignation and shame. I dropped my question cards at one point because I was so distracted – they just flew out of my hands. To my relief, the winning contestant didn't want to Turn the Tables – I didn't think I'd have coped – and, at the post-show party no-one mentioned the piece. My anxiety began to recede.

'Tom's right. People will forget,' I said to myself firmly as I got the taxi back to the office. 'It's tomorrow's chip wrappings.' But when I arrived Nerys told me that she had fielded no less than eight interview requests from the manufacturers of rival chip wrappings.

'They seem desperate to talk to you.'

'About what?'

'Well . . . about . . . your husband.' I felt sick. Look what that *Incognito* column had stirred up! This was just what I'd hoped to *avoid*. 'They all said they want you to "open your heart" about your, what was it . . . ?' Nerys looked at her notebook. 'Oh yes –' she fiddled with her locket – '"Secret Heartbreak".'

'Oh *shit*. And who are "they"?'

She peered over her glasses at her list. 'The *Daily News*, the *Daily Post*, the *Daily Mirror*, the *Daily Star*, the *Daily Mail*, the *Daily Express* . . .'

'The Daily Muck and the Daily Filth. I'm not talking to any of them,' I said. 'Why *should* I, just so they can sell more copies of their tabloid rags?' I silently cursed Felicity again.

'I'd do it if *I* were you,' Nerys said matter-of-factly as she took off her glasses.

'Why? I don't have to.'

'No, but if you *don't*, they'll never leave you alone.' Annoying woman – always prescribing.

'Thank you for your advice, Nerys,' I said coldly. 'But if I *don't* talk to them, then they don't have a story, do they? In my view, silence is golden.'

She shrugged. 'Up to you. But in *my* view you're making a mistake.' Blasted woman, sticking her oar in, as usual. 'Good afternoon. Trident Tee-*veee*. Tom O'Brien? Certainly . . . putting you *thro-ugh* . . .'

'At least the photo's nice,' Luke said consolingly when he phoned me at five.

'Although it gives me the creeps to think it was taken without my knowledge.' I imagined the camera trained on me, from a distance, like a sniper's rifle. 'And the piece was a farrago of lies and spite.'

'Well you've had loads of good publicity, so one nasty bit is hardly going to matter is it? Anyway, when can I see you again?' My mood instantly lifted. 'How about tomorrow? Why don't you come round and I'll cook supper.'

'Tomorrow would be fine – but do you mind if we watch the show? I'm not being vain – it's just part of the job.'

He said he didn't mind at all – he loves quizzes, whether or not presented by me . . .

'I enjoy releasing my inner nerd,' he explained as he turned on the TV the following night. 'And when's the one I was in being screened? I mustn't miss it.'

'Not till the end of March – there's usually six weeks between recording a show and broadcasting it. Did you tell Magda about it?' I asked as he poured me a beer.

'No, because I want it to be a huge surprise for Jess. I can't wait to see her face. I'll make sure she's with me that night.'

We sat happily on the sofa, Luke shouting out the answers. During the commercial break, Magda phoned.

'I can't chat – I'm just watching something,' Luke explained. 'Oh . . . this new quiz on Channel Four . . . You're watching it too are you?' My eyes widened. 'Yes, it *is* good . . .' I stifled a snort. 'No – *I* didn't know that Kilimanjaro was the world's largest volcano either. Yes – the presenter *is* excellent isn't she?' I emitted a squeak, and he grinned at me. 'No, Magda . . . I'm on my own. Oh, it's just starting again. Okay, Magda . . . yes . . . fine, Magda. Speak to you tomorrow then. Byeeee.' He hung up with a sigh of relief.

'She's in a good mood at the moment,' he explained. 'She's *almost* being reasonable. *Schoenberg*! I get the impression things are going well with her man. He clearly hasn't realized that she's nuts yet. *Wallace and Gromit*!'

'How long have they been seeing each other?'

'Six months. She's obviously been careful, but he'll twig soon. *Albert Einstein*!'

'Luke . . . why did you say you were alone?'

'Because she asked me if someone was there – *Wolverhampton Wanderers*! – and I didn't want to tell her.'

'Why *not*?'

'Because I don't want to rub her nose in our relationship. *Anagram*! I mean, *palindrome*!'

'But why should she care?'

'*Sharon Stone*!'

'She *left* you, Luke.'

'I know, but that doesn't mean she'll like it. *Frankenstein*!'

'I see. So she doesn't want you to be with anyone else.'

'I guess that's right. I *will* tell her about you, but I'll have to break it to her carefully. *Deoxyribonucleic acid*! Do you understand that?'

'In the circumstances – *no*.'

But as things turned out, it wasn't Luke who broke it to Magda at all.

His fridge was empty after the weekend, so we went round the corner to have supper at Café 206, and he told me all about his preparations for the forthcoming Craig Davie retrospective. And we were just walking out of the door at about ten thirty, feeling happy and relaxed, when a young man in a dark hooded top and baggy trousers suddenly loomed in front of us. For a moment I thought we were going to be mugged.

'Laura?' he said. I looked at him. There was a flash. 'Laura!' Then another. Oh *shit*. 'This way Laura!' I put my hand up to my face. Then there was another flash. 'C'mon Laura!'

'Go *away*!' I yelled.

'*Don't*!' Luke whispered as we walked away, fast, running now, the photographer in hot pursuit – I could hear his steps thudding behind. '*Don't* look at him and don't *say* anything.'

'One more, Laura!' we heard. 'There's a good girl! C'mon . . .'

I wanted to turn round and tell him to get lost, but Luke was propelling me down the street.

'Just *run*!'

We were unable to sleep, so getting up at six was easy. We went to the newspaper kiosk and bought all eleven dailies. We hoped the photo would be in one that no-one we knew ever read, like the *Mirror*. It wasn't. It was on page three of the *Daily News*.

There was a huge picture of us looking startled – and shifty – as we emerged, hand in hand, from Café 206. The piece was headed *QUICK WORK!* and was subtitled, *TV LAURA'S SECRET TRYSTS WITH MARRIED ART DEALER! EXCLUSIVE!* There was another shot of me trying to cover my face, a third one of me looking angry, then a smaller shot of us running away.

'Oh . . .' I said. I was too shocked to articulate anything more complex. For, in the hands of the *Daily News*'s mythmakers, I was *Troubled Quizmistress Laura Quick . . .* nursing a *secret heartache* over my *hero husband Nick's disappearance*. There was a 'quote' from a conveniently anonymous 'friend' of Nick's saying, '*Nick simply couldn't take any more ... he'd tried his best with Laura ... she's clever, but she can be so difficult and demanding.*'

'It's like reading about someone else,' Luke said.

There was an old photo of Nick looking serious – which was his natural expression – captioned *Haunted*. By now I was struggling to breathe. There was also an old snap of Luke and me smooching at a May Ball – God knows how they'd got hold of that. *Quick is now conducting an affair with her old flame from Cambridge – Luke North, a married father of one*, the piece continued. How had they found *that* out so fast? They'd done some pretty Quick Work themselves.

'It *isn't* an "affair",' I shouted. 'That's outrageous! We're both *single*.'

'Magda will go crazy,' Luke breathed.

I felt a stab of anger – he was thinking about *her* feelings, not mine. He was absolutely right though. She did. She phoned at ten past seven, having been alerted to the story by her mother who, apparently, rises early, and who has the *Daily News* delivered every day.

'It's a pack of lies,' I heard Luke say as I poured myself some strong coffee. 'That reporter should be writing airport novels.'

'Are you denyink that you're seeink her then?' Luke had the handset on speaker so that I could hear what he was up against. She sounded like the B side of Zsa Zsa Gabor.

'I'm not denying it, Magda – no. But I do deny that we're doing anything wrong. "Secret trysts"!' he spat. 'Laura's un-attached, and so am I.' I gave him an enthusiastic thumbs up.

'Yes,' she conceded coldly. 'You are ... But *only* because you *left* me.'

Luke's jaw hit the floor. 'N-o Magda,' he said slowly, as though talking to a recalcitrant five-year-old. '*You* left *me* – rem-*em*-ber?'

There was a momentary silence. I could almost hear her synapses firing as she tried to counter this inconvenient fact.

135

'Well . . . ok-*ay*. But . . . only because I *had* to. Because you were so *awful*. So, so . . . *ghastly. DOWN HEIDI! OFF* THE TABLE!!'

'That's rubbish! I was perfectly nice. You left me, Magda, because you were fed up with me and because I'd fulfilled my function as your sperm donor, and because you preferred your bloody *goats*!'

'You leave my goats *out* of this Luke! What have the poor darlinks ever done to *you*?' I nodded at him. She was right. 'I hope you're not blamink Phoebe and Sweetie for our separation.'

'No', said Luke, backtracking. 'I'm not.'

'It's been a *very* stressful time for them too. Yogi, in particular, has found it *very* hard adjustink. He's been exhibitink a *lot* of negativity and aggression lately.'

'Okay,' Luke said soothingly. 'I withdraw that.'

'And they were very . . . *fond* of you actually.' Her voice had cracked on 'fond'.

'I know, Magda.' Now he was looking upset.

'And I must say you were very *kind* to them, Luke.' I heard her sniff. 'I have *very* happy memories of you feeding them vanilla cream cookies.'

'Well,' he shrugged. 'I knew they liked them.'

'The way you used to scrape the icink out of the middles for them was rather . . . *touchink*.' I heard her swallow, and realized, to my surprise and disgust, that my own eyes were slightly damp. 'We had some *lovely* times,' she added tearfully. 'Didn't we?' Treacly sentiment was clearly her alternative strategy to naked aggression.

'We did have some nice times. Don't cry. Don't cry, Magda. Please *don't*. I can't *stand* it when you cry.'

'We were a *family*,' she wept. 'A sweet – uh-uh – little family – *uh-uh* – weren't we?'

'Yes,' Luke conceded. 'We were.' He must have been thinking about Jessica. He ran his left hand through his hair.

136

'I don't know what *happened*,' wailed Magda. 'Why did it all – *uh-uh* – go *wrong*?'

At this Luke suddenly seemed to come to. '*I'll* tell you why it went wrong, Magda. It went wrong because you were *awful* to me for a long time, and then you *left* me and started seeing someone *else*.'

'That's not . . . tr-u-*u* – *uh* – ue.' She was in full flow now. The phone was practically dripping.

'It *is* true, Magda. And I don't know why you're so upset about me having recently started dating someone, when you've been with this bloody Steve of yours for six months!'

'I'm upset about it because –' we heard a wet sniff – 'I didn't know that this, this . . . this . . . Laura, was your girl-friend at Cambridge.'

'Yes,' Luke replied wearily. 'That *one* sentence, at least, is true.'

'But you never mentioned her to me.'

'Didn't I?' he said vaguely.

'Not once, in all the time I've known you. Which can only *mean* –' I heard her voice fracture again – 'that she must have been very *special* to you.'

'No . . . I –' He shot me a guilty look. I shrugged.

'And that you've been *obsessed* with her all these *years*.'

'For God's sake, Magda.'

'Which means that *our* relationship meant *nothink*,' she steamed on. 'No-*uh-uh*-th-*uh-uh*-ink!' She was sobbing loudly now. I visualized her red eyes and puckered chin.

'That's simply not true, Magda.'

'I was just – *uh-uh* – second best!'

'Don't be ridiculous,' he said wearily.

'No more than a consolation – *uh-uh* – prize.' She was hysterical now. She *is* crazy, I thought calmly. She's the genuine article. A true loon. 'How – *uh-uh* – could you marry me so *dishonestly*?' she wailed.

At this Luke emitted a burst of dark laughter. 'I married

you very *honestly* actually Magda, because, if you remember, you'd got yourself *pregnant*, after only four months, *without* prior reference to *me*!'

There was a sharp intake of breath. Then silence.

'You. Heartless. *Bastard*! So you regret it do you? You regard your beautiful daughter as a mere "slip-up", I suppose!'

Luke's face was twisted with rage. 'Of *course* not, Magda. I'm just saying that I did the right thing.'

'How can you feel like that about your own *child*?'

'You are *so* twisted, Magda – Jessica's the most important thing in my life, as you *very* well know. I adore her. I would die to save her without a second's hesitation. And she is, may I say, the one, *wonderful* compensation for the mostly *miserable* eight years I spent with *you*!'

There was a shocked silence. Then a quiet sniff. 'You will live to regret that remark, Luke North,' Magda croaked. 'You. Will. Live. To. Re. *Grrrret*. It. Because you will not hear from me – or see your beautiful daughter – *ever* again.' She slammed down the phone. Then, seconds later, Luke's rang.

'Hello?'

'*Never* again, Luke! Do you hear?'

SIX

'I don't know *how* you put up with it,' said Hope a few weeks later. She'd come to meet me at Julie's wine bar because Luke had had to rush over to Chiswick mid-starter, and she lives nearby in Clarendon Road. She stared at Luke's soup. 'Is this gazpacho?'

I nodded. 'He only had a bit.'

'I see. So he's gone Hungary,' she added drily.

I handed her a clean spoon. 'Afraid so. Or you can have my salmon mousse if you'd rather. Look, I've only had this corner.'

'Awfully tempting I'm sure, but I'll pass on both, thanks.' She tapped the wineglass. 'And what's this?'

'Californian Chablis. He'd only had a couple of sips.'

'Hmmm . . . I'm not crazy about New World whites.' As she perused the wine list I told her about Magda's recent behaviour.

Hope's beautifully lip-glossed mouth hardened into a disapproving line. 'How awful.'

'She is. She's the Buda Pest.'

'I wouldn't be able to *stand* it,' Hope said. Normally slow to pass judgement, she was being unusually direct. I could see she was in a sharp, rather truculent mood. 'And poor Luke, having to live with all those threats.'

139

'They're mostly idle,' I said. In fact Magda's threats were bone idle. They were disgustingly lazy. They'd sit on their fat backsides all day, not lifting a finger. They'd want to be driven everywhere. For, as I told Hope, not only did Luke continue to hear from Magda as normal – 'normal' being, on average, every eight minutes – he now heard from her even more. He attributed this to the fact that she was determined to punish him for having a girlfriend, and to prove that she still 'owned' him, with her excessive demands.

'So the deal seems to be,' said Hope, 'that Magda leaves Luke and finds someone else, but that he must remain single so that he's at her disposal.'

'Precisely.' I rested my knife on my plate. 'And that's why so many of her things are still in his house. She didn't forget them, she left them there, deliberately.'

'Like a feral cat,' Hope observed. 'Spraying everywhere, to mark its territory.' I remembered that aggressive gleam in Magda's eyes.

Now, as Hope sipped her Semillon, I told her how Magda's favourite trick was to manufacture some sort of 'crisis' – a gas leak, a faulty microwave, Martians in the back garden – which invariably required Luke's help.

'Once she managed to get Luke to go over there because she'd broken a saucepan,' I said. 'And last week she demanded his presence because Ophelia and Yogi were fighting. When he refused, she threatened to call the police.'

'Whose role would have been what? To arrest Luke for non-compliance, or the goats for violence?'

'We weren't entirely sure. But what I can't stand is the way she shreds his nerves about Jessica, claiming that she's got "suspected meningitis" when it's just a headache, or an "abscess" when she's cutting a tooth.' I had come to loathe the sound of Luke's mobile. Its jaunty little tune would invariably herald a twenty-minute barrage of false alarms, threats and demands. But he couldn't ever turn it off in case of a *real* emergency. I tried to imagine the intoxicating sense of power Magda must have.

'I don't know how you put up with it,' Hope repeated, shaking her perfectly-coiffed head. She looked, as usual, as though she'd just walked out of the hairdresser.

'Well, I put up with it, because . . .' I thought of what Mike had once said to Fliss. 'It's a question of love. I love Luke, so that's the answer. But if I hadn't known him before, then, yes, I admit it would be hard. If it was a *new* relationship . . .'

'But it *is*,' Hope interrupted. 'You've only been seeing him for – what – six weeks?'

'Yes, but it's actually longer than that.'

'Why? Are you living in a parallel universe or something?'

'No. It's because we were together before. We've already settled into a comfortable routine because we have a history. Can't you see that?'

'No.' Hope was starting to annoy me in the way only my sisters can. They give me 'sistitis' – it can be very uncomfortable. 'I just think it's convenient for Luke. It means that after less than two months he knows you well enough to abandon you mid-date because his ex snaps her fingers.'

'Luke's life isn't easy,' I said firmly, 'and you have to be very understanding when someone's got kids.' I didn't add that, as Hope had never wanted them, she might not appreciate that.

'I'm sure that's true,' she replied, fiddling with the Tiffany gold teardrop earrings that Mike had got for her for her last birthday. 'All I'm saying is, don't let Luke put you in the comfort zone too early. He's got to woo the new Laura, not just take the old one for granted. You're a different person now – and so is he.'

'Well, yes. We *are* different in many ways – but our previous time together provides a firm foundation.'

She poured me some Evian. 'Does it?'

'Magda knows I *matter* to Luke. She can't dismiss me as

some passing fancy. Plus she's furious that I knew him before she did. That's why she's being so vile.'

'She's being vile because she's being vile,' said Hope matter-of-factly, 'and because she's clearly slightly deranged.' This was true. I now realized that my anxieties over whether Magda would try and get Luke back were ludicrous. A reconciliation was not on the cards. 'What main course did he choose by the way?' she added.

'Lamb.'

'Not too rare I hope?'

'Medium.'

She nodded approvingly. 'Side order?'

'Spinach and mash. Luke's just being cautious, that's all. He doesn't want to do anything to jeopardize his position with Jessica, given how tricky Magda's being at the moment.'

'So he has Jessica on Saturdays. But presumably you spend Sundays together.'

'Well . . . not at the moment.' I fiddled with my napkin.

'Why not?'

'Erm . . . because . . . . he tends . . . to go there.'

Hope looked at me as though I were mad. 'Are you saying he spends Saturday with Jessica, then Sunday with Jessica and *Magda*?'

I sighed patiently. 'Well, ye-es. Because ever since she found out about me, Magda's been inviting Luke over for Sunday lunch on the basis that they should spend family time together for Jessica's sake.'

'If she was so keen on them having family time together then she shouldn't have *left* him,' said Hope acidly. 'But that's a powerful weapon she's got there – roast goulash and all the trimmings.'

'It is, because Luke wants to see Jessica as much as possible, so, although he's torn about me, he wants to go. Plus Magda said that if he didn't go, she'd invite her boyfriend, and *he'd* end up being Jessica's dad.'

'Manipulative cow,' said Hope shaking her head. 'But doesn't her chap mind her playing happy families with her ex?'

'He plays golf on Sundays so apparently it suits him.'

'But I don't know how *you* can bear it,' Hope said. 'I know *I* wouldn't be able to.'

'I know it's not ideal. But twelve years ago my relationship with Luke ended because, well . . .'

'Because he was *unfaithful* to you,' Hope interjected.

'Ye-es.' Her angry tone had taken me aback. 'But he felt terrible about it and he begged me to forgive him, but I couldn't. I was . . . judgemental. I saw it in black and white. Now, older and wiser, and having been through some bad stuff myself, I intend to cut him some slack.'

'But now it sounds as though you're forgiving him too *much* – not judging him *enough*.'

'Look Hope, it's to his credit that he should put his child first – I wouldn't like him so much if he *didn't* do that.' I thought again of Tom, who had put himself before his wife and his newborn child – an act which, however much I liked him on one level, had seriously diminished him on another. 'Anyway, it's only until things shake down,' I added. 'Luke asked me to be patient.'

Hope shrugged. 'Well . . . it's *your* life. But *I* wouldn't let myself be treated like that,' she repeated. She drummed her perfectly-manicured nails on the table. 'Oh no,' she added vehemently. 'I would *not*.' She was getting *right* under my skin now so I changed the subject. I discussed the newspaper coverage I'd had. Being in PR, Hope knows how things work.

'You were a victim of the circulation battle between the *Daily Post* and the *Daily News*,' she explained as the waiter took away our plates. 'Their editors loathe each other.'

'Why?'

'It's partly traditional – they're after the same slice of Middle England – and partly personal, because last year

R. Sole nicked Terry Smith's wife. Thanks to Scrivens the *Post* got their nasty little "story" about your "drunken behaviour", so the *News* had to go one better with their "scoop" about your so-called "affair" – you were caught in a tabloid tug-of-hate.'

'And how would they have got hold of that old photo of Luke and me?'

'By blagging their way on to Friends Reunited and tracking down people you used to know.' I thought of all the university friends I'd dropped after Luke and I had split up. Why should they have been loyal? 'They could have found former colleagues of yours to give them a quote,' I heard Hope say. 'Or your hairdresser, or your neighbours...' I thought of Mrs Singh next door. 'Anyone who ever knew you. Journalists are *very* resourceful. Anyway, thank God it's all died away.'

'Thanks to the Minister for the Family.'

For the first time that evening, Hope smiled. It had been widely reported that the Right Honourable Eric Wilton, 'happily married father of four', had started hormone treatment prior to undergoing a sex change operation, and so my 'story' had gone off the boil.

'You'll still have to be on your guard though,' she warned. '*Don't* talk to journalists.'

'I'd rather eat my own leg.'

'And when's the show he was in being broadcast?'

'Tomorrow night.'

'Really? Well there'll probably be some press interest in that so you'd better brace yourself.' I felt sick. Now, as our main courses arrived, Hope talked about Fliss. 'The christening cost five grand,' she said. 'It was *crazy*. Another three months and they'll have to put the house on the market. Has she told you what she's going to do to make ends meet?'

'No. We haven't spoken for a couple of weeks.'

'She's putting Olivia out to work.'

'She should be reported then.'

'Baby modelling. She told me today that she'd sent a snap of Olivia to this "Kiddlywinks" child-modelling agency and they've signed her up on the spot. Fliss is thrilled – she's dying to see Olivia's face plastered on the cover of Babychops Magazine or whatever – plus she thinks it'll make them shed-loads of cash.'

I spooned some spinach on to my plate. 'What does Hugh think?'

'He thinks it's exploitative and undignified, but she told him that as he's not even earning because of his "silly inven-tions" he's in no position to object.' She had a sip of wine. 'She's got a point in a way, but don't you think she's mean to him?'

'I do. Although his ideas *are* mad.'

'They are. Did he tell you about the mudguards he's just designed for women to stick to the backs of their legs on rainy days?'

'No.'

'Or the PVC burka for bad weather, ditto?'

I shook my head. 'Patently absurd.'

'But at least he *tries*. Fliss'll be sorry, though,' Hope added darkly. 'She'll be *very* sorry if Hugh gets fed up with her and has an affair.' She pursed her lips, as though she was suck-ing on a lime.

'Do you think he would?'

She shrugged. 'Most men would, if they got the chance. Wouldn't they?' She looked at me intensely, as though solic-iting my opinion. 'I mean . . . *any* man would. Isn't that what they say?' she added feelingly.

'Hm . . . not all men.'

'That's what they *all* say,' she insisted. A distracted look came into her eyes. 'And I sometimes *even* wonder . . .' She put down her knife and fork.

'What, Hope?'

'Well . . .' She sipped her wine, then ran her middle finger around the rim of the glass and it began to emit a plangent hum. 'I sometimes even wonder . . . if . . . *Mike* might be having one,' she said, finally. 'Actually . . .' She paused. 'I think he *is*.' Now I understood why she'd been in this combative mood all evening. 'In fact I'm sure of it.'

I stared at her for moment. 'No way. He's not the type.'

'That's what I used to believe,' she whispered, but you know, Laura . . .' Her eyes had suddenly filled. 'I've got a rather difficult situation – in fact I'm glad to have the chance to talk to you . . .' Her mouth trembled for a moment, then she controlled herself.

'What's happened, Hope? Tell me.'

She dabbed the corner of her left eye with her ring finger, and the huge diamond Mike had given her for their fifth wedding anniversary flashed and sparkled. 'Okay,' she said. 'I *will*. I will tell you.' I realized that this was the first time that Hope had ever opened up to me about her marriage. Where Felicity is open to the point of imbecility, Hope is completely discreet. It wouldn't surprise me if I found out she'd been moonlighting for MI5.

She rested her face in her hand. 'Mike's been behaving in a very . . . odd way,' she began.

I thought of his sharp remarks at the christening, and his irritable behaviour.

'How?'

'He's been working late.'

'Since when?'

'The end of January. Every Tuesday and Thursday, without fail, he comes home two hours later than normal.' She fiddled with the salt cellar. 'At first I didn't even notice; and then when I did, I didn't think about it, because I've always felt so confident in our marriage.'

'Why shouldn't you?' I said. 'Mike's always been nuts about you.'

146

She shrugged. 'That's what I'd always believed.'

'You've both seemed incredibly happy.' She nodded, miserably. 'And you have a great life together.'

'I know. We've been so lucky – we've been in love, and we've also been very good *friends*. But now I feel it's all under threat. Because on Tuesdays and Thursdays he doesn't get home until about nine thirty. We're usually both home by half seven, unless Mike's working on something big, or is away on business, so it's very strange.'

'And you asked him why?'

'Of course. But he was unable to give me a satisfactory answer. He still hasn't. Every time I say something about it he just says, very shiftily, that he's been "working". So I felt that something wasn't right. Plus whenever I phoned him in the office at those times, he wasn't there. He didn't pick up either of his direct lines, and his mobile was switched off.'

'Really?' This didn't sound good. 'Did you challenge him about it?'

She nodded, then fiddled with the tiny vase of narcissi. 'He looked extremely uncomfortable; then he got very snappy with me, which is unusual.'

'So what did he say?'

'He said I must have dialled the wrong number, or that there must have been a fault on the line, or that there might have been no signal for the mobile, or that he must have been in the canteen, or in the bathroom, or in the lift.'

'Hmm.'

She pursed her lips. 'In other words – *crap*. He'd be completely incommunicado for about three hours, and when he came home, he'd be in this strange, rather . . . *emotional* mood. So finally, last week, I asked him straight out.' Her chin puckered. 'It was terrible.' She laid both hands, palm down, on the table, as though bracing herself against the pain. 'I just asked him if he was having an affair. And he looked at me so sadly that I thought he must be about to confess. Instead he said, "No. I am not having an affair, Hope. I have never had one, and I never would. Because I love you."'

'But that's a categorical denial – so why don't you feel reassured?'

'Because the situation has remained the same. Every Tuesday and Thursday Mike "works late", but cannot be contacted and will not tell me where he's been. He's out tonight, for example. That's why I was able to come and meet you because I knew he wouldn't be home until nearly ten. It's always the same story.'

'How weird. And have you looked at his credit card statements?'

She nodded, guiltily. 'I'd never done it before. It had simply never *occurred* to me to snoop on him.'

'And?'

She shook her head. 'Zilch. But he could just be paying for the Agent Provocateur and roses with cash.'

'Any alien scent on his clothes?'

'No. But I'm *convinced* he's got a mistress,' she said, her voice cracking. 'There's no other plausible explanation for where he is, or why he's so reluctant to explain, plus his odd mood when he gets home, plus we're coming up for the seven year itch.'

'Well . . . it does sound a bit odd.'

'My guess is that Mike can't bear to admit the affair, even to himself, because he *is* a decent person, so instead he just *lies* to me.' We were silent while the waiter took away our plates. Hope's lamb was almost untouched. 'They say that a wife's instinct is never wrong,' she continued miserably. 'They also say that you just can't tell – about *any* man,' she added with a painful shrug.

I thought of Tom, and of how decent he is, and of how, despite this, he'd behaved so callously.

'I mean, *you* could never have imagined that Nick would do what he did, could you?'

'No. I can safely say I never saw *that* coming.'

'You read these stories all the time,' Hope went on. 'About these women who say, "I never thought for a *second* my husband would stray. He just didn't seem the *type*." Or they say, "I thought I *knew* my husband – but now I feel that our whole marriage was a sham." Why should *I* be immune from that, Laura? Why should *I* be lucky? Lots of people suffer – I mean, *you* did –' her eyes had filled again – 'so maybe now it's simply *my* turn. Anyway, ' she croaked as she fumbled in her Kelly bag for a tissue, 'that's what's been going on in my life.'

'Hmm . . .'

She looked at me. Her eyes were pink-veined and her mascara had run. It was strange to see her looking so *distrait*. 'So,' she said quietly. She was fiddling with the stem of her wineglass. 'So . . .' she said again. 'So . . .' she repeated with a sigh. Why did she keep saying that? 'So what do you think I should do?'

'Oh . . .' I was taken aback. As I say, Hope has hardly ever told me anything personal, let alone sought my advice. To be honest, I found it rather scary. That Hope, whose entire adult life had seemed as unruffled as her salon-smooth hair, now had personal problems for which she needed my help.

'What should I *do*?' she repeated.

'I don't . . . know,' I replied truthfully. I didn't want to say what I thought – that Hope's instincts were probably right. That's why Mike was behaving so strangely at the christening, I now saw, because being in church reminded him, uncomfortably, of the marriage vows he'd made six years earlier. He was being aggressive because he felt bad.

'Will you help me, Laura?' she said quietly. I stared at her, shocked. She looked about twelve years old.

'Well – of course I will,' I stuttered. 'You can talk to me about it any time – day or night – you know that.'

'That's not what I mean.'

I looked at her. 'What *do* you mean then?'

149

She blinked a few times, then took a deep breath. 'I want you to follow him.'

'*What?*' My heart sank to the soles of my shoes. '*Don't* ask me to do that,' I murmured. 'I really don't . . .'

'Please, Laura,' she interrupted. 'I *need* you to.'

I shook my head. 'I couldn't bear to.'

'Why *not?*'

'Because if he *is* having an affair, I do *not* want to be the person to tell you, Hope. It could affect *our* relationship for the rest of our lives.'

She was shaking her head. 'But I'd rather hear it from you than from anyone else. And because we're sisters, I feel we could survive it.'

'I'm not sure about that – this kind of thing can be a mine-field.'

I felt uncomfortable seeing Hope like this. I found her sudden vulnerability disturbing when she'd always seemed unassailable.

'Look, Laura, I need your support, and it's not something I could ask of a friend. And, I helped *you* didn't I?' she added.

I had been so hoping that she wouldn't say that.

'You did help me, Hope – but that was very different. All you had to do was write me a cheque, which I repaid as soon as I could. But if I did *this* for you, I might end up paying a terrible price psychologically. Can't you see that? If you want Mike followed you should ask someone who's neutral – preferably a private detective.' She shook her head. 'Why not? You can afford it.'

'It's not the money.' She rolled her eyes. 'It's the *humiliation*! Having to explain it to a total stranger – plus you can't be sure they won't blab. But I know that you'd be discreet. Unlike Felicity. *Please* Laura,' she begged. 'I was going to phone you, but it's much easier asking you face to face. I'm glad Luke had to abandon you tonight as it's given me this chance to talk to you.'

'Couldn't you follow him yourself?'

'*No*.' She shuddered. 'It would be . . . awful. In any case, I'd give myself away. He'd spot me – I know he would – because he'd somehow *sense* that I was there, because of our emotional connection, but for that reason, I doubt he'd see you. Please, Laura,' she added. '*Please*. I'm in turmoil.' I looked at her anguished expression. I so wanted to help.

'I'm sorry, Hope. But the answer is no.'

I like facts. I find them comforting. Facts make you feel somehow secure. You can usually rely on facts in the way that you can't trust opinion and conjecture. Facts won't let you down. I don't just mean the 'Riga is the capital of Latvia' kind of fact, but facts in the broader, human, sense. For there were certain facts about Mike's behaviour, for example, which led painfully, but inexorably, to one conclusion. Which is why I refused to do what Hope asked.

If I'd thought she was barking up the wrong tree, I would happily have agreed to her request, in order to have the pleasure of proving her wrong. But I didn't believe that she was. For why else would Mike be behaving in such an odd way? If he was doing something quite innocent – going to the gym, or to an evening class – he'd be open about it. If he was having dinner with clients, he'd say. If he was going to see his parents, or his sister, he'd tell her, and in any case she always goes too.

It *was* possible that Mike was doing something that, for whatever reason, he felt self-conscious about. Seeing a shrink, for example, or going to church, or attending Weight Watchers (not that he's fat) or Alcoholics Anonymous (not that he drinks), or going to a lap-dancing club with some of his racier colleagues. But if that were all it was then he'd admit it rather than let Hope continue in the destructive belief that he was having an affair.

But he's refusing to enlighten her in any way about his

151

activities, whilst continuing to come home late twice a week. So the facts do, unfortunately, seem to support Hope's growing belief that Mike is 'embroiled'. That's why she was in such an unsympathetic mood I now realized. And *that's* why she was so tough on Luke. She was transferring all her anger and negativity about Mike's behaviour on to him.

Even so, I felt awful refusing to help.

'I'm sorry, Hope,' I said again. 'But I just can't do it.' I fiddled with my napkin.

'I know why. You're refusing because you're angry with me for criticizing Luke. Aren't you? Because I didn't say what you wanted to hear.'

'That's not the reason at all.'

'Yes it is. That's *just* what you were like when we were kids. You're trying to punish me.'

'No I'm not.'

She picked up her bag. 'Anyway, I'm going home. Kindly do *not* mention what we discussed tonight to *anyone*.'

'I won't. You know that, Hope.'

'Yes,' she said frigidly. 'I do at least know I can rely on your discretion – even if I *can't* rely on your support.' She gave me an '*Et tu, Brute?*' look and then left.

So, to confirm to myself that I had made the right decision, I imagined doing as she wished. As I sat there, sipping my espresso, I imagined following Mike from work, on foot, or by taxi, keeping a safe distance, hoping that I wouldn't be spotted by him, or by anyone else for that matter given that my face has become familiar through the quiz. I imagined watching him enter his girlfriend's house, or some faceless hotel, then having to hang around until he emerged, hair ruffled, tie askew – quite possibly with *her*. Hope would no doubt want photographic evidence. Now I imagined presenting her with a photo of them kissing perhaps, or holding hands. No, I said to myself again. No *way*. I'd happily give Hope one of my kidneys, my blood, my bone marrow, or my life savings – but I wasn't prepared to give her bad news.

For what if she confronted Mike with the evidence – evidence that *I* had gleaned – and he then, at last, confessed? What if they got divorced? For the rest of my life I'd have to live with the knowledge that *I* had helped them go down that road. What, alternatively, if Mike ended the affair, they went to counselling and everything was tickety-boo? That would be great, wouldn't it – except that they'd forever associate *me* with that horrible time. I'd be the chink in their marital armour. They'd resent me – especially Mike. And even if Hope forgave him, I'd almost certainly dislike him – it would be bound to turn relations sour. So I knew that I had to keep out of it but, as I say, I felt very bad. And I was just sitting there, replaying it all in my mind for the fourth or fifth time, and wondering what I *could* do to help her, when Luke called to say that he was on his way back, and would pick me up. So I paid the bill, then, feeling utterly wrung out, decided to repair my appearance before he arrived. And I was just making my way down the stairs when I glanced to my left and saw that the bar, which had been deserted earlier in the evening, had suddenly become busy.

There was a group of twenty-something women sitting in the window, two men in the middle, and a couple in their late thirties sitting at the end, nearest to me. Judging by the static crackling between them – and the champagne chilling on the counter – they were clearly on an early, but getting serious, date. The man was laughing and talking, and the woman was gazing at him, her face radiating interest and excitement. It was as though he were a film star, and she his number-one fan.

From time to time she lightly touched his forearm, or threw back her head, exposing her throat. His own body language was similarly 'open' and positive. His knees were practically touching hers. Now I saw him lean forward and touch her shoulder, then slide his hand downwards, almost stroking her breast, while she gave him an encouraging smile. They were the very picture of a couple in the throes of pupil-dilating attraction, oblivious to the rest of the world. So engrossed were they that I could have walked right past them and they probably wouldn't have noticed. But, as I knew them, it wasn't a risk I could take. And I was just hovering on the stairs, wondering what on earth to do, when, with characteristic courtesy, Hugh resolved my dilemma for me. He paid the bill, helped Chantal Vane on with her coat, held open the door for her, and then they left.

SEVEN

We're not doing very well on the marriage front, my sisters and I. All three have either failed already, like mine, or seem to be in danger of imminent collapse. I thought of how horrified Mum would be – not that I'd be telling her – she and Dad had their fortieth anniversary last year. As I drove back with Luke I remembered seeing Hugh talking to Chantal at the christening. She'd probably had a thing for him for years. And now, detecting marital fatigue, like a hyena detecting exhaustion in an elderly antelope, she'd seen her chance to close in.

Luke didn't notice how distracted I felt – he was fired up about Magda, going on about how difficult she was and how it hadn't been necessary for him to go over there, and how she'd only done it to spoil our evening, and about how she'd had a huge row with him and had made Jessica cry which was quite unforgivable.

'She has no *self*-control,' he snapped as he parked outside his house. 'Yet she thinks she controls *me*! Well she *doesn't*!'

'Of course she doesn't,' I replied as his mobile trilled again and he shovelled his hand into his pocket.

'*Yes* Magda,' he hissed. '*No* Magda. *Yes* Magda.'

Three bags full, Magda. I decided I'd take advantage of

his negative mood. As we were getting ready for bed, I asked him if he could take her clothes out of his wardrobe and return them to her. His toothbrush stopped in mid-stroke.

'I can't,' he said. 'It will only provoke her.' He bent his head to the tap, then spat neatly into the plughole. 'She'd feel I was rejecting her.'

'That's absurd.'

'I know.' He began to pull floss through his teeth. 'But she likes to have everything both ways. And she'd only tell Jessica that I'd "thrown" her things out of the house, and then Jessica would get upset. Anyway, whether or not some of Magda's stuff is still here doesn't matter, does it, Laura?' He took my hands in his, then gave me a minty kiss 'What matters is that we're together again. So can't you put up with it?'

'It's precisely because we are together again that I *can't*. I feel far more possessive about you than if we'd only just met. So I *can't* bear the thought of it, no. And the point is, it's not even ordinary stuff. I could cope with the odd pair of trainers, or an old sweatshirt – but she's left *sexy* stuff here as a form of provocation.'

'That's almost certainly true,' he conceded. 'She's very combative.'

'Why the hell do I have to look at her slinky dresses hanging next to your jackets, or see her lacy underwear and thongs in your drawers?' I tugged open the medicine cabinet. 'And I *don't* want to see her packet of Tampax when I'm getting out the toothpaste. When you come to my flat, Luke, what do you see of Nick's? Nothing,' I answered for him. 'Not a *thing*. You don't see his shaving foam in the bathroom. You don't see his Y-fronts when you open a drawer. Imagine how *you'd* feel if the tables were turned.'

'I'd hate it – but that's a completely different situation.'

'Yes,' I agreed. 'It is. My ex has left, but he's vanished – so he doesn't bother you at all. Magda's at the other extreme. She's left you but she remains omnipresent.'

'That may be true, but she's in my life. And she always *will* be because she's the mother of my child, and that's what you must *understand*. My relationship with Magda has to be a cordial one, Laura – even a good one – because I can't afford to antagonise her – especially while Jessica's so young.'

'You're in her power,' I said as he climbed into bed.

'I suppose I am,' he replied quietly. 'Like many separated fathers. But I won't do anything which might lead to my seeing less of Jessica.'

'That's fair enough but there are limits, Luke. So if you don't feel you can return Magda's things, would you at least put them away so that I don't have to look at them every time I come round?'

'Oh, I've had enough aggro for one night.' We were irritating each other, I realized. The honeymoon was over. He pulled the duvet over his head. '*You* do it,' he said. 'If you really feel you must.'

'Okay then,' I said quietly. 'I *will*.'

I went downstairs and got two carrier bags from the kitchen. Into them I neatly put Magda's clothes, her shoes and her underwear, then, with a small but significant sense of triumph, I pushed them under the bed. Then I removed her things from the medicine cabinet and put them in a bag in the bathroom stool.

Now, for the first time, I put away the few things that I wanted to leave in Luke's house – a beautiful pale blue silk kimono that Hope had brought back for me from Tokyo; a green cashmere cardigan and a pair of jeans; some underwear, a t-shirt and a small toilet bag. In the medicine cabinet I put a pot of moisturiser, my hair-straightening mousse and a few bits of make-up.

Feeling better now, I got into bed.

'Don't let's fall out, Laura,' Luke murmured. I felt his arm slide around my waist. 'That's precisely what Magda wants

– to drive a wedge between us.' I vowed not to let her. 'I love you, Laura,' he whispered. 'I'm so glad I've found you again.' I felt my indignation subside. 'I'm sorry I had to abandon you tonight.' I felt his chin on my shoulder, the stubble scraping my skin. 'Did you have a nice evening with Hope?' I thought of her marital problems, and of Felicity's, and of how complicated all our relationships were now proving to be.

'I had a lovely evening,' I lied.

I wanted to tell Hope that I'd seen Hugh with Chantal, but she wouldn't speak to me. I phoned her three times the next morning but her P.A. said she was busy. I could tell from her artificially bright tone it wasn't true. Being the youngest, Hope has always expected to get what she asks for, and, when she doesn't, she sulks. But I felt sorry for her because she'd exposed her vulnerability, without getting what she'd wanted. So I sent her a friendly text message with the numbers for three private detectives. Then I wondered what to do about Fliss . . .

I could casually let Hugh know that I'd spotted him with Chantal, but that would only make them more careful next time. I *could* ring up Chantal herself . . . No. I couldn't possibly. I shuddered. It would be awful. Downright *primitive* . . . So I decided I'd just go and see Fliss. She's so open – she should have been named Candida, I often think – that I'd be able to tell whether or not she already suspected. So I rang to say I'd pop round after work to drop off an Easter present for Olivia.

'That would be . . . lovely,' she said. She sounded distracted. 'Yes, yes, that would be . . . great. Erm, come round at about . . . ooh . . . I dunno . . . five, I suppose.'

'Are you okay Fliss?'

'Well – no. Actually, I'm not. In fact, I'm *worried* about something.'

'What's that?' I asked innocently. I heard a sharp intake

158

of breath. She knew. She knew about Hugh and Chantal.

'Because Olivia's got her first casting after lunch. It's for the Tiddli-Toes Baby Bouncer and we're really, *really* nervous – so please just keep everything crossed.'

So after we'd recorded the show I got the driver to drop me in Moorhouse Road. I climbed the steps to the front door, then rang the bell, clutching the musical rabbit I'd bought for Olivia. I was so nervous I squeezed it too hard and it began to play a lullaby. The door was flung open. Fliss was standing there, clutching Olivia, smiling dementedly.

'We've got the *job*!' she declared as she ushered me inside. 'Olivia's agent has just called. Isn't it *fabulous*?'

'Er, yes,' I said as I squeezed past the pram.

'All she had to do was twang up and down a few times, beaming for the camera! Bingo! That'll be seven hundred and fifty quid! The photographer said she was the prettiest baby girl he'd *ever* seen. Didn'themylickledarling?' Olivia clapped her podgy little hands. 'Thassrightmysweetiepops! Give yourself a *big* hand! You'reavewy*clever*babygirlaren't-you?!' she squeaked as she wiped infant dribble off Olivia's chin with the hem of her t-shirt. 'We've got another audition tomorrow,' she added, as we went down to the kitchen. 'Coochisoft non-bio fabric conditioner. All she has to do is sit on a fluffy towel looking adorable – *not* exactly difficult in her case – and if we get it, that'll be twelve hundred. Then she's got two TV castings at the end of next week. There are some babies who don't get out of their cots for less than five grand. I'm convinced Olivia's going to be one of them,' Felicity continued as she plonked Olivia in her playpen. She looked like a tiny jailbird as she stared out balefully through the bars.

'Give her a chance, Fliss, she's only just started.'

'I know. But she's *so* beautiful that she's bound to hit the baby Bigtime isn't she? Plus she has loads of *character*, which is what they're really looking for.' Olivia gave us a vacant stare. 'Some of the other mothers were *so* irritating though,' she snorted as she filled the kettle. 'They could have bored for England about their little darlings. Talk about proud parents.'

'Really?' I glanced at the framed enlargement of Olivia's thirteen-week scan. 'That must have been annoying for you.'

'Oh, they can't help it,' Fliss said indulgently. 'They don't even realize they're doing it. *Zero* self-awareness.'

'Uh huh.' By now Olivia was ripping the tissue paper off my gift and trying to stuff it in her mouth.

'That's a *sweet* rabbit isn'titdarlingit'salovelylicklebunny-wabbit! Thanks, Laura.' Felicity looked at me over her shoulder, and saw that there was a slick of regurgitated baby rice on it. 'Blast.' She dabbed at it with a sponge. 'That's always happening. Lapsang or Kenyan?'

'I'll have Lapsang – but I can't stay long. Er . . . where's Hugh?'

Fliss peered into the garden. 'In his bloody shed. He's spending inordinate amounts of time in there at the moment. Says he's got some brilliant idea.'

'What is it?'

'He won't tell me. Claims I'm not sufficiently supportive. But I imagine it'll be about as useful as a laundrette in a nudist colony. You know, Laura, I seriously think Hugh's going to end up being financially supported by his six-month-old daughter!'

'Felicity,' I said. I felt myself shifting from foot to foot. 'Look Fliss . . .'

'Yes?'

'Um . . .' I stared at her. 'Well . . .'

'What's the matter, Laura?' She peered at me. 'You look like the dog's just died.' Her smile suddenly vanished. 'Christ, has something awful happened?'

'No. I don't think so. At least – not yet.' I could hear the water begin to boil.

'What do you mean? Not yet?' Steam was misting the kitchen window. 'What *is* it Laura? Would you please stop being mysterious.'

'Well . . . I think you should . . . spend more time with Hugh, that's all.'

She shrugged. 'I see him every day.'

'But you don't go *out* with him. You don't do nice *things* with him.'

'We can't,' she said as she got down the teapot. 'We don't have a babysitter.'

'But you could easily get one. Through an agency.'

She looked horrified. 'Absolutely not! I refuse to leave Olivia with anyone I don't know!'

'Then *I'll* baby-sit for you. I wouldn't mind. In fact I'd love to.'

'Would you?'

'I don't know why you haven't asked me before.'

'Well,' she said as she put in two teabags, 'because Hugh and I never go out at the same time so it hasn't been necessary.'

'Exactly. Big mistake. But now she's over six months, I think you should. In fact I think that you ought to, maybe, go away together some time.'

'We are. We're going down to Hugh's parents tomorrow for Easter.'

'I mean, go away together – on your *own*. Why don't you stay in a nice little hotel somewhere? Maybe for your fortieth?'

'That's not 'till July – and anyway, we're skint. As you know, Hugh's income is zero, and my maternity pay's about to end. The Notting Hill Workhouse awaits us,' she added matter-of-factly. 'I just hope it's comfortable. I hear Stella McCartney designed the bedspreads.'

'Look, Fliss, a weekend away wouldn't cost *that* much. In fact I could give it to you, as an early birthday present.'

'Really?' She got down two mugs, both of them adorned with photos of Olivia. 'Well, that would be wonderful – and very generous of you.' She looked at me, uncomprehendingly. 'But why are you being so adamant about it, if you don't mind my asking?'

'Because I just . . . think it would be a good thing to do. A very good thing actually.'

She opened the biscuit tin. 'But *why*?' She peered at me. 'What are you *driving at*, Laura?'

'Oh . . . nothing.' I sat down at the table.

'I *know* you. There's something on your mind. Isn't there? Something you're not telling me.' The water was boiling loudly now.

'Well . . . okay, yes, there is – and it's that I simply think you're . . . neglecting Hugh. I've said it before, Fliss. You're so obsessed with Olivia that you've ignored him and that could have . . . consequences. Serious ones, quite possibly.'

Felicity had narrowed her eyes. 'What's going *on* here?' She tipped the scalding water into the teapot. 'What are you *getting* at, Laura?' The tarry scent of Lapsang filled the air. 'C'mon. Tell me, will you?'

'I think . . . you might be storing up problems, that's all.'

'*What* problems?' She gave me a challenging stare. 'You're talking in riddles – would you *please* be direct?'

'All right, then.' I took a deep breath, as though about to dive underwater. 'I saw Hugh,' I said. 'Last night. In Julie's.' She gazed at me as I told her, calmly and quietly, what had taken place. There was a stunned silence as she took it in.

'Hugh and Chantal?' Felicity repeated quietly. 'Are you saying that Hugh and Chantal . . . ?'

'I'm not saying anything,' I interjected. 'I just think you should be . . . aware, that's all.' Felicity sank on to a chair, while Olivia peered at her through the bars of her playpen, making little clicking noises.

'Are you seriously suggesting that Hugh – and *Chantal* . . . ?'
Felicity looked at me.

'Well. Yes, Fliss. I suppose I am. She was all over him like
chicken pox, put it that way.'

Fliss was looking at me dumbfounded. Then she shook
her head in disbelief. Now she was looking quite stricken,
and I saw I'd made a terrible mistake. Like Hope, Fliss
couldn't handle the truth. By now her face had gone red,
her mouth was twisted and, oh God, she had started to cry.
She leaned forward, convulsed with distress. I heard a high-
pitched whine, an odd little gulp, then she threw back her
head.

'That's the *funniest* thing I've heard all week!' She made
a loud, honking noise, which startled Olivia.

'It *isn't* funny.'

'I'm sorry,' she snorted. 'But it is.' Her shoulders were shaking.

'Look. I *saw* her flirting with Hugh.'

'There's no way Chantal would do that,' she insisted. She
poured two cups of tea.

'How do you know?'

'Because I've known her for twenty-one years. And I can
tell you that she's not . . . well . . . *like* that.'

'Then what were they doing having a drink?'

She shrugged. 'Why shouldn't they? He's her friend too.
Anyway, Hugh *told* me he was meeting her.'

'But why did he want to, without you being there?'

She sliced the end off a lemon. 'Because I've got Olivia to
look after, haven't I?'

'Then couldn't they have met up here?'

'Julie's is on Chantal's way home – it was more convenient. Plus Hugh wanted her advice.' I looked at Fliss. 'That's
the main reason, actually.'

'What sort of advice?'

'Professional advice – about this thing he's working on,

163

whatever it is, which he refuses to tell me – so I don't think he *wanted* me there.'

'But how could Chantal help him? She's a solicitor. I thought she did litigation.'

Fliss shook her head. 'She's switched to patent law. She's got a science background, so it suits her.'

'Oh.' As Fliss handed me the mug, I moved her electric breast pump out of the way.

'And Hugh wanted to discuss his "invention" with her.' She rolled her eyes.

'I see. But . . . he *touched* her, Fliss. I saw him. And she was encouraging it – *smiling* at him.'

'Look,' she said, 'Hugh's a very tactile man, and that's all there is to it, and Chantal's going to do a patent search for him, gratis, which will apparently save him two thousand pounds. He was probably just trying to give her a thank you hug. But I'll phone her up right now if you like and ask her.' She giggled. 'I know what she'll say!' She shook her head with mirth. 'Hugh and Chanty . . . That's a good one.'

I stood up. 'All right, Fliss. Whatever you like. I was only trying to protect you. I don't want to see you get hurt. You're my sister, remember?'

'Oh I know you meant well, Laura. And I'm very grateful. Honestly. It's just that you're totally wrong.'

I *wasn't* wrong, I told myself as I walked back to my flat. I knew what I'd seen. The body language was unmistakeable. I'd seen Hugh *touch* Chantal – I'd seen him practically stroke her *breast*. If Felicity believed that to be an innocent gesture then she was more of an idiot than I thought. She no longer saw Hugh as her husband, or treated him like one, and so, starved of respect, companionship and sex, he'd turned to Chantal, who was clearly offering him more than professional help. But I'd done my sisterly bit and now I'd wash my hands of it. Nor was I going to get involved with Hope's problems.

164

In any case I had big enough ones of my own. Meeting Jessica, for example. She was with Luke tonight, as Magda was going to a ball at the Savoy with Steve and a few of his key clients, so Luke thought it was a good chance for Jess and me to meet. We'd have supper together, then watch the quiz. I was very nervous, far more so, I realized, than when I'd met Luke's parents twelve years before.

At ten to seven, I rang Luke's bell. I heard light footsteps, then a scrabbling at the lock, then the door was cautiously pulled back. Jessica stood there in a tartan skirt and grey cardigan. She was wearing a pair of blue glasses. She stared at me for a moment, then gave me a cautious smile. I was nearly knocked down by a wave of relief. She hadn't slammed the door in my face, or burst into tears. Luke appeared in the hallway behind her, and blew me a kiss.

'Hello, Jessica,' I said. My heart was banging, and I was aware, despite the cold, that I was perspiring.

'Jess, this is Laura,' said Luke. She put her head slightly to one side, as though she were a naturalist and I some curious species she was encountering for the very first time. 'Why don't you let her in?' She stepped aside, flattening herself against the wall. The crown of her head shone in the spotlights like a halo.

'I saw you,' she said, sibilantly.

'Did you?'

She nodded. Her bespectacled gaze was disconcerting. 'On the TV.' She pulled up one of her socks. Her legs were as slender and pale as young leeks.

'Well, Jess,' said Luke, 'Laura's on the telly again tonight. Shall we watch her quiz programme?' She nodded again, while Luke winked at me. 'You might even get a surprise.'

'A surprise?' She looked at me enquiringly. 'Have you got a surprise for me?'

'Actually, I do have one. Here.' I handed her the carrier bag I was clutching, and she glanced at her father.

'It's okay, sweetie. You can open it.' She pulled out a large, pink-beribboned Easter egg sitting in a *Little Mermaid* mug. Her eyes widened. 'You lucky girl. And what do you say?'

'Thank you,' she said, wonderingly. It was as though she'd been expecting the Wicked Witch of the West, and instead Snow White had turned up.

'It's for this Sunday,' I explained as Luke took my coat. 'But you can open it before if you want to. If your Dad says it's okay. I like your glasses,' I added.

'They're new,' she said proudly. 'The petition said I needed them.'

'Optician, darling,' Luke corrected her. 'Optician. Can you say that?'

'Petition.'

He beamed. 'Very good.'

I began to relax. The evening had started well. We went down to the kitchen where Luke began to cook supper. There was a bag of groceries from Fresh & Wild on the table. As he unpacked them, Jessica told me that she'd just broken up from school. Then she showed me a collage she'd been making.

'It's lovely. Is that your Dad?' I asked as I pointed at a tall figure on the left of a tinfoil pond.

'Yes.' She absent-mindedly wobbled a loose tooth with her thumb.

'And that's you? In your blue coat?'

'Yes. And *these* . . .' she pointed to some balls of yellow tissue, 'are ducks.'

'It's lovely.'

'Where's the chicken?' I heard Luke mutter, as he rummaged in the bag. He tipped everything out on to the table. 'I must have left it in the shop. *Damn*.'

Jessica shot him a disapproving look. 'Don't say damn, Daddy.'

'No. You're quite right, darling. Bad word.'

'I'll go and get it,' I said.

'It's okay. You stay here with Jessica while I go. Is that okay Jess? Laura will stay with you while I'm out for five minutes.' She hesitated for a moment, then nodded. I was so relieved that she hadn't flatly refused, or phoned the NSPCC to report Luke for cruelty, that I gave her a pathetically grateful smile. As I did so, I took in her face. Her features were like Luke's – her mouth was the same shape, her nose was going to be aquiline, like his, but her eyes were a clear, pure blue with large, luminous irises. She was lovely. As we heard the front door close behind Luke she went to the dresser and came back with a gold biscuit tin. She pushed her book of fairy stories out of the way.

'Do you want to see my photos?' She pulled off the lid.

'I'd love to. Did you take them yourself?'

She nodded, then reached into her pink duffle bag, and took out a red camera.

'My mum gave it to me for my birthday. It's not a toy,' she explained as she handed it to me.

'It's great. And does it take good pictures?'

'Yes. Really good.' She took a wallet of snaps out of the tin. There were several, slightly blurry photos of the goats, which I exclaimed over. They seemed to be not so much miniature, as full-sized, but with stumpy little legs. The caprine version of the Dachshund, I decided.

'Do you have a favourite one?'

'Oh *no*.' She clearly thought the question improper. 'I love them *all* the same.' Then she pointed at a black goat with a white cap and giggled. 'That's Yogi. He fights sometimes,' she confided.

'Does he?'

'So Mummy puts him in the naughty corner.'

'Really?' She nodded, then giggled again. Then she handed me another photo. As I looked at it I felt my morale collapse, as though I were a puppet, and someone had just cut my strings . . .

Luke's arm was round Magda's shoulder, and she was smiling up at him affectionately, looking deep into his eyes. With a sudden sick feeling, as though I was on a boat, in rough seas, I scanned the photo for the date. I found it on the reverse, in tiny pale grey letters – 20-03-05. Last Sunday. Then Jessica handed me another, lopsided photo, again of Luke and Magda, taken the Sunday before that. They were sitting at a dining table somewhere, smiling into the camera, literally tête à tête, Magda's unpinned hair spilling on to Luke's shoulder. I felt as though I'd been knifed.

'Hmmm,' I heard myself say. 'That's a nice one too. And . . . where was it taken?'

'At Nagyi's house.'

'Whose house?'

'Nagyi's – granny's house – my Hungarian granny. She lives in Amersham.'

'Oh.'

'My English granny and grandpa live in Kent.'

'I know.' I remembered the house so well. Now Jessica handed me another snap. It was of her, Luke and Magda, standing in his parents' garden, by the weeping willow. Jessica was standing between them, holding their hands tightly, grimly almost, as though terrified that they were going to run off. She then showed me another ten or so, taken over the preceding month, all of which were of Luke and Magda, either standing or sitting together, arms round each others' waists, or shoulders, or linked at the elbow. I felt as though I'd been hollowed out with a trowel.

'Thanks for showing me,' I managed to say. I could feel tears gathering in my throat.

'My mum's very pretty,' Jessica said. It was said without mischief – it was simply a statement of fact.

'Yes.' I tried to keep the tremble from my voice. 'Like you.'

'She used to be a model.'

'Did she?' I said weakly.

'That's how she met my Dad. He did lots of drawings of her.'

'Oh. I . . . see.' *We met at life drawing classes . . .*

'And she was *so* pretty that he fell in love with her.' Jessica clapped her hand over her mouth, stifling a shocked giggle. 'She didn't wear any *clothes!*'

'Really?' I said faintly.

'No,' she said, in a scandalized tone. 'She was *bare.*'

My mind was suddenly filled with dismaying images of Luke brandishing a stump of charcoal, staring lasciviously at Magda who was draped along a chaise longue like the nude in *The Toilet of Venus.* I imagined him tracing the curves of her breasts and hips. Now I remembered what he'd said. He'd said he'd been 'very attracted' to Magda. Perhaps, despite everything, he still was.

'She was very pretty,' Jessica repeated happily. '*So* pretty that *he* fell in love with *her* . . . and *she* fell in love with *him,* and then they got *married* . . . and . . . *and* . . .' The words *lived happily ever after* hovered in the air, like a mirage. I heard a tiny, frustrated, sigh.

'. . . and then they had you. And they were very happy.' There was silence. I could hear the hum of the fridge. Jessica started shuffling through the photos again, then spread them all out on the table, scrutinizing them like a fortune-teller with a pack of cards. From upstairs I heard the clock chime half seven.

'My mum says . . .' she began quietly. Then she stopped. 'Yes?'

She blushed, then leant both elbows on the corner of the table, resting her face in her hands. 'My mum *says* . . .' she tried again. She was rubbing the back of one leg with her foot.

'What does your mum say, Jessica?'

'We-ll . . .' She took a deep breath, then scratched her nose. '*She* says you must be a horrible person.'

I felt as though I'd been punched.

'Why does she say that?' I asked quietly.

'Be-cause . . . your husband left you and he never came back.' She tucked some stray wisps of hair behind her ear. They were as light and fine as cornsilk.

'Well . . . my husband did leave me, that's true. And it's also true that he didn't come back. But it isn't true that I'm a horrible person, Jessica. I don't think your Dad thinks that.'

'No.' She shook her head. '*He* says you're nice.'

'But you can make up your *own* mind. If you get to know me a bit better. *You* can decide, Jessica. Okay?' We heard Luke's key in the lock, then the floorboards creaking overhead, then his descending footfall.

She gave me an oblique look, then nodded. 'Okay.'

Luke quickly cooked the supper, chicken fillets in bread-crumbs, Jessica's favourite apparently, and we all sat down.

'I've had such a nice conversation with Jessica,' I said as she squelched ketchup out of the bottle. 'She told me how you and Magda first met. She was your model apparently.'

He blushed. 'That's right. We met at life drawing classes – as I told you.'

'Hmm. Sort of. And she's been showing me some of her recent photos,' I went on pleasantly as I looked at them, still lying on the table. 'There are some really great ones of you and Magda together.' I felt tears prick my eyes. 'Like this one.' I picked it up, and held it out to him. Luke and Magda were chinking glasses somewhere, laughing into the camera, the picture of marital harmony.

He didn't blink. 'That's right. Jessica likes to take lots of photos of her mum and dad, don't you darling?' She nodded happily as she scooped up some peas. 'She's always getting us to pose for her, aren't you Jess?' She nodded again. 'She likes to have *lots* of happy family snaps for her album, so we don't mind how often she asks us. She can have as many

170

as she likes.' He gave me a pointed smile, and I suddenly felt mean and ashamed. Luke and Magda were just putting on a united front for their confused, upset, six-year-old child, whose only wish was that they had never split up.

'Finished!' Jessica announced.

'Put your knife and fork together, darling. That's it. Now, how about a meringue?'

She shook her head. 'I want to take another picture.'

'Okay. But you'll need the flash.' Jessica took a few steps back, and pointed the camera at Luke, and I was just scraping back my chair to move out of shot when the flash went off.

'That one won't come out very well,' he said. 'Try again.' He looked into the lens and smiled. Then I took one of them together – her head on his shoulder, her arms clasped round his neck.

'You've got six left,' I said as I handed it back to her.

'Keep them for this weekend,' said Luke, 'then we'll take it to Boots on Tuesday.' He suddenly glanced at the clock. 'Hey – Laura's programme's just starting – quick!' We ran upstairs and Luke turned on the TV just as *Whadda Ya Know?!!* was being announced. As the opening titles scrolled down – a montage of whirling question marks, mathematical equations, animals, planets and famous faces – Jessica jumped on to the sofa with Luke. His arm was round her, both hers encircling his chest, like a hoop. This is just like my dream, I thought. There they are, exactly as I imagined them. And here am I.

'Here to present *Whadda Ya Know?!!* is . . . Lau-ra QUICK!'

Jessica shot me an approving look.

'So let's meet today's four contestants . . .'

'I'm Christine Schofield . . .'

'I'm Doug Dale . . .'

'Hi, I'm Jim Friend . . .'

'I'm Luke North. I'm an art dealer and I live in West London.'

Jessica sat bolt upright. She pointed at the TV, her mouth a perfect 'O'. Then she turned and gawped at Luke, then looked at the screen again.

He grinned. 'That's your surprise, Jess!' She was wreathed in smiles. She looked at the TV again, then clapped her hands together in speechless astonishment.

'It was a surprise for me too,' I said wryly. 'A *big* one.'

'It's Monrovia . . . *Kerching*! . . . Juniper . . . *Kerching*! . . . The Minoans . . . Argentina . . . *Whoop*! . . . Caprine . . . Yellow . . . *Whooop*! Eagle . . . Michaelangelo . . . It was Michaelangelo. *KERASHHHH*!!!'

'You *won*, Daddy! You *won*!' Jessica was radioactive with excitement, jumping up and down on the sofa, squealing with laughter. 'You're my clever, *clever* Daddy!'

Luke and I had agreed that I'd leave after the show was over, so I went into the hall to get my coat. 'Mummy will be so surprised!' I heard Jessica exclaim as I unhooked it. 'She'll be so, *so* surprised when I tell her won't she?'

'She will darling,' Luke said as I picked up my bag. 'But, you know, Jess,' he added quietly, 'I think it's better if you *don't* tell Mummy that you met Laura tonight. Okay?' I felt the by-now familiar sagging sensation, as though someone was dragging me down by my ankles. I went back into the sitting room. 'Is that okay, Jess? You won't say anything about meeting Laura, will you?' She nodded, her euphoria gone, her shoulders slightly hunched, her head sinking towards her chest. 'Now,' said Luke, after a moment, 'no more surprises tonight – up to bed young lady.'

'I'm going home now,' I said. 'Bye bye, Jessica. It was lovely to meet you.'

She was standing on one leg, like a baby heron, as diffident now as when I'd first arrived. 'Bye,' she said quietly.

'I hope I see you again,' I said. She gave me a little half smile.

'Up you go then, sweetie,' said Luke. 'I'll come up in a minute and read you a story.'

'*Why* couldn't she tell Magda she'd met me?' I whispered as Jessica ran up the stairs. 'Magda's with Steve, and now you're with me – and that's all there is to it.'

'I know, but she's been making such awful threats. She said yesterday that if I involved you with Jessica in *any* way she'd reduce my access.'

'She *can't* – you were married, so you have automatic parental responsibility, don't you?'

'Yes. But the fact is that Magda can still do whatever she likes. If she wanted to be awkward she could simply refuse to let me see Jessica, and then I'd have to go to court, which would take time, and money, and yes, I'd get the contact order all right – but she'd flout it. That's what happened to a friend of mine. His ex-wife simply ignores the orders with the result that he hardly ever sees his two kids. I don't intend to let that happen to me, so I have to be *very* careful, which means I take Magda's threats seriously.'

'But people who make threats the whole time tend not to carry them out.'

'That may be so, but I don't want to rile her.'

I put on my scarf. 'But you don't mind riling *me*. And I feel sorry for Jessica, being told to keep quiet like that. It's not right, Luke.'

'She's already used to it, I'm afraid. The children of separated parents learn to be discreet – she never ever mentions Steve. But because you were on the TV I thought she might say something, and it's best at this stage if Magda doesn't know.'

'I see,' I said. I opened the door and a gust of frigid air chilled my face. I looked at him. 'I *hate* the way you kowtow to her, as though she were some effing ... *deity.*'

'That's because you don't understand how difficult my situation is.'

'I do,' I said. It was so cold, my breath was billowing out in little puffs, like cigarette smoke.

He shook his head. 'You don't. Until you've had kids of your own, you can't truly understand the nature of the attachment . . .'

'I suppose that must be true,' I said quietly.

'It's all-consuming.' He clapped his left hand to his chest. 'You're joined to them, *here*, at the heart. And if you're separated from them you feel so . . . anguished. Every day I live with the chronic fear that I will see Jessica much less, or that her mother will brainwash her into hating me, or that she might even take her abroad.'

I turned up my collar. 'Could she do that?'

'In certain circumstances, yes. She keeps saying that Steve wants to go and live in France and that if he asked her to go with him, she would. She also says that if it *doesn't* work out with him she might go back to Hungary. So in order for those things not to happen, I walk this tightrope with Magda. It gives me emotional vertigo, but I have to do it in order to be with Jessica as much as I can – not just for me, but for *her*. Children *need* their fathers, Laura.'

'Yes, of course, but –'

'When Jessica's here, I hardly sleep. Do you know why? Because when I've put her to bed, and tucked her up, and read her a story, then I sit next to her on a chair, and I stay there for hours, just sitting there, watching her sleeping, because I don't want to miss even *that*. I don't want to miss a single *second* of the time that I have with her.' His eyes were shining with tears. 'When Magda left me, she didn't just leave me – she took away my *child* – she took away my *family*. So please *don't* criticize me, Laura – please just try and understand. And if you *can't*, then perhaps we shouldn't be together.'

I felt myself panic.

'I *do* understand. I *do* . . .' My voice was thin and high.

'Maybe more than you think. But understanding is different from *feeling*.'

Luke blinked back his tears. 'I know. I know it is, and I'm sorry, Laura.' He reached for my hand. 'I'm sorry my life's not nice and simple like it was when we knew each other before – just you and me with no-one else to consider – but I couldn't wish it any other way, because of Jess. But *please* bear with me.' He pulled me to him, and wrapped his arms around me. 'I love you Laura,' he whispered. 'I don't want to lose you and I promise that it won't always be like this. I promise you that everything *will* change. Over time.'

EIGHT

The next day most of the tabloids had photos of Luke's quiz triumph, with typically inane captions. *LUKE WHO'S WON!* announced the *Daily Post* on page 9 beneath his smiling photo. *QUICK'S MARRIED LOVER WINS QUIZ!* announced the *News*. It knew about Luke's abandoned attempt to Turn the Tables during the recording. *Well, we'd like to Turn the Tables too. And the question WE'D like to ask Laura is – why did your husband go missing?* I felt sick. *Charity supremo Nick Little disappeared three years ago, but tragic TV Laura is being comforted by old flame, contemporary art dealer Luke North. However, North remains married to his wife of nine years, Hungarian interpreter, Magda de Laszlo . . . See pages 7, 8 and 15.*

'This is horrible,' I said to Tom as I read the piece again. We were in the tiny, windowless edit suite at the back of the building. He was editing yesterday's show. He used to be a film editor so he prefers to do the first offline cut himself. Sara usually does it with him, but she'd gone early for Easter. I watched myself hop-scotch across the screen, in a series of freeze frames. As he did the mixing, I sounded like the Voice of the Mysterons one moment, then the next moment like Minnie Mouse.

176

'Triton is the l-a-r-g-e-s-t ofwhichplanet's m-o-o-n-s . . . ? N—e-p-t-u-n-e . . . i-s- c-o-r-r-e-c-t. Neptuneiscorrect . . . is correct, is correct, is correct.'

'I am not being "comforted" – nudge nudge – by Luke. I'm going out with him. And how dare they say that Luke's still married to Magda – she left him almost a year ago.'

'It's because you've refused to talk to them,' Tom said as he tracked back and forth, digitising the tape. He glanced at the timelines on the adjacent monitor, then tapped some numbers on to his keyboard. 'They didn't get their "My Heartache" story out of you so now they're trying to imply that you're a marriage-wrecker.'

'Out of revenge?'

'No – it's just a different angle – however misconceived. They want to write about you, and they're not going to let the fact that they couldn't get an interview with you stand in their way.'

'But *why* do they want to write about me?'

Tom shrugged. 'Because there's this mystery in your background about Nick – and I suppose because they just . . . *do*. It's odd, but some celebrities are completely ignored by the tabloids – however risky their behaviour – while others get a pasting day after day. Plus the *News* and the *Post* have this rivalry, so they're like a pair of dogs fighting over a bone, and I'm afraid that, for the moment, that bone is you.'

'Nerys was right,' I said bleakly. 'She said I should give them just one interview, so that they'd leave me alone.'

'Nerys is very annoying, but she does, sometimes, just put her finger on things. The fact that you wouldn't talk to them seems to have made them more determined.'

I read the piece again. It was like looking at myself in one of those grotesquely distorting fairground mirrors. Bile bubbled at the back of my throat. I'd been wrong in assuming that if I didn't speak to them, they didn't have a story.

'Can't I sue them? Or get them to print an apology?'

'No – because he *is* still married, isn't he?'

'On paper. '

'Then there's no defamation. I'm sorry, Laura. It's rough.'

'Still, it's all good publicity,' I said acidly. 'Channel Four must be thrilled.'

'They can't say it openly – but they are. Of course they are. They'd have to have spent a fortune to get this kind of coverage.'

'I suppose *you* think it's wonderful too?'

Tom looked offended. 'I don't actually.'

'Be honest,' I said. 'You do.'

'No.'

'But you thought up the quiz so you must be pleased at the massive media exposure.'

'Not if it's at your expense. I hate seeing you getting so much . . . crap. In a small way, I know what that's like.' He was thinking of Tara. 'But I'm afraid that's –'

'– the risk I took,' I concluded bitterly.

'To be honest, it is. And we discussed it at the time, and you decided that the opportunity was too good to miss.'

'Which it was.'

'Yes – but now you're paying the price. I wonder if *Nick* has seen any of it,' he added as he edited the sign-off into the commercial break. I looked at the paper again and at the absurd come-on in the box at the bottom of the page.

Do YOU know where TV Laura's husband is? If so, please ring the Daily Post Hotline, in confidence, on 0800 677745. There was a mugshot of Nick, captioned *Wanted!* as though he was a cattle rustler.

'I do sometimes think about that. If he's still in the country he could easily have done; he might even have watched the quiz. But for all I know he's in Tasmania.'

I thought of the SudanEase slogan – *A Little Goes A Long Way*. Perhaps Nick had pondered that too, as he'd planned his . . . what? Flight from reality? He'd stepped out of his old life like a snake shedding its skin.

'Maybe he's in the Sudan?' I heard Tom say.

I looked at him. 'That's unlikely. a) He didn't take his passport, and b) if he had managed to get there, he'd have been spotted by one of the other aid workers and word would have got out.'

A silence descended, then Tom nodded at the photo of Luke. 'But you've moved on now.'

'I have. It's funny, but you told me it was time I had a new relationship – and I met Luke that very afternoon. You told me to seize the day – and I did. It was only six weeks ago, but it feels like six months.'

'So it must be going well, then – apart from this kind of garbage,' He tapped the newspaper.

'Hmm.' I thought of Jessica's snaps of Magda and Luke. 'It's . . . fine.' I thought of her dishing up the goulash on Sundays. 'It's great.'

Next question . . . N-e-x-t-question. Nextquestionnextq-u-e-s-t-i-o-n.

'And how's love the second time around?' I was surprised by this as Tom and I don't really discuss anything personal. 'Is it better than the first time?'

'It's . . . different, because his situation is more complex. His little girl's lovely though. I met her last night. She's adorable,' I added longingly.

'You become very fond of the children.' Tom didn't take his eyes off the screen while he completed the edit. There was a pause.

'What nationality was the jeweller, Fabergé? Whatnationalitywas . . . was . . . w-a-s . . .'

'In fact I'm in a similar situation myself.'

I looked at him. 'You are?'

'Russian . . . Ru-ss-ia-n . . . Thatiscorrect . . . c-o-r-r-e-c-t . . .'

'My girlfriend has a little boy.'

179

'Really? How old is he?'

'Three and a half.' I realized that that's exactly how old Tom's own son must be by now. 'He's a great little guy. I've only been seeing Gina since Christmas . . .'

'Gina? But I thought . . . .' I stopped myself.

He looked at me curiously. 'What?'

'That –' *her name was Sam* – 'you were single. I mean, you hadn't mentioned meeting someone.'

'Well, as I say, it's fairly recent – but I met Gina on New Year's Day, and Sam's her little boy.' *Ah.* 'He's a lovely kid. I've become very attached to him actually.' Into my mind flashed the Valentine card. So it was from *him* – that was sweet. But how *weird*, I then thought, that Tom could devote himself to someone else's child, having effectively abandoned his own.

'And how did you meet Gina?'

'In Ravenscourt Park. I'd been to some friends for lunch, and I was walking back when I saw this tiny boy coming towards me – I was vaguely aware of his mum in the background, pushing the stroller – and he was running along, laughing, waving this piece of tinsel, and he suddenly fell over, right in front of me. I hated seeing him cry so I helped him up; then she caught up and thanked me, and we got chatting . . .' He smiled. 'And she gave me her card.'

'That's romantic. And do you spend much time with Sam?'

'Quite a bit.' He clasped his hands behind his head. 'Gina's doing a part-time degree, and needs to study on Saturday mornings, so I take Sam to play on the swings. Then I read to him, or we watch CBeebies. I love my time with him; it's the highlight of my week.'

'Well,' I said awkwardly. 'That's great.' And then I didn't know what else to say, because, as I say, Tom and I don't normally discuss our private lives. Even when he was so kind to me after Nick left he didn't ask awkward questions. He was sympathetic, but discreet – he just helped.

'And what about Luke's ex?' I heard him ask casually. 'Is it okay on that front?' I felt my stomach muscles clench as I thought of Magda. 'I hope you don't mind my asking – I just can't help . . . wondering.'

'Oh. Well . . . Magda's . . . okay. She's . . . .' I was tempted to tell him the truth, but I didn't want to let Luke down. 'She's . . . *fine*.'

'That's lucky.' There was an odd little silence. 'Because it *can* be hell in these situations.'

'Hm,' I said. '*Exactly*.' Tom glanced at me. 'For some people,' I added quickly. 'And how about you?'

'Same, really. It's . . . you know . . .' he shrugged. 'Her husband's around sometimes, but it's . . . okay.'

'Untiln-e-x-t-weekg-o-o-dbye . . . G-o-o-d-b-y-e . . . good-byegoodbyegoodbye. Goodbye.'

Tom hit the hard return. 'Right then – so that's us done.' He looked at me intently and, for a moment, I thought he was about to ask me one of his 'very serious' questions. But he simply took the disc out of the hard drive, and labelled it. 'So . . . have a good Easter, Laura.'

I picked up my bag. 'You too. Have a great one . . .'

'Got nice things planned?'

'Oh . . . .Yes . . . definitely . . . I'm not quite sure what – I need to talk to Luke – but, well . . .' I stood up. 'I'll see you on Tuesday then, Tom.'

He smiled. 'See you Tuesday.'

So Tom was also dating someone with a child and an ex. This cheered me up for some reason; the thought that he was in the same boat as me. But as I walked up Westbourne Park Road on the way to Luke's gallery I thought again how strange it was that he'd spoken to me so openly of his affection for that little boy, when he must be aware that I knew what he'd *done*. That he'd had this *coup de foudre* as his own sister had said, which had left him estranged from his child. As I crossed Powis Square I decided that dating Gina must be an act of atonement. Suddenly my mobile rang.

'Laura?' It was Hope. She sounded stressed.

'Where are you?'

'At home. Packing for Seville. I'm in a bit of a state actually.'

'But you're not going till tomorrow morning.'

'*That's* not the reason! It's because . . .' There was a stifled sob. 'I've just *found* something. Firm evidence.'

'Oh God . . . *What?*'

'A receipt. From Tiffany's. It was in the jacket of the suit that Mike wore yesterday.'

My heart sank. So he'd been careless. 'And what was it for?'

There was a teary gasp. 'A silver bangle with a gold heart clasp. It's for *her*. I know it is, it couldn't be for anyone *else* . . .'

'How do you know it's not for *you*? He might have got it . . . for your birthday.'

'But my birthday isn't for *months*.'

'Then maybe it's just . . . a present. He's got you things from Tiffany before. Maybe he's planning to give it to you this weekend.'

'No.'

'Maybe it's for his mother, or sister.'

'It isn't for them. I know it's definitely for this . . . woman, because –' I heard her voice crack – 'the receipt listed an extra charge for "engraving" – and it gave details. She's called –' I heard another tiny sob – '*Clare*.'

'Clare?' I Googled my memory. No matches. I crossed over Talbot Road.

'But I don't *know* anyone called Clare – and *he's* never mentioned anyone called Clare. And to think – he's with her at this very moment!' Of course. It was Thursday. He was 'working late'. 'He's probably giving it to her right now – in *more* ways than one,' she added bitterly. 'It must be some-one at work. That's where most affairs start isn't it – by the bloody water cooler – and there are loads of attractive women at Kleinwort Perella – and he's a very handsome and success-ful man.'

'Yes, but it's *you* he loves Hope . . .'

'I'm not *sure* any more. Oh God, Laura . . .' She was weep-ing now. 'I've got to go to Seville with him tomorrow morn-ing and pretend that everything's fine between us when frankly things couldn't be *worse*.'

'Don't cry, Hope. Please don't.'

'I can't *help* it. You'd cry if you'd just found what I have.' I probably would. 'I can't eat. I can't *sleep* . . .'

'If you think this *is* the proof you've been looking for, then you should speak to him about it. When he gets back just quietly tell him that you found the receipt and ask him to explain it.'

'No!' she screamed.

'You might *have* to, Hope.'

'I won't confront him tonight.'

'Why not?'

'Because then he might stop seeing her.'

'But . . . don't you *want* him to?'

'No! At least, not *yet*. Because the point is I want him to go and see her on Tuesday, as normal.'

'Why?' I asked as I turned up Ledbury Road.

'So that you can follow him.'

I groaned.

'Please *don't* refuse me again, Laura,' I heard Hope say. 'You said no before because you didn't want to give me bad news – but the point is that I already *have* the bad news.' This seemed to be true. 'I now *know* that Mike's having an affair, but what I *don't* know is where he meets her, or what she looks like.'

'But why do you want to have your nose rubbed in it?'

Into my mind flashed the image of Luke with Jennifer all those years ago. I still remembered the almost physical shock.

'I *don't* want to – I just want proof. So that I can start proceedings.'

'Look, you're being incredibly rash. Even if Mike *is* doing something he shouldn't be doing, it doesn't have to mean it's the end. People work these things out, Hope. They go to counselling, they try to –'

'Laura, I know myself *very* well. And I know that if Mike *has* been unfaithful, then I wouldn't be able to get over it.'

'You *don't* know that, Hope.'

'I *do*. So on Tuesday night, when he leaves work, I want you to go after him.'

'Oh . . . God.'

'Please,' she said. '*Please* do this for me, Laura. I'm desperate. I have to know where he's going. *Please*.'

'Oh . . . oh . . . all *right* then. I don't *want* to. But I will.'

'What don't you want to do?' Luke asked as I arrived at the gallery. He kissed me. 'I just heard you.'

'Nothing. I was talking to Hope.'

'I've just been going through the guest list for the Craig Davie show on Tuesday night. There'll be a big crowd. You will be there won't you, Laura?'

I suddenly realized that now, thanks to Hope, I *wouldn't* be. I wondered about asking her if I could do my sleuthing on Thursday instead, but it seemed callous. Now I felt doubly annoyed. I didn't want to snoop on Mike – nor did I want to miss Luke's show.

'You *will* be there, won't you?' Luke repeated as he picked up his jacket.

I couldn't explain why I probably wouldn't be. 'Of course I will,' I said.

Luke set the alarm and double locked the door, then we wandered back to his house in the early evening sunshine, past front gardens filled with shocks of golden forsythia, and

184

clumps of nodding daffodils, and bushy, glossy camellias already displaying their fat blooms. And we were just having a drink on his tiny terrace, beneath his flowering cherry, which was encrusted with pink petals which were lifting off in the light breeze and drifting down over us like confetti, I was happy to think, when the phone rang.

'Ooh – who can *that* be?' I said.

It was Magda, of course. But then it was never not Magda. Luke spoke to her patiently and, it seemed, at inordinate length, while I sat there twiddling my thumbs. For once, amazingly, she wasn't phoning to berate him, but to seek sympathy. It seemed the charity ball had not gone well. Steve was being offhand. She was anxious. What was Luke's view? Did he think Steve might be cooling off? I found it amusing to see Luke cast, for once, in the role of agony aunt rather than whipping boy.

'I'm sure it's not anythink *I've* done,' I heard her moan on the speakerphone. 'DOWN YOGI! *OFF* the sofa! OFF, OFF, *OFF*!!!!'

Luke grimaced. 'No Magda – I'm sure it's not you . . . You're a very nice person Magda. Yes . . . Of course you are. You're a wonderful person . . . . I see. You had a little difference of opinion with one of his clients did you . . . ?' Luke grimaced at me. 'Well of *course* you were entitled to your view . . . Yes, Steve *should* be more understanding . . . Hmm . . . I think he's being intolerant too. Yes, Magda, he's *very* lucky to have you . . .'

'Especially as he's got baggage,' she whined. 'I mean, there he is with this *awful* ex-wife – she's *so* nasty to him.'

'Really?' Luke said, while I rolled my eyes.

'She's absolutely horrrrendous. She's just jealous of me of course.'

'Of course she is,' said Luke. 'Because you're probably much more attractive than she is.'

'Well, yes, actually, I think I *am*. I've seen photos and she's got this . . . squint. *NO* HEIDI! *OFF* THE MANTELPIECE!!! AT *ONCE* YOUNG LADY!! *Bad* goat! *Ba-aa-aa-d*! But she's constantly on the phone to him about the alimony, or complainink about her new husband – he's just lost his job – that's not the husband she married after she left Steve, by the way – that was Pete – this is Jake, he's the one she married *after* she left Pete because that marriage didn't last long.'

'I see,' said Luke uncertainly.

'So she's upset, because he was earnink loads in City – Jake, that is, not Pete – Pete was a teacher – and they've got *big* problems with their teenage son, Patrick – that's Steve's son, by the way. He was caught with some cannabis – Patrick, that is, not Steve – and he's been expelled. But they're going to appeal so that he can take his GCSE's in May – he's sittink eleven so he's quite a clever boy. *Anyway*, Steve is very upset about that, and then he's worried about his mother because she's gettink married again next month to her toyboy – he's only sixty-two and she's seventy-three. Maybe *that's* why Steve's so distracted at the moment . . .' Magda's voice trailed away.

And I was just sitting there thinking about the fact that in dating Luke, I was also dating Magda, and Magda's boyfriend, and *his* ex-wife, and his mother, and his *ex*-ex wife and *her* discarded husbands and assorted progeny. All these people, who I had never met, and who I probably never *would* meet – except, possibly, it suddenly occurred to me, morbidly, years hence, at Magda's funeral (unless I'd murdered her, in which case I would not be expected to attend) – all these unknown people – not to mention five vertically challenged goats – were now in my orbit, circling obliquely round me, making me feel dizzy and disturbed.

'Steve just doesn't seem . . . *happy*,' I heard her say. 'But then I've been rather tense myself, what with all this newspaper coverage there's been about you and, and, and . . .'

'Laura,' Luke said helpfully.

'So actually, Luke, I blame *you* for our problems, because if you weren't seeink this, this, this . . . Laura . . . then my relationship with Steve would be *fine*.'

'I don't really think that's fair, Magda,' Luke said sweetly. He was rotating his index finger by his right temple.

'And on that front, I was goink to tell you that this journalist phoned me today, after that piece about you and, and . . . her was in the papers. And he asked me how I felt about it, and when were we gettink divorced and I said I really didn't know. But I was feelink miserable about Steve, and I must have had a bit too much to drink at the ball because I had this terrrrible headache so I just said, "Look, I'm feelink a bit upset at the moment. No comment." So I'm certainly not givink the newspapers any ammunition, even if you are.'

TV LAURA STOLE MY HUSBAND! announced the *Daily Post* the next morning. *EXCLUSIVE! ABANDONED WIFE OPENS HER HEART!* There was a large photo of Magda, in her dressing gown, watering her tulips, captioned *Distraught Wife's Tears of Betrayal.* She'd obviously had no idea she was being snapped.

The wife of Luke North, the quiz contestant lover of tragic Laura Quick, spoke out from her modest home in Chiswick about the emotional devastation she's suffered since her husband left her for the troubled presenter of Whadda Ya Know?!! 'No, we're not divorced . . .' a clearly distressed Mrs North confirmed. What did she think about her husband's relationship? 'I'm a bit upset,' she said with quiet, understated courage. Asked what she thought of her rival, Mrs North blinked back her tears, and, with dignified restraint, said, simply, 'No comment'. There was a world of meaning in those two little words . . .

There was a hideous photo of me, taken last night, talking to Hope on my mobile, captioned, *Feeling the pressure – anguished Laura arranges assignation*; next to it was one of Luke kissing me as I arrived at the gallery – *Kiss me Quick* – and beneath, a smaller one of Sweetie and Yogi captioned *Kids devastated*.

I was so shocked, I almost walked out of the newsagent's without paying. Then I ran home and read it all, speechless with rage.

'I've just seen it,' Luke said from his car. 'I saw it at the garage.' He was going to Majestic to get the wine for the private view.

'I haven't stolen anyone's husband – I'll sue these bloody people – and I'd sue Magda too, if I didn't know *you*'d end up footing the bill.' I could hear the tick-tock of his indicator.

'There's no point – even if you had the half a million it would cost – because that *is* what Magda said. They've actually quoted her accurately but given it a completely different context to twist the meaning.'

I heard his car slow up.

'So she's furious too, I presume.'

'No – she's thrilled.'

'*Why*? It makes her out to be a complete victim.'

'Strangely, she doesn't mind. She *does* like to think of herself as having been "abandoned" by me, even though *she* was the one who left. I asked her whether she'd send them a solicitor's letter so that they'd print an apology and she said she has no intention of denying their story.'

'Do you think she did it deliberately?'

'No.' I heard him pull up the handbrake. 'She's not that subtle.'

'Right. Well, that's my day ruined. It's now, officially, No-Good Friday. And what's happening with the rest of yours?'

'I've got to take the wine back to the gallery, then I've got to collect the catalogues from the printers before two. At three Jessica's being dropped off, and I've got her this evening . . .'

'Oh. You didn't tell me that. I assumed I'd be seeing you.'

'I'm sorry, but Magda's out tonight, so I said I'd have Jess.'

'What about tomorrow? Will I see you then?'

'Well, it's a bit difficult, because I'm taking Jessica down to my parents.'

'Really? What about the evening then?'

'Well Jessica's staying, as normal, and then on Sunday we'll be over at Magda's.'

'How *lovely* for you,' I said bitterly. 'I'm so glad!'

'Well there'll be an Easter egg hunt and Jessica said she wants to be with us both – it's perfectly understandable as it's Easter Sunday. *Please* don't be cross with me, Laura, I can't bear it.'

'Well what about Sunday evening then?'

'I'll try . . .'

'Or *Monday*?'

There was a pause. 'Well . . . on Monday we're actually going to Magda's mother's.'

'Oh! Wonderful! So you've left me completely high and dry! All weekend! Bloody *marvellous*!'

'Well . . . it's *so* difficult when you've got children. I'm really *sorry* Laura. I *promise* I'll make it up to you.'

'Why couldn't I at least have gone with you to *your* parents? I'd love to have seen them again, and maybe they'd have liked to see *me*.'

'Of course they would – they've said that – they always liked you. But Magda would have gone *mad* if she'd found out that I'd taken you there with Jess. I couldn't risk it.'

'*Gone* mad? She already *is*. In any case you could have just said, "Sorry, Magda, but, as a single man, I'm at liberty to incorporate my girlfriend into my weekend arrangements if I *wish* to."'

'Yes. I could have done, and I know I *should* have done – and in future, I promise I *will*. But I'm not going to do that *just* yet . . .'

'Why not?'

'Because I'm taking Jessica to Venice for the May bank holiday weekend.'

'Oh. You didn't tell me.'

'I've only just decided. One of my artists is getting married there and I'm invited and I thought it would be lovely to go with Jess, and Magda's agreed to it in principle, which amazed me, so I *don't* want to rock the boat. I'm treading on eggshells here, Laura.'

'Yes,' I said crossly. 'And you're breaking them.'

I was furious with Luke, and also with myself for not having discussed the weekend with him in advance. I hadn't realized that he'd be unable to see me, and I'd got nothing else planned. Hope and Felicity were both away, and my parents were incredibly busy because Easter is the start of the tourist season, and in any case they needed all the beds. I'd simply have to occupy myself, I realized. Swim. Read. There were things to sort out in the flat – I'd neglected it since meeting Luke again. So on Saturday I spent a couple of hours in Holmes Place, ploughing up and down the pool. I went to the market and bought lots of plants. I did the small back garden – pruning and planting – then I tidied the front. And I was just standing in the bay window, putting young red and pink geraniums in the window boxes, when I saw a woman with a black and white Great Dane climb the front steps, and ring Cynthia's bell. Half an hour later, as I was putting out the rubbish, they reappeared, followed by Cynthia, elegantly dressed as usual, smiling benignly.

'Let me know how you get on,' she called to them from the door. 'We can always do a follow-up if you need it.'

'I don't think we will,' the woman beamed, 'but thank you, Cynthia. I feel *so* much better now. Come on, Dinky.'

Cynthia waved them off as the dog loped down the street.

'Another satisfied customer?' I said pleasantly.

'Yes. She'd come up from Godalming. She was desperate

to see me.' I could smell the sweet scent of Cynthia's *Magie Noire*. 'I was able to charge a bit more as it's Easter Saturday.'

'Nice of you to let her bring her dog.'

Cynthia looked puzzled. 'Oh, no – the dog *is* the customer or, rather, client.'

'Really?'

'I've been diversifying, you see.'

'Into what?'

'Psychic healing for pets. I realized that I wasn't making full use of my ability to connect mentally with animals; so I've just done a two-day course in Advanced Interspecies Communication. You can't imagine how useful it was.'

'No. I can't.'

'I put it on my website on Monday and, to my amazement, I've already had *four* bookings – two for today – so that should help keep the wolf from the door or, rather, get the wolf *through* the door. I've just had a very good session with Dinky. I was able to tune into her thought waves and identify the problem.'

'Which . . . *was*?'

'Well . . . I shouldn't really tell you. Client confidentiality and all that . . .'

'Oh. Of course.'

'But . . .' She lowered her voice. 'She was worried about her biological clock – she almost five so it's understandable – but her owner just wasn't picking up on it, with the result that Dinky was miserable. She told me she couldn't *bear* to see puppies. But hopefully a nice boyfriend will be found for her and she won't lose her chance to be a mum. Because that would be a terrible shame. You must never let that happen to *you*, Laura,' she added. '*You* should have a baby.' She peered at me. 'Shouldn't you?'

The infernal *cheek*! And I was about to tell Cynthia to keep her impertinent pronouncements to herself when I saw Mrs Singh from next door coming down her steps. She leaned over the wall, then laid her hand on my arm, her face, as usual, a mask of sincere, if slightly horrible, sympathy.

'I'm afraid I saw the piece about you in the newspaper yesterday, Laura.' My heart sank. '*But* . . .' She inclined her head. 'I just wanted you to know that I didn't believe a word of it. Not a *word*,' she added benignly.

'I'm glad you didn't, because it wasn't true.'

'I know you would *never* steal another woman's husband.'

'Thank you Mrs Singh.'

'I know I *don't* have to worry about Arjun.'

'You don't.'

'I *never* believe what I read in the papers,' said Cynthia. 'Because I know only too well what journalists are like. They are dishonest, dishonourable, deceitful, duplicitous . . . *scumbags*!'

'Well, the tabloid journalists certainly are,' I concurred.

'No – *all* of them! They're *all* like that! Take it from me – they are *all* completely mendacious, misleading, morally bankrupt . . . *bastards*!' She was so angry that the sinews on her throat jutted out like flying buttresses. 'Anyway . . .' She breathed in deeply through her nose. 'I have a troubled guinea pig coming in half an hour so I mustn't upset myself.'

As I followed Cynthia up the front steps I wondered why she should she be quite so bilious about journalists – perhaps she'd had some bad press when she was an actress. But that was a very long time ago. As she slammed her front door, I dismissed her outburst from my mind, deciding that she was simply eccentric, and carried on with my spring clean.

Now that I'd got the garden organized I tidied up inside. I had sorted out Nick's things in February but hadn't been through my own. So I opened the wardrobe and decided to take to Oxfam anything I hadn't worn since he'd left. And I was just standing on a stool to pull the things out of the top shelf when I noticed a cardboard box on the top of the wardrobe, right at the back, pushed against the wall. I pulled it towards me and lifted it down. It wasn't heavy, as it only contained one thing – an expensive-looking blue and white striped carrier bag. My heart turned over. I'd forgotten that it was there. Inside were two things which I could no longer bear to look at: a well thumbed copy of *What to Expect When You're Expecting* and, sheathed in tissue, the white babygro, patterned with tiny teddy bears, that I'd been unable to resist – or to dispose of.

You should have a baby, Laura . . .

Yes, I thought bitterly I *should*. *I should* have a baby – or, rather, I should have *had* one.

For once, Cynthia was right.

By Sunday afternoon I was climbing the walls. I'd scoured all the papers – to my relief there was nothing more about me – I watched the boat race in a bored sort of way, then I went for a long walk in Holland Park, lingering in the knot garden, which was cross-hatched with rows of pink and purple tulips. Then I decided I might as well go in to work. I could just sit there in silence and solitude, compiling questions for the second series – Dylan and I were behind. I have a key, so I let myself in. I sat at my desk, totally absorbed. It was the perfect distraction.

What sea is 1300 foot below sea level? (The Dead Sea.) What is bouillabaisse made from? (Fish.) At what stage of gestation can the heartbeat of a human embryo be detected? (Five weeks.) How do you express zero in Roman numerals? (You can't.) Why has Luke abandoned me for the entire weekend? (Because he's scared of Magda.) What is the chemical formula for carbon monoxide? (CO.) What is the golden rule when dating someone with kids? (Remember that you will always come *last*.)

To my surprise, I heard the front door squeak open.

'*Hi*,' said Tom wonderingly. 'What are *you* doing here?' I felt myself blush, as though I'd been caught raiding the

193

stationery cupboard. 'It's Easter Day – I thought you had . . . plans.'

'Well . . .' I shrugged. 'Nothing firm . . . and Dylan and I need to stock up on questions for the second series so I thought I'd come in and make a start.' He nodded sceptically as he took off his jacket. 'How about you?' I asked.

'Oh . . . I've got so much to do. I've got accounts to check – the April 5th deadline's looming – then I've got to rewrite the Lenin proposal for BBC Four, plus I want to think about Cannes – the Mip festival's in a fortnight.'

'And you're definitely going?'

'You bet I am – I want to sell foreign rights for the quiz.'

'Has there been much interest?'

'Yes, from the States, France and Germany – but I want to do any deals face to face.'

I fiddled with my pen. It was one of Nick's SudanEase biros. *A Little Goes A Long Way* was stamped on it. 'Anyway,' Tom went on, 'I've got things like that to do, and today's the perfect opportunity.'

'Yeah, perfect.'

'Plus, I wasn't that busy – as it turned out.' I looked at him. 'So, well, right, then.' He gave me an awkward smile. 'I'll . . . leave you to it.'

He went up the narrow stairs to his office on the top floor, and I carried on working, lifting the reference books off the shelf, and flicking through them for suitable questions.

What breed of dog is named after the largest state in Mexico? (Chihuahua.) The letter Delta comes where, in the Greek alphabet?' (Fourth.) What, in Russian culture, is a 'Dacha'? (A country house.) Where is my husband? (I simply don't know.)

I became aware that my mobile was ringing. I scrabbled in my bag.

'Laura, it's me.' I glanced at my watch. It was already half past seven.

'Are you on your way back?'

'Well no – that's why I'm phoning. I'm really sorry, because I was hoping to see you, but I can't leave yet.'

'Why not? You've been there since lunchtime. It's *my* turn now, Luke.'

'But Phoebe's not well –' he dropped his voice – 'and Magda's in a bit of state about it and she wants me to stick around a bit longer for moral support in case the vet has to be called.'

'I see,' I said blankly.

'I'm really sorry.'

'Never mind,' I said breezily. 'I'm getting used to all the disappointments.'

'I'm sorry – it's only temporary – I love you, Laura – ALL *RIGHT* MAGDA!!!! – I'llringyoulater.'

As the line went dead, I heard a sudden creak on the stairs.

'Still here?' said Tom gently.

'No. I left an hour ago.' He flinched. 'Sorry,' I muttered. 'That was rude. I'm just a bit . . . tired. Anyway,' I sighed. 'Have you finished what you had to do?'

'No, but I've broken the back of it. So . . . I guess I'll be off then . . .'

'Right. Well . . . I'm on a roll, so I think I'll keep at it.' I wasn't going to admit that I'd been stood up for a goat.

'Unless . . . Can I ask you a very serious question, Laura?'

'Hm?' I looked at him.

'Do you fancy a drink? If you're not going anywhere, that is.'

'No. I'm not,' I said sourly. 'A drink would be nice – if there's anywhere open.'

'Smitty's is always open.'

'That's true. Smitty's will be open on Christmas Day – '

'And probably Judgement Day too.'

'Smitty's it is then . . .' I picked up my bag.

'I thought you'd be having a nice romantic weekend away,'

Tom said as we sat in Smitty's Caribbean diner in All Saints Road a few minutes later.

I sipped my Red Stripe. 'No such luck.'

Get up, stand up, stand up for your rights . . . sang Bob Marley.

'Aren't you seeing Luke?'

Get up, stand up, don't give up the fight . . .

I shifted on my chair. 'Well, it's been a bit difficult this weekend because, being Easter, he's got –'

'Don't tell me. Family commitments.'

I nodded. 'That's why I'm in a bad mood actually.'

'I guessed. Not easy is it?'

'Well . . . it's rather tricky.' I fiddled with the table-cloth.

'Tricky's an understatement.'

'Yes – you're right. To be honest, this weekend's been a wash-out.'

Tom gave me a wry smile. 'Tell me about it.'

'You too?'

He nodded. 'The frustrations of dating someone with kids.'

'You have to be understanding, don't you?'

'Not understanding, Laura. *Saintly.*' He ordered another couple of beers. 'I've put myself forward for beatification because I have to tolerate so much crap.'

I snapped a banana chip in half. 'Like . . . what? Not that you have to tell me.'

'I don't mind telling you at all – in fact I'd like to. You don't mind do you?'

'No. Of course I don't mind. We're friends. '

'We are.' I looked at him. 'And I think you'd understand . . .'

He told me that when he'd first met Gina she was a single parent, her husband having left her six months before for another woman. But now he was trying to make a comeback.

'Gina hadn't seen him for dust. But then he heard I was

196

around – plus his affair hadn't worked out – and now he's trying to play the devoted family man as though I'm some interloper.'

That sounded familiar. 'What does he do?'

'He phones up all the time, especially late at night or disgustingly early, to see if I'm there. He tries to come round unannounced. I have to be over at Gina's flat, obviously, because of Sam, but I refuse to hide because I'm not doing anything wrong.'

'Does Gina let him in?'

'No – she talks to him on the doorstep.'

'And what about his contact with Sam?'

'This is the problem. Gina says he can see him every Sunday – but not at his flat, because she doesn't think he's responsible enough. Which means he has to see him at her place.'

'Which means that you can't be there.'

'Exactly.'

'And that they're spending time together.'

'Correct.'

'Which you don't like.'

'Who would? She was single when I met her, but now they have all this family time which I can't *stand*.'

'Well, it's *very* difficult,' I said. I could feel my jaw tense.

'They've gone to her parents today. That's why I came in to work, because I was so pissed about it and I needed to distract myself.' I smiled bitterly. 'Gina says that it makes Sam feel more secure to see his parents being friendly to each other but it's not on.'

'No, it isn't,' I said feelingly. 'Can I ask *you* a very serious question, Tom?'

'Yes,' he said.

'Why are you with Gina?'

'That *is* a serious question. Well . . . I . . . *like* her. She's nice, she's very smart – and she likes *me*. And then . . . I don't know . . .' he fiddled with his beer mat. 'I've become very fond of

Sam. I'd really miss that little boy if it didn't work out . . .'

'And Gina, presumably?'

He looked at me. 'Well yes – of course. But I have a problem with her ex being around so much. But then he needs to be around because he's Sam's dad.' He shrugged. 'And I'm not.'

But you are father to another little boy, I wanted to say. What about him? Don't you miss him? You must surely regret what you did? Isn't that the real reason why you're dating Gina?'

Tom had another sip of beer. 'It's . . . not easy.' He looked at me. 'And how about Luke's ex? I saw that piece about her yesterday. More crap, I presume.'

I nodded bleakly. 'Of the first *ordure*. She left Luke ten months before I set eyes on him again.'

'Have you ever met her?'

'No.'

As I sipped my beer I thought how strange it was that a woman whom I had never actually seen should be able to exert such an influence over my life. She was like God – invisible, yet omnipresent, and seemingly all-powerful.

'Do you think you *will* be meeting her?' I heard Tom ask.

I grimaced. 'Not if I can help it.'

He looked puzzled. 'But you said yesterday that she's okay.'

I fiddled with my beer mat. 'That was a lie. The truth is she's anything but. She left Luke, but doesn't want me to be with him. She's banned me from having anything to do with Jessica – she has no idea that I *have* actually met her. She deliberately takes up all his spare time – like today – in order to show me that she still "owns" him. She's got Luke by the balls because she's the mother of his child. She's a huge problem.'

'But *she* isn't the problem. Luke is. He should be setting boundaries.'

'He knows that,' I sighed, 'and he wants to be tougher

198

with her, but he's worried that if he does he'll end up seeing less of Jessica.'

'If he *doesn't*, he'll end up seeing less of *you*. He should be worrying about that too, Laura – I know *I* would be.' I looked at him. 'And *he* pursued *you*, didn't he? *He* came on the quiz. *He* asked you out. We all saw him. So, however tricky his situation, he has to strike a balance.'

'How do you strike a balance with an *un*balanced person?' I asked. 'Magda's slightly . . . unhinged. But in one way, I can't criticize Luke, because it would be like criticizing him for being too devoted to his child. And I'd rather he was like that, than not spending *enough* time with her. I mean, when you think of all the men who just walk away from their families and who *abandon* their children and their responsibilities, or who just give up the second the going gets tough and never even *see* their kids it's –' A red stain had spread across Tom's throat. 'Like . . . Gina's husband did. That's all I mean. But it's . . . hard for Luke. It's very hard.'

Tom nodded. 'I understand. Anyway,' he picked up the menu. 'I'm starving, and there's nothing in my fridge. I've got to eat. Will you keep me company?'

'Okay. Why not? I've had nothing since this morning.'

'What do you feel like?'

I pondered the pumpkin soup, the yam casserole, the fried jerk chicken, and the peas and rice.

'How about the fish fritters?' I heard Tom say. 'Or the red snapper – that looks good. So . . . what's it to be then?' He waved at Smitty. 'Have you decided?'

'Yes. I think I'll have the curried goat.'

NINE

On Sunday night Hope called from Seville. They'd just had dinner in a tiny restaurant near the Cathedral.

'I'm putting on a convincing show,' she whispered. 'Mike hasn't a *clue* that I know.'

'What's his behaviour like?'

'Normal, although he seems a little . . . on edge. There was an awkward moment this evening when he started saying something – I thought he was about to confess – but then he stopped, as though whatever it was, was too painful to talk about . . .' She paused, then I heard a quiet sniff. 'It's awful to think that this is probably our last holiday together.'

'Are you sure you want to do this, Hope?'

'Yes,' she said quietly. 'I am. I could bury my head in the sand – keep the life I've got – but he could end up leaving me anyway. I've got to *know*, Laura, so I can plan.'

'So you still want me to follow him on Tuesday?'

'I do.'

'And you'll take the consequences?'

I heard a sigh. 'I will.'

'And you swear that you will never *ever* blame me – whatever I find out – or hold it against me in *any* way?'

'I swear.'

'*However* unpalatable?'

'However unpalatable.'

'All right, then. What's his work address?'

'It's Tower 42 – the old NatWest Tower – at 25 Old Broad Street – you can't miss it.'

'And what time does he normally leave?'

'At about six thirty. There's a café on the ground floor that you can lurk in.'

'Won't he spot me?'

'No – because it's tucked away at the back, behind the escalators – but *you'll* see *him* as he leaves. And the walls of the building are glass so you'll easily spot which way he goes.'

So on Tuesday evening I got the tube to Liverpool Street, then walked out on to Old Broad Street, moving against the steady flow of City workers making their way home. There was an early heat wave, so I didn't feel too self-conscious in my sunglasses. To my left was the massive green-grey Gherkin and, ahead of me, Tower 42 soared into the sky, its windows flashing bronze and gold in the late afternoon sun.

I went inside and crossed the foyer to Café Ritazza, from where I kept a discreet watch on the two revolving doors. I sat there sipping my coffee, profoundly wishing that I could be anywhere else – preferably at Luke's private view. I'd phoned him at five-thirty to say I was caught up in something, but would try and get there later. I couldn't tell him the truth, but I didn't want to lie.

According to the leaflet I'd picked up about the building, Tower 42 was so called because it had 42 floors, of which Kleinwort Perella occupied the top four. I'd arrived a good twenty minutes early, so I put my mobile on mute – I didn't want it advertising my presence – and as I sipped my latte, I passed the time, as I often do, idly thinking up questions we could use on the quiz. What is the tallest building in the world? (The Sears building in Chicago). What is the name of the national relationship counselling service? (Relate.) Name the great Dane who designed the Sydney Opera House (Jörn Utzen.) How long is a normal human pregnancy? (Forty weeks.)

I glanced at my watch. It was six fifteen. In front of me, departing staff were floating down the glass-sided escalator and exiting through the two revolving doors. As they spilled out on to the pavement, some turned right towards Liverpool Street, while others stood there, waving at cabs. From where I was sitting I had a good view. As I looked at them in their charcoal suits and silk ties and Hermes scarves, I tried to decide on a collective noun for bankers – an 'interest' maybe, or a 'stripe', or a 'credit'. Suddenly my heart skipped a beat. *There* was Mike. Just stepping off the escalator. I'd already got to my feet, pulse racing, when I realized I'd made a mistake. I sat down again, feeling jittery, like a sprinter after a false start. I glanced round the café, hoping no one had seen me, but it was almost empty. I calmed myself with deep breaths.

Hope was right. There *were* a lot of attractive women working in the building. Twenty- and thirty-somethings mostly, uniformly slim, well-groomed and glossy-looking. Tempting. I wondered if Mike had strayed before. I felt angry with him for letting Hope down – and angry with her for involving me.

By now it was six twenty-five. I imagined Mike clearing his desk for the day, putting on his jacket, then picking up his briefcase, in which would be – what? Something skimpy from La Perla? Tiffany earrings to go with the bangle? I imagined him heading for the lift. By now the volume of people leaving had increased. I scrutinized the men through narrowed eyes. No, I thought. No. Not him. Or him. Not him either. No . . . No . . . No . . . Definitely not . . . No. I was watching both doors, my eyes darting back and forth between them; then I looked at the escalator again, down which another large knot of people was descending. No . . . no . . . no . . . no . . . *Yes!*

I scraped back my chair. *There* he was. No mistake. I saw

202

him step off the escalator, walk smartly across the foyer and spin through the revolving door and now, through the glass walls I saw him turn left out of the building. I followed him outside. I was so alert I felt radioactive. Adrenaline burned through my veins. I was pursuing him down Old Broad Street, half running now to keep up as he crossed the road, oblivious to my presence thirty yards behind him. A bus passed in front of me, obscuring him. Panicking that I'd lose him, I stepped off the pavement without looking, and a black cab hooted.

'You *stupid* cow!' a lycra-clad cyclist shouted, as he swerved to avoid me. Across the road I could just see Mike's dark head in the crowd as he walked down Threadneedle Street, past Pavarotti's sandwich bar and the Royal Bank of Scotland towards the Palladian splendour of the Stock Exchange. As I followed, trying to keep a neutral expression on my face, despite the tension I felt, I saw him going down into Bank tube. I felt like an assassin as I pursued him down the black and white-tiled tunnel, dodging commuters.

'Excuse *me*!' a woman snapped as I accidentally barged her. I muttered an apology, then saw the sign to the Central Line. But why was Mike getting on the Central Line at Bank, when Liverpool Street tube would have been nearer? Then I realized that he was following the signs for the Waterloo and City line – the 'Drain'. I rounded a bend, and saw him taking the stairway down to the platform – a long, wide, tunnel of shallow steps which gave me a clear view of him all the way down. As I followed forty feet or so behind, aware of my rapid breathing, I wondered why he was going to Waterloo. Presumably he was going to get a B.R. train out to the suburbs – or perhaps he'd get off at Clapham Junction, or Barnes. I wondered how old this woman Clare was, and what she looked like. I saw her as a twenty-five year old red-head – wild and abandoned. The opposite of Hope.

I had reached the foot of the stairs. And there was Mike,

walking to the end of the short platform. I could hear his footsteps snapping across the marble tiles. If he turned round now, he'd spot me, so I stood behind a tall, fat man in a beige raincoat. There was a distant rumble, a rush of warm air, and now the train was pulling in. The doors drew back, the passengers spilled out, and we all surged forward.

Mind the gap, intoned the automated guard. *Mind the gap . . .*

Out of the corner of my eye I saw Mike board the adjacent carriage to my own. As the train rattled off I could see him through the glass, standing by the middle door. He didn't look happy or excited. If anything, he looked rather sad. Perhaps he felt filled with shame at his betrayal – or perhaps the affair was coming to an end.

Now we were pulling into Waterloo and I felt the knot in my stomach harden as I realized how difficult it would be to keep track of him here in the rush-hour crowds. The doors trundled back, and I saw that the *Way Out* sign was to the right, so I lingered in the carriage for a few seconds to allow Mike time to pass down the platform in front of me. He walked past, quite unaware that I was standing just a few feet away, then I followed him along the platform and up the steps. He was only about fifteen feet in front now as I passed the signs for British Rail, then went up the stairs, watching him pause at the automatic gate, as he fumbled for his ticket. Now he was on the escalator, rising slowly above me as I stepped on, the glass roof of the station overhead, daylight flooding through. I felt a welcome cool blast of fresh air.

Please keep your baggage with you at all times . . . I heard over the tannoy.

As I pursued Mike across the station concourse I was dimly aware of the Eurostar entrance to my left, and then the British Rail platforms to the right, and I was just worrying that I didn't have a train ticket and in any case had no idea where Mike was going, when I realized that he wasn't heading for the platforms at all. He was walking towards the main station entrance. He was leaving. Side-stepping the milling commuters, I followed him as he passed the Body Shop and Delice de France, then went through the huge, stone archway, and down the front steps. I saw a sign for the National Theatre. Perhaps he was meeting Clare there.

Ahead was the huge rotunda of the Imax, and to the left, the Festival Hall. Below us was a line of waiting taxis, as black and shiny as stag beetles, but Mike walked purposefully on. He turned left into York Road, passing underneath the overhead walkway to the Shell Centre. The pavement was wide so I had an uninterrupted view of him now, about fifty yards ahead. He was walking confidently. Unhesitatingly. He'd clearly come this way many times before. Now, on the right, was the London Eye, its glass pods glinting in the early evening sunlight. I thought, with a pang, of Nick.

Mike had stopped at the crossing. As he waited to go over I hovered at a nearby bus stop in order to preserve a safe distance. Then, as the green man beeped him over, I set off in pursuit again. As he got to the other side he quickened his pace and I was aware that I had a stitch in my side and a grating in my throat. To my right was County Hall, and now I could see Big Ben and the Palace of Westminster, its gold-leafed turrets winking in the sun. We were on Westminster Bridge – the buses rumbling past – the river broad and brown and shiny beneath it, a stiff breeze blowing my hair.

Mike had walked to the other side, but as I waited for a gap in the traffic, glad to catch my breath, I saw that he didn't turn right, to cross over the river, as I'd imagined. Instead he went straight on. Now he was entering the grounds of St Thomas's hospital. As we skirted its perimeter I assumed he'd walk past it, on his way further down the embankment, but, to my surprise, he was following the signs to the main entrance, and now he was going through the sliding doors, sidestepping a patient in a green hospital gown and a foot plaster.

What the hell was Mike doing *here*? It was hardly the place for a romantic rendezvous. Maybe his girlfriend was a doctor, or a nurse and he was picking her up at the end of her shift. Perhaps he was visiting a friend? Or perhaps ... yes ... perhaps *he* was having treatment for something? *That* must be it, I decided as I passed the flower shop. I felt a sudden surge of relief. He had something wrong with him, but was protecting Hope. Except that it would be a strange time of day to be having outpatient treatment, and in any case what about the silver bracelet, with the gold heart clasp, engraved with the name 'Clare'? Unless it was *Clare* who was ill ... Yes. *That* was it, I now saw as I followed Mike down the corridor, towards the North Wing. Clare was a patient here. *That's* why he was looking so sad. She'd been in hospital for two months, so it must be serious. I imagined her sunken cheeks, and his tears.

He had stopped at the bank of lifts. As he pressed the button, I quickly retreated out of his eye line towards the café. I'd successfully followed him this far, and didn't want him to see me. But what would I say if he did? At least, here, I'd have a credible excuse. I'd feign astonishment at 'bumping into' him then tell him that I was visiting a friend. But Mike was in no danger of seeing me. He seemed oblivious to the eight or so people around him as he stared at the floor, totally absorbed. There was a ping, and they all drew back as the lift opened, disgorging its human cargo – then they all stepped on and the doors closed again. Mike had gone – and I had no idea where.

I rushed forward to get the next lift. It arrived within seconds and I stepped in then pressed all the buttons. There had been so many people on Mike's lift that it would probably stop at most floors, so I was going to make sure my lift did too. That way I might just catch a glimpse of him in the corridor as the doors opened each time.

First floor. Door opening, intoned the automated voice. I

peered out into the lobby. There was no sign of Mike in either direction. The door closed and we lurched upwards again.

Second floor. Door opening. I couldn't see Mike, but four more people got on so I made sure I didn't allow myself to be jostled to the back. A woman in a wheelchair glared at me for not moving, but I needed to keep my vantage point.

Third floor. Door opening . . . Fourth floor. Door opening . . . Fifth floor . . . Each time it stopped I peered out into the corridors, but I didn't see Mike. I'd lost him . . .

Seventh Floor. Door opening. The doors drew back, and suddenly there he *was*, fifteen yards or so to my left, waiting to be let into a ward – I couldn't see which one as he was standing in front of the sign. As I stepped out, he lifted his hand to the large red buzzer and pressed it. I crept around the corner, my heart banging with the tension of being so close, then I stood by a notice board, pretending to be absorbed in a poster about the MMR jab. I stole a glance at Mike, and saw him press the buzzer again, then I heard an exasperated sigh. He'd obviously been waiting some time. Now he rapped on the glass with his right hand, then suddenly lifted his left hand and waved. The door was opened for him, by a nurse in a green tunic and trousers.

'Hi Mike,' I heard her say. 'How are you?'

'I'm fine thanks, Julie. And how is she today?' he added anxiously as she ushered him inside.

'About the same. But she'll be all the better for seeing you.' The sign on the wall said *Post-Natal Unit. No Unauthorised Entry.*

I waited a few minutes, staring at notices about breast-feeding and the NCT, but taking in none of it. Then I went up to the door. I had no idea what I was going to do, but I simply had to know more. But I'd only be allowed in if they thought I was a visitor. And I was wondering how I'd get round this, when I heard the lift ping open behind me, and a man and a little boy came out. The man was holding a large bunch of white tulips, and the boy was clutching a big teddy bear with a blue ribbon round its neck. They came and stood alongside me, then the man pressed the buzzer. Now, through the glass panel, I saw a nurse advancing towards us. The door was opened.

'We've come to see my wife, Sandra King,' he said. The nurse – assuming that we were together – ushered us inside. I breathed a sigh of relief – I was in. Then, as I made my way slowly down the long corridor, aware of the smell of antiseptic mixed with floor polish, my pulse began to race again. I could hear babies crying. The sound shredded my heart – not just for the usual reasons, but because I knew that one of these babies was Mike's.

I tried to work out the dates. Hope said he'd been behaving suspiciously since the end of January. If he'd been coming *here,* twice a week, since then, that would mean that the baby must have been premature. Now, as I passed two empty incubators, I understood the true reason for his hostile behaviour at Olivia's christening. He must have been sitting there, consumed not just with guilt, but with fear. I thought of the baby's tiny body, its miniscule limbs, thinner than my fingers, attached to trailing wires and tubes. A christening was the last place in the world Mike would have wanted to be.

Now, as I approached the nurses' station, I tried to imagine the level of *deceit* that he'd had to maintain in order to conceal all this from Hope. Not just over the last two months, but long before that, as Clare's pregnancy progressed. I wondered how long they'd been involved. At least a year – maybe two or three. A nurse smiled at me as I walked past the desk, so I smiled back praying that she wouldn't ask me who I'd come to see. On my right now were the small side-wards, with visitors milling around each curtained bed, and the occasional glimpse of a recumbent mother, or of a swaddled newborn in its see-through bassinet. Now I turned left and found myself in another, vertiginously long, corridor.

A woman in a yellow waffle weave dressing gown walked slowly past me, gingerly clutching her abdomen – she'd obviously given birth not long before. And there, right at the very end, oblivious to my presence, was Mike . . .

He was holding a baby. *His* baby. He'd taken off his jacket, and had rolled up his sleeves, and had it on his left shoulder. I could see its tiny face, puce with distress. He was patting its back, and walking up and down with it, a few feet in each direction, gently bouncing it, or stopping and rocking back and forth on his heels. The baby was wearing a white babygro and a white hat, and it was crying in the relentless, rhythmic way that newborns do.

'*Araaah . . . Araaah . . . Araaah . . . Araaah . . .*'

As it stopped to draw breath I could just hear him comforting it. 'Shhhh . . . Shhh . . . Shhhh, darling. It's okay. It's *okay* my little baby . . . you'll be fine . . . you'll be fine. Shhhh now darling . . . Shhhh now my baby . . .'

'*Araaah . . . Araaah . . . Araaah . . .*'

I retreated further away, then sat on a chair, just watching him for two or three minutes as he walked up and down with the baby in his arms. I was so shocked I could hear myself breathe. And now I tried to imagine telling Hope . . .

Yes, Hope, I did follow Mike, and yes, I did see where he went – no, I didn't lose him – but I'm afraid it's not good news because . . . yes . . . he does . . . he does seem to have someone, and actually it looks as though it's a bit worse even than that because you see . . . well . . . you see . . . there's a baby, Hope, and . . . yes . . . a baby . . . yes . . . I don't know . . . I don't know . . . I don't know if it's a girl or a boy, but . . . that's right . . . it is . . . it is his baby . . . I'm sorry, Hope . . . because I saw it . . . I did, I definitely saw it with my own eyes . . . in the hospital . . . St Thomas's . . . oh please don't cry, Hope . . . please don't cry . . . I'm afraid it is true . . . it is . . . Yes, it was definitely Mike . . . I saw him walking up and down with this baby. Comforting it, because it was crying an awful lot because it must have been born prematurely, although it's not in an incubator any more, but it still seems to need medical care. And I think that that's what he's been doing for the past two months, going to the hospital to visit his baby – and that's why his behaviour's been so odd and so – what was the word you used? – emotional. That's it. And this is why. And you're just going to have to talk to him about it, and tell him that you know the truth now, you know the truth and then . . . I'm sorry, Hope. I thought you might be wrong, but you weren't wrong . . . you weren't wrong at all . . . I'm sorry, Hope . . . I'm really sorry . . .

'Can I help you?'

'Mm?'

As I came to I saw that the woman who was speaking to me was wearing a badge that said she was a senior midwife; *Special Care* it announced beneath. 'Can I help you?' she repeated. 'Who is it you've come to see?'

'I've come to see . . .' I glanced at Mike, and felt my throat constrict.

'Are you okay?' she said. 'You look upset.'

'It's . . . rather awkward. Could I just have a word?'

I walked out of the hospital twenty minutes later, in turmoil. How could Hope and Mike stay together now? It would be impossible. I hadn't spoken to him – I hadn't wanted to – but I'd found out everything I needed to know, and now I'd have to break it to Hope. I imagined her sitting at home, desperate for me to call, but I wasn't going to – at least not yet. So I left my mobile on answer mode then walked over Westminster Bridge in the fading light, crossed Parliament Square, then hailed a cab home. As we drove through Victoria I decided that I couldn't possibly tell Hope the truth over the phone. So instead of going back to the flat, where she could reach me, I decided I'd go and find Luke – not least because

I suddenly remembered I'd said I'd try and get to the party. It was a quarter to nine – he'd still be there.

I asked the driver to take me to Chepstow Road. As he dropped me outside the gallery I could see that there were a dozen or so people inside, clutching empty glasses, laughing and talking. I paid the driver, and went in. As I pushed on the door, I saw Hugh. This was all I needed.

'Hugh,' I said. 'What a surprise.'

'Hi Laura!' He kissed me on the cheek as though it was perfectly normal that I should catch him at a private view with a woman other than my sister.

'Hello Chantal,' I said pleasantly. 'How funny seeing you both here.'

'Well I like to support local arts events,' said Hugh. 'And Chantal and I have just been for a drink, so she decided to come along too.'

'That's right,' she said, blushing.

'But we were just leaving,' Hugh said.

'Well send my love to Fliss,' I added brightly.

'Will do,' he replied nonchalantly. What a *nerve*.

'Laura!' I heard Luke say. He kissed me.

'Sorry I'm late,' I said. 'I got delayed by something and . . .'

'Don't worry,' he said warmly. 'I'm just so glad you're here.'

'That was my brother-in-law,' I said with a nod through the plate glass window at Hugh's departing back. 'He's married to Felicity.'

'I know. I remembered meeting him with you once, years ago, and he introduced himself again. So who's the blonde he was with?'

'One of Felicity's friends, Chantal Vane. I think it's a bit . . . *off* actually.'

'Why? Oh. I see. Do you think they're . . . ?'

'I don't know. I hope to God not.' I'd had enough problems with my sisters' husbands. 'Anyway, how's it gone?'

He beamed. 'It's been fan*tastic*. We had a hundred and

fifty people here, and we sold *ten* paintings. Craig's already left,' he added, 'but let me show you his pictures.'

As we walked round the gallery, I was careful to exclaim over them even though they didn't do much for me – just primary coloured oils trowelled on to the canvas, *impasto*, in a vibrant, but seemingly arbitrary way. I tried to take in what Luke was saying about non-representational, abstract art and the intellectual challenges it presents – the way that discussing it takes you almost into the realms of philosophy – but it was hard to concentrate. I felt as though he was talking to me from the other end of a long dark, tunnel. Then he introduced me to some friends of his, Grant and Imogen, whose nine-month-old baby was his goddaughter.

'She's gorgeous,' Luke said. 'Jessica adores her too.'

'Is she your first one?' I asked Imogen politely.

'*My* first,' she replied. 'Grant has two lovely boys of twelve and nine. They adore Amelie – don't they darling? She's a lucky little girl.'

He nodded happily. 'She is.'

We exchanged a few further pleasantries, then they said they'd have to get back, and now the last stragglers were drifting away and Luke and I were able to go while his gallery assistant, Kirsty, cleared the last of the glasses and locked up.

'There was so much interest,' he said happily, as we strolled back to his house. 'I was worried that coming so close after Easter there wouldn't be, but everyone came and there was a real buzz. Are you okay?' he said suddenly. 'You seem a bit . . . quiet.'

'Well, I've got a . . . headache,' I said truthfully.

'Poor you. I'll make it go away.'

'I don't think you can.' I thought of Hope, still waiting and wondering, unable to get through to me. But I couldn't ring her now, even if I wanted to, because by now Mike would be back. I decided I'd call her first thing. But how could I possibly tell her something so grave over the phone?

212

I couldn't. It had to be done face-to-face. Suddenly I knew what to do. Yes. *That* was it . . .

'We'll spend the rest of the evening quietly,' Luke said, holding my hand. 'We could unwind with a film – a nice Hammer House of Horror, or we could see *The Mummy's Revenge*. That's fun.'

Now we were walking up Lonsdale Road, and we'd drawn level with the house, and Luke had just opened the gate when he suddenly stopped. Lying on the flagstones in his front garden was a pair of jeans.

'What in *God's* name are these doing here?' As he lifted them up I felt a sudden *thud* in my rib cage. 'And *these* . . .' He picked up a pair of white briefs, and a pink t-shirt which had been lying on the doorstep. 'What on *earth* . . . ?'

'They're mine,' I said quietly.

'They're *yours*?'

'Yes,' I said with a sick feeling.

'Oh. *God* . . .' He unlocked the door, turned off the burglar alarm, then we went upstairs. He switched on the light in the bedroom.

'Oh. *God* . . .' he repeated softly.

The first thing we saw was my silk kimono. It was hard to recognize, given that it had been slashed into about twenty pieces of varying size which were strewn over the bed and floor. There were bits of it on the chest of drawers, on the dressing stool, and on the bedside table. A piece had floated down on to Wilkie and had covered his head, like a handkerchief, as though he was sunbathing.

'Oh *God* . . .' Luke murmured again. 'I'm *sorry*, Laura.' He picked up a scrap of blue silk. 'I don't know what to say. I feel . . . *ashamed*. I'll get you another one,' he added impotently.

'No . . . Please . . . Don't bother,' I breathed, too stunned to express my outrage. 'Really . . .'

He sank on to the foot of the bed. 'I'm so *sorry* Laura . . .' He shook his head. 'She's just . . . *insane*.'

I went into the bathroom. The lid of the loo was down, and out of the side of it hung one arm of my green cashmere cardigan, as though it had been struggling to get out. As I lifted the seat I was, at least, grateful that the water into which Magda had plunged it appeared to be clean. She had written *Bitch!* in large capitals, with my lipstick, on the bathroom mirror, and had then smashed the remainder of the lipstick into the sink. She had sprayed my hair mousse all over the walls. She had tipped my make-up into the bidet, and squeezed toothpaste all over it. She had put my hairdryer, the flex cut off, in the bin.

I imagined Magda carrying out this destruction in a breathless frenzy – like a fox in a henhouse – fuelled by . . . *what*? Then I remembered.

'It's because I moved her things.' I looked in the wardrobe. Sure enough, her Liberty print shirt, her two dresses, her velvet jacket and her shoes had all been restored to their former places.

'*Jesus*,' Luke groaned. He was just sitting on the bed, still holding a piece of my kimono, shaking his head.

'But the question is . . . how did she get in?' He looked at me. 'How did she get *in*, Luke?'

'Well . . .'

'She didn't *break* in, that's obvious.'

'No . . .'

'So does she have a key? Please don't tell me she has a key, Luke.'

'She doesn't,' he said wearily. 'But she does know where I keep the spare. But I don't think she did this just because you moved her clothes.'

'Then why did she?'

'Because she'd found out that you'd met Jess.'

'Really?' He sighed, then nodded. 'How? Did she see the Easter egg I gave her?'

'No. She had Jessica's photos developed this morning and she saw you in one of them.'

214

'Ah . . .' I remembered the flash going off as I moved out of shot.

'She phoned me in a rage and I was incredibly busy hanging the pictures for the show, so I told her to get lost. I didn't think she'd do . . . *this*.'

'Are you saying she drove over from Chiswick, in order to cut up my things?' I felt almost flattered.

'No. She had to come over here anyway because Jess had a play date in Notting Hill, and while she was waiting, she must have let herself in, had a snoop, *then* seen you'd moved her stuff, and just . . . lost it. It would have been too much for her.'

I sat down next to him, still stunned. We didn't need to watch *The Mummy's Revenge*. We had our own version going on right here.

'I'll speak to her . . .' he said. 'I'll put it right with you, I don't know how, or what I can do . . .' He buried his head in his hands. 'It's such *hell*, Laura. You can't imagine the stress. It's like living on the lip of a volcano.'

'Magma,' I said quietly. 'Her name should be *Magma*.'

I put out my right hand to support my back. As I did so I could feel something hard under the duvet. I pulled it back. Placed in the middle of the pillow on my side of the bed, was the pair of large dressmaking scissors that Magda had obviously used to cut up my kimono, the blades open. I stood up.

'I don't think I'll stay here tonight.' I picked up my bag. 'I'm sorry, Luke. It's just . . . too much. And I've had a very stressful day as it is.' I thought of Mike, and the baby. 'Let's speak tomorrow.'

I walked down the stairs and out of the house. I didn't have the energy for anger – I was still subdued by shock. But as I made my way back to Bonchurch Road I thought how amazing it was that Magda should have wrought so much destruction, and at the same time exhibited such control,

215

carefully closing the window out of which she'd hurled my things, then diligently setting the burglar alarm and locking the door.

I heard a clock strike eleven. I looked at my mobile phone. I had eight missed calls – all of them from Hope – and when I got back I saw that she'd left five, increasingly desperate messages on the answerphone. I texted her to say I couldn't speak to her tonight, but that I'd call her first thing. But before I was even awake the next morning, she had phoned me.

'Why didn't you call me *back*?' she wept. I blearily glanced at the clock. It was six-thirty. I'd hardly slept. 'I've been going *crazy*!' she wailed. 'Why didn't you *call* me?'

'a),' I croaked, 'because it was impossible, and b) because I knew that by the time I *could* have done, Mike would be at home.'

'So . . .' I heard her draw in a breath. 'What did you find out?' I didn't reply. 'What did you find *out*?' she repeated. 'Where did he *go*? What's this Clare woman like? Is she younger than me? Is she more attractive? Did you get a photo of her? Will you *please* tell me what you saw? Please Laura. I can't stand it. I can't *stand* it! I've got to know. Just *tell* me, will you Laura! *Tell* me! Please, please, please *tell* me . . .'

I took a deep breath. 'No. I won't.' There was a gasp.

'What do you mean – you *won't*? You've *got* to. That's why you followed him. What are you *playing* at?'

'I'm not playing at anything. But I *don't* want to tell you what I saw.'

There was a shocked silence. 'Why *not*?'

'Because I want to *show* you – that's why. Tomorrow evening I want you to come with me, and I will show you what I saw. And you are to control yourself until then, and not pester me, or berate me, or cast aspersions on my integrity or my motives, or rant at me about how miserable you are because, actually, Hope, I've got my problems too . . .' My

216

throat was aching. 'And, believe it or not, I'm trying to do my best for you here.'

I could hear her crying.

'It's bad news, isn't it?' she wept. 'That's why you don't want to tell me. Because it's such bad news. It's the worst possible news.'

'Well . . .'

'Mike's in love with this . . . Clare,' she croaked. 'Isn't he?'

'Yes. I think he is.'

'My marriage is over.'

'Maybe . . . But I want you to trust me – and you are to say *nothing* to Mike tonight. Please don't confront him however much you may be tempted to.'

'Of course I want to, but I can't, because he's just gone to Brussels and he won't be back until tomorrow lunchtime – he left early to get the train. Maybe she's gone with him,' she added dismally.

'I think that's unlikely,' I said. 'Anyway, I'll meet you . . . where? Outside Westminster tube station at . . . 7pm tomorrow night.'

'But where are we *going*, Laura?'

'You'll see.'

TEN

I recorded the show the next afternoon – the winner got a very high score – and then, embarrassingly, as it turned out, she decided to turn the tables. The question she asked me was perfectly reasonable: 'In Greek mythology what effect does drinking the waters of Lethe produce?' But with all that's been happening my concentration was poor and I said 'sleepiness', when the right answer was 'forgetfulness', which I did know, although, ironically, I'd forgotten. Anyway, the audience sniggered at that, which annoyed me, and the contestant's prize money doubled to thirty-two thousand – which was a bit of a budget-buster – and then just as we'd finished the last re-take there was a power cut. All the lights went out because, we learned afterwards, there'd been some problem with the grid in this part of west London, so that wasted another half an hour as we sat there in the dark – there's no natural light in the studio – while someone tried to find a torch. Apart from the inconvenience, I hate the dark, so I was glad when the electricity was restored and we could all go home. Luke phoned me as I sat in the cab.

'I've just spoken to Magda,' he said. 'She's feeling pretty rotten about what happened . . .'

'About what *happened*?' I closed the glass partition so that the cabbie couldn't hear. 'About what she *did,* you mean.'

'She's very sorry, Laura, she's feeling . . . really . . .'

'Cut up?' I suggested.

'Bad. She admitted that she'd lost her temper.'

'No, Luke, she didn't "lose her temper". She went *berserk*!'

'But things haven't been easy for her lately, Laura.'

'Poor love. Still, nothing like a little recreational destruction to perk you up when you're having an unsatisfactory day is there?' We'd stopped at a red light.

'And she's worried that it's not going well with Steve. She's –'

'Don't tell me – for the chop?'

– 'not been feeling that confident – she was convinced it was over – and she *was* annoyed that you'd moved her things.'

'*I* was annoyed that they were *there*!'

'And sometimes, Magda just gets a bit . . . het up,' he went on, ignoring me. 'But now she's a lot calmer. Normal. Almost.' The lights turned green.

'Look Luke, I really don't want to hurt your feelings – I realize that Magda's the mother of your child, and must therefore be sanctified, or at least, not criticized, but the fact of the matter is, she's insane. For the purposes of this argument, I am Jane Eyre, you are Mr Rochester, and Magda is Bertha Mason. Except that she isn't locked up in the attic, she's rampaging through the house with a pair of dressmaking shears. How do I know it won't be a chainsaw next time? Or that she'll decide to cut up my clothes while I'm still *wearing* them!'

'Look, Laura, she's offering you an olive branch – and I really hope you'll accept it. She said that she'd like to meet you.'

I gasped. 'No way!'

'Please Laura.'

'Not after that! No! How could I? And in any case, what's the *point*?'

I heard Luke sigh. 'The point *is* that I have to have a

reasonable relationship with her, which means that *you* do too. Because we're going to be together, Laura. Isn't that what you want?'

I looked through the windscreen.

'Yes . . .' I said. 'It is.'

'Which means that Magda will be in your *life.*'

'I don't . . . really see why. There are a million step-families in this country, Luke, and I imagine that in the majority of cases the first and second wives have zero contact. The children are dropped off, and their mum zooms away. And if that's how it is with Magda then that's fine by me.'

'But it isn't fine by *me*. Look, Laura, I know she can be a bit . . . tricky . . .'

'You're sounding like Comical Ali.'

'But if you want to get on with Jessica, which I assume you do . . .'

I looked out of the window. We were in Chiswick.

'Of course I do,' I said quietly.

'Then however much you may hate the idea, you'll have to have a civilized relationship with Magda.'

'Which would be fine if Magda *was* civilized, but on the evidence of last night, she *isn't*.'

'*Please* Laura. She can be perfectly . . . rational . . . some-times.'

'You want me to appease her,' I said angrily. 'She behaves *horribly*, destroys my things – but the idea is that I now bow and scrape to her like you do. Well I'm not bloody well *going* to!'

'You don't have to. You just have to be nice. I want you to help me realize my goal of a happy and harmonious set-up for Jessica.'

'I'm sorry, but I don't think that's possible.'

'It *is*. You know those friends of mine you met at the gallery last night. Grant and Imogen? The ones with the baby?'

'Yes.'

'Grant and Rosie split up five years ago, and a year later he met Imogen, and last year they had the baby. Now, *they* all get on really well. Rosie likes Imogen, she brings the boys over most Sundays and they all have lunch; she also adores Amelie and sometimes even baby-sits her while Grant and Imogen go out. Sometimes they all go down to his parents together. They're all *friends*, Laura, and the children are happy and secure because of it – and that's how I would like it to be with *us*.'

'It sounds lovely,' I said. 'What could be more civilized? Utopian even . . . But the point is, Luke, that a) it sounds pretty unusual, and b) in your friend's case, wife number one is clearly a nice, normal, *sensible* person – unlike Magda. I'm sorry to be so uncooperative here Luke, but she turned my silk kimono into dust rags. And now you're asking me to sit down and take tea with her as though we're in some play by Oscar *Wilde*!'

'Well . . . .yes. I suppose I am. She'll be at the house tomorrow afternoon, and it would be wonderful if you could be there too. It would also help me, because I don't want Magda to change her mind about my trip to Venice so I need her to feel confident and calm. *Please* Laura. I know it's a lot to ask, but I hope you'll do this for me.'

Why are people always asking me to do things I don't *want* to do, I thought crossly? Why am I constantly being cajoled and coerced? But then, out of curiosity about Magda, as much as any desire to help Luke, I found myself saying.

'Ohhhhh . . . All *right* then, dammit. What time?'

The tabloid hacks, fresh from their Easter holiday freebies, have had another go at me. *IS TV LAURA LOSING HER WAY?* screamed the masthead of the *Daily News* this morning. There was a large headshot of me looking worried. On the centre pages was a splash by their showbiz editor about how my '*friends*' were worried that the '*strain of presenting the quiz*', the '*trauma*' of not knowing where my husband was, combined with the *emotional agonies* of dating a *married man* were beginning to get to me. There was a grainy photo of me dropping the question cards that time, captioned '*The stress gets to Laura*' – one of the audience must have taken it with a mobile. Beneath, one unnamed '*confidante*' was quoted as saying that the '*guilt*' I felt at having '*stolen Magda's husband*' was '*eating me up*', while another '*reliable source*' claimed that I wasn't eating at all, but was '*struggling with anorexia*'.

'You've got to get your side of the story across,' Nerys said when I went in to work. She patted her salon-stiff hair which, this week, was the colour of loganberries. 'In *my* view, you're letting them get away with murder. It's awful.'

'It is, Nerys. I'm absolutely sick of it.'

'Then you should do an interview yourself,' she said as she adjusted her headset. 'Just my opinion. Good *morn*-ing, Trident Tee-*veee*.'

'Nerys does have a point,' said Tom. 'This has been going on long enough. Maybe it's time you played the media game, Laura – I know that's what they think at Channel Four.'

'I thought they were delighted with the rising ratings – aren't we up to four million now?'

'We are, but they're worried about you. They feel you should respond.'

So when, later that day, Nerys took a call from a broadsheet journalist, I let her put him through.

'Miss Quick?' He sounded very earnest. 'My name's Darren Sillitoe. I'm from the *Sunday Semaphore*.'

'Yes?'

'First of all, can I just say that I'm a huge admirer of yours. I think the quiz is wonderful.'

'Oh. Thanks.'

'I saw that piece about you in the *Daily News* this morning.' I felt my face flush. 'I must say the tabloids have given you a pretty rough ride.'

'You're telling me.'

'It was obvious that the *News* had made up most of those quotes.'

'They had.'

'I know you've so far refused to speak to the press, but I was wondering whether you don't *now* feel that it's finally time to go on the record – with a "proper" newspaper.'

'Well . . . as it happens, I *had* been wondering that.'

'Oh . . . then I've called at the right time.'

'Maybe. But what would you want me to say?'

'Well, it would be a profile of you – a positive one – but we'd want the human story, which would, I'm afraid, mean talking about your husband's disappearance.'

My heart sank. 'Would I have to?'

'I'm afraid so, otherwise there'd be no point in doing the piece. But we would interview you very sensitively and then carefully report what you say. But while you're on the phone, can I just ask you, by way of background, what sort of things have especially bothered you about the coverage you've had recently?'

'Well . . . *everything*,' I replied. 'But mainly the suggestion that I broke up Luke North's marriage when his wife had left him ten months earlier, and that I'm difficult and demanding – I'm not.'

'Well . . . it's been very hard for you. But the *Sunday Semaphore* is at least a serious newspaper and for once the public would be reading about you in your *own* words.' There was a pause. 'I'll give you my direct line and you can let me know if you'd like to go ahead.'

'Would you let me see the copy in advance?'

He hesitated. 'That's *not* something we normally do.'

'Well, giving interviews is not something *I* normally do. So I'll only consider it if I'm allowed to see the piece beforehand.' I was surprised to hear myself sound so tough.

'Well – perhaps I *could* swing that – given the sensitivity of your position.'

'And would your paper donate a fee to the National Missing Persons' Helpline?'

'I'm sure that could be done.'

'Not less than five hundred pounds?'

I heard a quiet laugh. 'You're driving a hard bargain.'

'If you want me to talk to you, I'm afraid that's what it'll take.'

'We do want to talk to you – exclusively of course.'

'Yes, of course. But I'd like to have a think.'

After all the lies that had been printed about me, I was very tempted to agree, but I wasn't going to decide there and then. I had too many other things on my mind – not least my rendezvous with Hope. I was dreading it.

I arrived at Westminster underground a good ten minutes early, but Hope was already there. She was standing by the street map, her face as pale as papyrus. But although resentful at not knowing where I was taking her, she was at least reasonably calm. But as we set off across the bridge the atmosphere between us was strained; so, to distract her, I asked her about the request I'd had from the *Semaphore*.

'Well, I suppose at least being a sensible broadsheet they won't print brazen lies about you like the tabloids have done,' she said as we walked over the bridge.

'They also said they'd let me read the piece beforehand.'

'They'd give you copy approval?'

'Unofficially, yes.'

'In that case, there's no downside – go for it.'

'I might. But I've got too many other things on my mind to make a decision now. Not least . . . this.'

'So . . . where are we going then, Laura? *Please* tell me. I'm in agonies. Where are we *going*?' she repeated as we crossed the Thames, the wind whipping our hair.

'You'll see.'

She emitted a frustrated sigh. 'And how long will it take to get there, wherever it is?'

'Not long.' I looked away to the left. There was the London Eye, and the Oxo Tower behind it, and the elegant white masts on Hungerford Bridge. Terns were diving and swooping over the water. A pleasure boat passed underneath us, leaving a fan of water in its wake.

'So Mike will be there, will he?' I heard her ask, raising her voice above the rumble of the traffic. 'I'll see him?'

'Yes, you will.'

'I can't believe I'm *doing* this,' she said. 'Just allowing you to take me to this unknown place without a clue as to what it is or where it is.'

'Well you're doing it because you asked me to follow Mike, and now I'm going to show you what I found out.' We walked on without speaking.

'Is it much further?' she asked as we got to the other side of the bridge.

'No. It isn't.' I stopped outside St Thomas's. 'In fact we're here.'

'Where? This is the hospital.'

'Exactly.'

'We're going into the *hospital*?'

'We are. Come on.' We followed the signs round to the main entrance.

'But why?' I heard Hope ask. I didn't answer. '*Why?*' she repeated as we walked through the sliding doors.

'Because this is where we'll find Mike.' We passed the flower shop and the newsagents, and went through reception to the bank of lifts where ten or twelve people were waiting. 'This is where he's been coming.'

'I don't understand,' she whispered. 'He's not ill, is he? Please don't tell me he's *ill* Laura.'

'He's not ill.'

'Then what on earth could he be doing *here*?' The lift doors drew back and we got in. 'Is he visiting someone?' she murmured. I pressed number seven.

'Yes. He's visiting someone.' The lift stopped at the third floor, and the other passengers got out and no-one got on. We were alone.

'Clare?' said Hope. 'He's visiting Clare?'

'That's right.'

'Oh. Oh my God. *She's* ill . . . ?' I didn't reply. 'Is *that* it? He visits her because she's *ill*? Poor woman . . . but what's *wrong* with her? It must be serious if he's been coming here for two months. Why won't you just *tell* me, Laura? Why aren't you saying anything?'

'Because I want you to *see* it.'

'But I don't understand,' she groaned. 'Why all the mystery? And if she *is* ill she's hardly going to want her boyfriend's wife turning up at her bedside is she!'

Seventh floor. Doors opening . . .

As we stepped out, Hope saw the sign on the wall, then stopped. She'd gone white.

'Is this the right place?'

'It is.'

Her hand flew to her mouth. 'Are you sure?'

'I'm sure.'

'So . . .' there was a tiny gasp. 'Oh my God . . . there's a baby?'

'There is a baby, yes.'

'Oh my God,' she repeated. 'A baby. There's a *baby* . . .' She was shaking her head. 'Oh *God* . . . I can't go *in*, Laura.'

'I think you should.'

'I *can't*. I can't *possibly*.' Her eyes had filled. She was staring at me accusingly.

'Trust me.'

'Trust you? Why *should* I? You're being vile. *Vile* . . .' Her mouth was twisted in distress. 'Sadistic and *vile*. To bring me here.'

'You may think so, but actually, I'm not.'

'Then why *have* you brought me here? To rub my nose in

it? To see my pain? I don't *understand*.' She was rummaging in her bag for a hanky. 'I wish I'd *never* asked you,' she wept. 'I wish I'd never, *ever* asked you to help me!'

'Well you did,' I whispered back. I pressed the red buzzer and a nurse opened the door.

'Hi,' she said. 'You were here a couple of nights ago weren't you?'

'That's right. This is my sister.' Hope managed a watery smile.

'Just go straight down. You know the way.'

By now Hope was whimpering with distress.

'You . . . *cow*,' she croaked as we washed our hands in the visitors' loo, as requested. 'What are you *thinking* of? Forcing me to come in here so that I can see that my husband has not only had an affair, but a *baby*. Why are you *doing* this to me?' she hissed as she grabbed a green paper towel. 'What kind of sick pleasure is it giving you to see me . . . *suffer* like this?' She stamped on the pedal bin and threw the towel in. I didn't reply. 'Is it something from when we were kids? Something you want to punish me for twenty years later?'

We walked down the corridor, not speaking now, just listening to the crying of the babies and the respectful murmurings of visitors. We could hear our shoes squeaking across the lino.

'Why are you *doing* this?' Hope repeated, *sotto voce*. 'What did I ever do to *you* to justify such cruel behaviour, Laura, such deliberately cruel, manipulative, *horrible* behaviour, I mean *why* are you doing this to me, *why* for God's sake – it's so *vile* of you and I just don't under . . . stand . . . I . . . *Oh* . . .'

In the distance, oblivious to our presence, was Mike. His shirtsleeves were rolled up, and he was walking back and forth, with the baby in his arms, his face filled with compassion and tenderness.

'Shhh . . . my darling. Shhhh . . . don't cry now. Please

don't cry my little girlie . . . come on now . . . that's it . . .
Shhhh . . . you'll be fine . . . Shhhh . . . Shhhh . . . Don't cry
now . . . don't cry . . .'

Hope stood rooted to the spot, as she watched Mike walk
the crying baby up and down.

'I can't take this.' She was shaking her head. 'I can't . . . I
just . . . *can't* . . . .'

'Shhhh . . . Don't cry now . . . Don't cry.'

'*This* is where he's been coming?'

'Yes.'

'All this time?'

'No need to cry . . .'

'All this time.'

'I can't *bear* it,' she croaked. 'I feel *si-ck* . . . Oh *God* . . .
Oh my *God* . . . a baby. A *baby*. And where's this . . . Clare,
then?' she murmured. 'Where's *she*? I want to see her – now
that we're here. I want to *see* the woman who's had my
husband's child. The woman who's destroyed my marriage
and my future and my whole . . . *life*. Where *is* she? Where
is she? Where is *Clare*?' she demanded. 'Why don't you *tell*
me, Laura?'

'He's holding her,' I said quietly.

'What do you mean?'

'He's holding her.'

She blinked. 'But . . . I don't understand.'

'Clare's the baby.'

'Clare's the *baby*? Oh. Then . . . who's the *mother*?'

I shrugged. 'I don't know. Nor does Mike. He's never met
her – and he never will.'

Hope was looking at me as though I were speaking in
tongues.

'Then . . . what . . . ?'

'Clare's mother is a heroin addict, so Clare was born one
too. And the babies of drug-dependent mothers suffer with-
drawal symptoms, so they need someone to hold them and

228

cuddle them, and walk them up and down because they tend to be very jittery and they cry a lot. And their muscles are very tense, making it hard for them to go to sleep, so they need extra holding and soothing, which the nurses don't always have time to do. So that is what Mike, along with a number of other volunteers, has been doing for the past two months. He has no idea that I know, or that I spoke to the nurse who organizes the programme.'

'Oh,' said Hope. She was still staring at Mike. Her mouth quivered. Then I saw a tear slide down her face.

'Shhh my little baby,' we heard him say. 'Shhhh . . .'

'Oh,' she whispered. 'I *see* . . .'

'Shhh darling . . . Shhhh, it's okay . . . it's okay my little girl . . . you'll be fine . . . you'll be fine . . . don't cry now . . . please don't cry . . .'

'So . . . he *hasn't* had an affair?'

'No.'

'So . . . he was just doing it . . . ?' She blinked in bewilderment.

'To be kind, Hope.'

'But then . . . why didn't he *tell* me? Why *hide* it Laura?'

Mike chose that moment to look up. He registered our presence, then stared at us, his eyes shining with shock.

'That's something you'll have to ask him.'

The next day, when I got to work, there was an e-mail from Hope.

I've taken the day off. Meet me for lunch? Hx

'My treat,' she said quietly when I met her at Zucca's. 'It's the least I can do.' She still looked pale – but less tense than she had for a long time, as though a screw in her chest had stopped turning.

'I'm sorry,' she began as we sat in the window. She picked at her salad. 'I'm sorry for all the horrible things I said to you last night.'

229

'That's okay. *I'm* sorry I had to keep you in the dark. I knew it would be very stressful, but I didn't want to say anything beforehand.'

'You were right not to,' she said. 'I needed to see it for myself. I needed to be shocked by it – and I was.'

'So what happened? After I left?'

'Mike was just so . . . *amazed* to see me. He asked me to go home. Then, when he got back, we stayed up until half two, just talking. That's why I've taken the day off – I was just so *exhausted*, so I called in sick. Plus the emotional stress of it all had got to me. But . . . I didn't *know*,' she said wonderingly. 'I didn't realize . . .'

'How much he minded?'

'I had *no* idea.' She was shaking her head. 'Until I saw him last night. We never *talked* about it. It was a closed subject.'

'Why didn't he open it up?' There were tears standing in her eyes.

'Because he knew I wouldn't change my mind.'

'I see . . .'

'He told me how much he loved me, and that he hadn't wanted to lose me. So when he heard about the Cuddlers' Programme at the hospital . . .'

'How *did* he hear about it?'

'Through someone at work. She was a volunteer, and she happened to mention it to him just before Christmas, so he applied – they vet them very carefully – and he was accepted. He said that he didn't tell me about it because he knew that if he did, it would lead to a very painful conversation, but he said he'd wanted to hold a baby so much . . .' She leaned her face in her hand. 'He said he wanted to know what it felt like to really hold a baby in his arms. And that little baby, Clare, had been in the unit longer than the other babies because she's had particular problems – so it was always Clare who Mike walked. But he was told she'd be going home at

230

the end of this week, so he wanted her to have something from him.'

'The silver bangle.'

She nodded. 'Because he knows he'll never see her again. He'll never know her second name, or who her mother is, or her father, or where she lives, or anything about her. All he knew was that she needed to be held.' She blinked back her tears. 'He'd become very . . . fond of her. He cried when he talked about not seeing her again.'

'So he *had* fallen in love with Clare.'

'Yes.' She pulled a tissue out of her bag. 'He had.'

'So . . . you talked half the night.' She nodded. 'With any . . . result?'

There was a pause. 'No. But I'm glad that I at least *understood*. I finally understood how *deprived* Mike had felt.'

'But why hadn't you *guessed*?'

'Because, not only did he not talk about it, he behaved as though he wasn't remotely *interested* in babies – but now I know that that was only a front. He said that when we got married he'd thought he wouldn't mind, but how it had then started to eat away at him, especially as our friends began to have children. He said that every time he had to go to another christening he'd come away feeling bitter and depressed. He said that having Hope meant that he was "hopeless". It was his sad little private joke.'

'So that's why he behaved strangely at Olivia's christening . . .'

'Yes. And that's why he was never keen on going round to see Hugh and Fliss. He said Felicity got him down, boring on about Olivia the whole time.'

'I know the feeling,' I said.

'But last night, as we sat there, Mike looked around our lovely cream drawing room, and he said how he longed for children to trash it, and scribble on the walls, and spill things on the carpet, and make chaos and mess and noise – all the things I've never wanted.'

231

'So?'

'So . . .' She shrugged. 'I don't . . . *know*. I'm just so glad it wasn't what I thought. Mike *wasn't* having an affair, and he *was* telling the truth when he said he wouldn't ever have one. But how can I stay with him now? How *can* I Laura?' Her eyes had filled again. 'It wouldn't be fair. He loves me, but he wants children. And those two things are incompatible.'

My heart sank. 'So you don't think you could . . . change your mind?'

She sighed. 'I have *never* wanted children. You know that. I have never wanted to go through a pregnancy or endure the broken nights, or the noise and the stress. I've never wanted the awful *responsibility*, or the anxiety – the white-knuckle ride of parenthood.' She fiddled with her knife. 'Not everyone *wants* children. You can have a lovely life without them, can't you?' I didn't answer. 'And I can't help how I feel.'

'But couldn't you . . . ? *Couldn't* you . . . ?'

She looked at me. 'Be persuaded?' She shook her head. 'No . . . I don't think I could.' She breathed a deep sigh, then looked at me. 'What are you thinking?'

'I'm thinking that a couple of years ago, Felicity asked Mike whether he minded not having a family.'

'Really?' she murmured.

'And he just said . . . that it was a question of love.'

'Oh. Well . . . that was a nice thing to say.'

'Yes. That's what we thought.'

'That's what *you* said to me, Laura, when I asked you how you could stand Luke's situation.'

'Did I?' I looked at her. 'Oh, yes. I remember that now . . .'

We sat there in silence, then she called for the bill. 'Thank you for helping me, Laura.' She picked up her bag. 'I know you didn't want to.'

'I wish I hadn't had to.'

We pushed back our chairs. 'So . . . are you going back to work?'

'No. Tom said I could take the rest of the day off because I came in over Easter.'

'So what are you doing now?

'I'm going to have tea with Luke.' I pulled on the door. 'And Magda.'

'*Magda*? You're seeing Magda?'

'I am.'

'If this is an April Fool, Laura, I'm afraid you've missed the twelve o'clock deadline and in any case I'd never fall for it.'

'It *isn't* an April Fool,' I said.

Although April Fool's Day *was* an appropriate day on which to be meeting Magda, I told myself a few minutes later as I sprang the catch on Luke's gate. I glanced up at his bedroom window and had a sudden vision of my jeans and t-shirt being flung out of it. Or perhaps they'd jumped, to try and save themselves . . . I realized that I was sweating, despite the fresh breeze. As I lifted my hand to the bell, my heart was hammering in my ribcage.

'There you are!' said Luke. He was smiling broadly, but I could see the whites of his eyes. 'Magda and Jessica are already here.'

'Lovely . . .' I said impotently.

Suddenly, Magda appeared. As she advanced down the hallway she smiled at me warmly, as though greeting a cherished friend.

'Laura! How *nice* to meet you properly. Jessica darlink do take Laura's coat for her.'

Jessica, looking subdued and confused, did as she was told. Magda extended to me a cool, dry hand, which made me aware that my own was horribly damp. I felt like Alice in Wonderland, except that I was accumulating a pool not of tears, but of sweat. As I gave her a clammy handshake I hoped she wouldn't smell my fear.

233

'Come and sit down,' she said.

As I went into the sitting room I registered two things – resentment at being graciously welcomed into my own boyfriend's house, by his ex-wife; and searing, excoriating jealousy.

Magda was beautiful.

The photos I'd seen of her hadn't done her justice. Her skin was pale, with the blue-white translucency of alabaster; her exceptionally long hair was as heavy and glossy as silk; her eyes were big, and wide set, with the same large blue irises that Jessica had and the same elegantly exposed eyelids; her feet and hands were small, as was her waist. She was . . . classically beautiful. Like a lovely porcelain doll.

I wanted to hate her, with my own idiosyncratic features and my griddle-panned hair and big feet; but I couldn't even dislike her, I realized, as she sat there chatting to me animatedly in her delightfully accented English, putting me at my ease, koshing me with her charm, while Luke hovered in the background, his mouth, like mine, a rictus of anxiety, his upper and lower eyelids just that bit too far apart.

Hungary had produced Edward Teller – inventor of the atomic bomb – and Estée Lauder. Terror and beauty. Magda to a tee.

She was talking to me about the quiz.

'We *love* watchink it, don't we Jessica, darlink?' Jessica nodded. 'You are *so* clever,' she said smoothing the front of her floral silk dress. 'But Luke said that you were always *verrry* clever when you were students together.'

'Oh she was,' he said. 'Top notch.' *Top notch*? Luke *never* said things like 'top notch'. 'Tea anyone?' he added. I thought he was going to produce a tennis racket.

'I'll have Darjeelink,' she said. 'You don't mind makink it do you Luke? What about you, though, Laura? What would *you* like?'

'I'd like a herbal tea,' I muttered. Something calming, I

234

thought to myself. That's what I need. 'Erm . . . camomile would be great. If you've got it,' I added, as though I had no idea that Luke had two boxes of the stuff. I didn't want to enrage Magda by reminding her that I had an association with the house that entailed a familiarity with the contents of the kitchen cupboards.

'Righty-o,' Luke said, clapping his hands together. I had never ever heard him say 'Righty-o' in his life. Perhaps you could slip something pharmaceutical into it, Luke, I wanted to add as he went down the stairs. A valium, preferably. Or half a bottle of whisky. A general anaesthetic, maybe. *Anything* to reduce the tension of this bizarre encounter. Oh and could you go and get me the can of Sure while you're at it because there's a damp patch the size of Bangladesh under my left arm.

But Magda was talking away, as though she was the Queen putting some minor Commonwealth official at their ease, or rather, yes, *that* was it, as though she was Luke's *mum* – meeting the nervous girlfriend for the first time and doing her best to be kind and welcoming, reserving judgement about the poor girl's pasty complexion, or thick ankles, or gauche manner or patent, spot-it-a-mile-off let's-just-forget-this-shall-we unsuitability. And it was on the tip of my tongue to tell Magda how very, *very* strange this was for me, sitting there, talking to her in this pleasant way, given that she'd trashed my things a mere forty-eight hours earlier. As she sat there, bludgeoning me with her charisma – she was talking about Chiswick now, something to do with Jessica's school – I tried to imagine her orgy of destruction but found it impossible. I thought of the dismembered dressing gown which, even now, lay in a black bin liner at the front of the house, like a butchered corpse. I was itching to ask her what emotions had gripped her as she slashed and sliced – but somehow the question would have seemed in poor taste.

And now here Luke was with the tea. He was a good ten feet away from me but I could see that his brow was beaded with sweat. And now, just *like* a nervous girlfriend desperate to impress, I asked Magda about the goats. It was a good move. Her face lit up. And as she began her exposition about pygmies I made a mental note to try and incorporate some caprine questions into the quiz.

'So what qualities should one look for when choosing a pygmy goat as a pet?' I asked her politely.

'Well the most popular ones are the "wethers",' she explained. (Q. What, in goat husbandry, is a "wether"? A. No idea.) 'These are castrated bucks. I *much* prefer them castrated,' she went on, as I stole a glance at Luke, 'because, when they stop thinkink about sex the whole time, then they seem to develop their intelligence and . . . I don't know,' she gave an elegant little shrug, 'their . . . *personality*.'

'Goatonality,' said Luke affably.

'*Person*ality,' she corrected him with a smile. 'And you see, the lack of testosterone makes them more interested in socializing with *people* rather than their four-footed friends.'

'Really?' I said.

'Oh yes. Our pygmies follow us around like dogs, don't they, Jessica?'

Jessica nodded. 'Especially Sweetie.'

'They bleat when they hear our voices. They like to sit on our laps.'

'*How* adorable.'

'But we do *not* allow them on the sofa or beds. Do we darlink?'

'No,' said Jessica seriously. '*Or* the table.'

'Well, that's . . . sensible. And what do they eat?'

Magda smiled. 'Oh, that depends. We call Heidi "Pig Me!" because she's such a greedy little guts, don't we Jess?'

Jessica nodded. 'She'll eat *anything*.'

'But the others are fairly picky. But all pygmies need hay in their diet.'

'Alfalfa hay!' I almost shouted, suddenly remembering

something Luke had once said and desperate to drop it into the conversation.

'Alfalfa hay – *yes*, that's *right*.' Magda smiled at me delight-edly, revealing a row of orthodontically perfect white teeth. 'But the problem with alfalfa hay . . .'

'Yes?' I said.

'Is that it has a very high sugar content.'

'Oh dear.'

'Which could lead to increased weight, even obesity, and the chance of kidney stones.' I arranged my features into a mask of anxiety. 'And they need a lick-block of minerals and salts. That's *verrry* important,' she added.

Jessica nodded sagely.

'Is that why Phoebe was ill recently?' I asked solicitously.

'Yes. It was a mineral deficiency. She had a bad fever, but she is *much* better now.'

'And what do they sleep in?' I asked. 'I've often wondered.'

'Well they have to have shelter of course. In Chiswick I have two large igloo-shaped dog kennels. They can climb on top of them and play "I'm the king of the castle." That's their favourite game.'

'And they can sleep inside,' said Jessica happily.

'Or just have some private time during the day,' said Magda. 'But they like to go to bed early . . .'

'With a good book?' I suggested gaily.

Puzzlement momentarily distorted Magda's lovely features. 'No, Laura. Pygmy goats can't read. What I am *saying* is that they are creatures of *habit*. They retire at dusk and get up at dawn.'

'They don't like getting wet,' Jessica added.

'No they *don't*, do they, darlink. You'd think they were made of *sugar*!' We all laughed. 'But you can take them for walks on a lead, you know.'

'Do you do that with yours?'

'Yes, because I show them, so that's all part of the training.'

'Any prizes yet?'

'Oh yes, Laura. So *many*.' She then launched into a list of all the rosettes Sweetie and Yogi had won at the Surrey County Fair, and the Royal Show, and at Windsor. 'Phoebe was expected to take gold at the South of England show,' she added. 'She was definitely best in her class, but I'm afraid she only got bronze.'

'Really?' I felt a flicker of genuine disappointment.

'But between you and me – it was *fixed*.'

'Fixed?'

She and Jessica were nodding slowly. 'I'm afraid the world of pygmy goat showing can be quite corrupt,' Magda went on, pursing her lovely, curved lips. 'But my pygmies have done very well. Yogi is currently Goat of the Month on the Pygmy Goat Club website.'

'You must be very proud of them.'

'Oh I *am*. They are such delightful animals – and *so* intelligent.'

'I'm not sure about that,' Luke said. 'Let's face it, Magda, goats have an IQ of thirty-five.' There was another quiz question, I realized. Q. What is the Intelligence Quotient of the average pygmy goat? A. Thirty-five.

'No! They are *verrry* intelligent,' Magda insisted. She looked at her watch. 'My goodness I must go. I have to feed the darlinks their supper, then Steve and I are going to a party. So I must get my skis on.'

'Skates,' Luke corrected her benignly.

She smiled at him. 'Yes, of course. Anyway, it's been delightful meetink you, Laura.' She embraced me warmly and I hoped she didn't notice the stench emanating from my armpits. 'Bye bye Jessica my darlink.' She kissed her. 'Be good for Daddy my little angel. Goodbye Luke.'

He saw her out, then came back into the drawing room, smiled, then clapped his hands.

'Well,' he said. 'Wasn't that *fun*?'

ELEVEN

'How bizarre . . .' said Felicity a few days later when I told her about my encounter with Magda. She was feeding Olivia at one breast while expressing milk from the other. I suddenly imagined the cross section of the lactating breast with its network of milk ducts, alveoli and Montgomery's tubercles. 'So she shreds your clothes and is then delightful to you. How . . .'

'Capricious?' I said as the electric pump droned away like a dentist's drill, the silicone valve lifting up and down as though the gadget was breathing.

'I *was* going to say "weird". Perhaps she's got bipolar disorder or something. You get massive mood swings with that. The two halves of the brain aren't on speaking terms.'

'She was so charming,' I said wonderingly. The bottle of milk was already two thirds full. I wondered if Fliss ate grass to have such a good supply. 'But it was obvious that she was quite mad.'

'Mad Magda,' Fliss said. 'But Luke must have been relieved that she was at least civilized to you.'

'He was.'

'And did she apologize for what she did to your clothes?'

'No. On the contrary, it was as though *she* was generously

forgiving *me*, graciously choosing to overlook *my* appalling behaviour.'

'How Magdanimous of her.'

'I think being pleasant was as near as she could get to saying sorry.'

'But why her volte-face?' She switched off the pump, then gestured to me to put the yellow top on the filled bottle. As I took it in my hand, it felt slightly warm.

'Luke says it's because Magda seemed to be genuinely contrite – she realizes she'd overstepped the mark, even for her. He also thinks it's because it's going well with her boyfriend. They had a dodgy moment when she had a punch-up with one of his key clients – but they're back on track now, apparently.'

'What does he see in her?' she asked as she flopped her left breast back into her bra.

'What Luke did, I guess.'

'Which was?'

I imagined Luke's hand trembling slightly as he drew her naked form for the first time. 'She's absolutely gorgeous.'

'Really?'

'She's . . . beautiful. You can't help staring at her.'

'How annoying,' Fliss said. I was touched by her loyalty.

'I do, meanly, wish she was more ordinary, but unfortunately she looks like Catherine Deneuve.'

'But Luke wasn't happy with her, was he, Laura?'

'That's true. Her behaviour was so bizarre that he fell out of love with her.'

'And it's *you* he wants.'

'That's what he says. He's told me that he wants us to be together.'

'*Good*. That's obviously his agenda now. And what about children?' she asked as she sat Olivia up and burped her. 'Presumably he'd like to have more?' She wiped a dribble of regurgitated milk off her shirt with a crumpled tissue.

'We haven't discussed it, but I'm sure he does.'

'That would be wonderful,' she said as she put Olivia on my lap. Then she opened the freezer and put in the bottle of expressed milk. I could see several more already in there, lined up like skittles. 'It's such *bliss* being pregnant, Laura.'

'I know,' I said. She looked at me. 'I mean – you've told me often enough.' And I thought, *but I've never told you. I've never told anyone but Nick that I was once pregnant.*

'It'll be *such* fun if you could have one soon – Andwouldn't-thatbeLOVELYforyoumydarlingbaby!' she said, stroking Olivia's nose with her index finger. 'AlicklecousintoPLAY-wivwouldn'tatbeLOVELY?'

'Khosaalthagazagoyagoya,' Olivia replied.

'It's such a pity Hope doesn't want the stork to visit *her*,' Felicity added.

'Yes, that *is* a shame,' I said. I'd told her nothing of Hope's problems.

'Not that Mike seems to mind. He's obviously not that bothered.'

'Hmmm.'

'Do you know where that business about the stork comes from?' I heard her say.

'No.'

'It's from a Norse legend that the souls of unborn children live in watery areas such as marshes and lakes. And since storks are known to visit such areas, they were thought to have gathered up the babies' souls and delivered them to the parents. Isn't that lovely?' she sighed.

'Yes. It is.'

As Felicity took Olivia, I wondered where *my* baby's soul had lived – in a spring or a stream, or by a river. I imagined the stork scooping it up, and carrying it towards me with its big, slow wing flaps. Then suddenly turning round in mid flight.

'I've never asked you this, Laura, but did Nick want children?'

I felt a wave of bitterness. 'I'm not . . . sure . . . But in any case it's not really worth thinking about is it?'

'Still no news then?' she asked. I shook my head. 'Even with all this publicity?'

'No. The *Daily Post* were asking readers to phone in if they knew where he was, so the *Daily News*, not to be outdone, have got two of their top investigative journalists on the case.'

'Then they might very well find him.'

'I don't think they will – he's the invisible man.'

'And what would you do if they did?'

I looked at her. 'God . . . I don't know. That's a scary question.'

'Well, you might have to answer it – if they do track him down.'

'They won't,' I repeated, 'because they won't commit resources to it for more than a few days, so if they *were* going to, it would have to be soon. By the way did Hugh *tell* you that he'd seen me at Luke's gallery the other night?'

'Yes. He was there with Chantal.'

'I thought she looked . . . *embarrassed*, Fliss. She was blushing with self-consciousness when she saw me.'

'I know you've never liked her much, Laura, but you shouldn't always think the worst of her.'

'And *you* shouldn't always think the best. I'm telling you, Fliss, she looked . . . shifty. She's *after* him.'

'Look, I *know* Chantal – and it's fine. The reason they were there together is because they'd just had another meeting about this mysterious "invention" of Hugh's – and he's now told me what it is.'

'Really?'

'Yes. The patent application's been registered, so they can talk about it.'

'So what is it then?'

'Well . . . it's a baby thing. You know how I'm always

complaining that I never have a muslin to hand when I need one?'

I gazed at her posset-spattered t-shirt. 'Yes.'

'And how when I *do*, the damn thing always slips off?'

'Yes.'

'Well this is what gave Hugh the idea. What he's come up with is a burping bib – but it's not a loose cloth, like a muslin, it's attached. It consists of a piece of pvc-lined flannel – it goes over the front and back *here*, so that you're completely protected – but it's shaped so that it sort of goes round *here* and then down . . . *here* . . .' She was gesturing, awkwardly, by her left shoulder. 'Actually, it's easier if I demonstrate on you.' Fliss leaned forward, touched my left shoulder, then ran her fingers down it, just brushing against my breast. 'It tapers under the arm, *here* . . . where it either ties, or is fixed with Velcro, and there'd be a hook or something *here* –' she touched my neck – 'so that it could be securely attached to the collar.'

'You just touched my breast,' I said.

'Sorry,' she said.

'No – it's not a complaint. I've just realized something.'

'What?'

'Well, I think *that* may be why I thought that Hugh was groping Chantal.' I cast my mind back to that evening at Julie's. 'He and Chantal were obviously discussing the bib thing . . .'

'They *were* – as I said, that's why they were there. Chantal's done all the patent work on it, which involves a very detailed technical description, so she had to know exactly how it worked, and how it fitted.'

'And Hugh was simply explaining it to her?'

'Yes.'

'*Ah.*' I realized that I might have been totally unfair. I replayed the scene in my mind again. Then again. I *had* been unfair. I felt a pang of guilt. 'So *that* was what he was doing.'

There was a perfectly innocent explanation! 'But I still think they looked suspiciously happy.'

'They were happy,' Fliss said. 'But only because they think the bib is a real possibility. I'd kept telling Hugh to invent something that we really need, and I think this may be it. With this there'd be no more hunting for muslins, or wiping off baby sick. The bibs would be sold in a packet of five, and the idea is that you just put one on in the morning, then replace it as needed, putting the used ones in the wash. I think it's a good idea.'

'It is – good old Hugh.'

'Yes – he might even make us some cash. He and Chantal are quite excited about it – she's putting some money in to develop it properly – although it could take a long time to come good, and we're down to our last few grand. But, luckily,' she went on, 'Olivia got the Coochisoft ad – didn'toomy-cleverbaby? – so that should keep us going for another month or so – and then she's got those two TV castings at the end of this week so I'm holding out for one of those, and that'll be three thousand at least because of syndication rights . . .'

Then Fliss told me about all the auditions she was taking Olivia to, and the mums she'd met, and about how nauseatingly competitive they were etc. etc., and then she started droning on about how Olivia had already grown out of the Baby Einstein videos and had graduated to *The Fimbles* and was 'obviously' following the stories, even though it's aimed at two to four year olds, so I was relieved when my mobile went. It was Darren Sillitoe phoning me again to see whether I'd made a decision about the interview.

'I *can* understand why you're hesitating,' he said. 'But I just wanted to let you know that my editor has given me an undertaking that if you *do* agree, not only will we make a donation to the National Missing Persons' Helpline, we'll actually make it our chosen charity for our Christmas Appeal this year.'

'Really?'

'And as we have a readership of over two million, that would bring in a lot of money – at least two hundred thousand. Possibly more.'

I thought of how supportive the charity had been to me when I was in the depths of despair. I thought of my case-manager, Trish, who had phoned me three times a day for those terrible first four months when I hadn't known whether Nick was even alive.

'Think what two hundred thousand pounds could do,' I heard Darren say. His voice was low and soft. Almost tranquillizing.

'Well . . .' It would be selfish of me not to do it plus, yes, I *did* want to put the record straight. I *did* want to correct all the rubbish and lies. 'All right then,' I said. 'I *will*. But only if you put it in writing that I will have copy approval.'

'Yes, of course I'll do that,' he said.

The next morning I went up to Tom's office to tell him about the *Semaphore* interview. He was reading the paper, and smoking a rare cigarette.

'Tom?' He looked up. 'Good God!' I exclaimed. 'What's happened to *you*?' He looked as though he'd skied into a large rock. The entire socket of his right eye was the colour of a damson, with a glowing yellow corona. Through the swollen lids you could just see the watery blue of his iris.

'Oh.' He gingerly tapped his temple. 'I had the pleasure of meeting Gina's ex properly last night.' He stubbed out the cigarette. 'He's a charming guy.'

'So I see. What *happened*?'

'He turned up at midnight, drunk as a monkey. He was just trying to see if I was there. Gina had left the chain off and he managed to force his way in, so I politely suggested he should leave. He didn't like it.'

'Was there a fight?'

Tom shook his head. 'He just launched himself at me, socked me in the eye, then left muttering that the next time he found me there he'd kill me.'

'Did you call the police?'

'No. Because if it went to court he'd have a record, which would hardly help Gina – or Sam, poor little boy. But he'd better not try it again. It's embarrassing though, because I'll be in Cannes next week and I don't want everyone thinking I've been brawling. I'll have to wear sunglasses.'

'Well they'll all be wearing sunglasses, so I wouldn't worry – anyway it'll be much better by then.'

'And how's *your* ex?' he asked. 'I mean, Luke's.' I told him about the kimono. His good eye widened in horror, then he shook his head. 'So she's a Scissor Sister.'

I smiled wearily. 'It was vile. But a couple of days later we sat down to tea and now the plan is that we're all going to become best friends and live happily ever after.'

'Really?'

'Maybe,' I laughed. 'I don't know. That's what Luke wants.'

'It's a perfectly honourable objective.'

'But I'm not sure it's achievable. The problem is that Luke's got these friends who are desperately civilized about it all – Sunday lunch together, shared Christmases, that kind of thing – in other words, the dream scenario – and he wants *us* to be like that too. He's got this fantasy of the perfect blended family; but I suspect that Magda's idea of blending me into her family would involve a large Magimix. Anyway, I wanted you to know that I'm going to go on the record with the press. I've just agreed to an interview in the *Sunday Semaphore* because I can't stand this tabloid crap about me *any* longer.'

'Well, I think that's a good move. As long as the journalist's kosher.'

'He seems sympathetic. His name's Darren Sillitoe.'

Tom shook his head. 'Never heard of him.'

'Nor had I – but we had a good rapport over the phone.'

'Check him out with Channel Four first.'

'I might do, but I feel fine about it because I managed to get copy approval. He's just put it in an e-mail.'

'Then there's no downside – you might as well go for it.'

The interview was the following Thursday afternoon. I'd thought Darren would want to meet me in a club or hotel, but he'd said that I'd appear more sympathetic if I was interviewed at home rather than in some glamorous eatery. I was touched by his concern that I should come across well. The Channel Four Press Officer had asked me if I'd like her to be there, but I said I felt I'd be fine on my own.

The photographer arrived first and quickly fired off two rolls of film.

'Don't you want me to smile?' I asked him as he pointed the lens at me.

'Not really – the journalist said they're looking for "gravitas". That's it. Just nicely serious . . .'

At four-thirty the buzzer went again, and there was Darren. He'd sounded fortyish over the phone, but looked twenty-five. He was tall, bespectacled, and slightly weedy – his schoolboyish appearance being in stark contrast to his confident, urbane voice.

'How long have you been a journalist?' I asked him as I made him some coffee.

'About a year and a half.'

'Do you take milk?'

'Cream, if you've got it. And I don't suppose you've got a biscuit have you?'

'Sure.'

'I missed lunch.'

'Well would you like a sandwich? I could make you one.'

He shook his head, so I put some chocolate digestives on to

247

a plate. 'And what were you doing before?' I asked him as I put it all on a tray.

'I worked in the City. Then I went into venture capital. But I thought journalism would be more fun.'

'And is it?

'On the whole, yes.'

I asked him who else he'd interviewed, and he said that he'd been doing stuff for the sports pages and that this would be his first major profile for the feature pages. So that was why his name hadn't meant anything – plus I rarely read the *Semaphore*.

As we sat in the sitting room he said he'd like to have a brief off-the-record chat with me first, and would only switch on the tape recorder when we were both ready to start. He expressed surprise that I lived in such an ordinary little street, given the huge success of the quiz. I explained that I'd been unable to move.

'Would you *like* to upgrade from Ladbroke Grove?'

'I don't know how about "upgrade", but I'd leave it like a shot. Not because I don't like the area – it's marvellously cosmopolitan – but because it's got bad vibes for me now for obvious reasons.' He nodded sympathetically. 'Plus my neighbours drive me nuts.'

'Why's that?'

'Because of the gossip – it's a small, curtain-twitching sort of street. They're nice people, but I would love to live somewhere where I can be a bit more anonymous.'

'There's not much evidence of your husband about the place is there?' he said glancing around.

'I put all his stuff away. I couldn't bear seeing it any longer.'

'You wanted to wipe the memories?'

'No – but it was time to move on, and the physical reminders that he had lived here were holding me back emotionally.'

'I understand. So it must have been a relief.'

'It was. It was liberating actually, although it made me feel a bit ruthless; but I needed to try and free myself from the past.'

Darren quickly ran through his list of questions with me, and asked me to give him a rough idea of what I'd say to each. First of all, he wanted to know how the quiz came about, and about what makes a quiz work; then he wanted to know what I thought of the other quizmasters – Anne Robinson, for example. I said that I wouldn't be answering that question as I wasn't really a fan and didn't wish to say anything negative.

'I agree,' he said. '*The Weakest Link is* pretty dire, isn't it?'

'Well . . . it's just that the questions are rather low-grade. But it's still very popular, so she's obviously doing something right.'

'And what do you think of Jeremy Paxman?'

'Well, he *can* seem overbearing and impatient, but at the same time he has this humorous authority which I find very appealing, and of course he's terribly clever, so . . . no, I don't mind talking about him.'

'The one *I* can't stand,' he suddenly confided, 'is Robert Robinson on *Brain of Britain*. He's pretty grim – don't you agree?'

'Well . . . I must say, I do rather.'

'His naked astonishment when a female contestant gets a correct answer!'

'I know,' I giggled.

'Oh well *done*, Mrs Smith! That is the *right* answer! How in*credible*!'

I rolled my eyes in agreement. 'To be honest I can't listen to it, otherwise I'd have to chuck the radio out of the window.'

We chatted in this light-hearted vein for a bit longer then Darren asked me if I was ready to begin. I nodded. He pressed the red button on the tiny tape recorder and pushed it towards me.

'Right,' he said. 'Here we go then. Your starter for ten . . .'

I'd never been interviewed before, but the Channel Four press officer had advised me to keep my replies short. 'When you feel you've said what *you* want to say, then "zip the lip"', she'd said. '*Don't* try and be "helpful" by filling the gaps – gaps can be traps.' It was sensible advice, but at the same time I recognized that Darren needed good, vivid copy in order to have an interesting article. I decided to strike a balance between a friendly openness and natural circumspection.

He asked me about Cambridge, and about my early career at the BBC and about meeting Tom there, before I went to work for him; then we talked about the quiz, and how I came to present it. He didn't ask me about the other quiz show hosts, which I was relieved about. We talked about Luke and I was able to set the record straight about his personal circumstances and about the timing of our relationship. Then he came on to Nick. I told him about his work for SudanEase, and about our marriage. He asked me why there was so little of his stuff on show.

'I decided to put it all away,' I explained again. 'I'd waited three years and felt it was finally time to move on. I wanted to start *living* again.'

'Who could blame you?' he said. 'Three years is a long time. But could you tell me about the day Nick disappeared? How it all unfolded?'

As Darren sat there, nodding sympathetically, I recounted it in detail, down to the month I'd spent searching for Nick, to the two silent phone calls which I believed had been my last ever contact with him. Once or twice I had to stop and compose myself, but I was proud of the fact that I managed not to break down. I didn't want to be portrayed as a victim.

'What's been the hardest part of it for you, Laura? Apart from Nick's actual absence?'

250

'The false sightings – there were a few of those at the start – and then the milestones have been very hard. When I realized that Nick had been missing for a thousand days, for example – that was very painful; when it was his birthday; or mine, or our anniversary. Our tenth wedding anniversary is coming up in early May so I'm bracing myself for that. Christmas is always hard of course, as is New Year's Day because that's when it happened.'

'When you heard from the Missing Persons' Helpline that Nick was okay, but that he wanted no contact with you, how did that make you feel?'

'Well . . . crushed of course. And terribly hurt.'

'And surprised?'

I stared at him. 'Yes of course. Of course I was surprised. Very surprised.'

Then Darren asked me about the tabloid coverage, and I told him how hard it had been, having to read so many lies about myself.

'Lies – and innuendo,' he added. 'The innuendo that you had . . . I don't know . . . in some way been responsible for your husband going missing.'

I didn't answer for a second. 'That's right.'

'That you might somehow have caused it.'

'Yes. That's been the subtle suggestion in some quarters.'

'But how *could* you have done?'

'I don't know . . . I suppose they think that I might have . . .' I looked out of the window. 'That I treated him badly I suppose . . . or that I hurt him . . . or that I drove him away . . . That's what they've tried to suggest.'

'Is there *any* truth in that?' I felt my face heat up. 'I'm sorry to have to ask you,' he quickly added. 'But I'm only doing it so that you can deny it.' I looked at him.

'There's no truth in it whatsoever,' I said. 'No truth at all.'

'So you don't feel guilty then?' he added quietly.

'Well . . . I *do* feel guilty – but only because anyone in this awful situation *does*. It's natural, because your partner's gone and you don't know where.'

'Or why?'

There was a pause. 'Or why. So you feel . . .' I sighed, 'that you . . . might have let them down in some way. So, yes, of course there's . . . guilt.'

'Even though it's not your fault?'

I felt shame and regret flood my chest. 'Yes.'

'So you sit there wondering whether it was something you said, or did – or failed to do?'

I shifted on my seat and sighed. 'Yes. You pick over your conversations again and again – quite obsessively.'

'If it *was* your fault then –'

My eyes strayed to the skirting board. 'It *wasn't* my fault.'

'But if it *had* been, then how would you feel?'

'How would I feel?' I looked at him. 'Well how would anyone feel? Just . . . awful, of course. Absolutely devastated. But as I say, it wasn't my fault.' I zipped the lip.

'It's funny, isn't it,' Darren went on after a moment, 'that you're a quiz show presenter, and yet here you are with this huge, *un*answered question in your own life.'

'That irony hasn't escaped me,' I said.

'And has the media frenzy taken you aback?'

'Totally. I knew there might be *some* interest in me once the papers got hold of the story, but I never expected that there'd be so much.'

'Can you understand people's curiosity about you?'

'I suppose I can. If it wasn't actually happening to me, I guess *I'd* be curious. If I read that, say, Carol Vorderman's husband had been missing for three years, then every time I saw her on TV or read an article about her, I'd probably wonder where he was and how he'd been living, and what she'd done to try and find him, and whether she'd ever see him again.'

252

'And why he'd gone?' He looked at me. 'Wouldn't you wonder that?'

'Well . . . I don't know . . .'

'Surely you'd wonder what had caused him to do it? What the story was?'

'Perhaps, although . . .'

'You'd wonder what might have gone on between them?'

'Look, it's obviously very complex. People who go missing have all *sorts* of reasons for doing so. Don't they?'

'But they must be unhappy and confused. Was Nick unhappy and confused?'

'I . . . I don't know. I guess . . . yes . . . perhaps . . .'

'Otherwise he wouldn't have done what he did?'

'I suppose not.'

'And *why* do you think he *was* unhappy and confused?'

I stared at Darren. 'I don't . . . know. His father had died not long before. I think that was part of it.'

'But had anything else happened?' *Zip the lip.*

'No. Nothing. Nothing at all. Maybe you could ask me another question now.' There was a slight pause, then Darren asked me a few more things about the quiz, so I told him about the second series which would start in September, and about the programmes we were developing, thanks to the success of *Whadda Ya Know?!!*

'So the company's on quite a roll.'

'Yes. The format for the quiz has just been sold in eight countries – including the States – which means that we can expand. We're currently recruiting new staff, we're having the building refurbished. Trident's doing very well.' I felt a burst of pride.

Darren leaned forward and stopped the tape.

'Well, I think that's it, Laura. Thanks very much. I'm pretty sure I've got enough now and I don't want to keep you.'

'That's okay. And you'll show me the quotes?'

'I will. I'll either fax them to you or read them over the phone.'

'And when do you think that'll be?'

He was rummaging in his briefcase. 'Not for a couple of weeks because we've decided to run it on Sunday May 1st as that coincides with the start of National Missing Persons' Month.'

'Oh that's a *great* idea,' I said. 'It'll help hugely with the fund-raising. I'll let the charity know that's what you're doing.'

I went to show him out, and as I lifted my hand to the latch, the front door was pushed open from the other side, and there was Cynthia, with two bags of shopping.

'Hello Laura,' she said wearily. In the weak sunlight she looked exhausted and suddenly frail. Then, as she noticed Darren, I saw her face redden.

'Cynthia, this is Darren Sillitoe.' She flinched. Then she gave him a tight little smile, unmistakable in its hostility. I saw a look of surprise cross his face.

'Do you know her?' I whispered as she went upstairs.

'No. I've never laid eyes on her.' How curious. On the other hand she can be quite odd.

'Well thanks for coming, Darren. I hope it's not too hard to write up.'

'I don't think it will be.'

As he walked down the steps, I heard Cynthia's door open again.

'Has he gone?' I heard her hiss in a theatrical whisper.

'Yes.' I turned round. 'Why? What's the problem?'

'I'll tell you what the problem is,' she said as she came downstairs. 'The problem *is* – that he's a fucker!'

'I'm sorry?'

'That young man is a fucker,' she repeated vehemently.

'That's a bit rough, Cynthia. He seemed all right to me.'

'Well he *isn't*. None of those fuckers are.' She obviously meant journalists. Her *bêtes noires*. But . . . how did she know he *was* a journalist given that I hadn't told her?

Perhaps there was something to this psychic business after all.

'They are all disingenuous creeps,' she added. 'Darren Sillitoe indeed!'

'Well – that's his *name*, Cynth.'

'It *isn't*. He was lying. His real name's Darren Fucker.' I looked at her non-comprehendingly. '*Fucker*. F, a, r, q, u, h, a, r,' she enunciated contemptuously.

'Oh.'

'And it's a great pity you didn't tell him to Farquh off when you had the chance. So he's just interviewed you has he?'

'Yes.'

'Oh dear.' She was shaking her head. 'Oh *dear*.'

'What do you mean – "oh dear?" He seemed perfectly okay – nice even.'

'He would do,' she said. 'But he *isn't*, he's a little . . .'

'Cynthia,' I said, panic rising in my chest. 'Would you please tell me *what* you're talking about? You've got me *worried*.'

'All right. I *will*. Come with me.'

I followed her upstairs to her flat. It was the first time she'd invited me in. The furniture and furnishings were in good taste but it was clear that, like Cynthia, they'd seen better days. The Chinese brocade on the *chaise longue* was badly frayed, as was the silk shade on her standard lamp. The velvet cushions on her sofa had bald patches, and the fringes on the large Persian rug had been pulled. On the mahogany sideboard were about eight silver frames all containing black and white photos of Cynthia in her younger days. As she made a pot of tea, I glanced at them. She was glamorous enough now, but she had been a true beauty. A British Claudia Cardinale.

'Darren Sillitoe, my *eye*,' she muttered as she brought in the tea tray. 'His real name is Darren *Farquhar*. Sillitoe is his mother's maiden name.'

I felt my stomach turn over. 'How do you know all this?'

'Because . . .' her hand trembled as she lifted the silver pot, 'I know his father. We had a long . . . association.' Suddenly Hans appeared and began winding herself in and out of Cynthia's legs.

'Who *is* his father?'

'Sir John Farquhar.'

'He's a big-shot at the *Sunday Semaphore*, isn't he?'

'He is,' she said acidly as Hans curled herself up in her lap. 'He's the chairman.'

'But then why didn't Darren recognize you if you know his father so well?'

'Because Darren and I have never met. But I've seen many photographs of him. My relationship with his father was . . . unofficial. I was his . . .'

Oh. 'Friend . . . ?' I suggested.

'*Mistress*. I won't mince words. I was his mistress, Laura – for twenty-five years.'

'That's a long time,' I breathed.

'Don't I know it?' she said wearily. She passed me a chintz-patterned china teacup. 'But in many ways I couldn't complain. I had a lovely flat, in Hans Place. I had a gener-ous monthly allowance, and an account at Harrods. I used to go to Marrakech and St Bart's. I sat in the stalls at the Opera House. I dined at the Ritz; I wore couture . . .' So that explained the elegant clothes. 'Of course I longed to be John's wife,' she went on. 'But I told myself that I was his *real* wife. His soul mate.' Her voice had caught. 'That's what he said I was. He said he couldn't do *without* me.' She ran her hands over the cat to try and calm herself.

'How did you meet him?'

'At the royal premiere of *The Spy Who Loved Me* in '77. I was 36, and John was ten years older, a handsome, power-ful man; he'd been a journalist for twenty years, but through clever manoeuvring had managed to get on the board of a number of media companies, including the one which had financed the film. I fell catastrophically in love with him despite – and I am not proud of this – knowing that he was married. But he said that his marriage was loveless and that his wife totally neglected him for their children. Darren, the youngest, was a baby. I suppose that doesn't say much for John does it?' she added with a bitter sigh.

I thought of Tom. 'I don't think it does.'

'Time went on, and John remained with his wife. Whenever I became upset about it he would claim that it was because she was ill, and a divorce might kill her; sometimes he'd say he was waiting until the children were older. It was the old, old story.' She fumbled in the cuff of her silk shirt for a tissue.

'I see. So he never left her then?'

Cynthia looked away while she struggled with her emotions.

'Oh no,' she said bitterly. 'He *did*. That was what was so awful. He *did* finally leave her.' Her mouth quivered again. 'But not for *me*!'

'Oh . . . I'm sorry.' Hans was purring loudly, quite oblivious to Cynthia's distress. So much for inter-species communication.

Cynthia wiped her eyes, then took a deep breath.

'A little over a year ago, John told me that he was going to leave Mary. I was *so* happy to think that my years of living in the shadows were coming to an end. He came to the flat and I cooked him supper, and he told me that she had agreed to a divorce and that the flat in Hans Place would have to be sold. So I asked him where we would live. But he didn't reply.' She fiddled with her crystal beads. 'Then he explained that Mary would get the house in Mayfair, and that he would move to Hampstead. So I said that Hampstead would be wonderful – I didn't mind where we lived, as long as we were together. Then he dropped his bombshell. He said he was sorry, but that he'd fallen in love with someone else – a woman I'd never even *heard* of.'

'Who was she?'

'Some American journalist called Deborah, thirty years his junior, a hard-faced creature, with legs like toothpicks, huge feet and –' she lifted her left hand to her generous décolletage – '*no* breasts.'

I vaguely remembered now seeing Sir John Farquhar in one of the gossip columns with an anorectic, beady-eyed brunette.

'I've seen pictures of her,' she went on tearfully. 'She's not even *pretty*. Not in the way that *I* had been . . .' I glanced at the photo again.

'You were beautiful Cynthia. You still are. Age has not withered you,' I added consolingly.

'I did play Cleopatra once,' she said regretfully. 'I was too young. But my *God*, I could play her *now*. But . . . John ended our relationship.' Her eyes welled up again. 'He told me that I had three months to find somewhere else to live before the lease on Hans Place expired.'

'Didn't he help you, financially?'

'He said he couldn't because his divorce was going to ruin him. It was a lie of course. And I had been with him for so long – *twenty-five years*. I had given up my career because he was so jealous of me being with other men.' So that's why she hadn't wanted to talk about her later film roles. There hadn't been any. 'I had also given up . . .' her eyes had filled again . . .'a respectable family life; the chance of *children*.'

'Did you want them?'

'Yes. Very much. But in those days unmarried motherhood was still very much frowned on, plus I wanted to keep the life I had. So it's my own fault.' She shrugged. 'I know that. For allowing myself to be . . . *kept*, and for believing that I would ultimately be rewarded for my patient devotion. Instead I was flung out like an old dog.'

'How terrible for you.'

258

'It was – in every way. It still is. I had no pension, fool-ishly thinking that I'd be with John for the rest of my life. We had been together so long that I couldn't imagine it ever ending. So there I was, at the age of sixty-three, faced with the prospect of no longer having John, *and* having to make my own living – while he started an entirely new life with a younger woman. Not that I believe it'll last,' she added bitterly.

'But didn't he help you? At least to try and cushion the blow a bit?'

'He gave me a cheque for twenty-five thousand pounds. I wanted to tear it up – it was so insulting – but I knew I'd *need* it; he also said I could keep what was in the flat. The furniture's very good although it's had a lot of wear, as you can see. But I had quite a lot of jewellery that he'd given me over the years, so I sold that, and put the proceeds towards the deposit on this place. But I still had to take out a mort-gage, which is why I became a psychic. I realized it was the only way I could make *any* money.'

So that had been the 'major turning point' in her life that she'd referred to when we'd met.

'Did you consider taking legal action? To try and get more money out of him, or some . . . I don't know . . . settlement?'

'Oh no.' She looked appalled. '*So* undignified. So . . . *mercenary*. I resolved that, however hard it might be, I'd at least keep my pride. But it has been very, very difficult, Laura, enduring both the loss of my relationship, and my "security", as I foolishly saw it.'

'So, in a funny sort of way, you must be grateful that you had that accident on the cliff top that day?' There was a silence. 'Otherwise you might not have become a psychic.'

'It wasn't an accident,' she said quietly. 'The drop was a good twenty-five feet, so I hoped I'd die. But then, when I regained consciousness, and found myself at *real* risk of dying, I realized how much I wanted to *live*. That no man was worth losing my life over.'

'No, of course not.'

'That every day we have on this earth – however hard – is precious. That life is all we've *got*. It's not something to be thrown away in a moment of depression, or discouragement, or fear of the future.'

'It isn't.'

'But since then I have been struggling to adjust to a lifestyle *utterly* different from the one I had been used to while he . . . he . . .' Her eyes were shimmering again. 'The *injustice* of it . . .' Her hands sprang to her face. Now I understood her loathing of 'mendacious, misleading, and morally-bankrupt' journalists. 'But this Darren,' she went on, as she wiped her eyes, 'is a *most* unpleasant young man.'

I felt my stomach clench. 'He seemed okay.'

'He isn't. He does nothing in a meritorious way. He got into Eton on family connections, then strings were pulled to get him into Oxford. But he was thrown out for failing his first year law exams; he'd wanted to change to art history but the college refused because they simply didn't like him. So then he went into banking and flunked at that; then he tried venture capital and failed dismally there. I remember how his father despaired. Then, eighteen months ago, not long before John left me, Darren decided he'd try journalism. But his father made him start right at the bottom, first selling advertising space, then as a junior sub-editor on the sports desk, so he's impatient to make his name. He will not be kind to you in this interview Laura. Let me warn you. He will *not* be kind because he is a complete and utter . . . a complete and *utter* . . .'

'Fucker?' I said dismally.

'Yes.'

TWELVE

The following morning I spoke to the Channel Four press officer, Sue. She looked up Darren's byline and found a number of short pieces by him about horse racing but said that he was *not* on her list of journalists who mustn't be approached without a string of garlic and a Bible. She told me that she would talk to the *Semaphore*, and phoned me back within the hour to say that she had been told that the interview would not be appearing for two weeks.

'If there *is* anything negative, there'll be plenty of time to deal with it,' she said. 'So let's not worry until we see what he's written, but I hope you didn't say anything that could possibly be used against you.'

'No, I didn't. We were both quite clear about what was on the record and what was off it, and I was very careful how I expressed things. There were one or two awkward questions, which I half expected, but I kept my replies short and gave nothing away.'

'Well we'll wait to see the advance copy, but I think it'll be fine.'

On Sunday morning I bought the *Semaphore* so that I could get some idea of how Darren wrote. I looked at the sports section first and saw that he'd done a small piece about golf.

Now I glanced at the review section, where he'd said his interview with me would appear, and got distracted by an article about the Royal Ballet. Then I idly flicked through the main news section. And froze . . .

MY REMORSE was blazoned across the top of page five. Beneath was a huge photo of me, looking mournful.

LAURA QUICK CONFESSES GUILT AT HUSBAND'S DISAPPEARANCE.

It was as though I'd been pushed off a cliff.

An enlarged 'quote' had been placed centre page, in bold: *I treated him badly . . . I hurt him . . . I drove him away.*

Heart pounding, my eyes raked the page.

Troubled TV presenter Laura Quick has spoken exclusively to the Sunday Semaphore about her husband, Nick Little's, disappearance. In this candid interview she reveals that she believes she caused the 'unhappiness' and 'confusion' that led him to go missing three years ago. Interview: Darren Sillitoe.

My hands were shaking and my face was aflame. The piece had gone in immediately, not as a 'soft' feature, but as a hard news piece, as though it was a 'scoop'. Worse, I had been completely stitched up.

The 'off-the-record' preamble had been used *on* the record, and in the most negative way possible, through ruthlessly selective quotation and crude editorializing. My comments about Bonchurch Road, for example, were evidence, apparently, of my 'intolerant streak'.

Quick says that if she could, she would leave Ladbroke Grove 'like a shot', describing it, with a patronizing roll of the eye, as 'marvellously cosmopolitan'. She dislikes the quiet, pleasant little street in which she lives, and is disdainful of her 'curtain-twitching' neighbours who have nothing better to do than 'gossip' about her.

Significantly, her split-level flat contains no reminders of her husband, despite the fact that they were married for six years, because, by her own admission, she 'couldn't stand seeing his stuff any longer – it was holding me back.' Quick goes on to confess that expunging his things was 'liberating' if, admittedly, 'ruthless'.

The piece wasn't so much a hatchet job as a chainsaw job. All qualifying or balancing remarks had been excised to fit a pre-determined portrait of me that was grotesque. Sillitoe had said – what was it? – that he would interview me 'very sensitively and then carefully report' what I said. 'Carefully.' That was the word he'd used, I now realized – not accurately. He'd done it carefully all right, filleting my quotes with a boning knife, then plunging it into my back.

As for her relationship with old flame Luke North, Quick claims that his wife had left him 'ten months' before she met him again . . . I didn't 'claim' that he had. I stated that he had, because it was a factual truth. The word 'claim' was intended to sow doubt.

We begin to talk about Whadda Ya Know?!! To my astonishment, Quick is soon happily dissing rival quiz presenters. Anne Robinson, for example, is dismissed as 'low grade'; Jeremy Paxman is 'overbearing and impatient'; as for poor Robert Robinson, affable presenter of Brain of Britain, Quick finds him so 'grim' that she claims to be unable to listen to the popular Radio 4 quiz in case she has to 'chuck the radio out of the window'. She may be a newcomer, but it soon becomes clear that Laura Quick is not one to mince her words about more established talents.

Now I remembered, with a sick, sick feeling, how nice Darren had seemed, and how concerned, touchingly, that I should come across well. But his agenda had clearly been to effect the opposite. Even my struggle not to cry had been made to look like a lack of feeling. *When it comes to discussing the day her husband disappeared, Quick remains curiously dry-eyed. I expect the tears to flow, and they don't.*

I had been worried that Darren would make me look like a victim; but he'd done the opposite – he'd portrayed me as a heartless bitch; one, moreover, with a fragile conscience. This was clearly the point of the piece.

When I ask Quick – who admits to being 'difficult and demanding' – why her husband might have felt compelled to leave, Quick bridles. The famous inquisitor may cope with having the tables turned on her on Whadda Ya Know?!! but, in real life, she clearly objects. Her repeated, clumsy assertions that her husband's departure was not her fault smack of the lady protesting too much. And so it seems. For, finally, under gentle but persistent questioning, she breaks down. 'Yes . . . I do feel guilty,' she confesses tearfully. 'Very. Of course I do . . . I treated him badly . . . I hurt him . . . I drove him away . . . I feel just awful . . . absolutely devastated . . .'

I got to the end, my stomach dry-heaving with speechless outrage, my mouth as dry as dust. Sillitoe had planned it all along. Even the unsmiling picture of me had been premeditated. He'd told the photographer that he wanted me to look serious. But it wasn't 'gravitas' he was after, but 'guilt'. He had manipulated me into making unguarded comments, off the record, which he had fully intended to use. Not only had he used them, he had wilfully distorted them. The fact that it was in my 'own words' made it so much worse.

I banged on Cynthia's door.

'The. Little. *Shit*,' she breathed as she read it. She pursed her mouth, then lowered her reading glasses. '*Now* do you see what I mean?'

'*Yes*,' I croaked. 'But why did he *do* this? What have I ever done to *him*?'

'Nothing. But that's not the point.'

'Then what *is*?'

'The point is that he's desperate to make a name for himself. This is *so* nasty that he knows it will get him talked about and make him appear "controversial" – rather than dull and insignificant. As he hasn't the talent to do it honestly, he has to go about it in an underhand way.'

I soon discovered how underhand he'd been. On Monday the head of the Channel Four press office complained to the *Semaphore*'s editor but I decided I'd speak to Darren myself. The staff on Sunday newspapers get Mondays off, so the next morning I called his direct line.

'Darren Sillitoe speaking.' He sounded nauseatingly pleased with himself. I imagined the spring in his step as he'd gone in to work, smugly anticipating congratulatory comments from his colleagues.

'This is Laura Quick.' There was a tiny hesitation.

'What can I do for you?' he enquired impertinently.

'I'll tell you what you can do, Darren. First, you can explain why your piece went in two weeks early.'

'Well . . . a . . . news piece got pulled at the last minute, and as I'd already written up your interview they used it to plug the gap.'

'Really?'

'Really,' he said indolently.

'Then why didn't you fax me the quotes?'

'Well, in the circumstances I'm afraid there wasn't time.'

'I don't believe you.'

'You're not calling me a liar, are you?'

'Yes. I am. Because you planned to run the piece when you did. That's why you'd already written it up. You planned to run it as a news piece, not a feature. And you were never going to read me the quotes. That's all obvious to me now.'

'You can believe what you like – I don't care.'

'Well *I* care that you wrote such mendacious, malice-filled crap! *I* care that you lied *to* me, and *about* me.'

'I made nothing up. You *did* say those things.'

'But you know I didn't say them like *that*! You hacked the quotes about to make them mean the *opposite* of what you knew I'd intended.'

'It was a matter of . . . interpretation. I was reading between the lines.'

'So I was left reading between your *lies*. I mean, who would describe themselves as "difficult and demanding"? *No-one* would, and *I* didn't.'

'Well you're certainly being difficult now.'

'No, I'm not being "difficult" – I'm being justifiably angry. I don't even know where you *got* that quote. I never said to you, "I am difficult and demanding".'

'Yes you did. You used those very words.'

'When?'

'When we first spoke. On the phone.'

'I didn't.'

'Yes you did. I have it on tape.'

'You what?'

'I have it on tape,' he repeated calmly.

It was like a punch to the solar plexus. 'You were *recording* me?'

'Yes.'

'From the moment I picked up the *phone*?'

'Correct,' he said shamelessly.

'But . . . that's illegal.'

'No. How many times when you phone a business do you hear the automated voice telling you that the call may be recorded for training purposes etcetera?'

I felt my jaw open, then close, in impotent, mute protest. 'But the point *is* they *tell* you that *first*. You *know* you're being recorded. They don't record the conversation *covertly*, like *you* did, Darren, like some fifth rate little spy.'

'Insult me if you like,' he said airily, 'but what I did isn't illegal.'

'But it *is* unethical. How . . . *low*.'

'I always record. I recorded everything you said.'

'No you didn't. Your machine was switched off for the first twenty minutes of the interview. Then you turned it on. I saw you do it.'

'I recorded *everything*,' he repeated. 'So that there could be no dispute later.'

'But I don't . . . understand, I . . . Oh . . . I *see*,' I said quietly. 'You had another tape recorder running.' There was silence. 'In your pocket or your bag. How . . . *underhand*.' He didn't reply. 'But the first part of our conversation was *off* the record. We discussed it and you assured me that it was *off the record*, remember?'

'There is no such thing as "off the record",' he said pleasantly.

I felt my mouth gape. 'If you have *any* integrity there *is*. And I repeat that I did *not* say that I am "difficult and demanding" – I said that *that* was one of the tabloid lies. Nor did I say . . .' I stabbed the paper with my finger '. . . that "I treated Nick badly . . . I hurt him . . ." etcetera . . . I said that that is what the *tabloids* had tried to *imply*. But you deliberately attributed those quotes to me to . . . to . . . make out that I blame myself for my husband leaving. I do not.'

'But you *do* blame yourself. Don't you?'

'No, I don't, I *don't*. I –'

'It was obvious to me that you do. I could see how uncomfortable you were with that question so it was my duty, as a journalist, to report that. I'm sorry you're disappointed with the piece but, as we're both busy people, may I suggest this concludes our conversation?'

'No Warren, you may *not*, because I haven't fin –'

But the receiver had already gone down.

My attempt to set the record straight had left it as twisted as a bagful of snakes. How naïve I'd been to think that I'd be better off talking to a broadsheet newspaper than a tabloid. It had been far, far worse.

'The *News of the World* would have behaved more decently,' I said to Hope when I finally managed to speak to her on her mobile, late that afternoon.

'Quite possibly,' she replied. 'But the piece was so vile, it was obvious that this Warren . . . Silly*arse,* or whatever his name is, had an agenda against you. And it was quite clear he'd taken everything out of context because none of your so-called "quotes" were longer than three words – you could see his saw marks all over them. It was crap journalism.' In the background I could hear traffic. I wondered where she was.

'You only noticed that because you're in PR. Most people who read it will think I *did* say those things.' I felt sick as I thought of it again. 'I haven't eaten since Sunday. I've hardly slept. I've had to send flowers to my neighbours and letters of apology to Anne Robinson, Jeremy Paxman and Robert Robinson, God help me.'

'Sillitoe's an earthworm,' Hope said.

'Wrong. An earthworm has ten hearts – he has none. I mean, there he was, sitting in my flat being pleasant to me, while I fixed him coffee with cream – he actually asked for *cream*, can you believe – *and* chocolate biscuits – he asked for those too – knowing, all the time, that his second tape recorder was quietly whirring away.'

'It's vile,' Hope repeated. 'Pure entrapment and deliberate misrepresentation. So. Are you going to take action of any kind?' She was slightly out of breath now, as though she was hurrying to get somewhere.

I groaned. 'I don't know. I've taken advice from Channel Four but it's *very* difficult. This is what newspapers rely on because they know that most people won't sue because the costs are so high and the damages so low. Not to mention the stress. And if you start something, and then drop it, *that* becomes the story: "Quiz Presenter Drops Libel Action – *Semaphore* vindicated".'

'But I'd say you'd have a very good case.' She lowered her voice. 'I mean, that awful bit where he made out that it was your fault that Nick went missing and that you'd basically caused his breakdown – *that's* your libel, isn't it?'

'Hm.'

268

'Although . . .'

'Although what?'

'Well I suppose in order to refute it in court, you'd have to have a statement from Nick to say it wasn't true.'

'Yes, I . . . suppose I would.'

'And let's face it, you're not going to get *that* are you?'

I stiffened. 'Why not?'

'Well . . . because Nick isn't *around*.'

I sighed with relief. I hadn't been thinking straight. 'Of course.'

'But you should discuss what to do with Tom.'

'I can't – he came back from Cannes on Friday, then he had to go to Montreal for a few days for his Dad's seventieth and I don't want to bother him with it when he's on leave.'

'Anyway, can we talk about this another time, Laura? I've got to turn off my mobile now.'

'Where are you then? At the tube?'

'No. St Thomas's.'

'Really? Why? What are you doing?'

'I'm meeting Mike here.'

I glanced at my watch. 'But it's only 6.30. He doesn't finish until nine.'

'I'm doing the cuddling programme with him.'

'You are?'

'They vetted me last week. I start tonight.'

'Gosh – that's nice.'

'Well . . . . regardless of what's happening with Mike and me, I decided I'd like to do it too.'

'That's good. But . . . why?'

'To . . . I don't know . . . keep him company, I suppose. He's walking a new baby tonight – a little boy. And then I don't do enough for other people. I give money to charity and all that,' she added. 'I go to lots of fund-raising events – but I've never done anything hands-on, have I?'

269

'Well, cuddling a baby is about as hands-on as it gets.'

'And it's so easy, Laura. Just walking up and down with a little baby for a couple of hours. The poor little things,' she added. 'The poor little . . .' I heard her voice catch. 'It's so awful to think of them suffering like that before their lives have even started.'

'Yes it is – but at least they do get well. But it's wonderful that you're doing it too.'

'You know what my real reason is though, don't you?'

'Erm. No.'

'Can't you guess?'

'Well . . .'

'My *real* reason . . .'

'Yes?'

'Is that I see it as my penance, for having been such a suspicious cow.'

'Oh.' I felt disappointed. 'I see.'

'Poor Mike,' I heard her say.

'But he *was* behaving suspiciously. He didn't tell you what he was doing – and you couldn't have guessed.'

'That's true. Anyway I'd better get up there, Laura. I don't want to be late on my first evening. Chin up. And try not to worry about the *Semaphore* – the whole thing just looked fishy – and I imagine you're getting lots of support from Luke.'

Luke was being supportive, up to a point. He was outraged by Darren's piece, but apart from expressing the desire to tear him limb from limb he didn't talk about it much because he was worrying about his trip to Venice. He was convinced that Magda would try to kibosh it at the last minute.

'I can just imagine what she'll do,' he said as he sketched me sitting in his tiny conservatory the next afternoon. 'Keep still, will you?'

'Sorry.' I could hear the soft scrape of his pencil across the pad.

'The day before we're due to leave, she'll say that she thinks it's a bad idea for Jessica to go, or she'll suddenly remember something she'd got planned for her here – or she'll decide that Jessica's not well enough, or she'll pretend she can't find her passport. *Please* don't fidget. And can you relax your features a bit?'

'No, I can't. I've had too much stress. I feel as though my face has been reverse-Botoxed into a permanent frown.'

'I'm sorry,' he said.

'I'm sure Magda will be fine,' I went on. 'Things are obviously going well with Steve which is why she's behaving in such a benign way.'

She still phoned Luke fifty times a day, but the difference now was that most of her calls were to have cosy little chats with him, rather than to rant.

'Give me a rrrrink,' we'd hear her say, very sweetly, on the answerphone. 'I'd love to have a little word with you, Luke . . .'

So he would dutifully phone back, and she'd ask him whatever it was, but although she was being reasonable, she couldn't resist turning the conversation round to how happy she was with Steve, and how well it was going, and how successful/attractive/reliable and charming to goats he was etcetera, etcetera. Luke habitually had the phone on speaker, so I always got to hear.

'Steve is such a *kind* man,' she'd say. 'I feel I've really fallen on my feet – at *last*.'

'I'm so glad you're happy,' Luke would say calmly.

'Oh I *am* thank you Luke. I'm *very* happy. Steve's a *wonderful* man.'

'I'm *delighted* to know that, Magda,' he'd say. 'You deserve *no* less and I *couldn't* be happier for you.'

'He's invited me to his mother's wedding.'

'How nice,' he said indolently.

'It's next weekend.'

'Oh. Well that *is* good news,' he said, visibly brightening. 'Next weekend?'

'Yes. There's going to be a huge family party on the Saturday night – black tie.'

As Luke put the phone down he grinned. '*Great.* That means she won't monkey about with my trip to Venice. Steve, *I* love you too,' he smirked. 'You gorgeous man, you.'

'And where in Venice will you stay?'

'At the Hotel Danieli. It's a restored palace near St Mark's Square.'

'How lovely. So have you stayed there before?'

There was a flicker of hesitation. 'I have actually.'

'When?'

'On our honeymoon.'

'I see. So you must have happy memories of it.'

'Well, we *were* happy then, that's true. Not that it lasted long,' he added balefully. 'Anyway, it's a beautiful hotel – very expensive, but I want to spoil Jess.'

'It sounds blissful,' I said wistfully. I glanced at his sketch of me. I looked sad and anxious.

'I wish you were coming too, Laura, but it'll be my first holiday with Jess on my own.'

'It's okay. You don't have to explain.'

'But we *will* go on holiday together soon. After Venice everything will change. And as Magda's talking about taking Jessica away in the summer with her and Steve, she can hardly object to my doing the same with you can she?'

'No – but she probably will.'

'We'll go somewhere lovely,' he went on happily. 'Maybe Crete. Would you like that?'

'No,' I said. He looked surprised. 'I mean yes – but not Crete.'

'What have you got against Crete?'

'That's where Nick and I had our last holiday.'

'Oh I see. Bad vibes then?'

272

'Sad vibes. That's when *we* were last happy.' And with good reason. But within a month everything had changed. His father fell ill, and then died, and from then on things spiralled downwards, culminating in our nightmare before Christmas, and its continuing aftermath.

'How about Corsica?' I heard Luke say.

That Friday, Tom returned from Canada – his black eye now faded to a lemony yellow – and filed a formal complaint about Darren Sillitoe to the Press Complaints Commission.

'Paragraph Ten of the PCC Code forbids the covert use of "clandestine listening devices,"' he said, showing me a copy of the letter. 'So I've based the complaint on that.'

'And what about the deliberate inaccuracies?'

'That's harder.'

'But they were outrageous.'

'I know. But the Code allows the selection of the material for publication to be a matter of "editorial discretion". I'm sorry I encouraged you to do the interview now,' he added. 'But none of us could have known.'

Except Cynthia, I thought ruefully.

'What about his e-mail saying I'd have copy approval?'

'I asked the Channel Four lawyers about that and apparently it's not enforceable – there are ways round it.'

'I see. But he's defamed me, Tom.'

'Yes. But do you *really* want to start legal action? It would inevitably focus on your *marriage*, Laura. Who of us would want that?'

'He's libelled me, Tom. He's reduced my standing in the eyes of others.'

'You may have to live with the injustice of it. I'll do my best to get some sort of apology through the PCC, but don't even think about litigation because you will end up bankrupt – and stark, staring mad. Any kind of legal proceedings are just . . . awful,' he added. He was obviously thinking of his divorce. 'Anyway, can I change the subject, Laura, because there's something *very* serious I need to ask you . . .'

'Really? What?'

He swung a book of carpet samples on to his desk. 'Which one of these do you like? The refurb's being done next weekend, so we've got to choose today. They're all in stock, apparently, but you can decide.'

I flipped them over, then stopped at a green speckly one.

'This one,' I said. 'Green's restful – which is exactly what I need after all the shite I've had to deal with.'

'Okay – and here are the paint cards.' I flicked through the colour tiles, held them up to the scuffed-looking walls and picked out something complimentary. 'This guy I know, Arnie, is going to do it,' Tom went on. 'He's given me a good price, but he's incredibly busy, so he wants to get it done on the bank holiday Monday. Dylan and I are going to shift the stuff the day before.'

'And how was Canada?'

'It was okay,' he said absently. 'Stressful though.'

I wondered why. Perhaps he'd seen his little boy and it had disturbed him – or perhaps he'd *wanted* to see him, and his ex-wife hadn't let him. I was curious, but couldn't possibly ask. Although he'd confided in me about Gina, his failed marriage has always been off limits. Not that I'd have known what to say. *Sorry to hear you've left your newly delivered wife for another woman, Tom. Sorry to hear that you've let down your baby son. Sorry to know that you won't get to see much of him now, if anything. Sorry that you really screwed up.*

'How's Luke?' he said suddenly.

'Oh . . . he's fine.'

'And the ex? How's she?'

'Okay. Things are going well with her man at the moment, so that's good news for us.'

Later that night, as Luke and I were watching Channel Four News, the phone went.

'Luke?' I heard Magda sniff. The loudspeaker was on, as usual.

'Hi,' he replied. 'I was just about to call you, to say good-night to Jess.' We heard another sniff. 'You sound as though you've got a bit of a cold there.'

'Uh-uh-uh . . .'

'*Magda?*' She didn't have a cold. She was crying. 'What's the *matter*, Magda?'

There was a stifled sob. 'Oh Go-od-od,' she said. 'It's so – uh-uh – awful.'

'What is?' said Luke.

'Somethink terrible's happened.'

'*Jessica?*'

'No, no, no, nothing to do with Jessica,'

Luke clapped hand to his chest. '*What* then?' He was blink-ing in bewilderment.

'It's just *so* terrible. It's Steve uh-uh . . .'

'What's happened?'

'Uh-uh-uh-uh . . .'

'*What's* happened to him?'

'Uh-uh-uh. I can't say it.'

'Will you please just *tell* me, Magda.'

'Steve's d – uh-uh-uh.'

He's dead, I thought, with an equanimity which surprised me. She's trying to say the words, 'Steve's dead', and she can't. I had visions of him plastered all over the M25, or collapsing at the eighteenth hole. Or perhaps he'd been tram-pled to death by Yogi. I braced myself.

'Steve's d-d-d – uh-uh-uh – d-d-d . . .'

'Dead?' whispered Luke, horror twisting his features. 'Are you saying that Steve's *dead?*'

'No! I wish he *was*! Steve's d-d-d – *dumped* me!' she wailed.

THIRTEEN

'It couldn't have come at a worse time,' Luke groaned, when he put the phone down an hour later. 'Why the hell did he have to do it *now*?'

I mentally replayed the conversation in my head. Magda had said she'd just been to Harvey Nichols to buy something to wear for his mother's wedding, and how she'd spent £200 on a new dress; and how she'd been on her way back to Chiswick in a cab, when Steve had called her.

'So I began tellink him about the new frock I'd just bought,' she'd explained between teary gasps. 'And about how much I was lookink forward to meetink his family and about the – uh-uh-uh – lovely present I'd got for his mum. Then there was this awkward pause, and he said that he was very sorry – uh-uh – but that he didn't think I should – uh-uh-uh – go after *all* . . .'

'How awful for you,' Luke had said sympathetically. 'So he invites you, then uninvites you. *Why*?'

'He said – uh-uh – that he feels it would be unfair to introduce me to his entire fam-uh-uh-ily, when he doesn't think it's goink to work out.'

Poor Magda, I thought. Especially as she'd thought it was going so well.

'And what reason, precisely, did he give?' Luke asked, evincing all the indignation of an outraged father. I half expected to see him reach for a horsewhip.

'He said – uh-uh – that he felt that we were – uh-uh – fundamentally incompatible. He said he found me very – uh-uh – attractive and charmink . . .'

'You are,' said Luke indignantly. '*Everyone* says so.'

'Thank you,' she sniffed. 'But he said that he didn't feel – uh-uh – that I was . . . *right* for him. But I *am* right for him,' she wept. 'Of course I *am*. I mean, I'd just spent *£80* on a *very* nice present for his mother when I don't even *like* her.'

'Of course you're right for him,' said Luke crossly. 'The man's a *fool*!' I didn't know whether this was genuine spousal loyalty, or irritation at the potential impact this would have on him.

'He said – uh-uh – he'd been tryink to find the right way to say it for weeks.'

'It's got nothing to do with his work has it?' Luke asked her. 'That client of his that you had that little disagreement with?'

There was a pause. 'Which one?'

'The one you called an idiot?'

'Oh, no, it's got *nothink* to do with that,' she wept. 'That horrrrrible little man's gone to another firm now so no, *that's* not the reason.'

Luke rolled his eyes.

'Is dumping her Steve's revenge then?' I asked as we absorbed it all a few moments later.

Luke shook his head. 'No. He'd liked her – he must have done to have stuck with her this long – but he obviously realized that she was too high risk. A man like that wants a well-behaved, corporate wife, and that's not Magda – but this is *very* bad news for me.'

'Do you think she'll still let Jessica go to Venice?'

He gave a defeated sigh. 'No. She'll be so miserable that she'll want her at home.'

'Poor Jessica,' I said. At one point we'd heard her say, 'Don't cry, Mummy. *I'll* look after you. *Please* don't cry Mummy . . .' It was heartbreaking.

I kept expecting to hear that Venice was off. I even wondered, guiltily, whether, if Jessica couldn't go, Luke would take me instead. But as the days went by, nothing was said. Magda phoned up just as much, but Luke didn't put the speaker on any more as he said he thought it unfair to her, in her distressed state.

'So it's still happening then is it?' I asked him on the Wednesday, two days before he was due to go. We were watching the quiz. The commercial break had just started.

'Yes,' he said. 'It is.'

'Magda's letting you take Jessica?' He nodded. 'Do you think she'll put a spanner in the works at the last minute?'

'No. I . . . don't think so.' He seemed slightly on edge. He was obviously still worried that she might do exactly that.

'Well, it's good that she's not being selfish about it – especially as she's so unhappy.' I felt a surge of respect for her, which took me aback.

'I've got something for you,' Luke said.

'Really? What?'

He reached behind the sofa, and pulled out a carrier bag, on which was printed *Georgina von Etzdorf*. Inside was a silk dressing gown, of exquisite loveliness, with a pattern of pink tulips.

'Thank you.' I kissed him. 'It's beautiful.' I put it on.

'Well, it was the least I could do. I meant to get one for you before, but I've been too busy.'

'I love it, and I'll cherish it.' I slipped my arm through his. 'So tell me again how long you'll be away?'

'Four days. Luckily the school's closed on the Friday for teacher training, which gives us an extra day, and we'll be back on Monday night.'

'And when's the wedding?'

278

'On Saturday afternoon.'

'And where are you staying again?' He looked at me. 'It's just that I'd like the phone number there. You said it was called the Hotel . . . what was it? I can't remember.'

'Well . . . I'll have my mobile on. Hey, the quiz is starting again.' We stared at the screen.

Where, after the fall of France, in June 1940, were the headquarters of the French state located?

'Vichy!' shouted Luke.

Correct.

I didn't see Luke again before he left for Venice, because Jessica was staying the night with him. I phoned him at Heathrow as they waited to board.

'Is Jessica excited?'

'Yes, she is. Aren't you darling?' he called. 'Jessica!'

'Yes,' I heard her reply, a little way off. 'I'm *so* excited!' I was glad that, apart from seeing Venice, she'd have a break from her mother's misery.

'What time will you get there?'

'About two, and we'll check into the hotel then go exploring.' *Bing-Bong.* 'The flight's being called – I'll ring you later.'

I missed Luke, but I was happy for him as I visualised the two of them, floating along the lagoon on a gondola, or taking the Vaporetta. I imagined Jessica's face as she saw the canals and churches and palaces and paintings. I imagined her listening to Luke as he told her a little bit about Georgione, Titian and Veronese. She was just old enough to appreciate the trip.

Luke and I spoke briefly that night – they'd been to Murano, to see the glass blowing – and he rang me at breakfast time the next day. Then they were going to be at the wedding, so I didn't ring him again. But by eight I thought it would be nice to speak to him, but his mobile was switched off, so, to distract myself, I turned on the TV. A drama about

Gallipoli had just started, scheduled, according to the paper, for its 90th anniversary. There was a scene in a field hospital, and I suddenly saw Tara McLeod. She was playing the female lead – a nurse who falls in love with a wounded officer, but he's married with a baby so they can't do anything about it. It was the reverse of what had happened in real life. As the final credits rolled, I wondered whether Tom had been watching it too, and how he might have felt.

By now it was ten. I'd heard nothing from Luke all day and was beginning to feel anxious. I dialled his number. He'd still be awake.

'This is Luke North. I'm sorry I can't speak to you, but if you leave me a message . . .' I hate answerphones, so I didn't.

I slept badly, and woke early. I glanced at the alarm – it was ten past seven – ten past eight there. Ten minutes later I dialled him again, but he still wasn't answering. I wished I had the number for the hotel so that I could try him in his room before he and Jess went out for the day. What was it called again? The Hotel . . . *Danieli*. That was it. I got the number from directory enquiries. There were three long beeps as it rang.

'Pronto . . .'

As I drew back the curtains, I asked to speak to Luke North. No, I didn't know what his room number was. Mr Luke North from London.

'Luca North. I 'ave it now,' the receptionist said. 'Signor and Signora North.' Signor*ina* North, I mentally corrected him. '*Un atimo, per favore.*'

The dialling tone changed as the phone in the room rang. Once. Twice. Three times. He wasn't there. Five times . . . He and Jessica must be at breakfast. Or perhaps he was in the shower and couldn't hear it. Perhaps they'd already gone out. I imagined them crossing St Mark's Square, scattering pigeons. Suddenly the phone was picked up.

'Hello?' said a bleary, but familiar voice.

I felt a sudden flood of warmth in my chest, then my knees buckled beneath me like a stunned animal.

'Hello?' she repeated as I sank on to the bed. *Signora.*

'*Magda?*' I croaked. There was silence. I could hear my heart banging beneath my ribs. I felt sick and breathless. 'Is that Magda?' There was no reply, then I heard a grumble of noise as the phone was passed over.

'Hello?' I heard Jessica say anxiously.

'Jessica, it's Laura.'

'Hello,' she said again.

'Jessica . . .'

'My dad's not here,' she said. 'He's eating his breakfast.'

'Was that your mum?' I said weakly.

'Yes,' she said. 'I mean – *no*. Do you want to speak to my dad? He'll be back soon.'

'It's okay,' I murmured. 'I don't want to. Goodbye Jessica.'

I heard a little sigh of relief. 'G'bye.'

I replaced the handset and stared at the wall.

That was why he'd been reluctant to give me the number for the hotel. That was why he'd had his mobile switched off most of the time – in case I heard Magda's voice. That's why he hadn't had his home phone on speaker for the last few days – in case she accidentally mentioned the trip. That was why he'd been so confident that she wouldn't sabotage it – because she knew that she was going too. And *that's* why he'd given me the dressing gown, I realized, bitterly. Because he knew he was about to betray me. Again.

I sat on the bed for quite a few moments, too shocked to move. Then, I thought – strangely perhaps, given the circumstances – but then who's looking after the *goats*?

By now the phone was ringing, as I knew it soon would.

Hi, this is Laura, sorry I'm not here . . .

It rang again. Then my mobile trilled out and I ignored that too, and then my landline rang a third time. The red light remained illuminated. He was leaving a message.

'Laura,' I heard. 'Pick up if you're there will you? Please Laura. I'm really sorry. But I couldn't tell you because I knew you'd go crazy and I know it looks awful, but Magda was totally hysterical about Steve – she was really depressed – and so she said I couldn't take Jess, so we had this huge row, and I said it was wrong to penalise Jess for her own unhappiness, so then she said that I could take Jess – but only if she came too; and of course I didn't want her to come, but she was making all sorts of threats and then she got Jessica to apply pressure as well so I was put in a position where it was impossible to say no, and I didn't want Jess to miss the trip – she'd been looking forward to it so much. But I felt so bad about you, and I didn't want to hurt you. I upgraded to a suite so that of course Magda's not in the same room as me – she's sharing the room next door with Jessica – but I told her not to pick up the phone.' I heard him groan with frustration. 'I told her not to pick up the phone,' he repeated dismally. 'But look, we'll have a nice weekend somewhere together, just the two of us, maybe Prague or Budapest, no not Budapest obviously, I meant Bucharest, or maybe Barcelona. I haven't been to Barcelona for years and I'd love –'

I pressed 'Stop'. Then I showered and dressed. Today was May Day. The first of May. But I am *dis*Mayed, I thought. I put on flat shoes, and went out.

I walked up Portobello, where a few market traders were already starting to set up their stalls, then I went up Kensington Park Road, passing E & O with a pang, remembering Luke's anguished telephone conversation with Magda on our first date; then I went through Ladbroke Square, and along Holland Park Avenue, past the tube, and now I was at the top of Clarendon Road. I stopped on the corner. I could see Hope's house, the curtains drawn back. I rang the bell. No reply.

'Hi Laura,' she said, on her mobile a few moments later.

'Are you there?' I asked her.

'No,' she said, giggling. 'We're *here*.'

'Where's "here"?'

'At Babington House. It's Mike's birthday.'

'So it is. Sorry – I forgot.'

'Don't worry. I decided to whisk him off for a long week-end. It's heaven – we've just been for a swim – and how are you?'

'I'm . . . okay.' I didn't want to spoil her happy mood. 'Give me a call when you're back.'

I phoned Fliss.

'Hello?' I heard her croak. She sounded exhausted. She'd obviously had a rough night with the baby.

'Fliss – can I come round? I've just had a bit of a shock you see and –'

'*You've* had a shock?' she interrupted. 'Well you're not the only one! I've had a bloody *nightmare* – Hugh and I have had the most *awful* scene.'

'Why?'

'Because last night my computer crashed, so I logged on to his laptop – I know his password – and I found these e-mails. From *her*.'

'Who?'

'Chantal! You were *right*, Laura. I didn't believe you – *fool* that I am – I thought it was just a business thing, but you were *absolutely* right. He said he couldn't wait to see her again, and how he'd like to take her away for the weekend somewhere and . . .' I heard a sob. 'And her e-mail said she couldn't wait to see *him* . . . But how *could* he? How could Hugh *do* that to me? He's such a *bastard*. There we are with a seven month old baby – ooh can't talk. It'sallrightdarling-mummy'scomingdon'tcry . . .'

She hung up. I was relieved – I couldn't cope, I had enough problems of my own. Now I crossed the road and went into Holland Park, up the steep slope and into the cool of the woods, last year's leaves compacted and dry underfoot as I walked along the sun dappled path.

I told Magda not to pick up the phone. I told her not to . . .

So if only Magda had done as he'd asked, I would never have known. Was that it? Worse, he'd involved Jessica in the deceit – he must have done – because he knew she might blurt it out sometime, or show me her photos. Now I remembered the other time when he'd asked her to keep quiet.

You won't tell Mummy that you met Laura tonight will you?

I remembered the droop of her head.

I was so angry my feet hardly touched the ground as I powered round the park, barely registering the thrusting lushness of everything, the carpet of bluebells in the woods, the flowering cherries in the Japanese garden, the glorious wisteria flowing over the walls of the Belvedere in a wash of lilac, the peacocks screeching on the lawn. Then I skirted the cricket pitch and left the park and now I was walking up Kensington High Street, some of the shops already open for Sunday trading, then along Kensington Gore past Kensington Palace, then I came to the Albert Memorial, Albert refulgent in the bright sunshine, beneath his gothic canopy, and turned in. I walked through Hyde Park, dodging the helmeted cyclists and abstracted looking roller-bladers, the Sunday fathers pushing buggies, the dogs running and playing, and, worst of all, the happy couples strolling hand in hand beneath the oaks and the London planes or canoodling on the chlorophyll grass.

Is that Magda? Still energized by anger, I walked up the eastern edge of the Park and found myself at Speakers' Corner where the loonies were shouting out their insane beliefs.

– AN ALIEN INVASION IS IMMIMENT . . .

– THEY'RE POISONING THE WATER SUPPLY . . .

– SO LET'S PUT THE GREAT BACK INTO GREAT BRITAIN . . .

– PRINCESS DIANA'S ALIVE! . . .

I pushed through the crowds of bystanders who were looking variously interested, bored, puzzled, or amused. I wanted to get up on a soapbox myself and deliver the deranged monologue which had been running through *my* head for the past hour and a half.

Now I cut back across the park and skirted the Serpentine, where ducks and moorhens bobbed about on the silty water; and now I was passing the Lido and the café, where people were sitting outside, having coffee, their faces uplifted to the sun. I pressed on, my left hip beginning to ache now as my feet pounded the path.

'Laura!' I heard. I stopped – then groaned inwardly. This was all I needed. 'You look like you need a little sit down if you ask me.'

'Nerys.'

'How *nice* to see you.' She was smiling at me with genuine delight. I felt a spasm of guilt for not being friendlier to her at work.

'What are you doing here?' I asked. 'Sorry – I just mean, I'm surprised to see you.'

'My flat's not far away – in Paddington.'

'Of course. I'd forgotten.' Today her hair was the colour of teak.

'So I come here every Sunday – whatever the weather. I feed the ducks. I watch the world go by.' She gestured to the other side of the lake. 'I watch people boating. There's nowhere like it,' she concluded happily.

'That's nice,' I said as her features began to blur.

She patted the bench. 'I should have a breather if I were you, Laura. You look all in.'

'I think I will.'

I sank down next to Nerys, suddenly glad of her company. In front of us, at the water's edge, some coots were squabbling over a piece of bread. I tried to remember the collective noun for them. What was it? I'd committed so many of them to memory, but my mind had gone blank. I knew it wasn't a 'flock' or a 'flight', or a 'gaggle'... A 'cover' – that was it, wasn't it? A 'cover' of coots?

'Are you all right, Laura?' Nerys asked; she gave me an oblique but penetrating glance.

I swallowed. 'Yes, thanks Nerys. I'm fine.'

'Are you *sure*?' she said kindly. That was it. Now, at last, I burst into tears . . .

'It was the shock of it,' I wept.

Nerys shook her head. 'So that's your day ruined then – oh dear. *Oh* dear,' she tut-tutted. For someone normally so full of herself, she was a sympathetic listener. 'So his ex picked up the phone. Don't upset yourself, Laura.' She handed me a tissue. 'But he shouldn't have done that – he really should *not* have done that.'

'It never occurred to me that he *would*.'

'But from what you say, he spends a lot of time with her.'

'Yes,' I croaked. I pressed the tissue to my eyes. 'It's so that he can be with his child. It's the price he pays.'

'No, Laura.' She shook her head. 'It's the price *you* pay.' I didn't reply. 'Anyway, children or not,' she went on briskly, 'he can't go away with his ex when he's got you – that's not on, is it? He should have cancelled the trip if you want my opinion.'

I smiled. For once I was delighted to have her opinion.

'He didn't want to disappoint his little girl,' I stared across the lake. The sun glinted on the water.

– *Jessica means everything to me. I miss her.*

– *Sometimes I just sit on her bed and cry.*

– *The separation's been hard for her.*

 . . . just watching her sleeping . . .

– *You're joined to them – here – at the heart.*

'He adores her,' I went on. 'His love for her overshadows

286

everything else, which means I often draw the short straw. It's been so . . . frustrating, Nerys. We've been together for three months, but I've yet to spend a *Sunday* with him. I still feel as though I'm waiting for our relationship to start properly.'

Across the lake, a teenage boy was struggling to make one of the rowing boats go forward. His oars kept catching.

'Why do you put up with it, Laura?' I heard Nerys say.

Hope had asked me that too, and I'd replied that it was a question of love. But I knew now that wasn't the answer.

'It's because . . .' I felt my throat constrict. 'You see . . . the last three years . . .' Nerys' face had blurred again. I looked down at my lap, and watched, with a detached interest, as a large tear splashed on to my hand. 'All my confidence had *gone*. I didn't know how to be with anyone. How to have a relationship. I hadn't been on a date for so *long*. Not since I first met Nick over ten years ago.'

'There there, Laura.' I felt the light consoling pressure of her hand on my arm.

'I'd made this decision to move on, but I was terrified . . . But then, out of the blue, there was Luke, and he wanted to be with me so I said yes. I was trying to seize the day.'

'No,' said Nerys. 'You *weren't* trying to seize the day.' I looked at her. 'You were trying to seize *yester*day.'

I stared out over the lake, her words rippling through my mind as though she'd just lobbed in a huge stone. *You were trying to seize yesterday* . . . It was so, so true. I'd resolved to move forwards, but had gone backwards.

'Can I give you some advice?' I heard Nerys say.

'Yes,' I replied. For once I wanted to hear it.

'What I've always thought is . . .' She hesitated. 'I've worked with you both for over two years now . . . and, well, every time I see you together I just think how well you get on, and how sort of "right" you seem together . . . No?' I was shaking my head. 'He thinks the world of you, Laura. He'd be lost without you – he often says that.'

I looked at her. 'Does he?'

'Yes. He often says how marvellous you are – and how clever.'

'I'm not clever,' I said bitterly. 'I'm a mug.'

'He says how attractive you are too.'

'No. I'm a "*jolie laide*" with delinquent hair and size forty-one feet.'

'But he feels you've never seen him in that way,' she went on, ignoring me.

'To be honest . . . I don't think I have.'

'Why not, Laura? You like him, don't you?'

'Yes. Of course I do. Tom's wonderful.'

'Then what's the *problem*?'

'Well . . . He's seeing someone apart from anything else.'

'*That's* not going anywhere,' Nerys said with a dismissive wave of her hand. 'Come on Laura, what's the real reason?'

I didn't want to tell Nerys the real reason and diminish her respect for Tom. She hadn't been working for him at that time. It would be disloyal to him, and unfair on her – she admired him so much.'

'Is it because he's your boss?' she persisted.

'Yes,' I said. 'That's the reason. It's too . . . difficult.'

'I don't know.' She shrugged. 'People often date their colleagues.' I thought of Hope – she used to work at Kleinwort Perella, she met Mike on a training course. 'Anyway, don't miss your chance, Laura. I missed mine,' I heard Nerys add, 'twenty-five years ago. Not a day goes by when I don't regret it.'

'Really?'

'I knew such a nice boy – Patrick – we dated for two years in our mid-twenties, and we got engaged. But then I had my head turned by this other boy – Alan – and I broke it off with Pat. Pat held a candle for me for three years but by the time I realized my mistake, it was too late – he'd got married. He had three kids and is still happily married apparently, while I . . .' Her voice caught. 'I've always regretted not marrying Patrick when I had the chance because, for whatever reason, another chance never quite came my way.' She wrapped her fingers around her gold locket. But how sad to keep a photo of him, I thought. A constant reminder of what might have been. Nerys saw me glance at it. 'Here . . .' she said gently. 'I'll show you.'

'Don't Nerys,' I said. 'Really. It's too personal.'

'It's fine,' she said. 'I don't mind showing you.'

She prised it open with a crimson thumbnail.

Two tiny, avian faces stared out at me, one yellow, one green.

'That's Tweetie,' she said, pointing to the left hand side, 'and that's Pie. I've had them for eight years now. *Lovely* company, they are – they whistle their little hearts out they do, the darlings.' Suddenly her mobile trilled out. 'Hello, Tom. What? Oh *dear.*' She was shaking her head and tut-tutting. 'Oh *dear,*' she repeated. 'Poor Dylan. Well I *kept* telling him to be careful on that motorbike of his didn't I? I said to him, you want to be careful on that motorbike of yours, Dylan. *He's come off his bike,*' she mouthed. '*Broken his wrist.* I see, Tom . . . So you need help . . . Of course you do . . . no, it's definitely too big a job for one person . . . Well, as it happens, I've just bumped into Laura. We're sitting by the Serpentine . . . Yes. It *is* nice. Very nice . . . Lovely day for it. No . . . she says that's fine. She'll be with you in twenty minutes. She's delighted to help.' She snapped her phone shut.

'Er . . . I *don't* mind, Nerys – but is there any reason why you didn't *ask* me first?'

'Because I knew I didn't have to,' she replied.

289

FOURTEEN

I got to the office twenty minutes later. As I walked down the Mews, I saw that the front door was wide open, and suddenly there was Tom, looking fraught, in a white tee shirt and jeans, an emergency cigarette in his mouth, a bulging bin liner in each hand.

'Thanks for coming,' he said as he swung them into the yellow skip that now occupied the parking space. 'The guys will be here early tomorrow to give the place two coats; then in the afternoon they'll pull up the old carpet and lay the new one – which means everything's got to be cleared by tonight. It's a much bigger job than I realized, and I was relying on Dylan but he's in casualty.'

'We'll manage,' I said. My anger with Luke still filled me with a manic energy that made the idea of physical work appealing – and it was more constructive than smashing plates.

'Are you okay, Laura?' Tom said, peering at me. He drew on the cigarette, then stubbed it out on the wall. 'You look a bit . . .'

'I'm fine,' I said briskly. I didn't want to talk – or think – about Luke. I picked up one of Tom's rubber bands, and tied up my hair. 'Let's start.'

We disconnected the computers and printers. Then we spent a couple of hours moving the furniture, putting the desks and chairs in the tiny courtyard at the back of the building, under plastic sheeting. Then we began to clear the cupboards and quickly filled several bin liners with old video tapes, presenters' show-reels, box-files of redundant publicity material and long-concluded correspondence.

'We should have dealt with all this junk ages ago,' Tom said as he dumped a pile of old *Broadcast*s into the bin liner. 'Nerys has been going on at me about it for months, but I couldn't face it.'

We worked for a couple of hours – the skip was filling, and Tom's t-shirt was getting grubby and grey – then he glanced at his watch. 'It's two thirty. We'd better eat something – I'll run out and get some sandwiches.' He returned ten minutes later with two small paper carriers.

'What are you smiling at?' he asked as he handed one to me. He overturned an empty crate and sat on it.

'At this.' I held it up. 'I found it while you were out.' It was a photo of Tom and me, surrounded by packing cases, on our first day in All Saints Mews. 'Remember that? September '99?'

'Yes.' He looked at the photo. 'It was exhausting because there was that late heat wave, wasn't there – it was eighty degrees – and I was in a state at what I'd taken on. I'd borrowed so much money – I never thought I'd be able to make it work.' He passed the photo back.

'Well I told you that you would – and you have done. Brilliantly.'

'*We* have,' he corrected me. 'And what's that other photo you've got there?'

'Oh.' I wasn't going to show him this one. I handed it to him and I noticed him colour slightly.

We were sitting at our table at the Bafta awards in the spring of '01, smiling for the camera. We'd been nominated for the Helen of Troy documentary, and with us were our other halves. There was Tom and, on his left, Amy, who was then six months' pregnant. She looked lovely in her pale blue dress with a rose in her hair, but at the same time I could see she was tense. With hindsight it was obvious why – she was probably aware, even then, that Tom had fallen for Tara, who was sitting on his other side, luminously beautiful, leaning into him just a little too far. And there I was, in the foreground, with Nick on my right, looking big and handsome in his DJ, his arm stretched along the back of my chair. Within months of that picture being taken, all our relationships had imploded. The photo seemed to vibrate with nostalgia and angst.

Tom handed it back without speaking, then unwrapped his cheese roll.

'We look so young,' I said, just to break the silence.

He shrugged. 'It was a long time ago.'

'Shall we keep it?' I asked, though I knew the answer.

'I don't want to. But I do want to keep this.' He held up a large snap of Tom, me, Sara and Nerys celebrating the commissioning of *Whadda Ya Know?!!* We were waving a bottle of Krug at the camera and Tom was hugging me. He was smiling so much you could hardly see his eyes.

'Now that was a happy moment. And it's all thanks to you, Laura.'

'No – you came up with the format.'

'But you started the whole idea. When you told me about the question-setting you were doing. Don't you remember?'

'Yes. But then if it hadn't been for Nick going missing I wouldn't have been doing that, so, in a funny sort of way, we owe it to him – not that he'd have the slightest idea.'

Tom nodded sympathetically.

'It's our tenth wedding anniversary tomorrow,' I went on. I pulled the ring-pull off my can of Coke. 'I don't think we're doing anything special.' It felt strange even remarking on it, slightly desperate, like trying to celebrate someone's birthday after they'd died. As I opened my packet of crisps I wondered whether Nick would notice the date, wherever he was. The tabloid hacks had all given up.

Tom and I carried on sorting and discarding – by now it was gone five – then we began to take everything off the walls. We put all the reference books into crates – the fat Compendiums and the Oxford Companions and the sturdy Cambridge Guides. I heaved the *Encyclopaedia Britannica* off the shelf, and here, now, was my old Latin dictionary, and next to it, I now saw, my Horace. So that's where it was. As I pulled it out, it fell open at a well-thumbed page.

See how Mount Soracte stands deep in dazzling snow
and the struggling trees cannot bear their loads,
and the rivers are frozen with sharp ice . . .
Heap high the fire, and bring out, O Thaliarchus,
your finest, four year old wine . . .
Entrust all else to the Gods . . . don't ask what tomorrow
will bring, and whatever days fortune bestows,
count them as profit.
Now is the time for sweet love affairs and dances,
while you are young, and crabbed old age is far off;
So, for now, let the playing fields and the piazzas,
laughter and soft whisperings at nightfall be your
pursuits . . .

'What's that?' Tom asked. I passed the book to him. 'It's beautiful,' he said. 'And this one – on the facing page.'

'"Don't ask what final fate the Gods have given . . . "' he read, '"and don't consult Babylonian horoscopes. Much better to accept what shall be; whether Jupiter has granted us many more winters or whether this may be our last, which now hurls the Tuscan sea against the facing cliffs. Be wise, strain the wine, and don't look too far ahead. Even while we've been talking Time has been swiftly flying. So seize the day . . . " Seize the day . . .' he repeated.

'Not yesterday,' I murmured. Tom gave me a quizzical glance.

Suddenly my mobile rang. Without looking at the screen, I answered it.

'Laura!' It was Luke. 'I just needed to speak to you, Laura, to explain everything in person – you see I didn't lie to you, because I didn't say that she wasn't going –'

I snapped the phone shut. A moment later, it trilled again, and I ignored it. It rang a third time and I hesitated for a second, then tapped in the code which would block the number.

'Are you okay?' said Tom.

I was aware of his curious gaze. 'Yes,' I said quietly. 'I'm okay.'

Now we dragged the crates of books to the back, then Tom unscrewed the rickety shelves and we flung them in the skip, and took the pictures and posters off the walls. Then we went upstairs and cleared everything there. By the time we'd done that, it was eight. My back was aching and my temples were damp.

'So . . . is that it?' I said, looking around. The light was fading.

'Well, there is just one more thing,' Tom said. 'But you don't have to stay.'

'Of course I'll stay – what is it?'

'Arnie said I should give the walls a quick wipe so that they can dry overnight. He said the paint will look much better if we do. It'll probably take us about an hour but as I say, you don't have to – you've already done so much and I'm really grateful that you came to help me and – where are you going Laura?'

'To fill the bucket.'

We had a large sponge each – I loved plunging mine into the warm water, then wiping away the dust and grime in strong, sweeping strokes as though I was waving to someone a very long way off. My shoulders ached, but I didn't care. It was satisfying and distracting. Just what I needed.

'This is Radio 4. And now it's time for Word of Mouth with Michael Rosen.'

Tom had found his small transistor, so, as we worked, we listened to a discussion about whether the word 'actress' has had its day when 'authoress' and 'priestess' have long since been abandoned. Then there was an interesting feature about all the foreign words that have found their way into the English language – 'zeitgeist', 'fiasco', 'karma' and 'bonsai.'

'The best ones are French,' said Tom. '*Esprit de corps, crème de la crème, joie de vivre* – that's a nice one isn't it – *embarrass de richesses . . .*'

'*Cause célèbre,*' I mused. '*Crime passionel . . .*' I love that. 'Only the French could romanticize murder.'

'*Femme fatale,*' said Tom. 'And of course, *coup de foudre* . . .' he added with a jaundiced air.

'Hmmm . . . *coup de foudre.*' To be stunned or dazzled by love.

By now, dusk had descended, and by the time we'd got to the top floor night had fallen and we were working by artificial light.

'Almost finished now,' said Tom as we worked away in the boardroom. I felt a bead of sweat slide into the small of my back. 'Hey!' he suddenly yelled.

We'd been plunged into darkness.

I heard Tom sigh as he went over to the light switch and flicked it up and down. 'It must be the bulb,' he muttered. 'There's a spare one in the kitchen. I'll get it.'

'It isn't the bulb,' I said, glancing through the open door. 'The lights downstairs have gone too.'

'Then it's the fuse,' he said. 'I'll have to fix it. The fuse box is by reception.'

'Don't leave me on my own, Tom.' I felt a fluttering of panic. 'I don't like the dark. In fact, I *hate* it.'

'Then come down with me. But be careful.'

Now, as we stepped gingerly on to the landing, feeling for the handrail, we saw that the entire building was without light.

I glanced out of the window. 'There are no lights on anywhere.'

The Mews was in total darkness, and, beyond it, the Lucozade glow of the street lamps had been extinguished. There were the sounds of doors being opened as people stepped outside to see what was happening, or threw up their windows. In the distance we could hear the wail of police sirens, and the honking of cars.

'Maybe it's just a local failure,' I said.

'No,' I heard Tom say. 'This is a blackout. The traffic lights are down.' I remembered the power cut we'd had a few weeks before at the studio.

I stretched out my hands in front of me. 'Where are you?' I said, my pulse racing. 'I can't see you. I can't see *anything*.' I suddenly saw the fluorescent points on Tom's watch face float towards me, then felt his hand on my wrist. I heard the click and sigh of his lighter, then the room was filled by a halo of light. Now we could see each other, our features distorting in the flickering flame, our shadows dancing across the bare walls.

'We interrupt this programme to bring you a newsflash,' we heard. 'Large parts of London and the south east have been hit by a power failure. The cause is unknown but a spokesman for the National Grid company, Transco, has said that terrorism has been ruled out . . .'

'It'll probably last a few minutes,' Tom said as he held the lighter higher. We could see the tongue of flame reflected in the window, our faces aglow on either side of it, as though we were figures in a Rembrandt. 'Let's just sit and wait.' We went back into the boardroom where we sat on the big brown leather Chesterfield that had been too heavy to move out.

'You are advised to stay at home until the electricity supply is reconnected. We'll bring you further updates, but there is rolling coverage now over on Radio 5. Meanwhile here on Radio 4 . . .'

Still holding the lighter, Tom turned the dial.

'. . . the advice is to stay at home, avoiding, wherever possible, the use of naked flames, and, if you were about to set out on a journey, you should delay leaving until power has been restored. So joining me in the Radio 5 studio now is . . .'

'If you want, I could walk you back to your flat,' Tom said as some energy expert chatted away in the background. 'It's a cloudy night, so it's pretty black out there . . .'

'Don't we have a torch?'

'No. But we could take it steadily.' I thought of bumping into a lamppost and having my nose broken again, or falling off the kerb and snapping an ankle – or being mugged; that could happen, couldn't it? Worse, I thought of being alone in my flat in the dark.

'I'd rather wait, Tom. I'm sure it won't be that long.'

'I'd better save my lighter. There's not much left.' He took his thumb off the catch and we were enveloped in inky blackness again.

'Are you okay?' he asked. I heard the leather creak as he settled himself more comfortably on the sofa.

I pulled my legs up under me. 'I'm okay.'

'At least, being a Sunday night, it'll affect far fewer people than if it had happened on a week day,' we heard the radio presenter say. 'Like that power cut in August 2003, remember?' There was then an animated conversation about that. Then a woman guest pointed out that many people were away, as it was Bank Holiday so that was a good thing too. I thought, dismally, of Luke. Then there was a discussion about the massive

North American power outage in 2003 when fifty-five million people were plunged into darkness when twenty-one power stations failed. Then we heard further updates as to what was happening in London as the radio reporters began to file.

'–Hundreds trapped on tube trains . . .'

'–Hospitals have back-up generators, of course . . .'

'–People pouring out of cinemas . . .'

'–Strange atmosphere . . . so quiet . . .'

'–Traffic gridlocked . . .'

There was speculation as to whether the disruption might be due to a solar flare – but an astronomer phoned in to scotch this idea. They then discussed whether it could be an act of industrial sabotage by anti-capitalists, as a curtain-raiser to the May Day demonstrations the following day.

'I don't believe that for a minute,' I heard Tom say. 'It's just a cock-up.'

From outside we could hear people talking, and even laughing. Someone was playing the guitar. As the programme addressed other matters, Tom turned the radio down. 'It's ten fifteen,' he said. 'The lights will be back on by half past, probably sooner.'

Twenty minutes later the power still hadn't been restored, so, unable to do anything else, we just sat there, side by side, in the velvety black, talking, or rather, whispering, as though the darkness had sapped our confidence. We could hear each other breathe.

'It's like being at the movies, without a movie,' said Tom. 'I know . . .' I heard his hand scrape into his pocket then he turned on his lighter again. 'Hold it for me will you? Right . . . up a bit . . . like that . . .' He sat forward, then placed his hands together, then held them up to the wall in front of us, his fingers pointing downwards, his thumbs upraised. The hand shadow blurred, and then sharpened. 'What's that then?' he said.

I peered at it. 'Well . . . it looks like . . . a dog.'

298

'It's not a dog. Here's a clue . . .' It began to 'hop' across the wall.

'Is it a rabbit?'

'No. Rabbits don't have such upright ears.'

'Is it a horse then? A horse – jumping over something.'

'No.'

'A llama?' I said, desperately.

'Llamas don't jump.'

'But they do have very upright ears.' Jump . . . 'A kangaroo! It's a kangaroo isn't it?'

'No. But close – it's a wallaby.'

'Oh.'

'You can tell from the shape of the nose. Wallabies have shorter snouts than kangaroos.'

'Right . . .'

'But of course it's a bit hard to see because the flame flickers a bit – you really need a torch. Plus I'm out of practice. We used to do this when we went to our cabin at Lake Memphremagog when we were kids.'

'Where's that?'

'In South East Quebec, not far from Montreal. It's beautiful. We used to canoe and fish . . . and make hand shadows.'

'You obviously took that very seriously.'

'There wasn't much else to do in the evenings. My mom could do a very creditable elephant.'

'African or Indian?'

'Hey, the lighter's really low now – I'd better save it. Brace yourself.' The flame vanished and everything became as black as anthracite again.

I shuddered, audibly.

'You do hate the dark, don't you?' I heard Tom say.

'Yes. I'm not too bad if someone else is there – but I can't cope with it if I'm on my own. Don't laugh . . . but I still sleep with a little night light on.'

'Really? And your teddy bear?'

'No. I gave him to Luke years ago – and he's still got him. But I won't be seeking custody,' I added. 'Or even contact visits come to that.'

I was aware of Tom shifting slightly next to me. 'That doesn't sound very good.'

'It isn't. It's rather bad actually.'

'So where is he now?'

'In Venice.'

'Uh huh.'

'With Magda.'

'Oh . . .' I told him what had happened.

'Jesus . . .' he breathed. 'What a mistake. So . . . is that it then?'

I heaved a sigh. 'Yes. I think it is . . . Not because he took her there – and not even because he's bent like a sapling to all her demands, however unreasonable - but because he's been untruthful.'

'He lied to you?'

'Oh no. Luke never lies. He just leaves things out. Important things. Like the fact that he was taking his ex to Venice. He must have known for a week beforehand, but he left it out of our conversations, to protect himself.'

'He's been leaving you out too,' Tom said.

'Yes, he has.'

'I'm sorry. I could see you were upset when you arrived.'

'Well . . . I feel better now. Not least because today I realized – with Nerys's help actually –' I felt another spasm of guilt – 'that I've been with Luke for the wrong reason.'

'Which was what? Trying to finish unfinished business?'

'No. It was simple fear. Fear of the unknown. Fear of a new start. And I think that's why he was with me. Because he'd had a lot of emotional pain, and I reminded him of a happy time in his life.' Luke had been trying to seize yesterday too.

'But today, Nerys made me ask myself that question – why are you with him – and I realized that was the answer. And it's not a good enough reason to be with someone.'

'Better to end it then,' I heard Tom say. I could hear his gentle, regulated breathing, and could just make out his profile in the gloom. 'And I've told Gina that it's not going to work out.'

So Nerys was right then – again.

'I saw her yesterday and asked her if we could just be . . . friends. I'd still like to see them, and play with Sam, but I don't want a big emotional thing with her because . . .'

'Because it was just too messy, with the husband?'

'No. It was actually much simpler than that. It was because when I was away, I realized that it wasn't Gina I was missing. It was Sam. I didn't really think about her, but I thought about him. I imagined him playing on the swings, or riding his trike, or sitting in his little armchair, watching CBeebies.'

'You're very fond of him.'

'Yes . . .' His voice caught. 'I am.' I saw the illuminated watch dial rise up to where his face was, then fall again. 'But I knew I wasn't in love with her. If it hadn't been for her giving me her card that day, nothing would have happened. She promoted the relationship. She also promoted my relationship with Sam.' I thought of the Valentine card he'd 'sent'. It was sweet, but it was also manipulative. 'She was looking for someone to fill the Daddy Gap.'

'But weren't you tempted?'

I heard him sigh. 'At one level I was. If I'd had stronger feelings for her, then I would have loved to play that role in Sam's life – I could even have coped with her oaf of an ex. But I wasn't in love with her – and I don't think she was in love with me. We were both in it for the wrong reasons. She was looking for a replacement dad while I was . . .'

Looking for a replacement child . . .

'What were you looking for, Tom?' I could just make out the sheen of his eyes as he turned his head towards me, then looked away again.

There was silence.

'I guess . . . I was looking . . . for my son.' From somewhere we heard a church clock strike the hour. 'I miss him,' Tom murmured.

'I thought so. But as you've never talked about it, I've never mentioned it. But I knew how painful it must be.'

I heard a tiny exhalation. 'It's been like a hole in the heart. When he was taken away from me I thought I'd die.'

'So . . . don't you ever see him?'

'No. But I'm always looking for him. I see little boys his age, and my heart stops.'

'You have no contact with him?'

'No.'

'Even though you were married to Amy? That's tough. But then it must have been very tough for her too.'

'That's what she said. That it was breaking her heart.'

'So I suppose she just can't face seeing you – is that it?'

'Yes. She said she couldn't bear even to look at me . . . knowing . . .' I heard him swallow.

'That you'd just . . . left her? That you'd walked away?' I realized that I was probing, but I couldn't help it. I wanted him to *talk* to me about it, so I'd understand.

'I did walk away,' he said miserably. 'It's true. But she made me . . . suffer, Laura.'

'But can you honestly blame her, Tom? I mean, please don't mind me saying this, but what you did – I've never been able to comprehend it. I mean . . . sorry – I don't mean to sermonize and I know there's often this big gap between one part of a person's life and another – but you see I like you so much and I've always respected you a lot – and I just . . . can't . . .'

302

'Laura – what are you trying to say?'

'I'm trying to say . . . Okay – I'm trying to say that I could simply never understand how you could do that. How you could leave Amy – let alone at such a time.'

'Because I had to,' he said flatly.

'*But you didn't have to* – I'm sorry, Tom, I know it's not my business, but I just don't get it, because you're such a wonderful person and you see I want to understand . . .' My throat ached with a suppressed sob. 'I want to understand how someone I like and admire so much could just leave his wife a month after she's given birth, and . . . *go off* with another woman.'

There was a stunned silence. I'd really offended him. I should have kept quiet.

'But . . . I didn't do that,' I heard him whisper.

'What?'

'I didn't go off with another woman.'

'But you did. You fell in love with Tara and you left Amy, even though she'd had the baby only a few weeks before. Why are you denying it?'

'Why am I denying it?' he repeated. I could just make out the glimmer of his eyes, staring at me in the dark. 'I'm denying it because it isn't true. Where the hell did you get that cracked idea from?'

'Well . . .' I could feel myself blinking in non-comprehension. 'From what I understood at the time and . . . and from your own sister actually.'

'Christina? How?'

'When we had lunch. Don't you remember? You got up to take a call and while you were away from the table she explained what had happened – she suddenly started talking to me about it – she seemed to want to unburden her feelings about it.'

'But she wouldn't have told you *that*.'

'But she did, Tom. Why else would I be saying it?'

I heard the sofa creak as he sat up. 'Tell me what she said.'

I cast my mind back. 'She referred to your leaving Amy and she said that . . . it was a "*coup de foudre*" – that's what she actually said – I've a very good memory, remember. And she obviously meant that you'd fallen catastrophically in love with Tara and just couldn't . . . help yourself.' I could feel the intensity of Tom's gaze as we stared sightlessly at each other.

'Laura, that's not what she meant, and it's not what she would have said. Because it wasn't *true*.'

'No?'

'No. For the simple reason that the "*coup de foudre*" wasn't mine.'

'What?'

'It was Amy's.' There was silence. 'I think that's what Christina was trying to say.'

'Amy's?'

'*She* had the "*coup de foudre*". *She* had the affair. She "went off" – I thought you knew that, Laura.'

'No,' I said faintly. 'I didn't.'

'I assumed you all knew. When it happened, I assumed you must have talked about it – I wouldn't have blamed you if you had.'

'No. No-one ever discusses you in that way, Tom, so I have no idea what the others thought, but I thought . . .'

'What? That I'd walked out on Amy, when she'd just had the baby, because I'd fallen in love with Tara McLeod? Is that what you thought?'

'Yes,' I croaked. 'It is. That's exactly what I thought.'

'Do you seriously think I would behave like that? Walk out on my wife when she's just given birth? Let alone abandon my child?'

'Well, no . . .' my voice caught. 'I don't think that – which is why I couldn't understand. I was just amazed by it at the time, because I remember how happy you were when Amy was pregnant, and how much you were looking forward to being a father, and how thrilled you were when Gabriel was born. And we all cracked open the champagne with you and we tied blue balloons to your chair. I'll never forget how happy you were.'

'I *was* happy.' I heard his voice catch. 'The day Gabriel was born was the happiest day of my life. "Nothing will ever better this," I told myself.'

'I'm really sorry, Tom,' I said. I felt my eyes fill. 'I misunderstood. I've misunderstood all this time, but you see, I thought – but I was wrong - so it was ... Amy.' It was a *coup de foudre*. 'Christina was talking about *Amy*. But ... then ...'

'You obviously don't know, Laura – do you?'

'Know what?' And then I realized.

'Gabriel wasn't my baby.'

'Not ...' My chest had tightened.

'Not my baby,' he croaked.

'Oh,' I said quietly. *Oh* ...

'It's four years now, so I can talk about it. And maybe the only reason I *am* talking about it is because it's pitch black, and I can't see your face, or your reactions, so this makes me feel more bold and reckless than normal, and at the same time, strangely, more safe. And also because I don't mind you knowing, Laura – as I say, I thought you did. But Amy was seeing someone else. I had no idea ...'

'So ... how did you find out?'

'Well ... she was acting in a strange way after the birth. She bonded well with Gabriel, but she cried a lot of the time, and if I cuddled him, she'd get upset. I thought it must be the baby blues – plus he'd been severely jaundiced, so she was anxious. So I was just extra nice to her, but that only seemed to make her worse. And then ... when Gabriel was almost three weeks old, his jaundice got worse, and he was admitted to St. Mary's.'

'Yes, I remember that ...'

305

'They advised a transfusion, called an exchange transfusion, where they basically replace all the blood. But they said that the donated blood would have to come from the Rare Blood Bank, because Gabriel's type was very unusual – AB Positive with RzRz antigens. And I said that this was impossible, because my blood group is the most common type – O Positive – and Amy's was A Negative, and it wasn't possible that Gabriel could have this rare blood type so they must have made a mistake. I added that I knew a bit about it because a good friend of mine from Canada had this RzRz thing, and he'd inherited it from his great grandfather who was Native American. But the doctor insisted that there was no mistake, and all the time Amy was becoming very agitated, but I thought that was just because Gabriel was so unwell. I still didn't understand.

'Then the doctor left the room – I didn't know why she'd done that, though I realized afterwards – and Amy broke down and cried, and she kept saying that she was sorry, over and over, how sorry she was, and that she hadn't meant to do this to me. And I said, "Do what to me? What is it you've done to me?" I thought it was something to do with Gabriel being ill. That she felt it was her fault in some way . . .' He paused. 'And then she told me. She told me that Gabriel wasn't mine.

'I felt as though I'd fallen into a crevasse . . . So I said, "What do you mean Gabriel's not mine? Of course he is – how could he not be?" My brain was simply refusing to process what she was saying. But then, I finally understood. And then of course, she didn't even have to say his name. I just got this terrible sensation. Here.' I heard him bang his chest with a dull *thud*. 'As though everything had collapsed inside.'

'Was he a close friend?'

'Yes. We'd been at McGill together. He was working for CBC and he'd been posted to London. He'd never actually met Amy

– he hadn't made it to our wedding. So I invited him round not long after he got to London, and we all had dinner, and they just . . . fell in love. She told me afterwards that it had been a '*coup de foudre*' – that's how she tried to explain it to me, and to herself. Their affair went on for most of that time. And I remember being surprised that she didn't seem happier when she got pregnant. But she was secretly in the most terrible state.' I thought of that photo of us all at the Baftas. And now I understood the real reason for the tension in Amy's face.

'What did you do when you found out?'

'I didn't know what to do. Whether even to pick Gabriel up. I longed to, but at the same time I felt I shouldn't – that I'd lost the right. And Amy told me that she loved me, but that she wanted to be with Andy, so it became obvious what I had to do. But even now, four years on, I still think of Gabriel as "my" baby. My little baby boy. But he wasn't. Anyway, that's what happened,' I heard Tom say. He clapped his hands together with mock joviality and a tiny echo bounced off the walls. 'We've all got our sad stories, haven't we – and that's mine.'

'It is sad.' At a stroke, he'd lost his wife and his baby – and his entire sense of himself as a father, and a family man. All the things that Luke had talked about, but infinitely worse. The Harpies had swooped down and snatched up his feast.

'So that's why you became so attached to Sam.'

'Yes. He's exactly the same age.'

'And do you ever see Gabriel?'

'No. Because he's no more my child than Sam is. I have no role to play in his life – now I'm simply his mother's ex. Amy and I parted on terrible terms, and she went to Canada with Andy, and in time I learned to think of Gabriel in a different way. But when I go back to Montreal it's hard, because I have to pass within a mile of where they live.'

'So that's what you meant when you said your trip had been "stressful".'

307

'Yes. But of course I have to go, because my folks are there. So that's what happened, Laura. And the reason why Christina said what she did was because she assumed you knew the truth, and didn't want you to think badly of Amy, who she'd always liked. But you got it all back to front and ended up thinking badly of *me*.'

'I'm really sorry. But then . . . you see, the stuff in the papers confused me as well. There were a couple of pieces saying that you and Tara were an item and that Amy was distraught about it.'

'Laura, what have you learned recently about what you read in the tabloids – and the broadsheets come to that?'

'Well, yes,' I sighed, 'but it sounded convincing, and the thing is, Tom, that you never *denied* it. You never came in to work and said to us, "Look there's something about me in the papers today, but I just want you to know it's not true."'

'Ah. Well you do have a point there,' he said. 'Tara had a very pushy agent at that time, and he fed the story to the press about me "seeing" her – I think he thought that a little controversy would be good for her career. I didn't like it – but once it had gone in, I didn't deny it, no, because I preferred people to think I'd been a cad rather than . . .' His voice trailed away. 'So, yes, I can see why that fed your misapprehension. But the fact is that Tara and I were friends – no more than that. I couldn't have looked at another woman, let alone . . .' I heard him sigh. 'I was a total mess.'

I cast my mind back. 'You concealed it well. I could see that you were very low, but I assumed that it was because of the divorce. Plus you never talked about your personal life – not even when you used to come and bring me things in the first few weeks after Nick disappeared. You could have talked about it then. I wish you had done – then I would have known the truth, instead of which –'

'I didn't want to talk about it – plus you had such big

308

problems of your own. And at work I hid my feelings because I didn't want people to feel sorry for me – you should understand that – and because I had a business to run. I wanted to fall apart – but I couldn't. I did talk to Tara about it, though. We went to the movies and to the pub. She consoled me. But not in the way you obviously thought.'

'I did think that . . . although deep down I still couldn't believe it . . .'

'You did believe it.'

'But only because it appeared to be *true*, because a) that's how it looked, especially with the newspaper coverage and b) I was misled by that awkward conversation I had with Christina . . .'

'You never seem to get beyond a) and b), do you Laura,' Tom said wearily. 'But what about c) to z) – which were that I would never do that. You should have given me the benefit of the doubt – you knew me well enough.'

'Yes, I did. I'm sorry. I was judgemental.'

'You were – but, you know, Laura, I've never been judgemental about you.'

'That makes me feel even worse.'

'You've had such crap thrown at you these past few weeks, but I know that's all it is – crap – and that Nick had his own reasons for doing what he did. And if anyone had asked me whether you were capable of hurting your husband so much that he'd have a breakdown then I'd have answered, "absolutely not".' I didn't say anything. 'All this "guilt" rubbish the press have tried to pin on you – especially that nasty piece of work from the *Semaphore*.'

'Yes. But then . . .'

'What?' We could hear the clock chiming the three quarters. It would soon be midnight.

'But . . . actually, Tom . . . he was *right*. I do feel guilty about Nick leaving.'

'Why?' There was silence. 'It wasn't your fault. You weren't responsible for what was going on in his head.'

'Wasn't I? I think I was.' From outside we could hear the wail of an ambulance.

'What do you mean?'

I paused. 'Something happened . . . something he couldn't get over.'

'You don't have to tell me, Laura.'

'I want to tell you. But you're the only one I will tell.' I realized now that I had never told Luke. 'We had that car crash – a few days before Christmas.'

'Yes, I remember – Nick took a bad knock to the head. You said afterwards you thought it might have precipitated what happened to him.'

'Yes, I did say that – but I didn't believe it, because I knew the real reason. I've known it for the past three years. It was something I did, or rather *said*, that he couldn't cope with.'

'What did you say?' Tom asked.

I could hear myself breathe.

You killed our baby . . .

'I made this terrible accusation . . .'

You killed our baby . . .

'I was pregnant . . .' I explained. Then I told him what I'd said to Nick.

'You were pregnant?' Tom murmured.

'Yes. In the autumn of 2001.'

'I had no idea.'

'I didn't tell you – or anyone – and in any case you had so much else on your mind – it was a couple of months after Gabriel was born. And it hardly showed, plus I had very little morning sickness.'

'So . . . was it that . . . ?' He paused. 'Did Nick want you . . . to have a termination? Was that it?'

'Oh . . . *no*. No, he was thrilled about it – we both were. We'd found out in late September, when we were on holiday

310

in Crete.' I remembered Nick, standing on the hotel balcony, in that blue silk shirt of his with the tropical fish, his face alight with joy. 'But then I had a slight scare in the October, so we decided not to tell anyone – not even my sisters - until I was at least sixteen weeks. At fourteen weeks I had the first scan, and it was fine.' I paused, remembering hearing the rapid beat of the baby's heart – like a bird's – as the Doppler was pressed on to my abdomen; then the miraculous sight of the tiny form rocking in its uterine cradle, one dainty hand uplifted, as though in greeting.

'So we decided that we'd tell everyone on New Year's Day: I was worried about telling Felicity, because she was desperately trying for a baby herself. But that's when we planned to let them know.'

'So what happened then . . . ?' Tom murmured. As we sat there whispering in the dark, I felt as though I were in the confessional, and that he was the priest.

'On the Saturday before Christmas, we'd gone to a party in Sussex – it was a fund-raising thing for SudanEase, so we had to go, although I hadn't really wanted to, as I hadn't been feeling that great. But as we were driving back, we had the accident – we spun off the road and went into a ditch. We were taken to hospital, and I told the nurses I was pregnant, and they said that I'd be fine, and not to worry, because babies are so safely cocooned. And when I got home I looked it up in that book – *What to Expect When You're Expecting* – and it said that women can be in really serious accidents and break their bones, and still not lose their baby. So I must have been very unlucky, because I hadn't been seriously hurt, but two days later I lost mine.'

Suddenly I felt Tom touch my right hand, then he cupped both his hands over it, as though it was an injured bird.

'I'm sorry, Laura,' he whispered. 'And I'm sorry that I didn't know.'

311

'I got Nick to tell you that I had 'flu – but I was in hospital. The doctor told me that it was a girl.'

'I'm sorry,' Tom said again. 'I must have been too wrapped up in my own misery to notice yours although, I do remember, now I think about it, how sad you seemed then.'

'I was. Nick and I were both distraught. And three or four days later, we had this awful row. He'd had a glass of wine at that party, so I'd told him that I'd drive home, but he insisted that he was okay, plus he knows I hate driving in the dark. He was well under the limit, but I became obsessed with the idea that it had affected his judgement . . . and I said this terrible thing. And the next day I said I was sorry, and that it was only because I was still so distressed, but I don't think it was enough. Because, although on the surface he seemed to be coping, it was ten days after that, that he went – on January the 1st.'

'On the day when you were due to tell everyone.'

'Yes. And he'd clearly planned to go, because he'd drawn £5,000 out of his account ten days before he went. So yes, I do feel responsible for Nick going. I did "hurt him," I did "treat him badly", I did "drive him away". "My Remorse" was just about the right headline.'

'Oh Laura . . . But it's understandable . . . in the circumstances. You were in a very bad way –'

'But Nick had other things going on at the time – his father's death six weeks before had hit him badly – they'd had a terrible row and hadn't made it up – so he was already in a fragile state. But to feel that losing the baby might have been his fault and to know that I blamed him – and that I might always blame him. I suppose that's what he couldn't bear.'

'He probably did blame himself, Laura.'

'Yes – so he didn't need me saying it as well. But that's why he went missing.' I could hear Tom sigh. 'So that's *my* sad story.' I thought of Cynthia's psychic reading that night, and how disturbing I had found it.

312

There isn't one person missing from your life – there are two.

'I think of her often – she'd be almost three. A little girl in a pink dress and Startrite shoes.' We heard the clock strike twelve.

'But how terrible then to leave you – whatever his turmoil.'

'Yes – because we could have got through it, in time, and put it behind us. Tried again.'

'But he left you . . .'

The last chime sounded. It was the second of May. Our anniversary.

'Yes, he did. Just when I needed him most.'

FIFTEEN

Tom and I had no idea what time the power had come back on, because after that we fell asleep. He offered to sleep on the floor, but we slept on the sofa, with him slumped against one arm, while I was half stretched out, my head on his lap. We awoke, aching in every joint.

'God, it's five past seven,' Tom croaked. He reached for the radio. '*Ow*, my neck.'

'Power has now been restored. The failure is thought to have been caused by a fault at the Hurst substation, near Bexley in Kent. It lasted a total of six and a half hours . . .'

We heard a van drawing up outside. Tom got up and looked out of the window.

'It's Arnie. He said he'd be here at seven.' We heard the van door open, then slam, then male voices. I looked out; there were three painter-decorators in white overalls. Tom ran downstairs to let them in.

'Morning,' said one of the painters as I came down the stairs. He was clutching a huge tub of paint in one hand and a step-ladder in the other.

'Good morning . . . I'm just going.'

'Thanks for your help,' said Tom. He hugged me, then held me to him for a moment. 'I'll call you later.'

I went home, blinking in the bright sunlight as I walked through the deserted streets – then crawled into bed, and slept.

I woke at midday, still aching, and steeped myself in a hot bath, with a flannel over my face, thinking about the conversation of a few hours before.

. . . like a hole in the heart . . .

–She made me suffer

–She had the "coup de foudre" . . .

–Do you seriously think . . . ?

. . . abandon my child . . . ?

–You should have given me the benefit of the doubt.

I should have done. Instead, I'd spent three years believing that Tom had done something awful. If I hadn't thought that – how then might I have regarded him, I wondered . . .

Through the open bathroom window, I could hear the shriek of whistles, and the honking of bicycle horns. May Day protestors. The streets would be full of them, especially with the General Election. I decided I'd go and look. As I got dressed, my mobile beeped – there were five missed calls – three from Luke, and two from Felicity. Then I listened to the answerphone. Luke had left three messages, and Fliss had left two. Suddenly the phone rang. It was her.

'Where have you *been?*' she said accusingly.

'Oh . . .' I was too tired to explain. 'Working,' I said, which was true.

'Well it's been absolute hell here – he's out with Olivia so he can't hear – but when I confronted him about the e-mails he admitted that he'd been getting far too cosy with Chantal.'

'Did anything actually happen between them?'

'No – but *thank God* I looked at his computer when I did, otherwise it would have done – he said so himself. But it's been the most terrible twenty-four hours – and then just to top it all off, that bloody power cut! I looked in the freezer this morning – I had sixteen pints of breast milk in there, all ruined! OhgodHugh'sjustcomingbackcan'ttalkbye.'

And I was just wondering quite why Felicity had sixteen pints of breast milk in the freezer – when the phone rang again.

'Laura!' It was Luke. 'Thank God. I couldn't get through to you on your mobile for some reason – this annoying woman kept saying that calls from this number were not being accepted or something, anyway, I'm just on my way to Marco Polo airport and I'll be back later and then we'll talk and I can't wait to see –' I hung up, then tapped in the code.

'Calls from this number are now barred,' said the automated voice. 'Thank you.'

Then I picked up the dressing gown, still in its carrier bag, unworn. It was so beautiful, with its pattern of pink tulips – but now it was tainted and spoiled. I wondered what to do. Give it to Oxfam, I suppose, or to Hope or to Fliss or to my mum, that would be nice or . . .

'OOHHHH!' *THUMP! THUMP!!*

Cynthia. I'd give it to her. I put it back in its bag and went upstairs.

'OOOHHHH!' *THUMP! THUMP!! THUMP!!!!*

I knocked hard so that she could hear me.

'Laura!' she said, opening the door. She beamed at me. 'How lovely. Come in!' As I followed her inside I noticed that she was wearing yet another scent – what was this one? Oh yes – that new one by Chanel – *Chance*. 'Have a cup of coffee with me,' she said. 'I've just made a pot.'

'Okay – thanks – but I won't stay long. The weather's so gorgeous that I want to get out there and –'

'Seize the day,' she finished. 'Good idea. Make the most of it my girl. To quote Philip Larkin, "Days are where we live . . . They are to be happy in" –' *THUMP!!* – 'But this damn television . . .'

'What are you trying to watch?'

'ITV are doing a two-hour special – *The World's 100 Worst Ever Films* – and I really want to see it.'

'Why?'

'Because,' she said proudly, '*seven* of them are mine.'

She banged the TV again. I bent down and examined the console, then twiddled one of the buttons at the back. The picture wobbled again then stabilised. 'There.'

'Oh *thank you*, Laura. Which button is it again?'

'This one, here.'

'I never knew that,' she said.

'And were you okay in the power cut?' I asked her.

'I was fine – I like the dark. I see everything more clearly. Can you understand that?'

'Ye-es,' I said. After last night, I could. 'I've got something for you, Cynthia.'

'Really?' I handed her the bag, and she opened it. 'Oh, I say.' She held up the dressing gown. Then she slipped it on – it was wonderful on her – and looked in the mirror over the fireplace. 'How lovely, Laura,' she said as Hans batted at the belt with her paw. 'But you shouldn't be giving it to me, I mean, it's so sweet of you but –' she blinked in bewilderment. 'Don't *you* want it?'

'No. It was an unwanted gift,' I explained.

'Oh. From . . . ?' I nodded. 'Not going well then?'

I shook my head. 'I'm afraid your prediction was right.'

'I knew it,' she said, as she poured me a cup of coffee. 'The second I saw him. It was his aura, you see. Too much orange – it clashed with your lilac.'

'I was very dismissive about what you do,' I said. 'I was very judgemental. I'm sorry.'

'You thought it was "bunkum",' she said good-naturedly.

'I did think that. But I'm a little less sceptical than I was before.'

'So there *are* more things on heaven and earth . . .'

'Yes, there clearly are.'

I picked up one of her flyers. *Let Psychic Cynthia predict your past, present and future.*

As I sipped my coffee, I realized how much of my life Cynthia had got right – I *had* been missing two people: *You didn't know them for long . . . you loved them. You didn't want it to end . . . .* That was so true. Her reading of my current life had been accurate too. *Romance is in the air. But not with him.* As for the future . . .

'An ending is coming, Laura. I can see it . . .' I heard her say. She meant my ending with Luke – but to me, that had already happened twenty-four hours earlier. 'And there's a new beginning.' She sipped her coffee, then closed her eyes. 'I see a lake,' she said after a moment.

I smiled. 'Really?'

'Yes. A beautiful lake – in a vast wilderness. The leaves are all gold. It's autumn. And there are some animals. I'm connecting with them now.' Her eyelids flickered. 'I'm not quite sure what species. Hold on a moment . . .' She cocked her head on one side. 'How *odd*,' she said, her brow furrowing. 'It looks like . . . a kangaroo . . .'

'It isn't a kangaroo,' I said happily. 'It's a wallaby.'

From outside we could hear the shrieking whistles and loud cheers of the May Day protestors.

'Anyway, thanks for the coffee, Cynthia. I'm going for a walk now. It sounds rather jolly out there.'

'Well thank you, Laura – for this.' She patted the dressing gown. 'I shan't ever want to take it off.'

I walked to the end of Dunchurch Road and, there, coming up Ladbroke Grove, were the Reclaim the Streets cyclists – peddling up the hill, maybe two hundred of them, all blowing their whistles and hooting their horns – and with them, in force, the anti-capitalist demonstrators in their Bush and Blair masks and their fat cat suits. It was a bit like the Notting Hill Carnival.

No Bombs, Bosses, or Borders! announced banners. *Split The Pea – Not the Atom!* Slogans were emblazoned on backs,

318

fronts, and huge placards. *Solidarity with Asylum Seekers – Free Movement of People Not Goods! More Jaw Jaw Less War-War!* Protestors were dressed as clowns, Vikings and vicars or just wrapped in pages from the *Financial Times*. One cyclist was in cricket whites, with *Smash Capitalism for Six!* emblazoned on his shirt. Two anarchists held up a huge banner: *Why Should the Police Have a Monopoly on Violence?* Meanwhile the policemen themselves were nervously eyeing the protestors whilst trying to look relaxed.

'One more word and I'll arrest you,' I heard one officer say to a man wearing a lacy wedding dress.

'Sod off copper!'

'One more word and I'll arrest you.'

'Sod off copper!'

'One more word and I'll arrest you.'

'Sod off copper!'

My mobile rang.

'Laura?'

'Tom.' I turned up the volume so that I could hear him. 'How are you?' I said, pressing my index finger to my left ear.

'I'm fine. And you?'

'I'm fine, thank you.'

'Good. Now I have a very serious question for you.'

'Yes?' I smiled. 'What is it?'

'Well . . . did you really tell Nerys that in your opinion I was the most gorgeous, handsome, wonderful, marvellous, sexy, brilliant man you'd ever laid eyes on? Because she's just dropped in to see how it's going here, and she told me that you said all those things to her, no exaggeration. Of course I'm much too modest to believe it,' he added. 'So I thought I'd better check. So . . . did you?'

I hesitated for a second.

'*All You Need is Love.*'

'Yes, Tom,' I said. 'I did.'

* * *

319

I walked up to the top of Ladbroke Grove with the protestors, then left them as they turned towards the West End, while I veered right to Holland Park. As I went through the gate, I felt a thousand times happier than I had done when I'd gone there twenty-four hours before. Somehow, telling Tom everything had made me feel lighter. Today I didn't avoid the toddlers' playground as I usually did. In fact I stood there for a few moments, watching the children being pushed on the tiny swings, or bounced on the springy horses, being helped up the climbing frames or just happily scraping and digging in the sandpit. And I knew the chances were that, one day, I'd be doing that with my child too. I had been pregnant once, after all, so maybe it could happen again. And if it didn't – then there were other ways to have a family.

I believe that if you truly want children in your life, then one way or another, children will come.

I'd bought a copy of the *Evening Standard* from the newsagent's at the top of Ladbroke Grove and I sat on a bench, reading it. As it was a Bank Holiday it was a thin edition – there was quite a bit about the power cut, and its aftermath, a couple of pages on the May Day demonstrations, some pre-election coverage, some foreign news, and then something caught my eye in the media diary: *NORMAN SERVICE WILL NOT BE RESUMED*. It was about Scrivens. It said that R. Sole had sacked him for buying shares on his behalf, in a company that was apparently involved with animal experimentation. R. Sole was, famously, an animal nut. I thought of the awful 'Incognito' piece, and the horrible coverage it had unleashed, and the pain and turmoil it had caused me, and couldn't help a little smile.

It was half past six. I went back to Dunchurch Road and cooked myself an omelette, and by now it was eight thirty.

Bzzzzzzzzz. I went to the door.

'Laura.'

'Luke.' He looked tired and dishevelled, five o'clock

320

shadow darkening his jaw. He'd obviously dumped his suit-case and come straight round.

'Look, I know you're very cross with me Laura, and I do understand it, but there was no need to block all my calls.'

'But I didn't want to talk to you, and you kept ringing.'

He looked at me imploringly. 'Don't be like that, Laura.'

'Luke,' I said patiently. 'You told me that, after Venice, everything would change – and it is going to.' I shut the door.

Bzzzzzzzzz. Reluctantly, I opened it again.

'*Did* you know,' he said, 'that in Florida it's illegal to sing in a public place while wearing a swimsuit?'

'No,' I said wearily. 'I can't say that I did.'

'And did you know that bamboo can grow thirty-six inches in a single day?'

'No.' I shook my head. 'I didn't know that either.'

'And did you also know that the ancient Egyptians trained baboons to wait at tables?'

'That's absolutely fascinating, but can we please leave it now, Luke? There's really no point.' I shut the door.

Bzzzzzzzzz. I opened it again.

'And did you *also* know . . . that for reasons which no-one understands, twins are much more common in the east than the west?'

I stared at him. 'No I didn't know that. And did *you* know – that I really don't care. I like you very much, Luke – but we're not going to be together. We can be friends again, at some indeterminate time in the future, but our relationship is not going to resume. We've been round the block twice – and that's enough. We are not Charles and Camilla.'

'I'm sorry, Laura,' he said. 'I know I've let you down . . . in many ways . . . with Magda. I feel so bad . . .'

'Well there's no need to,' I sighed. 'It was only because you love Jessica so much. But you know, Luke, why don't you answer that sad little prayer of hers – the one about her mum and dad living together again?'

'Oh God . . .' He was rolling his eyes.

'Why not? Then you'd have Jessica with you all the time. Okay, Magda's insane – but no-one's perfect. And it isn't going to work out with me. Goodbye for now, Luke. There's nothing of mine at your house, so we won't need to speak. And please don't ring the bell again.'

I shut the door, then went back inside, feeling more upset than my sardonic tone might have implied, although I knew that I'd done the right thing. I went downstairs. My omelette was cold and leathery – not that I was hungry. I binned it, then filled the sink.

Buzzzzzzzzz.

Right, I thought. I am now going to get very cross.

I flung open the door. Shit. This was all I needed. One of those day-release guys with their bloody holdalls . . . Tall and thin, cropped hair and a short dark beard, black leather jacket. I heaved an exasperated sigh.

'Please don't shut the door in my face . . .' he began.

'Look, can we just cut the tragic sales pitch,' I interrupted. 'I promise I *will* buy something from you, because I always do, but I do *not* want a long sob story on my own doorstep and, while I'm at it, can I just say that I wish you guys didn't *always* have to turn up when it's dark and –'

He had started to cry. Oh shit. The man was crying. I stared at him, too shocked even to breathe. Then he looked at me, and his features became more distinct now. Familiar. Oh. *Shit* . . .

'Laura.'

I felt my mouth quiver, then the sudden *thump* in my ribcage. My eyes had filled now, too.

Nick.

'Laura,' he murmured again.

'I . . . didn't . . . recognize you,' I whispered. The Nick I knew was a big bear of a man. This Nick was . . . thin and lean and hard looking – like a plank of wood. And he was

322

sun-tanned – his face and neck a ruddy brown – and there were deep furrows at his eyes and brow. His hair, which had been thick and wavy and the colour of mahogany, was very short – and sprinkled with grey. I'd had to hear his voice again, to be sure.

He was staring at me. 'Can I . . . Do you mind . . . if I . . . ?'

I had rehearsed this moment so many times – the things I would say – the *sang froid* I would display, or, more likely, the bitter rage. But now that it was here, I could barely speak, except to utter the most mundane of sentiments.

'Oh . . . You want to come in?' I croaked. 'Yes . . . of course.'

As he stepped over the threshold I saw that he was wearing jeans – Nick had never worn jeans – and was probably three stone lighter than the Nick I knew. He was a different man. Everything about him seemed changed – his face, his physique, his gait, and even his hands. As he put down his brown canvas holdall, I saw that they were rough and reddened.

We went into the sitting room and just stood there, staring at each other in semi-silence, like strangers at a dismal drinks party.

'Do you . . . want something to eat?'

'No,' he murmured. 'Thanks. I hitched a lift – and we stopped at a café.' I noticed that his intonation was subtly different – he didn't say '*kafay*' – but 'ka-*fay*'.

'You hitched a lift . . . From where?'

'Harwich.' He looked around the sitting room. 'It's different in here. You've changed it. The colour.'

'Yes . . . I've . . . had it decorated . . . Not that long ago actually . . .'

'Do you mind if I sit down?'

'Of course . . . I don't mind. Erm . . . would you like . . . a drink?'

'No. Thank you. It's okay.' That slightly odd inflection again.

We sat on either side of the fireplace. Intimate strangers. It was as though we were facing each other across a canyon, although we were less than six feet apart.

'You've been living in Harwich?' I murmured. My mouth was dry and I was clenching my jaw.

'No. Not living there. I got off a boat.'

'From where? *Where*? I want to know . . .' I could feel my heart begin to pound. 'I want to know where you've been? Where *have* you been, Nick? *Where*?' My voice was thin and high as though I was keening. '*Tell* me. Where have you *been*?'

'In Holland.'

'In Holland?' I repeated. 'But why . . . ? Doing what?'

'Working. In agriculture.'

'Farming?' I said. Nick had hated the countryside. He was an urban person.

'Not farming exactly. Flowers. Tulips. I work in the tulip fields . . .'

A jolt ran the length of my spine. I stood up.

'Where are you going?' I heard him call.

'I think we both need a drink.'

'I'd been trying to come back for a long time,' Nick explained a few minutes later. He had taken off his jacket, and I saw how toned and muscled his arms had become. They were as tanned and weathered as his face. His neck looked thicker, and more sinewy.

'Then why didn't you?'

He stared into his tumbler of Glenmorangie, tipping it this way and that. I noticed that his fingertips were calloused and cracked.

He sighed. 'Because I didn't know *how*. I kept thinking of you . . . feeling so terrible . . . and so ashamed. But it was easier to stay where I was than face it all.' We could hear the tick of the carriage clock.

By now the initial shock had subsided and the whisky – which I never normally drink, but had fallen upon like an alcoholic – had started to sedate my mangled nerves. I began, slowly, to ask the questions that had been cramming my throat.

'You've been in Holland *all* this time?' He nodded. 'So when you left the car in Blakeney, is that what you'd planned . . . ?'

He shook his head. 'I had no idea what I was going to do. I only knew that I had to . . . escape. Not from you,' he added. 'From myself. From the mental mess I was in. I can talk about it now, because things are different for me – but I couldn't have explained it to you then.'

'Where did you sleep that first night?'

'In the car. And in the morning I walked down to the harbour, and there was this big fishing boat and I overheard someone saying that it was going to The Hague. So I paid the skipper to let me come on board. It was a very rough crossing. We arrived the next day.'

'And then?'

'I got a bus to Leiden, and I stayed in a hostel for a while. And there was a notice on the board about this bulb farm, at Hillegom, a few miles to the north, and they were look-ing for casual labour. So I bought a bicycle – and a tent . . .'

'A tent?'

'You have to camp. I didn't mind. In fact, I liked it. And I started to work.'

'Doing what?'

'Grading lily bulbs at first – in the warehouse. Sorting them by size. The calm monotony of it was . . . a relief. My hands were busy, but my mind was free.' He lifted his tumbler to his mouth again and I heard the ice cubes in it chink. 'I was paid forty guilders a day. Then I worked in the green-houses with the tulips, planting them, picking them, tying them into bunches of ten, packing them in boxes; and later in the year, after the harvest, peeling the tulip bulbs ready for export.'

'And no-one ever asked who you were, or why you were there?'

'No. There were a lot of us – mostly men. Many from Turkey and Eastern Europe. But no-one asked questions.'

'And how long did you think you'd be there?'

'I had no idea. I made a decision to live day to day. I thought I'd come back, eventually . . . but then . . . time just kept passing and . . .' His voice trailed away.

'So why have you come back *now?*'

He looked at me, and I noticed how worn he looked, hollow at the cheeks and temples, as though the wind had eroded his face.

'Do you believe in signs, Laura?' he asked quietly. 'I don't think you do, because I remember that you used to dismiss the idea of anything that couldn't be accounted for in purely rational terms.'

He's standing in a field of flowers.

'I know I did.'

He's surrounded by them – it's a marvellous sight.

'But I've changed my mind lately.'

'Why's that?'

'Because . . . I've learnt that some things just can't . . . be explained.'

'I believe I had a sign,' he went on. 'A short while ago, something . . . happened. And that's why I've come back now.'

'What happened?' I said. 'What was it?'

'It was . . . exactly two weeks ago.' He took a deep breath, then exhaled. 'I was in one of the tulip fields. It was the height of the season – the tourists coming in their thousands, every day; getting off the coaches to take photos.' He had another sip of whisky. 'It was a wonderful day,' he went on. 'Bright and sunny, but with this very strong breeze blowing in – it's often windy there, because it's close to the sea. And it was about three o'clock and I'd been walking through the rows of tulips since the morning, checking the plants for disease. We plant single variety crops, so first I went through a field of yellow ones, called "Golden Flame", then into a field of deep pink ones with a white stripe; "Burgundy Lace" –'

'I know that one.' I thought of Luke, on Valentine's Day, his arms filled with them.

'– then through a field of red ones – "Fringed Appledoorn". And a tour group had just stopped in the café area, for tea – they were pensioners. A short while later they left. And I suddenly saw, in the distance, that the guy who ran the café was trying to catch this newspaper – it was flying all over the place – and he was catching the pieces. But one bit of it blew right away, and it was flying across the field – flapping across the tops of the flowers like a big white bird. It was coming towards me, swooping and twirling in the strong breeze, turning over and over. And eventually it came to within a few feet of me, and I grabbed it. And I was just about to screw it up and put it in my bag, when I saw that it was an English newspaper from the day before. And I turned it over. And saw you . . .'

My Remorse

'The shock of it . . . not just that it was you – but your sad expression, and the terrible headline and your guilt and despair. I stood there, as rooted to the spot as the flowers around me and I felt so . . . bad.'

But even though he's standing in this field of exquisite flowers he's looking mournful and sad . . .

'I knew then that I must come back. You might say,' he went on, 'that it was chance. That on one level a British tourist left their copy of the *Sunday Semaphore* on a picnic table, and it blew away, and I just happened to catch the particular piece of it which just happened to feature you. But on another level, you might say it's a sign . . .'

'It is a sign,' I said quietly. 'You don't need to convince

me. But you've come back with what in mind, Nick?'

'To . . . talk to you . . . to explain. I couldn't have done it before, but now, things are different for me – and I can try and explain what happened . . . why I did what I did.'

'Well I've certainly deserved an explanation, ' I said bitterly. 'And I must say, it's really nice to know what it was that detained you that day three and a half years ago. Oh, and thanks for phoning the National Missing Persons' Helpline that time so that I could stop trudging round The Embankment peering under cardboard boxes, or having nightmares about you lying dead in a ditch – or rather a dyke, as it turns out – that *was* considerate of you. Pity you didn't do it after three days rather than three months though wasn't it? I presume you heard me on the radio?' I added.

'I did. I had a small transistor and I picked up Radio 4 on long-wave. So I called the Helpline.'

'But then when they told me that you didn't want to see me or even talk to me . . . I couldn't understand it. If you were able to phone *them*, then why couldn't you have phoned *me*?'

'I did try actually. Twice.' I remembered, now, the silent phone calls. 'But I put the phone down, because I knew that if I spoke to you, even for a few seconds, then a dialogue would begin, which would make it inevitable that I'd have to come back. But I wasn't ready to. I wanted to come back in my own *time* . . .'

'I see,' I said quietly. 'So now you have. And I suppose you think you're doing a marvellous thing, deigning to return now *you're* good and ready . . .' my throat was aching, 'to tell me where the . . . *fuck* . . . you've . . . *been* . . .' My hands sprang up to my face. 'You crash-landed my life . . . I hardly left this flat . . . it was as much as I could do to get dressed . . . I couldn't sleep . . . I was a *wreck* . . . the stress of it – I didn't *eat* . . .'

'I'm sorry, Laura,' he said again. 'I'm very sorry.'

I shook my head. 'You could say sorry to me every day for the next twenty years and it still wouldn't be enough.

You have caused *mayhem*,' I said. My throat was aching with a suppressed sob. 'The *turmoil* you left behind – the day-to-day difficulties – not to mention the agony of those first three months when I didn't know if you were even *alive*. I used to walk around this flat at night, wringing my hands!'

'I'm sorry,' he repeated. His eyes were shimmering.

'You didn't have to *go missing*,' I wept. I extended my hands towards him, as if in supplication, the fingers splayed and stretched. 'You could have just said, "Listen Laura, I don't want to be with you any more. Let's separate."'

'But I didn't see it, clearly, like that. I saw nothing but my own . . . pain. I felt I was disintegrating. That I'd been . . . dismantled, somehow . . . first, my father dying like that . . .'

'That still doesn't justify it,' I sobbed. Tears streamed down my face. '*Nothing* justifies it. Nothing justifies what it does to the people left *waiting*.'

'I hadn't spoken to him for two months. I was angry with him, and I wanted to make it up, but I didn't know how. And I kept hoping that he'd phone and say "come on Nick, let's have lunch". But he didn't do that, and *I* didn't ring *him* – and then he ran up a flight of steps, and *died*. And I couldn't bear knowing that the last time he saw me I was *angry* with him.' Nick's left hand covered his face. 'I'd wanted to have him put his arms round me just once more . . .' He was crying again now. 'But I never got the chance. And then you lost the baby and I blamed myself for that too – and *you* blamed me for it. What you said to me, Laura – that terrible, terrible thing . . .'

'I know – I know – I'm sorry. It was wrong.'

'And it probably *was* my fault, but it was too *much* – all at once. And we'd seen her . . . that was what was so unbearable – that we'd *seen* her, waving to us . . .' He buried his head in his hands.

'We were unlucky, Nick. A tear seeped into the corner of

my mouth. 'The crash shouldn't have caused it – the impact wasn't that great. And I hadn't been feeling well that day, and we'd had that earlier scare so maybe it was going to happen anyway . . .We'll never know . . .'

I heard him groan. 'I was . . . overwhelmed by guilt and regrets. My father, and then my child . . . I couldn't . . . absorb it, Laura. I couldn't cope with it.'

'. . . we could have had another chance. But then you *went*. So there were to be *no more* chances – *that's* why I've been so angry. On top of all the other stresses, I felt doubly deprived. I felt I'd never recover.'

We sat there in silence, smashed by emotion. I stared at the floor.

'It said in the paper that you're with Luke,' I heard him say. 'I remember you used to mention him sometimes.'

'I was with him. But I'm not any more. And you?' I croaked, looking at him now. I wiped my eyes. 'How's *your* love-life? It must be a bit tricky in a tent,' I added bitterly.

'I don't live in a tent any more. That was just for the first few months. I live in a small house on the farm. I'm the foreman there now.'

'Oh. That's good.'

'I have a dog – a Rhodesian Ridgeback. Betsy. She's very sweet.'

'You always wanted a dog . . . we couldn't have had one here with both of us out at work. It wouldn't have been fair.'

'Laura . . .' There was a mark on the carpet. It needed attention. 'There's something else I want to tell you.'

'What?' I said. I was suddenly *very* tired.

'Well . . . I have a partner now. Anneka.'

'Congratulations. I hope you'll be very happy, tiptoeing through the tulips together. I'd offer to be a bridesmaid but we're not divorced yet.'

'She's a very nice, kind person.'

'Well that's lovely Nick, delighted to hear it, I hope you'll be happy, and above all, I hope that you will NEVER do to her what you did to me.' I stared at the mark on the carpet again. It needed stain remover. What was that stuff called again? Of course. *Vanish*. How could I forget that?

'We have a child.'

Or maybe just warm water would do it. If I rubbed hard enough.

'She's ten months,' I heard him say. No detergent though. It might bleach the colour. 'Her name is Estella.'

'That's nice.' I looked at him. 'After the tulip I suppose? Estella Rijnveld?'

'That's right.'

But things are different for me now . . .

'So that's why you're able to . . . talk about what happened, isn't it?'

'Yes. I feel that I'm . . . I don't know.' He shook his head. 'Back in the world . . . I'd felt that everything I loved was dying. That's why I liked the work at the farm – knowing that inside each bulb was a life, coiled up, waiting to unfurl if I looked after it in the right way.'

'Do you have a photo of her?'

He dug his hand into his back pocket and pulled out his wallet from which he produced a small snap. He handed it to me. She was sitting next to a huge vase of red and white tulips. She had a sweet, smiley face, and a mop of dark shiny hair.

'She looks like you.' I wondered if *our* little girl would have looked like this. 'She's lovely.' She probably would. 'Did your partner – Anneka – did she know about me? Did you tell her?'

'Not until two weeks ago. But then I showed her the newspaper article. She was very angry that I hadn't told her before. She said that I had to come back; she said I had imprisoned you, and that I had to set you free.'

'Well . . . she's right.'

331

He stood up. 'I think I'd better go now.'

'Where are you staying?'

'At a hotel in Bayswater.'

'What about your stuff? I've kept most of it – contrary to what you might have thought from that article. It's all packed away in the spare room – your clothes . . .'

'They wouldn't fit me.'

'That's true. You're so thin now, Nick.'

'It's no bad thing – it's the outdoor life.'

'What about your books? Your pictures?'

'We wouldn't have room. Do whatever you like with them.'

'I'll take them to Oxfam. No. There's a SudanEase charity shop now. I'll take your things there.'

'But I would like the photos of my parents.'

'Of course. I'll get them.'

I went into the spare room, and came back with a bag.

He took it. 'Thanks.'

I handed him a piece of paper. 'Would you write down your address for the divorce papers? It should only take a couple of months.'

He took a pen out of his pocket and began to write.

'Niklaus Gering?' I said as I read it.

'That's how I'm known. It's just a translation of my name. No-one there knows who Nick Little is.'

'Do *you*?' I asked him.

'I do now,' he said.

'You'll get your half of the flat,' I said as he put on his jacket. 'It'll go on the market tomorrow.'

'That's not why I came back, Laura.'

'I know that.'

'You don't have to sell it. Stay here if you want.'

'No. Thanks, but no. I don't want to. It's spoiled. In any case, you'll need the money – you have a child.'

'Where will you live, Laura?'

'I really don't know. I think I'll rent somewhere, for now.

So . . .' He picked up his bag. 'Well . . . What do I say? Thanks for dropping by.' We went out into the hall. 'It's our wedding anniversary by the way.'

He blinked. 'So it is. I'm sorry. I forgot . . .'

'Never mind,' I said. 'It really doesn't matter.'

He lifted his hand to the door. 'Don't think too badly of me, Laura.' I didn't reply. 'Perhaps, who knows, we'll even stay in touch.' He smiled a sad little smile.

I shook my head.

'No, Nick,' I said. 'We won't.'

EPILOGUE
SIX MONTHS LATER

It's the last Friday in October. Tom and I are sitting in the kitchen of Moorhouse Road, the late afternoon sunshine pouring through the open back door, while Felicity and Hugh are upstairs packing for one of their not infrequent weekends away. We are to baby-sit Olivia – *in situ* – as we have done on two other weekends before and which we very much enjoy. Over the baby monitor – which, for some reason, is always on – we can hear Fliss clattering about in the bedroom opening cupboards and drawers, while Olivia yodels indignantly at her from her cot.

'It'sALLrightsweetiedarling,' we hear. 'Mummy'sJUST-coming. Oh there you are Hugh – get my weekend bag off the top of the wardrobe for me will you – now what do you think of *this* little number? I bought it yesterday in Agnès B.'

'Hmmm – delicious,' we hear. 'Especially now that you've lost that last stubborn four stone.' We hear neck-nuzzling noises, then Felicity squeals with laughter and Olivia squawks.

'It'sALLright darling,' Fliss says. ' 'It'sALLrightsweetie-darlingMummyandDaddyarejustPLAYING.'

'You really were a bit of a jumbo mumbo, Fliss.'

'I know. And look at me now.'

'A *scrummy* mummy . . . mmmmmmmmmm.' There are more squeals.

'You really should flirt with my friends more often Hugh,' we hear Fliss say. 'Nothing like the stress of that for making the weight fall off.'

'But I don't *want* to flirt with any of your friends,' says Hugh. 'I only want to flirt with *you* . . . mmmmmmmmmm. Hope we've got a four-poster at Chewton Glen.'

'She has to keep the weight off now,' I say to Tom. 'Now she knows that Hugh *could* be tempted. Best thing that could have happened to her.'

'I am now *so* slim,' Fliss says proudly, 'that I could probably wear Hope's cast-offs.'

'I don't know about that, darling, but she could certainly wear yours.'

'That's true – she's *huge* – you'd think she was having triplets!'

Felicity's annoyance that Hope had become pregnant at the first try is tempered by her happiness that, at five months, Hope is already enormous and has a face like a melon and feet like footballs. To Felicity, this seems only fair.

'I always *thought* she'd change her mind on the issue,' she opines. 'Very nice of Mike to go along with it like that – he didn't seem remotely interested. I mean, he never wanted to come round here much did he – showed *no* interest in Olivia – I was rather offended actually. Some men just have no feeling for babies, do they? Don't know *what* they're missing.'

I smile at Tom – who by now knows the whole background.

'But what a guy,' we hear Hugh say, as I flick through Felicity's copy of *Mother and Baby* magazine. I turn to page five, and there is Olivia in her Tiddli-Toes baby bouncer. 'I mean, not only prepared to do that baby cuddling programme that Hope got involved with –'

'That's what did it of course,' Fliss interjects. 'Made her go all broody.'

'– but also prepared to take a three year career break to look after the kid himself in case she doesn't take to the whole "mummy" thing.'

'Well so much for *my* three year career break,' Fliss says, as I turn the pages. 'I'm frantic.'

'Ironic really, because we could actually have afforded for you not to work.'

'I know. Funny isn't it?' We hear a snorty laugh.

I am staring at a photo of Hugh, accompanied by a two-page article all about the BurpaBib which he designed and developed and has now sold, under licence, to Mothercare, Asda, JoJo Maman Bébé and Little Urchin, as well as to the massive Babies'R'Us, in the States, where they are doing a particularly roaring trade. The article mentions *en passant* that Hugh's business partner, Chantal Vane, has just become engaged to a senior Vice-President at Babies'R'Us and is moving to the States.

'How romantic,' I say to Tom. 'Brought together by baby sick.'

The article goes on to say that Hugh is now developing a line of baby products, including a range of shaped cloth nappies with Gore-Tex outer wrappers and flushable liners called Top Bots.

'I'm frantic,' we hear Fliss say again. 'Happy though.'

'Well what you're doing now really suits you,' says Hugh. In addition to doing the product development and PR for Hugh, she has become an NCT teacher, where she can indulge her passion for boring on about babies for hours on end – but to a rapt audience. She is also working on a pilot for a baby care programme, *Baby Talk*, which Trident would make and she would present. Tom says she has screen presence – as I always thought. It would be the first such programme on network TV.

'Okay Hugh,' we hear her croon. 'I'm ready. I'll just change the baby . . .'

'I don't *want* you to change her,' he replies, right on cue. 'She's lovely as she is.'

'ComeonmylickleSWEETIEchops.' There are gurgled protests as Olivia is put on the changing station. 'Don't wriggle, my girl. These nappies of yours are *so* nice, Hugh,' we hear Felicity say. They are using the Top Bots prototypes. 'You *are* clever, darling – all your wonderful ideas.'

There is silence.

'I love you so much,' we hear Hugh say.

'And I love you so much,' says Felicity.

'We *both* love you, darling.'

'Alathatdobeylyerlgoyagoyagoya,' Olivia replies.

Five minutes later they all come downstairs. Fliss and Hugh open a bottle of champagne and we all have a glass, except for Hugh, who's driving, and we show them the details of the garden flat we're buying in Stanley Square, a quarter of a mile away. We gulped at the price – but Tom is getting great royalties from overseas for the quiz – particularly from the States.

'It looks wonderful,' Fliss says. 'Three bedrooms, one en-suite – and access to the Stanley Square gardens.'

'I know,' I say happily.

'There's a lovely little playground in that one,' she adds. 'With swings and a sandpit and a roundabout.'

'Well . . . that's what attracted us to it,' Tom says. 'We think that might be . . . useful.'

Now we quickly show them our Canadian photos from the trip Tom and I took there ten days ago. There are the photos of Montreal, and his parents outside their house in Westmount, and Christina and me walking in the Botanical Gardens, and Tom and me up on Mont Royale, looking out over the city, and then of our trip to Lake Memphremagog a couple of hours' drive to the south.

'How beautiful,' Fliss says. 'The colours of the trees . . .'

'It was wonderful,' I say. 'It's twenty miles north of

Vermont. Tom's parents have a chalet there. They've been going for years.'

'Do you see many animals?' Fliss asks. 'I imagine there are bears aren't there?'

'Yes there are,' Tom says. 'And deer.'

'And eagles,' I say. 'We saw a very good eagle.'

'A "good" eagle?' says Hugh, narrowing his eyes.

'Yes, it was really good – you could see it quite clearly. I also saw an ostrich.'

'An ostrich?' says Fliss.

'Ostriches are a bit harder to see,' says Tom. 'But it's not impossible.'

'And there were a few elephants,' I add.

'Indian ones,' Tom explains.

Fliss is rolling her eyes. 'Have some more champagne you two. Anyway, we'd better get going if we're going to be there in time for dinner. Bye-bye Babyboots.' She kisses Olivia's cheek with little smacking sounds, while Hugh strokes Olivia's head. Her face crumples and goes crimson as she realizes that her parents are going – and tears spill from her scrunched up eyes. I carry her up to the sitting room to distract her with something on the TV.

'What's it to be?' says Tom as I cuddle Olivia on my lap. She has stopped crying, and he is looking at the stack of her videos and DVDs. He holds up a Fimbles case. '*Let's Find The Fimbles?*'

'No, seen it too recently.'

'*Fimbly Bimbly Finding is Fun?*'

'Hmmm . . . I *quite* like that.'

'*Glitter Stars and Sparkly Things?*'

'That's a possibility – there's that lovely "snowflake" song that Florrie sings, remember?'

'I do, but let's have this one – *Get the Fimbling Feeling.*'

'Fine.'

And I have a very nice fimbling feeling myself as Tom and

I sit there, with a happy, sleepy baby and the Fimbles, and each other and a glass of champagne, on a Friday evening at the end of a pleasantly busy week. The DVD finishes, and then it's Olivia's bedtime, and I tuck her up, while Tom winds up her musical lullaby toy, and she falls asleep in *seconds*, her teddy clasped under one arm. And Tom and I go downstairs where we can hear her little snorts and sighs over the baby monitor as I get our supper out of the fridge. And I think how happy I am. How happy I am again – the trauma of Nick's disappearance – and return – behind me at last.

I pour Tom another glass of champagne. He's sitting at the kitchen table, looking through our photos.

'It *was* a wonderful trip wasn't it,' he says.

'It was.'

'But you know, when we went down to Lake Memphremagog, and we were sitting watching the sun set that evening over Owl's Head Mountain, there was something I really wanted to ask you.'

'Uh huh.'

'A question.'

'I see.'

'But somehow I didn't quite get to do it . . . And then the next day we walked to the top of Bear Mountain, and we had that fabulous view beneath us of the whole lake and the hillsides all red and gold – I wanted to ask you my question then. But again, I didn't. So I think I might as well ask you it now. It's one of my very serious questions. In fact –' he stands up – 'it's so serious that I think I'd better whisper it.' He comes up to me, and stands next to me, slipping his arm round my waist, then bends his head, and murmurs it into my ear. I feel my body suffuse with warmth.

'That *is* a very serious question,' I say.

He looks at me expectantly. 'And . . . ?'

I smile. 'The answer is yes.'

AFTERWORD

I would like to thank Janet Asprey, Mary Newman and Sophie Woodforde of the National Missing Persons' Helpline for their invaluable assistance during the planning and research for this book. The National Missing Persons' Helpline number is 0500 700 700.

I would also like to point out that the medical programme described in Chapter Ten does not actually take place at St Thomas's hospital in London. I have transposed it from the Volunteer Cuddlers' Program at the Royal Women's Hospital, Carlton, Victoria, Australia.

PERMISSIONS